CW00480937

A SCORE TO SETTLE
Part One (Revised Edition)
By Kim Hunter

Kim Hunter
Copyright © 2018 By Kim Hunter

The right of Kim Hunter to be identified as author of
this work has been asserted in accordance with
sections 77 and 78 of the Copyright, Designs and
Patents Act 1988.
All rights Reserved
No reproduction, copy or transmission of this
publication
may be made without written permission.
No paragraph of this publication may be reproduced,
Copied or transmitted save with the written
permission of the author, or in
accordance with the provisions of the Copyright Act
1956 (as amended)
This is a work of fiction.
Names, places, characters and incidents originate
from the writers imagination.
Any resemblance to actual persons, living or dead is
purely coincidental.
Copyright:
https://www.123rf.com/profile_photoshkolnik'123RF
Stock Photo

OTHER WORKS BY KIM HUNTER

WHATEVER IT TAKES
EAST END HONOUR
TRAFFICKED
BELL LANE LONDON E1
EAST END LEGACY
EAST END LOTTERY
PHILLIMORE PLACE LONDON
EAST END A FAMILY OF STEEL
FAMILY BUSINESS
A DANGEROUS MIND
FAMILY FIRST
Web site www.kimhunterauthor.com

ACKNOWLEDEMENTS

Heartfelt thanks to Kevin Plume for all your
editing and proofing.

To my Jenny, for once again saving me
emotionally when times get tough.

To Paul, many years, many books,
past and present. Thank you.

Last but by no means least, to each and every
one of you for purchasing my books
and allowing me to do what I love.

FOREWORD

Revenge is an act of passion, vengeance
of justice. Injuries are revenged, crimes
are avenged.
Samuel Jimson 1709 – 1784

Prologue

For the first few weeks after her arrival, Shauna had taken regular daily strolls through Soho Square observing the tourists and the world in general. On numerous occasions she had glanced up at St Bartholomew's and felt nothing but pity for the poor women, who for whatever reason, were now housed inside. Never in her wildest dreams had it ever crossed her mind that it would one day be the place she would eventually end up. When the proverbial shit had hit the fan, Neil Maddock, true to his word had let her know in advance and also told her in no uncertain terms to get the fuck out of London as fast as she could. Now after being cooped up in the room for almost two days Shauna knew that time was rapidly running out. By running she knew it would only be a matter of time before they found her but staying wasn't an option, if she did then pretty damn soon she would be dead. Not being in control of her own destiny, something she hadn't felt for years, made her angry. Shauna had phoned the refuge in advance and using the ruse of domestic violence, had secured herself a temporary safe haven.

It was now ultimately time to leave St Bartholomew's, so picking up the small suitcase Shauna took one last lingering look at the tiny room, a room so tiny but which would never be forgotten as her place of safety. The building, a refuge for countless abused or homeless women, had been the only place she could think of going to at such short notice and thankfully when she had turned up on their doorstep apart from taking her name, no detailed questions had been asked.

About to place her hand on the brass door knob, the knock was brief and sharp and came sooner than she had anticipated. For a moment she thought her time was finally up, her entire adult life had been spent knowing this day would eventually arrive, it was inevitable and the only possible conclusion. Checking that the safety chain was in place and secure, she slowly opened the door just enough to be able to glimpse out into the hallway and she half expected to see a gun pointed at her head. She wasn't thinking rationally but Shauna O'Malley was sadly in anything but a rational state of mind, she hadn't been for years, not since the day she had lost her dear sweet Vonny. She let out a gasp at the sight of the man but it shouldn't have been a surprise, the world these people lived in made it possible for them to gain access to just about anyone, anywhere and at any time. He slammed his foot against the jam, making it impossible for her to close the door.

His gruff voice with its distinct cockney twang, which in the past has made her laugh, now only filled her with fear. His huge frame filled the gap in the doorway and he wore his most menacing look.

"Fran you know why I'm here but thank fuck I found you before any of the others. Now open the door and let me in, or do I have to break it down?"

Shauna knew her voice would tremble and make her appear weak and pathetic but even so she was still prepared to beg, to plead for her life if it would in any way help her. She had known this man since first becoming his boss's girlfriend and while most people feared him, moved out of his way to allow him to pass, he had for some insane reason always made her feel safe. A stupid feeling she realised but even now, looking into his face, knowing that he had come to kill her, she had difficulty in accepting her fate. As she struggled to speak Shauna stared into his eyes, desperately searching for a glimpse of emotion, anything that might tell her she at least had a chance.

"I suppose you'd better come in then."

Following her inside, he quickly scanned the room for any signs of a threat.

"Right! Enough with the little girl lost look, after what you've done you've got some fuckin' guts still being in London."

Glancing down, his eyes fell upon the suitcase, such a tiny little thing that held her entire worldly goods within. His feelings started to get the better of him and he instantly wanted to reach out to her, touch her, console her but the moment passed a quickly as it had come.

"Why the fuck did you do it girl? The Boss wants your blood and he won't fuckin' rest until you're six feet under. He's got every fuckin' slag in London out looking for you, he's finished and he knows it but it doesn't change a thing. You know him well enough and he won't give up until he knows you're dead and he won't give a flying fuck how you die."

Shauna let out a huge exasperated sigh. She was tired of having to explain herself and didn't want to go through the whole sorry mess all over again.

"It's a long story. I couldn't begin to explain and you'd never understand anyway."

"Try me."

"How long have you got?"

He desperately wanted to say forever, wanted to say

she could take an eternity if it meant he could stay with her but he didn't, he couldn't.

"As long as it takes but it won't change anything, the ending will still be the same. It has to be I have no choice."

Anger started to build up inside her and her voice lost the childish innocent tone that he was so used to hearing. Somehow she now seemed older, wiser, as if she'd lived a thousand lives and finally didn't care if she never saw another day.

"Then why the hell are you putting me through this? For God's sake, can't you just finish this and give me some peace?"

He couldn't tell her that from the moment they had met he had fallen head over heels in love with her, would've walked barefoot over broken glass for her but also couldn't tell her that he felt as if he was slowly dying inside. It wasn't his way and instead and in true gangster style his face once again wore a mask of hardness.

"Because I have to know, I have to live with myself and the only way I can do that is if I am sure in my heart that it was you, you who really did set him up."

Shauna didn't answer but she continued to stare inanely straight into his eyes and it felt as if she were boring into his very soul. They stood staring at each other for what seemed like an eternity and when she couldn't stand it any longer she at last broke the silence.

"Before I tell you, please say you won't hurt Cecil or any of his family, they're good people, honest people and shouldn't have got involved in any of this."

"Of course I won't hurt them, it's nothing to do with anyone else. Now are you going to fuckin' tell me how this shit load of trouble happened and why, or not?"

"Okay but it's not a pretty picture and you probably won't believe half of what I'm about to tell you but to be totally honest, it's got to the point where I actually don't care anymore, I actually don't give a shit!" Lowering his huge frame down on the bed, he beckoned for her to join him but Shauna ignored the gesture and remained standing. If she was to lay her life open like a book, then she didn't want to relax but to stand tall for everything she and her family had suffered and been forced to endure and ultimately, for everything she had taken upon herself to do. Just standing there in the middle of the room staring, Shauna knew this was shit or bust, knew that she had to get this right. Slowly she breathed in and pursing her lips held her breath for a few seconds. Finally she exhaled and uttered the life changing sentence that would shock him to the core.

"Well, to start with my name isn't Fran, its Shauna, Shauna O'Malley."

CHAPTER ONE
1995

"Jesus, I feel like fuckin' shite."

Violet O'Malley emerged from the bedroom with a face like thunder and a throbbing head to match. As she felt the first stirrings of vomit begin to rise in her throat she resembled a woman much older than her thirty-four years. Violet was well known for being able to hold her drink but just lately it was starting to take its toll. In the past she had always told herself that it was the Irish blood running through her veins which enabled her to sink even the hardest of drinkers under the table. The thought crossed her mind that maybe she was working too hard. Jesus, she slogged her guts out for those ungrateful little bastards and what thanks did she get? They were either crying or whining that they were hungry.

"Shauna! Shauna!!! You lazy little bitch. Get your skinny arse out of that bed and get me a fuckin' cuppa, do you hear me girl!"

Hearing her mother's voice Shauna O'Malley could feel her knees begin to tremble and she prayed that the vibration wouldn't wake Vonny who lay nuzzled beside her. It had been after two by the time she had finally gotten her off to sleep and the last thing she needed now was for her little sister to wake up. It was a foregone conclusion that with their mother in this mood they would both get a thrashing. The family had moved to the flat when Shauna was just a baby and she couldn't remember it ever being any different. The paint on the walls was peeling from the damp and in the winter the mould grew in black patches around the windows. Apart from a solitary rug in the front room there were no carpets just bare boards. The children didn't know any better and thought that in reality this was how everyone lived but in all honesty it was just one step up from being homeless. Shauna lifted her small frame off of the damp bed and feeling around for her thin cotton dressing gown, she quietly closed the door behind her. The floorboards in the hallway were bare and rough on her feet and yesterday she had been careless. Running instead of taking her time she had managed to get a splinter in her foot which now hurt like hell. Tonight when her mother went out she would go next door and ask Mrs O'Dwyer for help. For anyone in need the old lady always had a pot of stew on the stove and a warm smile. Mary O'Dwyer made stews that were legendary and many times a bowl of it had kept the hunger pains at bay for the two small girls. Shauna knew that Mary constantly worried over her and Vonny but like many others, didn't dare say a word to Violet or she was liable to get a black eye for her trouble.

"Shauna!!!! If I have to fuckin' call you once more you're really going to get it."

Violet was only slight in build but her fist could pack a punch and Shauna reeled from the blow as she walked into the kitchen.

"I might lay on my back all fuckin' night trying to earn a crust for you ungrateful brats and you can't even bring me a **cuppa** in the morning. Jesus! I don't know why I fuckin' bother, I wish I'd had you ripped out of me when I first knew I was up the duff,

2

you and that whinging little cunt in the bedroom."
Shauna heard her mother's words but they washed
over her, it was all she'd heard from the day she was
born and nine years later it meant very little. The
pattern was always the same, Violet would get drunk,
stay out for most of the night and when she did deem
to come home, would more often than not have some
stranger in tow. It was Shauna's job to look after
Vonny and a good job she did too. At nine years old
she was more of a mother to the little girl than Violet
had or ever would be. All of Shauna's days began
with a set routine, once she had made the tea and
gotten her mother's cigarettes Violet would go back
to bed which then left Shauna time to concentrate on
Vonny. The smell of urine was strong in the flat and
Shauna couldn't tell if it was from her and Vonny's
room or Violets, as all of them wet the bed on a
regular basis. It wasn't Vonny's fault, after all she
was only three and had never been potty trained and
Shauna was a bundle of nerves most of the time but
her mother was a different matter, all her mistakes
were alcohol induced. Now into the second month of
living without hot water the best she could manage
was a cold wash. Vonny's nappy rash had been
getting worse and the sores were yellow and weeping,
Shauna made a mental note to ask Mrs O'Dwyer
about this later. As gently as she could Shauna
touched her sister's arm but Vonny cried out when
her sister tried to wake her.
"Shush Von, if you wake mum she'll thrash me,
maybe you as well."
Hearing the threat the tiny girl was instantly silent
and an hour later the two of them were dressed and

3

sitting in front of the small television. Both knew that it would be hours before their mother would wake and start to get ready for her night shift. Shauna called this their special time, time to laugh a little and imagine what it was like to have a family like the ones on the television. She loved the programmes where there was a mum and a dad and everyone was smiling and happy. Vonny didn't really understand what was going on but would laugh and clap her hands when she saw Shauna smile with a faraway look in her eyes.

"Shauna I'm wet."

"Not again Von, you haven't had that one on long."

Vonny's eyes filled with tears.

"It's ok baby, come on let's go and get you dry."

Shauna was old enough to know that her sister shouldn't still be wearing nappies but toilet training was beyond her capabilities so washing the towelling squares was all she ever seemed to do and the cold water made them grey and rough. Shauna would never dare ask her mother for disposables as it was hard enough getting any kind of money for food out of the woman let alone the luxury of nappies that could be thrown away. As sure as night would fall, Violet woke up at six and started screaming blue murder for her eldest daughter. Shauna hurriedly made her way from the living room to her mother's bedroom where she found Violet sitting at the dressing table.

"Help me with my hair you lazy little bitch, I suppose you've had your arse in front of that fuckin' box all day?"

"No mum, I washed Vonny then gave her......"

4

"Oh shut the fuck up Shauna, I can't be doing with your rambling tonight, now do my hair!"

This was one chore that Shauna actually did like to do. Brushing Violet's hair made her feel close to her mother, feel that she at least had some kind of relationship with the woman, some kind of normality. Shauna would gently brush the long copper mane over and over again while her mother sang one of her many Irish songs but a few minutes later the brush would be snatched from her hands.

"Get lost, I have to get ready. I'm meeting Davey Wiseman tonight and I want you in your bed when I get back. He won't want to look at your ugly boat, that'll really put him off his stroke. I knew I'd strike it lucky one day I just wish I didn't have you pair of fuckin' leeches around my neck."

Shauna closed the bedroom door and sighed. An hour later Violet emerged from the room, unrecognisable from the woman who had slept her day away. Slender and with the most glorious head of red hair, Violet was a vision of beauty. By seven thirty her mother was heading off in the back of a black cab and Shauna had managed to get Vonny into bed. As quietly as she could, Shauna opened the front door and slipped out onto the landing. Knocking on Mrs O'Dwyer's door it took several minutes before the woman opened up.

"Hello my lovely, what brings you round on such a cold night?"

"Vonny's bum is real sore Mrs O'Dwyer and my foot is bad, can you help me?

Mary O'Dwyer felt as if her heart would break and leading the little girl through to the kitchen sat

Shauna down at the table and gently removed her sock.

"Oh Shauna love how did you do this?"

Shauna didn't answer but at the same time her cheeks flushed with embarrassment. While Mary bathed the girl's foot she inquired about Vonny and could feel her own tears well up when she was told how the sores on Vonny's backside were now weeping with puss. With the splinter removed and the little girl now tucking into a large dish of stew Mary O'Dwyer started to hunt through her medicine chest for some type of cream that would alleviate Vonny's pain. The chest, just an old biscuit tin kept in the back of the kitchen cupboard, didn't contain much more than a few plasters and some ointment. Since her brood had flown the nest it wasn't required like it had been in the old days. On the door step Shauna thanked the woman for her help and kindness and standing on tiptoes she kissed Mary on the cheek.

"You know your mum loves you Shauna?

They looked into each other's eyes, both knowing this wasn't true but neither of them wanting to add anything further. Mary O'Dwyer didn't speak for fear of hurting the child and Shauna didn't speak because there really was nothing to say. Shauna O'Malley closed the door to her flat and leant against the cold paintwork. Sliding down the wall she sat on the hard floor and all at once the tears started to flow. Shauna cried more than ever before, wracking sobs that made her entire body shake. Finally exhausted and overwhelmed, sleep at last came. She must have lain in the hallway for several hours before she heard her mother's shrill laughter outside. Scrambling from the

6

floor Shauna ran to the bedroom, just in time to hear
Violet putting her key in the lock. Luckily Vonny
had slept through all of the crying and Shauna gently
climbed in beside her sister. She lay in the damp bed
listening to her mother and the stranger trying to work
out if it was a punter or another new uncle but in all
honesty she didn't care as long as he made her mum
happy because if Violet was happy, the girls were left
alone.

Going to school was the only real respite Shauna got.
Violet allowed this, not because she wanted her
daughter to be educated but to keep the officers from
the door, she'd already had several fines from the
courts and Shauna had received numerous beatings as
punishment. The little girl was able to make it to the
classroom only after she had dropped Vonny off at
the Community crèche on the way.

Suddenly things changed and one particular Monday
turned out to be like no other before. Shauna woke
Vonny, got them both washed and dressed, all the
time her mouth-watering at the delicious smell
wafting from the kitchen. Hand in hand the two little
girls crept along the hallway and peeping through a
crack in the door Shauna saw her mother at the stove
frying up eggs and bacon. Violets hair was brushed
and she was wearing full makeup, at seven thirty in
the morning this was a sight Shauna had never seen
before. Sitting at the table reading a newspaper was a
strange man.

"Fuck Vonny!" Shauna whispered to her sister,
"He's got nice gear on."

Vonny giggled and Shauna tried to quieten her by

putting a hand over her mouth but it was too late, their mother had already heard them.

"Come on in my little sweethearts, do you want some breakfast?"

The girls looked at each other and back to their mother but neither answered as the man put down his paper and looked in Shauna and Vonny's direction.

"Is that anyway to answer? If my mother asked me a question and I didn't reply I would have had seven bells of shite knocked out of me."

"Now Davey!" Violet smiled at the man and motioned for her daughters to take a seat. "Let's just all have a nice breakfast shall we?"

Neither the girls nor the man spoke again and breakfast was eaten in silence.

Tuesday morning Shauna woke up and hoped her mother would be in the same mood as she had been yesterday. The smell of bacon and eggs again hung in the air and smiling to herself she gently woke Vonny. They walked along the hallway and once more peered into the kitchen. Again their mother was at the stove with her new friend seated at the table but there were no kind words or offers of breakfast. Instead Violet sneered in the girls' direction.

"Get back in that fuckin' bedroom before I break both of your scrawny little necks. Don't come out again until I bleeding well tell you to."

In fear, they both scurried along the hallway and it would be after ten before their mother called again.

"Shauna, get your bony arse in here now!"

The child knew what was coming but for the life of her couldn't think what she'd done wrong. As she

8

walked into the poor excuse for a living room, Shauna
felt the blows start to rein down on her.

"Mum! Mum! Whatever have I done?"

"What have you done, what have you done? You
fuckin' spoil everything that's what you've done.
Davey don't like kids and I've got two around my
neck that's what you've fuckin' done you little cunt!"
The ferocity of Violets fists was more brutal than
usual and Shauna put her hands around her head
trying to protect herself. All the cries of pain woke
Vonny but still Violet raged. Five minutes later
Shauna sat on the bathroom floor nursing a bleeding
lip, nose and two eyes that were sure to be black by
the morning. The beatings had become a daily ritual
and Violet always vented her anger on her eldest
daughter but it had never been as intense as it was
today and now her ribs were so sore it hurt to breath.

Mary O'Dwyer listened daily to the screams that
could be heard through the walls, each one pierced
her heart as surely as if it were one of her own
children being hurt. She hated the silence that would
follow, not knowing if Shauna had even survived.
Every day she tried to think of a way to help the girls
but in this area of London no one dared to stick their
nose into anyone else's business. If she called social
services it would be her word against Violets unless
the girl was still marked and the label of a grass
would make life more unbearable for the old woman
than it already was. Mary had moved to Shepherds
Bush fifty years earlier. Back then it had been a nice
place, a respectable place, a place where everyone
looked out for each other. Her husband had spent all

9

of his working life on the local markets until his death fifteen years ago. Mary's faith had seen her through his passing and although she never saw her children, just the thought of them swelled her heart. She had given birth to three daughters and a son. Her boy Gabriel ran his own Company in America and could only spare the time to call her on holidays or on her birthday but Mary accepted the situation without question, she knew he was very successful and far too busy. Her eldest daughter Rose had died aged nine, the day she passed a part of Mary had died with her and she often wondered if the love she had for Shauna was somehow a replacement for the child she had lost It was true that Shauna with her jet black hair and startling blue eyes bore more than a striking resemblance to Rose. Mary's other daughters, Sharn and Lorna, had married well and chosen to move away from London. Both had large houses, new cars and holidays abroad but Mary knew they competed with each other over everything. The only thing they didn't compete over was Mary and neither could be bothered with having her visit. For a fleeting moment Mary thought they may be embarrassed or ashamed of her but she dismissed the thought as quickly as it had entered her mind.

On Wednesday morning Shauna woke at seven, kneeling on the bare floor she whispered 'Please just let us get through the day God amen'. True to form both her eyes were black and it was a school day but there was no chance her mother would let her leave the house. Violet showed no emotion when she saw her daughters injures, she actually believed it was

Shauna's fault, as far as she was concerned, everything in her miserable life was Shauna's fault. Today was the little girls tenth birthday but there would be no celebration. Not a single thing would be done to mark the significance of the day but Shauna didn't expect anything and after all, what she'd never had she couldn't miss. The only thing she wished for was to get through the day without another beating, well that and to make sure Vonny was safe. The only thing Shauna O'Malley cared about in the whole wide world was her little sister.

CHAPTER TWO

Davey Wiseman was born at Golders' Green hospital,
North London in 1944. The fourth son of Jewish
immigrants he cared little for the religion his parents
practiced. To Davey nothing mattered more than
making cash and he didn't care who got hurt or
trampled over in the process. From the day he
learned the value of money nothing felt or smelt as
good as those crumpled notes. Many times in his
early years his father had tried to tell him how they
came to England, tried to make him understand just
how lucky he was and that he should be grateful but
all Moishe got for his efforts was a sneer.

Moishe and Rebecca Wiseman arrived from Poland in
the autumn of 1939 after Moishe had seen the war
start and had a premonition of how it would end.
Until the day he died he would praise the Lord for
getting his family away from the encroaching Nazis.
Rebecca, a petite ill offensive woman had given birth
to her first two sons before leaving Poland, Joshua in
1935 and Samuel in 39. She had been reluctant to
move, wanting to stay close to her family but her
husband had insisted that as his wife she must obey
him. Moishe had also been adamant that they must
take no belongings that would reveal they were Jews.
It broke Rebecca's heart to leave behind all her
worldly possessions. The family menorah that was
given to her and Moishe on their wedding day, even
his yarmulke was thrown onto the fire. A few clothes
and as much dried food as their cart would hold were

the only things she took. That cold October day was the saddest of her life and waking the boys early, the family had begun their journey before dawn. Their small hay cart had taken them from the outskirts of Warsaw, through terrible weather and terrain, mile after mile. The dried food had enabled them to survive the journey until they reached the small port of Dartowo. Moishe found the family shelter in a deserted barn where they would wait until nightfall and then walk the three miles to the quayside where a boat was waiting to take them across the Baltic Sea to Sweden and safety. Moishe had friends who thankfully had arranged the family's passage at no cost. The next month was spent in Vaxjo, a small City that was rapidly expanding due to the demand for high quality glass products. That time was used to rest up and as soon as it was safe a light aircraft was organised to fly them to England.

The Wisemans made it to London on November the 20th, exactly six weeks after leaving Warsaw. The relief Moishe felt could not be measured but it was a different story for Rebecca. She pined terribly for her brothers and sisters and not being able to write to them was unbearable. With the help of friends the family moved to Bridge Lane in Golders Green and the small terraced house was everything Rebecca had dreamed of. The following November she gave birth to a son Matthew and the couple now felt that their family was complete but in 1963 and in the middle of her menopause Rebecca unexpectedly revealed that she was once again pregnant. David Yosef Wiseman came into the world kicking and screaming one hot and sticky day in July. With the other children now much older everyone spoiled the newest edition to the Wiseman household and it got to a point where neither of Davey's parents could control him. At first the family would laugh at the boy and at the daily scrapes he got into but as he grew and became a bully it was no longer funny. By the age of sixteen Davey was out all hours of the day and night. Moishe had tried to discipline his son but Davey just ignored his father's advice and things finally came to a head when Rebecca tried to intervene. "Mum, don't even try to live my life for me.

I'll go where I want and see who I want, and don't tell me the old man worries about me because he doesn't give a fuck. The only thing he worries about is himself and what the Rabbi will say, well fuck him, fuck the Rabbi, in fact fuck you all, I'm out of here!" All Rebecca could do was place her head in her hands and sob. Life carried on this way for several months and the only time the couple saw their youngest son was when he came home to sleep. Davey was making his own way and earning a reputation amongst the East End underworld. Whatever he was asked to do he did without question and was soon trusted in criminal circles. Get away driving became Davey's speciality and the better he became the more lucrative the jobs on offer were. Life was pretty good but Davey wanted more, so approaching several of the faces he'd worked for and borrowing as much money as he could, saw him able to afford a deposit on a small club in Gerrard Street, Soho. The repayments were crippling and he was forced to work all the hours God sent but eventually the place became a roaring success. It catered for the underbelly of the City and the Jackson and Reid firms were happy to frequent the club which instantly gave Davey kudos in the world of villainy. Everyone knew it was a safe location to carry out meetings and Davey would have the private rooms swept on a daily basis for any kind of bugs. With money rolling in and after another heated argument with his father, Davey Wiseman finally left his parents' house in just the clothes he stood up in. He would never again set foot over the threshold, not even on the day of his father's funeral and if he met a member of his family on the street, which was seldom, he would walk straight past them.

The Jacksons had run a successful criminal outfit in London for many years and no one dared to cross them. The sadistic level of violence they regularly resorted to was unprecedented at the time and what was often exaggerated soon became true, with Chinese whispers spreading like wild fire among the smaller firms. Billy Jackson the youngest of the brothers, was one of the most respected villains in the East End and if something was going down, you could be sure Billy was involved somewhere along the line. From the moment the two men's paths had crossed Billy Jackson and Davey Wiseman formed an instant friendship. Davey, aware that Billy was homosexual, knew when making deals he could use the man's sexuality to his advantage. Now and again he would flirt with Billy, just enough to keep the man interested and allow Davey to get his own way when it came down to making the more important decisions. The friendship became so strong that the two were often asked if they were brothers, though behind closed doors their relationship was viewed as far seedier. The Wiseman empire grew rapidly and it was the Jackson firm that provided protection. Davey had a thing for the ladies and it could be any lady he wasn't fussy. In each club he kept a small room for entertaining which he liked to call his interview room. All the new girls that came looking for work had to go through an interview Davey Wiseman style. It didn't matter if it was for hostess or bar work, they were all subjected to his sexual desire and if they didn't agree to this then there would be no job. Tongue in cheek by his associates and definitely out of earshot, Davey Wiseman was soon referred to as the hardest interviewer in London. The girls would go in, undress, perform a blow or hand job and then exit fully employed. Any that obliged were given jobs and some days there were more girls working than paying customers. Around the time Davey was planning to open his third club, Violet O'Malley came into his life. She wasn't his usual type, Davey like them young, really young in fact but the fiery temper and amazing red hair had him instantly mesmerised. He had to make her subservient and knew that with Violet it would be difficult but he would break her, if it was the last thing he did he would control her entirely. The club was usually quiet on Mondays and tonight was no exception. Suddenly the doors swung open and in walked the most attractive woman that the doorman, Stevie McNamara, had seen in a long time. Violet was known to a lot of the regulars as a part time brass though strangely not to Stevie, who asked if he could help her.

"I'm looking for some work and I wondered if there's anything going here."

"Take a seat and I'll have a word with the boss, what's your name darling?"

"Violet, Violet O'Malley."

"Ok Violet, you sit tight for a minute and I'll see what I can find out."

Stevie crossed the small wooded area that could in a bad light pass as a dance floor and knocked on Davey's door.

"Whoever it is you can just fuck right off! I'm about to start an interview."

Stevie moved closer and tried to limit who could hear as he was forced to speak through a closed door.

"Sorry boss but there's a woman out here who's looking for work and I think she probably has what you're looking for. Davey already had his hands full for the evening but he couldn't resist a look at his next possible conquest. Opening the door just enough to be able to see in the direction of the foyer he gave Violet the once over.

"Not too bad I suppose. When I've finished here, give me a minute then show her in Stevie."

Davey went back into the office and motioned to the young girl to leave.

"But Mr Wiseman, have I got the job?"

"I'll give it some thought, but you'll need to improve on your mouth action love, I struggled to get a hard on. Come back tomorrow and you can try again sweetheart."

The girl left the office in tears just as Stevie and

17

Violet approached. The young woman looked Violet straight in the eyes as if trying to warn her of what was to come but Violet just smiled. She had guessed what had gone down or rather who and chuckled to herself. When would these teenagers learn that nothing comes free in this world not even a job in seedy back street club. Davey introduced himself and asked Violets name, she answered the question and sharply added that she didn't take any shit from anyone.

"So is there any work going or am I wasting my time?"

Davey was taken aback but also amused by the creature that stood before him. No one, especially a woman, would normally dare speak to him like that.

"Well Violet O'Malley I like a woman who stands up for herself, maybe you should come and show me where your talents lie."

"What like that poor little cow that just left? No chance Mister, I came for a job and nothing else. Here's my number, call me if you have anything."

With that she walked out of the office slamming the door. Davey stood speechless, something he'd not been in a long time and then a smile crept over his face. What he didn't realise, was the fact that Violet also had a smile on her face, her plan had gone smoothly. Did Davey Wiseman really think that she was as naive as the stupid little whores he usually fucked? Violet had seen him on the streets a few times, liked what she saw and decided that it was time she had a man to take care of her and the brats. It had taken a few days to find out who he was and where he hung out and then she had put her plan into action.

18

The fiery woman with the flame coloured hair wasn't going to succumb easily, it was going to cost him dearly but it would take many years for him to find out just how dearly. Stevie was called into the office within five minutes of Violet leaving.

"What do you reckon?"

"About what Boss?"

"About, the bit of skirt that just left."

Stevie shrugged his shoulders, he couldn't deny that she was easy on the eye but apart from that he hadn't taken much notice and to be truthful he wasn't really interested.

"Don't know how to answer that Davey but I can see you're fuckin' taken with her."

"You're right Stevie and I think this one could turn out to be a bit special. Now I want to know where she lives, where she hangs out, I want to know everything about her. Do you get me?"

Stevie had never seen his boss like this and didn't really know what to make of the situation. He also knew a chancer when he saw one and Violet was defiantly a chancer. Stevie wasn't the brightest bulb in the box but he was savvy enough to know when to keep his trap shut and he wasn't going to be the one to tell Davey that he was making a mistake.

"I'll see what I can do boss."

"Don't see what you can do you tosser! Just do what I've fuckin' asked."

Stevie McNamara left the office and as he slowly walked across the dance floor, wished he had never let Violet O'Malley through the front doors.

CHAPTER THREE

From the moment Shauna and Davey's paths crossed
the little girl had taken an instant dislike to the man.
It wasn't anything he said or did but the fact that he
hadn't even tried to be friendly or gain their trust in
anyway. "I don't like that man", was the first thing
Vonny had said after they had eaten their surprise,
never to be repeated again breakfast. Shauna bent
down and whispered "me neither" into her sisters ear.
Once the girls realised they wouldn't be invited to eat
with Davey and their mother again they tried to stay
clear of him whenever he was in the flat, but it didn't
turn out to be that easy. Violet was totally smitten
with her new man and he always seemed to be
around, much to the girls dislike. It was just in the
evenings but when you're young and shut away in a
bedroom with nothing to do, a few hours can seem
like forever. A month later and Davey still didn't
know much about the woman he was starting to have
strong feelings for. In truth it had only taken Stevie
McNamara a couple of days to find out Violet's
history but out of fear he had kept the news to himself
in the hope that Davey wouldn't ask him again. His
luck was out on the day that he was summoned into
the office, he knew what was coming and he wasn't
looking forward to passing the information over to his
boss. As he knocked on the office door he could
visibly see his hands trembling.
"Come in Stevie. Now it's been a while since I asked
you to look into Violets background, found anything
out yet?"

"Well I have boss but you're not going to like it."
"Oh for fuck sake, just spill your guts, it can't be that bad."
Behind his back Stevie clenched his fists as he began to speak.
"It seems your new lady friend is on the game."
For a few seconds Davey just stared at the man without uttering a single word and then he suddenly laughed out loud.
"Don't be fuckin' stupid. Violet might be a bit of a rough diamond but she's no whore."
"I'm sorry Boss but you're wrong. Seems she works around Shepherds Bush, only part time mind. My snouts tell me she lives on the Mile End road with her two little girls."
"I know all that you fuckin' idiot but are you sure about her being on the game?"
"That's what I was told and from more than one source I might add."
For a few seconds Davey didn't continue, he felt a total and utter fool and knew that Violet had really tried to mug him off. The atmosphere in the office was making Stevie feel so uncomfortable that he broke the silence in the hope of easing the situation.
"So Davey, is there anything else you want me to do?"
Davey could only glare at his employee as he shook his head. With the revelation, his opinion of his new girlfriend had drastically changed, if she thought she could get away with lying to him she could think again. The relationship, although Violet wasn't aware of the fact, was already over and in the next few weeks the girls were about to witness the real

side of Davey Wiseman. He had slept over on the Tuesday night and the next morning Shauna was trying to get Vonny washed so that they could get to the crèche on time. The bathroom was always empty at this time of the day so the girls didn't think to knock before going in. Davey stood urinating in the toilet bowl and both girls just stared.

"What the fuck are you two looking at?"

Neither replied to the question and Shauna couldn't help but stare at the man's genitalia.

"I told you before to answer when you're fuckin' spoken to, you little cunts."

Davey lashed out and hit Shauna across the face with the back of his hand knocking her sideways onto the bath rim and the last thing she heard before blacking out was Vonny's screams. When Shauna finally regained consciousness she was shivering and her head was hurting badly from the blows. She tried to stand up but it took real effort as her legs felt like jelly. Suddenly Vonny came into her thoughts and from somewhere she found strength and flung the door open. Everywhere was in darkness but after stumbling along the hallway she at last felt the bedroom door handle. Opening the door Shauna could just make out Vonny's tiny silhouette lying curled up on their bed. The clock on the cabinet glowed red and when she saw five pm, she realised that she had lain in the bathroom for nine hours. Flicking on the switch, a bare bulb which was the only source of light illuminated the room and Shauna gasped at the sight before her. Vonny's mouth and nose were covered in dried blood and a lump the size of a golf ball stood out on her forehead. Shauna was

22

enraged and whispered under her breath. "That bastard, that bleeding fuckin' bastard." Climbing into bed beside her sister she wrapped her arms tightly around the little girl.

The following day Violet was the first to wake, Shauna hadn't bothered to get her sister up as she knew there was no way they would be allowed out of the house. Shauna was cuddled up to Vonny but when the small child woke she instantly began to cry with pain but Shauna didn't know what to do to make her feel better. She wanted to go and see Mrs O'Dwyer but now that her mother hardly went out of the flat it wasn't easy to just nip next door. They could hear Violet moving about in the flat but she hadn't called them yet, by this time Shauna was normally getting a right ear bashing so something was going on. The girls looked at each other and without a word between them climbed out of bed and tip toed along the hallway. Vonny timidly stayed two paces behind her big sister, petrified that the nasty man was still there. Entering the kitchen they found their mother just sitting at the table staring into space. Shauna put the kettle on to make Violet's tea and the silence seemed to last forever as they waited for the water to boil but finally when Shauna put the cup onto the table she asked if her mother was okay but Violet didn't reply.
"Mum are you alright?" Shauna asked again. As if coming out of a trance Violet looked at the girls and just nodded, neither sister could believe they hadn't received a mouthful of abuse.
"Come on Von let's get you washed."

Shauna led Vonny in the direction of the bathroom and at the same time wondered if it was just a case of too much gin last night but deep down she knew it was much more than that. Violet always vented her anger on Shauna and to date the abuse Vonny received had only ever been verbal, well it had been up until last night. Her thoughts were broken when Vonny suddenly started to talk in her innocent, infant way.

"She feel better soon Shauna, we going to school? I like school, when I a big girl I going to your school."

"No not today Von but we'll watch the telly and have a nice time."

Vonny looked up at her big sister and smiled.

"I love you Shauna."

"I love you too Von."

Next door Mary O'Dwyer was becoming increasingly worried about the girls. Except for a couple of quick glimpses out on the landing she hadn't seen much of Shauna lately but even then Mary had noticed that the little girl had appeared thinner than ever. She knew of the beatings and nightly shouting but she wasn't aware of just how bad things truly were. The two little girls entered Mary's thoughts as soon as she opened her eyes in the morning and they were the last thing she thought about when she closed them at night.

On hearing Stevie's revelations Davey had instantly stopped taking Violet out. Now he treated her as the whore she was and only called at the flat when he wanted sex. Careful of risking his health, he made sure he always left money on the bedside table, which at least stopped her having to go out and earn. Davey Wiseman was rotten to the core and as a punishment he had recently introduced Violet to heroin. While drunk and in a desperate attempt to please him, she had caved in under his pressure in the hope that by doing what Davey asked he would stick around. Violet had thought this man was different thought that maybe he would even marry her and couldn't for the life of her work out why he had changed so suddenly. A couple of days went by and when Davey hadn't been to the flat the girls hoped it was the last they had seen of him, however when Friday night came their mother began to get ready. They both knew the routine by now and as soon as he knocked on the door they disappeared into their bedroom. After the incident in the bathroom Davey had told Violet that he didn't like the girls and if she wanted him to call in then they had to be out of sight. Each day Shauna noticed her mother becoming quieter and more subdued. Violet had stopped getting dressed unless she was seeing Davey and even then she didn't put make up on and her hair was lifeless and dirty. One night as the girls sat in their room listening to their mother and her new friend they heard Violet cry out in pain and Davey start to shout.

"You dirty whore, you fuckin' stink. When was the last time you had a wash?"

"I'm sorry Davey but I'm so tired, don't be mad, I love you."

"Oh fuck off Violet you're just a dirty filthy slut who makes her living on her back."

Realisation finally hit Violet, he'd found out about her past. She could have punched herself, how stupid to think that a man like him wouldn't find out and now the chance of a decent life had just flown out the window. The girls heard the blows that landed on their mother and both hid their heads under the covers hoping it would stop but it didn't. When the flat was at last silent Shauna guessed that her mother and Davey had fallen asleep. She slid out of bed, tiptoed past her mother's room and opened the front door. Mary O'Dwyer heard the tapping on her front door but was a little scared to answer at this late hour of the night.

"Who's there?"

"It's me Mrs O'Dwyer, Shauna. Oh please let me in, please!!!!!!"

Mary took the chain off as quickly as she could and Shauna almost threw herself into the woman's arms.

"Oh Mrs O'Dwyer I don't know what to do, he beat me and Von and my Mum's........."

"Slow down child, I can't understand a word you're saying, now come in will you and I'll make us both a nice cup of tea."

For the first time, Mary ushered the little girl into her living room and sat her in one of the armchairs. Shauna was so small that the large comfy chair felt like it was wrapping itself around her and she snuggled down into the soft fabric never wanting to move again. Shauna looked around the room in amazement, until now she had only been into Mrs O'Dwyer's kitchen. The room though small was warm and inviting and it reminded Shauna of the houses she'd seen on the television. Suddenly she started to cry, racking heart breaking sobs that made Mary want to cry too.

"Now my love, don't carry on so. Come on sweetheart, tell Aunty Mary what's wrong."

"My Mum's got a new fella and he's horrible, he knocked me out the other day and he hurt Vonny and made her nose bleed. My Mum said she wouldn't see him again but she let him in tonight. Oh Mrs O'Dwyer we're both so scared."

This poor child didn't speak like a little girl, her words were direct and were spoken like an adult. Shauna had been denied any kind of childhood and Mary, aware of the dilemma she was in, also knew that she finally had to do something. Whether she was labelled a grass or not, she couldn't stand by and see these children suffer a moment longer.

"Now you listen to me Shauna, first thing in the morning I'm going to call Social Services and put a stop to all this carrying on once and for all."

Shauna didn't answer she just looked up at the woman with tears rolling down her cheeks. The next morning when Shauna heard Davey close the front door she went into her mother's room. The covers were heaped up in a pile in the middle of the bed and gently moving them sideways she saw her mother's bruised and battered face. Violet struggled to open her eyes, they were both black and swollen and she winced as she gingerly licked her fat bottom lip. Shaun could feel the tears fall onto her cheeks but for once she didn't wipe them away.

"Why do you let him do this to you mum? We got along better before he came on the scene didn't we?"

Instead of the usual barrage of abuse, through her terribly swollen eyes Violet just looked at her eldest daughter.

"Shauna he pays the bills and gives me stuff. I can't manage without him so what am I supposed to do?" It was the first time she had heard her mother admit that she was now hooked on heroin and it had only started when Davey had appeared on the scene.
"Why mum? Why did you take it? You never needed anything before."
"Because I thought he was different sweetheart and I just wanted to keep him happy."
Her mother hadn't called her sweetheart since she was small. Suddenly Shauna felt like the parent, she wanted to sweep her mother up into her arms and tell her that everything would be all right just like Mrs O'Dwyer said it would be but she didn't, instead she pleaded like never before.
"Please Mum, if he comes round again don't answer the door. Please mum, don't let him in here, please oh please Mum!"
'No Shauna I won't, I promise."
The following evening they were all in bed by ten o'clock and Shauna prayed that Davey wouldn't make an appearance but half an hour later the knock came at the door. Shauna flew out of bed as fast as her legs could carry her and ran to her mother's room just in time to see Violet putting on her dressing gown.
"Mum please you promised, please don't let him in!"
"I have to, I'm nearly tearing my bleeding hair out. You don't understand I need something from him, just this once Shauna then I'll never let him in again."
Shauna ambled back to her room and closing the door climbed into bed. Cuddling Vonny she began to cry and at the same time stared up at the ceiling as she

28

asked God why? With every passing day Violet
became worse, she didn't buy food for the girls or
bother about the flat. Shauna would wait until her
mother and Davey were asleep, and then sneak
around the house looking for any spare money that
Davey had lain down but mostly it was only two or
three pounds and just enough to keep her and Vonny
in chips. Every day Shauna pleaded with her mother
not to let Davey in and every night her mother's reply
was the same.

"Just tonight Shauna, I need a little help but after
today I'm going to clean myself up I promise."

In the end Shauna gave up trying. True to her word
Mary had telephoned Social Services first thing the
next day but it would be two weeks before anyone
called at the O'Malley flat, two weeks too late!

CHAPTER FOUR

Every passing day saw Violet sink deeper and deeper into the murky cesspit of heroin addiction, spending every waking hour waiting for her next fix. As the clock ticked Violet would become more and more agitated and when the signs began to show, the girls knew to stay in their room. The day would start off quietly enough and usually they would all manage to make it through to the afternoon but the atmosphere would become charged as the evening drew closer. The girls whiled away their time playing but Violet was oblivious to their presence. By late afternoon and just like a switch being flicked on, the need to satisfy her addiction would kick in and Violet started to pace the floor sweating and cursing at anyone and anything. Suddenly she called out for her eldest daughter and when Shauna ran into the room the strong smell of faeces hit her nose with both barrels. When her mother started to cluck, a term Shauna thought sounded funny, it usually resulted in Violet releasing her bowels and it could happen anywhere.

"Mum, mum? Should I call a doctor, you look really ill and you're so white."

"A fuckin' doctor! You idiot! What do you think a doctor would do, write me out a prescription?"

"I dunno but you need some help, you really, really do. Pleeeease Mum!!!!"

"For Christ sake Shauna! The only help I need, Davey will bring me."

'Oh Mum' was the only reply Shauna could give. Violet's pacing became quicker and she clutched at her stomach trying to stop the pain. Her nightdress was soaking wet, perspiration stood out on her brow and she knew that he was making her wait on purpose. What a cunt he was but in her own sad way she still loved him.

"Come on Davey, don't do this to me, please, please no!!!!"

"Please mum, don't let him in. I'll help you I promise I promise! You don't need to take that horrible stuff, pleeeeeease!"

"What the fuck do you know? I told you before I just need a little help and then I'll get myself straight." Shauna sighed a little too loudly and maybe too visibly. Before she knew it her mother's hands were around her throat. As Violet squeezed with as much strength as she could muster, white spittle formed at the sides of Shauna's mouth.

"You're a cocky little cow, do you know that? I'm going through hell here and all you can do is moan and whinge. I take oath on it Shauna, one of these days I'll fuckin' kill you, trust me I will."

For a second she loosened her grip and Shauna fell to the ground coughing and spluttering. The girl's eyes felt as if they were about to pop out of their sockets and tears flowed freely down her cheeks. She looked round for her sister and saw Vonny standing in the doorway, motionless watching her mother and sister. Even though her throat was burning Shauna somehow managed to whisper.

"You all right Von?"

The little girl didn't answer and just continued to stare at the carnage in front of her. The front room was normally messy but today and after her mother's

31

latest outburst it was worse. The coffee table had been upended and the remnants of a cup of something were now splashed up the wall. Getting to her feet and taking hold of Vonny's hand Shauna gently led her little sister along the hallway to their room and closed the door. It was all too much for the girl and she needed to take a break, if only for a while.

"I can't take anymore Vonny I really can't. What can I do, I can't help her, I don't think anyone can." Vonny started to cry and while Shauna hugged her she hummed her little sister's favourite song by the Stylistics. 'Sing baby sing, the world is getting better'. Normally this would have Vonny giggling but all she could manage was a half-hearted smile.

Davey didn't arrive until after nine and even then he had to force himself to go inside. Violet was fun in the beginning, well until he found out she would open her legs for anyone with cash. Double standards he thought to himself but he couldn't help it, any girl he really liked had to be clean, no skeletons, no one able to walk up to him and laugh because of who he was sleeping with. He'd thought Violet was that and more, thought they could have gone places and when he found out the truth, well it sickened him to his stomach. Davey always had to get his revenge, he was known for it and the last few days had all been nothing but a ploy to get back at that dirty whore. When he eventually entered the room Violet was in a terrible state.

"Where the fuck have you been? You know I needed you here by seven."

"Shut the fuck up you slut, nobody tells me what I should and shouldn't do. I've only come to tell you that I won't be around here again."

"What do you mean? You can't stop coming now, not after you got me hooked on that shit. I thought we had something good Davey, I love you."

"No you don't Violet, the only thing you love is this stuff."

He waved a small plastic bag in front of her. The dirty brown contents were like gold, gold for which she would do anything to get her hands on. In desperation she snatched at the bag but she wasn't quick enough.

"Not so fast scag head."

"Whose fault is that?"

"You didn't take much persuading did you?"

"Oh pleeeeease Davey, I'm dying here. Just let me have it and I'll do anything you want."

"Anything I want? That's a laugh, I wouldn't touch you again with a fuckin' barge pole. Now listen and listen good."

He threw Violet onto the settee with a hard shove but she didn't take her eyes off of the little bag. The cramps in her stomach were terrible and she knew that before much longer she would start to throw up if she didn't get what she needed.

"You're a bastard Davey Wiseman! Why are you tormenting me?"

"Because I like to watch you squirm you dirty cunt! You thought when we met I wouldn't find out you were a Brass, didn't you?"

"No Davey I was going to......"

Before Violet could finish her sentence he punched her hard in the face. She didn't react, the need for a fix was stronger than any physical pain, and the only thing she could feel was the warm trickle of blood as it ran down her chin.

"After this I don't ever want to set fuckin' eyes on you again, do you understand?"

Violet vigorously nodded her head and he threw the small bag down as he turned to leave. Looking over his shoulder Davey uttered the last words Violet O'Malley would ever hear.

"It's good gear Vi, the best you'll ever have."

She didn't care that he had gone, didn't give a thought as to who would supply her hit tomorrow, all Violet could think about was getting the drug into her vein as quickly as she could. Grabbing the small tin from the hearth she removed the rubber tube and tied it tightly around her arm. Slowly she sprinkled the bags contents onto an old spoon, her hands were shaking badly by now and Violet prayed that she wouldn't spill any as she added a small amount of citric acid and water. She then flicked on her lighter, Violet didn't even notice how dirty and stained her finger tips were as she proceeded to hold the flame under the bowl and watch as the powder turned to liquid. Placing a small sponge on top she carefully siphoned the liquid gold into a syringe. With the ritual of preparing the drug over she eased back and began to inject, slowly pushing on the syringe Violet could feel the rush as it engulfed her. Euphoria enveloped every part of her body but seconds later she was plunged into oblivion. This feeling was all that she craved and had been longing for, Violet didn't know and didn't care about the purity of the drug she had taken. As her life ebbed away the two little girls slept huddled together, blissfully unaware of what was happening in the room next door. For a while Shauna had laid listening to her mother and Davey having one of their regular arguments but after she heard the door slam she was so tired that she went straight to sleep. Shauna slept soundly, so soundly in fact that she didn't hear or feel Vonny climb over her in the early hours of the morning. The little girl made her way along the hallway and finding the living room door ajar, walked inside. Seeing Violet on the settee Vonny pulled the needle from her mother's arm and held it up to the light. So many times she had watched her mummy do it and now she was a big girl she was going to be just like her. Vonny innocently inserted the syringe into her arm and let out a small cry as the needle broke her skin. The sleepiness came over her straight away, a sleepiness that felt warm and nice but one from which she would never wake.

At the usual time Shauna rubbed the crust from her eyes and felt around the damp bed for her sister. When she realised Vonny wasn't there panic reared its head, Vonny never ever got up before her, where was she?
"Von, Vonny where are you baby?"
Shauna called out several times not caring if she woke her mother but there was only silence. Jumping out of bed she ran along the hallway but all the doors in the small flat were closed, all except the one to the front room. She breathed a sigh of relief, Vonny must have worked out how to switch on the television and the worry stopped as she pushed on the door and entered the front room. The horrific sight that greeted her would stay with Shauna for the rest of her life.

The stench inside the room was as usual rancid and she looked around for only a second before spying Violet sprawled out on the settee. The entire colour had drained from her face and Shauna knew that her mother would never wake up again. Violet would never beat her or shout at her ever again but no tears fell, Shauna just stood and stared. It wasn't until she noticed the tiny body lying at the side of the settee that she let out the most piercing, heart breaking scream, a scream that didn't sound remotely human. Mary O'Dwyer was about to go down to the market and was just writing out her shopping list when she heard the commotion. Grabbing her coat Mary rushed out of the door and within seconds was banging on her neighbour's door and shouting for someone to let her in. There was no reply so Mary peered through the letterbox and saw the little girl huddled in a tight ball on the hallway floor.

"Shauna, Shauna love, come on sweetheart its Mary let me in darling!"

Shauna just stared and it was a stare Mary had never seen the likes of before, as if the girl was looking straight through her, just the shell of a child with no one inside.

"Jesus in heaven help us."

The police arrived in less than fifteen minutes and by London standards that was quick but it felt like an eternity to Mary O'Dwyer. The young constable, who Mary guessed was no more than thirty years old, approached the flat at a slow pace as if he had all the time in the world.

"Excuse me Madam, are you the member of public who made an emergency call?"

"Yes I was, now for Christ sakes get this door open will you?"

"I'm sorry but I can't just break into a property. You can appreciate I have to have some details before any action can be taken."

"For fucks sake you stupid little man, a child is hurt in there! Now are you opening this bleeding door or do I have to try and break it down myself?"

It had been years since Mary had used such language but at this precise moment she didn't give a damn. The young man looked through the letterbox and met Shauna's gaze, moments later he had forced open the door and he and Mary rushed into the flat. Immediately Mary went to Shauna's side as the officer entered the front room and seconds later Mary heard the sound of vomiting and then the officer calling for back up on his radio. After help arrived all hell broke loose, an ambulance and police cars filled the small square below the flats and the landing was cordoned off. The constable was gentle with Shauna, his trauma training was in full force as he led her to the police car with as little fuss as possible. Mary stood on the doorstep with tears rolling down her cheeks. She was in total and utter shock as she watched them lead Shauna away before explaining to the plain clothed detectives who she was. She offered up as much information as she could, though what help it would be she didn't know. The guilt had started to take over, guilt at letting the situation carry on for as long as it had and when Mary walked back into the O'Malley flat no one tried to stop her. Violet and Vonny were still in the same position as they had been when Shauna had found them and Mary screamed at the officer standing by to cover them up. "For crying out loud, give them some dignity will you. Lord knows they had little in life so at least let them have some in death."

A young police woman of no more than twenty led Mary back to her own flat and made tea for them both."

"I'm sorry madam."

"For what?"

"That you saw what you did, it's a terrible situation."

"A terrible situation! You don't have an inkling regarding what's been going on in that flat! Those babies suffered for years and no one cared, no one bothered, no one batted an eyelid."

"That's right Mrs O'Dwyer no one did."

With those words Mary felt a terrible grief, grief for Shauna, for Vonny, for all the times she knew she could have done something but had stood by and let the badness happen.

"What will happen to the child?"

"She'll be taken to a local care home for the time being, from then on who knows?"

This made Mary feel even worse but she kept quiet, the only thing on her mind was the fact that she could have prevented this terrible tragedy if only she had acted sooner.

"Can I see her?"

The policewoman felt sorry for Mary, she had seen so many people suffer from guilt, guilt she knew Mary was feeling at this very moment.

"It's probably best if you don't. That little girl has a lot of things to come to terms with and seeing you will only bring back memories that need to be buried, at least for the time being."

Mary didn't answer but silently she prayed to God that one day Shauna would forgive her. The drive to the care home took about an hour and in that time Shauna didn't utter a word as all of her thoughts were of Vonny and how this could have happened. Hadn't she taken good care of Von, always keeping her safe? What would she do now, who would take care of her? The driver, a dark haired middle aged woman by the name of Amanda Burt, tried to make conversation. She'd been told not to mention what had happened but to try and get the child to relax, sadly everything she said fell on deaf ears.

"Are you alright my love?"

There was no reply.

"You'll like the place we're going to, everyone's so nice and friendly."

Still Shauna didn't reply and the child's silence made Amanda feel stupid and somehow inadequate. The poor little mite had just had her entire family wiped out, what did she care if it was a nice place or not. Amanda decided it was best not to say anymore, the child had far too much on her mind to make polite conversation.

CHAPTER FIVE

The late sixties had been a wonderful time and Jacqueline Silver had tried to be one of the in crowd but for some reason she just didn't gel with the last of the hippies. This hadn't stopped her trying and it had taken until 1970 to finally realise she was the butt of most people's jokes and would never fit in. The position at Sunrise Children's Home in Essex had become available and although she didn't think she stood a cat in hells chance, had applied anyway. The manager Jim Brackson, himself a follower of free love had taken to Jackie straight away and much to her surprise had offered her a job on the spot. By the time Shauna arrived at Sunrise Jim had moved up to area manager and Jackie had been promoted to manageress. Now twenty five years later she had seen many youngsters walk through the door, all frightened and alone. She had also witnessed them gradually integrate and become part of a large extended family and with the exception of a few, had seen them turn into decent human beings, before leaving to start new lives. Frankly nothing in all those years had prepared her for the feeling that would overcome her the first time she set eyes on Shauna O'Malley. Parking up on the drive Amanda opened the car door and after ushering Shauna out into the sunshine, faced Jackie and started to talk about Shauna as if she wasn't there.

"I think she's still in shock, she won't talk, in fact she hasn't uttered a single word for the entire journey."

"It's not surprising after what she's been through and

I would prefer it if you didn't talk about the children in front of them."

Amanda Burt took offence at Jackie's tone, she had been driving for Social Services for years and the least this jumped up manager could do was show some respect.

"Well sorry I spoke, I was only trying to give you a bit of insight."

Jackie knew she had ruffled the woman's feathers but that was the least of her problems. Today she was welcoming one of the saddest cases she had ever come across and nursing a middle aged woman's ego was bottom of her list of things to do.

"Listen to me, every child that passes through this door is in more emotional pain than you or I will probably ever experience. You drop them off, make your stupid comments and then leave us to try and sort out the mess."

Speechless Amanda got back into her car and slamming the door, drove off leaving Shauna and Jackie standing on the gravel driveway. Jackie slowly shook her head in disbelief, it never ceased to amaze her how selfish and unfeeling human beings could be. Sighing heavily, she plastered on a smile and then bent down so that she was at eye level with the child.

"Hello there, my name's Jackie and you must be Shauna."

Shauna looked the woman up and down for a second. She had a friendly face but her clothes were weird, her skirt was long and she had those funny sandals on her feet. Shauna remembered her Mum telling her all about the hippies and what they had got up to. At the thought of her mummy, hurt instantly filled her and she just stared straight through the strange looking woman.

"I expect you're hungry after your journey, come inside and I'll fix you something to eat. Everyone here is nice and friendly and we've got your room all ready."

Jackie continued to talk for what seemed like an age, hardly pausing for breath. Past experience had taught her that if a child wouldn't speak it was the best way, you either broke through the barrier or they eventually got so fed up with your voice that they replied just to shut you up but this wasn't to be the case with Shauna O'Malley. Over the next two weeks Jackie tried every trick in the book but nothing worked. The police came and went several times but no one could get a word out of the child. Shauna spent all day in her room only venturing out for meals and Jackie would often stand outside the bedroom listening to the little girl talk, to who she would later find out was the child's dead sister.

"It's Okay Vonny I'm here. Nothing will hurt you now."

In the end Jackie was at the end of her tether and about to give up when Shauna finally uttered her first words since her arrival.

"Can I go home soon Miss?"

Jackie was so stunned that for a minute she didn't reply but staring into the little girls large and very sad eyes, Jackie felt as if her own heart was about to break.

"No my darling, you have to stay here."

"I won't see Vonny again, will I?"

42

'"No, no you won't but you can say goodbye when we go to the funeral. That's if you want to go, no one would think anything less of you if you decided to stay here on the day."

Shauna's eyes misted over with tears, she didn't answer but nodded her head so hard Jackie thought that the girl would do herself some serious harm. Later alone in her flat she went over the conversation she'd had with the strange little child and one thing kept coming to the fore, not once had Shauna mentioned her mother. All the children talked about their mums, even if they were imaginary super mums who didn't exist. This wasn't true of Shauna O'Malley and until the day she left care she never ever mentioned Violet to Jackie or anyone else.

The funeral was a dismal lonely affair, the only mourners being Shauna, Jackie and Mary O'Dwyer. As soon as Shauna saw the old woman she broke away from Jackie and running over, threw both arms as tightly as she could around Mary's waist.

"Hello my angel, how are you?"

Shauna started to cry and Mary felt the familiar tearing at her own heart.

"Oh my little darling, I'm sure everything's going to be aright and Vonny wouldn't want to see you crying now would she?"

Hearing Mary's words Shauna wiped her eyes, she had to be strong for Von. When both of the coffins had been lowered into the ground, the cortege albeit small, walked out of the graveyard. Jackie held the car door open for Shauna to get in and Mary headed towards her taxi. Again breaking away Shauna ran over to Mary and grabbing the woman's hands began to plead.

"Please take me with you, don't leave me! Please Mrs O'Dwyer, I don't like it there I want to go home."

"Oh my precious I would if I could but I'm getting old and I won't be able to look after you properly."

"I don't mind. I looked after Vonny and I can look after you, please Mrs O'Dwyer please take me with you."

"I know you could sweetheart but you shouldn't have to. Now go with Miss Silver and start again. Shauna you need a life of your own child, you need to learn how to be a little girl. I will never forget you and I beg that one day you will forgive me but I have to do what's right my little darling."

When the taxi pulled away Shauna sobbed and sobbed until she felt her heart would break and past experience had taught Jackie Silver that at times like these it was best to say nothing.

The next few months went slowly by and very few at the care home were ever informed in any great detail as to what had exactly happened to Shauna's mother and sister. It was just expected that the O'Malley child would move on with her life and hopefully a foster home could be found. This never happened as the beautiful dark haired little girl would turn into a monster whenever placed with a prospective family. In later years Jackie and Shauna would laugh when they reminisced, the longest any family survived with her was nine days.

As Shauna's eighteenth birthday drew closer and her time to leave the home became imminent Jackie tried to prepare her for the big wide world but Shauna blocked her every step of the way. When they discussed jobs, there was nothing she wanted to do, when accommodation was mentioned Shauna would just say "I'm not living in that flea pit". Finally Jackie knew that she had to take a harder line with the young woman and sitting Shauna down her voice took on the tone of authority.

"Now listen to me Shauna. With your attitude we're not getting anywhere and time is now of the essence. You've only got two weeks left here so what is it that you want?"

For the first time in years Shauna began to cry, which made Jackie get a lump in her own throat.

"Oh why are you doing this Shauna, it's a fresh start, the beginning of something new."

There was only silence and Jackie was becoming increasingly annoyed.

"Well? You still haven't answered my question Shauna?"

"Alright, alright just give me five minutes will you!" Jackie decided it was best to leave the girl on her own for a while so using the ruse of making coffee she left the room. It was common knowledge among her colleagues just how deep her affection was for this particular young woman went and even though the girl was now approaching eighteen, to Jackie she was still the same little girl who had stepped out of that car eight years earlier. When she came back into the room Shauna was sitting by the window with her back to the door.

"I'm sorry Jacks. I suppose I'm being a little arsehole because I just don't want to leave here. After I lost Vonny I thought my world had ended but you showed me how to care again. I love you Jacks and I just don't think I can cope on my own."

"Of course you can. Now I've never told you that it would be easy but life isn't easy Shauna. I'll be here for you every step of the way and I could never stop caring about you even if I wanted to."

Both women smiled at each other and Jackie gave Shauna one of her special winks.

The next two weeks were hectic beyond belief and as difficult as it had been, Jackie had managed to secure a room for Shauna in Essex, a shared house with two other girls. Work wise it was a different story and the job at the local factory was not what Jackie had planned but beggars couldn't be choosers and for all intents and purpose that's what Shauna was or would be if she didn't take this job. It had taken a whole day to get moved into the tiny room. She hadn't realised that Shauna had so many bits and pieces but Jackie quickly found out that the girl never threw anything away. All her clothes were neatly folded and the gifts and toys given to her over the years were packed away in labelled boxes.

"Shauna you really should think about giving some of this stuff to charity. Let's face it, half the items in these boxes wouldn't fit a twelve year old let alone a girl of your age."

"I know, but it's hard to part with any of it. When I lived at home we didn't have anything and the first time you brought me something it was so special I cherished it, I still do. I cherish everything you have ever given me, even this"

Shauna held up a small brown bear which had been a gift to her in the first few days of her arrival at Sunrise.

"My God, you kept it all this time?"

Jackie started to laugh and Shauna stared at her then laughed too. When it was finally time to leave Jackie held her close.

"Remember if there is anything, anything at all just call me, night or day, I mean it Shauna."

"I know you do, but I have to learn to stand on my own two feet, I realise that now. I can never repay you for all that you've done and I know it went much further than doing your job."

Shauna gently kissed the woman on her cheek and then turned and went into the house. As Jackie walked to her car she felt the pain as total and utter loss consumed her and at the same time wondered if this was how parents felt when they lost a child. Alone in her room, Shauna also felt lost and for the first time in ages she thought about Vonny and wished that she was here. Quietly she muttered under her breath.

"I miss you Von."

The voice in her head was soft.

"I miss you too Shauna."

The work that Jackie had found her at the factory was mind numbing and the two girls she shared the house with were not much better. All they talked about were boys and makeup and it crazed Shauna, crazed her so much that she spent most evenings locked

47

away in her room and the only relief came when Jackie visited. It was mostly on Sundays and they would go for a walk in the park or stop at some little café for lunch. This was precious time for Shauna, a time that was just for her. The mundane factory job was only bearable when she thought about the weekend and her visitor but Jackie was becoming increasingly worried about the girl.

"Shauna you should get out more, make some friends. I won't be around forever you know, wouldn't you like to meet a nice man and have a family of your own one day?"

"No!!!!!!"

"Okay, okay, there's no need to bite my head off."

"I'm sorry Jacks, it's just that when I think of family I picture my own and I couldn't put any child through what Vonny and me had to endure."

"Just because you had a bad time doesn't mean you would treat a child of your own like that."

"I wouldn't take the chance."

"Alright sweetheart I didn't mean to upset you, we'll leave it for now, but I just wish you didn't spend so much time alone in your room."

"I like it, it's the only time that I feel really safe."

It would be a while, almost ten years in fact but it was in that small room that a plan would begin to form, a plan that would shape the rest of her life and one that Shauna O'Malley knew she had no control over.

CHAPTER SIX

2013

Ten mind numbing years at the factory had taken its toll on Shauna but after all the late nights of overtime she had managed to save almost six thousand pounds. It wasn't a King's Ransom but it would finally enable her to start putting her long drawn out plan into action. Without fail Jackie still regularly called by once a week and even though she was now in her early sixties she still worked part time at Sunrise. To any passing acquaintance Shauna would introduce Jackie as her aunt making Jackie's heart swell with pride. They spent every Christmas together, talked often on the phone and each summer would take a week's holiday in Bournemouth. It was on the last of those holidays that Shauna realised just how much she loved the woman and knew she could totally trust her with her life.

"I've saved some money."

"Hey well done, that's great Shauna, we all need to put something away for a rainy day."

"It's not for a rainy day it's to help find Vonny's killer."

For a moment Jackie was speechless and stared at Shauna with a quizzical expression.

"What do you mean Vonny's killer? No-one knows what really happened to your sister or your mum."

"I do but I just need to find out what happened to the bastard that killed them!"

Placing her cup down onto the table Jackie checked

around the cafe in case anyone was listening to their conversation.

"Shauna, whatever are you talking about? The police never came up with anything, what makes you think you'll have more luck?"

"Jack's, for an intelligent woman you can sometimes be so fuckin' dumb. I was there, remember? Just because I didn't speak to the police doesn't mean I didn't know what happened."

"So what are you saying, you knew who killed them and you need to find out if he's still alive?"

"Something like that, anyway, what shall we do today?"

"Slow down a minute! You can't come out with a statement like that and then not continue!"

"I know but I haven't finalized things yet so I'd rather not talk about it."

Jackie was lost for words and knew she had to find out more, had to stop her friend doing something that she could later live to regret but just how she would go about it, she didn't have a clue. Several times over the next week she brought the subject up but each time she was blocked with Shauna refusing to discuss it. When they arrived back at Shauna's home late that Sunday night Jackie could see that the young woman was exhausted.

"I'll pop over during the week love we both know that we can't leave things like this. We need to talk but I think tonight what we both really need is some sleep."

Shauna only nodded her head and after kissing Jackie on the cheek closed the car door and made her way inside.

Sleep didn't come easily for Jackie Silver that night or for the next two nights. In fact by Wednesday she was walking around Sunrise like a zombie which didn't go unnoticed by Jim Brackson when he called for an impromptu Case Meeting.

"My God Jackie, whatever is the matter?"

"Hello Jim, it's nothing, really, I just haven't been able to sleep for a few nights and it's starting to catch up with me."

"Well that's an understatement if ever I heard one, have you been to the doctors?"

"Doctors? No of course I haven't, it isn't anything that a good night's sleep won't solve. Now getting to sleep in the first place is an entirely different matter."

"Come with me, I know what you need."

Jim opened his old office door and ushered Jackie inside. Delving into his briefcase he pulled out a small green bottle and handed it to her but instantly Jackie began to protest.

"Oh no Jim I don't take prescription drugs."

"They are not prescription Jackie, let's just say I became aware of them back in my days of err, free love."

He winked at Jackie and smiled.

"Get yourself home now and I don't want to see you at work again until you feel one hundred percent back to normal."

"Thanks Jim, I really appreciate it."

Jackie then drove to her flat and after making herself a cuppa swallowed two of the little pills. Managing to stagger to the bedroom she then fell into the most wonderful sleep she had ever known. Waking up around noon she saw it was a beautiful sunny day and

51

switching on the radio was shocked to hear it was Thursday, she'd slept for twenty-four hours solid. Whatever those pills were, they had been a Godsend but she wouldn't be broadcasting their miracle abilities as she had a sneaking suspicion that they weren't exactly legal. After a shower Jackie got dressed, all the while thinking of what she would say to Shauna. The unsavoury topic, not mentioned since their return, had to be brought up. When Shauna turned into the driveway after her shift had finished she immediately saw Jackie's car. Normally she would have been so pleased to see her friend that she'd run into her open arms but tonight it was different. It had been a hard day and all Shauna wanted was a hot bath and to go to bed but there was no chance of that happening when she saw the look on Jackie Silvers face.

"How long have you been here?"

"That's a nice greeting, I'm fine thanks for asking."

"I'm sorry Jacks but I'm really tired and not in a very good mood."

"I can see that. We both know that there are things to discuss, things that were left unsaid after the holiday."

"I know but does it have to be tonight?"

"Yes I'm afraid it does. I've spent the best part of a week walking round in a daze worrying about you Shauna, the least you can do is give me an explanation."

In the tiny room that Shauna called home Jackie learnt the true history of Shauna O'Malley's early life. Shauna left nothing out and included every last horrendous detail, details that even with all her experience Jackie could never have guessed. It was

obvious when Shauna arrived at Sunrise that she had
gone through a terrible experience but Jackie hadn't
been prepared for what she was now being told.

"So what do you plan to do?"

"I told you I'd saved up some money, well now I'm
going to hire a private investigator to track down that
bastard Wiseman."

"And then what?"

"I'm not sure but he's not going to get away with
what he did. He will pay, if it's the last thing I do on
this earth, I'm going to make sure he pays."

Shauna's words scared Jackie, she had spoken with
such venom, and it was as if all the years of rage, rage
that had been deeply buried in some dark place, had
surfaced all at once.

"Shauna I don't think any of this is a good idea,
you've told me how violent this man was. You can't
come up against someone like that and have a hope of
winning."

"It has nothing to do with winning, it's about Vonny
and the life she, we, lost."

"But what about your life Shauna, you could have a
good one if you only wanted it."

"All I've ever wanted and wished for is to see him
suffer. I don't expect you to understand or try and
help me but don't even think about standing in my
way Jacks. As God is my witness, he will pay for
what he did."

"Sweetheart, God's not keeping score."

"Maybe he isn't but I am."

Jackie was bright enough to know when she was on a
hiding to nothing and decided not to argue the point
further. She couldn't condone what Shauna was

doing but nor would she stand by and see her get into trouble.

"I don't agree with this Shauna and I don't know if I can support you all of the way because I'm not sure where it's all going to end, but the least I can do is make sure you don't get ripped off by some sordid little prick who calls himself a private dick."

As soon as the words were out of her mouth they both burst out laughing and Shauna was relieved that the tension had broken between them. She knew that her dearest friend wouldn't let her down and was grateful for the offer of help but she also knew that not much further down the line they would have to part company. This thought saddened her but for Jackie's own safety it would have to be this way.

Over the next twelve months there was little word from the short balding man that Shauna had hired. After meeting four or five men from different agencies Shauna had thought Mr Simmonds was the best option but now she wasn't so sure. Most people would have given up but that wasn't Shauna's way, if she had an idea about something she would follow it through to the bitter end, no matter what the consequences.

Jackie Silver's telephone rang out at seven thirty one Saturday morning and she groaned in annoyance as she rolled over the bed to answer it.

"Hello! Whoever you are its far too early in the morning to call me."

She was just about to hang up when she heard Shauna's voice.

"Oh Jacks, Jacks he's finally come through."

"Who's come through Shauna, what are you on about?"

"Mr Simmonds, that's who! I've just received papers giving me all the information I need on Davey Wiseman."

"That's great love but don't you think it's a little early to do anything about it?"

Shauna shouted down the phone so loudly it almost deafened Jackie and she had to momentarily pull the handset away from her ear.

"Early? What are you talking about? I've waited my whole adult life for this."

"No, no listen Shauna I meant early as in Saturday morning lay in. Some of us need to sleep you know, I'm not getting any younger."

"I'm sorry Jacks. It's just that I'm so excited, can I come over later and show you?"

"Of course but can we leave it until lunch time love, I'm absolutely knackered?"

"Sure we can, see you later alligator."

With that Shauna hung up. Jackie snuggled back down in the bed and tried to resume her sleep but no matter how hard she tried it wouldn't come, so after half an hour of bed wrestling she got up. At twelve o'clock sharp Shauna rang the doorbell and Jackie opened up looking drained and unkempt.

"Well for someone who's been in bed all morning you don't look very relaxed, in fact you look as if you need another twenty four hours."

"Morning Shauna and for you information I couldn't get back to sleep thanks to you!"

Shauna just grinned and walking into the kitchen she

placed the large envelope onto the table and proceeded to make them both a coffee. Ten minutes later Jackie placed the last of the papers back into the envelope.

"This Davey sure leads a colourful life and he's wealthy too by all accounts but just where do you think you come into the equation?"

"I haven't thought about it yet but forget about him for a minute I've got something else to show you." Taking a second envelope marked Morgan Jones and Earl Solicitors from her bag, she handed it to Jackie.

"Go on feel free, it came in the same post as Mr Simmonds information."

Jackie opened the letter and began to read.

Dear Miss O'Malley

Regarding the Last Will and Testament of the late Mary O'Dwyer we have been instructed to contact you. We have pleasure in enclosing a cheque for the sum of eighteen thousand and three hundred pounds. Mrs O'Dwyer requested that her entire estate be bequeathed to you. Unfortunately there were no other instructions, other than to pass the money on and to apologise on Mrs O'Dwyer's behalf. If we can be of any assistance in the future please do not hesitate to contact our office at the above named address.

"I'm so sorry Shauna, I know you thought a lot of that lady."

"I did once. She was kind to Vonny and me but it was a long time ago now and I haven't seen her for years."

Jackie heard an icy tone in Shauna's voice, a tone she had never heard before and didn't much care for.

"I know you haven't but it was still kind of her, what

are you going to do with the money?"

"It will help me fulfil my plan, well not fulfil it but make things a little easier along the way."

"I don't know if I want to hear this Shauna."

"It's alright, I'm not going to tell you. I think it best from now on if I keep things to myself."

"Well that's nice I must say! I've supported you through this for years and now you don't want my help."

"It's not a case of not wanting your help Jacks, I love you but I don't want you getting hurt. The less you know the less chance you have of becoming involved. I have to watch out for you Jacks, you don't know what these people are capable of."

"And exactly who will be watching out for you?" Shauna didn't answer and they drank their coffee in silence, both hurting from the pain they were causing one another.

Three days past and Jackie still hadn't heard a word from Shauna, by the fourth day she was becoming increasingly worried. Calling the factory was something she didn't want to do but the phone at Shauna's house hadn't been answered and Jackie knew that the girl never went out except to go to work.

"Good morning Benson and Son. Julie speaking, how may I help you?"

"I'm sorry to bother you but I need to speak to Shauna O'Malley."

"I'm sorry caller but employees are not allowed to take personal calls."

"This is an emergency, I must speak to her."

57

"Hold the line please and I'll see if I can locate her."
Jackie waited receiver in hand, for what felt like an eternity.

"Hello caller. I'm sorry but Miss O'Malley no longer works at Benson and Sons."

"What do you mean no longer works there? She's worked there for over ten years."

"I'm sorry but I have been informed that Miss O'Malley resigned from Benson and Sons on Monday."

Jackie was stunned and snatching up her coat she rushed from her flat and drove over to Shauna's in record time. Screeching to a halt outside the house she barged past a young girl who was just about to close the front door. Jackie sprinted up the stairs two at a time ready to break the door down if she had to. She didn't, Shauna's door stood ajar with the key still in the lock. Entering the room she knew what she would find but desperately wished it wouldn't be so. The bed had been stripped of all linen and the wardrobe doors hung open revealing nothing inside, nothing to tell that Shauna O'Malley had ever lived here. Scanning the room hoping for some clue as to where her precious girl had gone, she didn't have to look too far. The small white envelope stood out against the dark slate fireplace and Jackie hands trembled as she tore it open.

My dearest friend

I'm so sorry that I had to leave you like this but there was no other way. I knew that if I told you what I was planning to do you would only try to stop me and I didn't want to argue with you again. I love you Jacks and we will see each other again one day, I promise.

Love Shauna.

Jackie read the note over and over again but she still couldn't take it in, Shauna, her beautiful Shauna had gone. Somehow she made it back to the safe haven of her flat but the place now seemed strangely different. Where she had once felt so cosy and at home, it now felt grubby and for the first time she noticed the peeling wallpaper and damp patch on the ceiling. Suddenly she realised that for years her whole life had revolved around Shauna and nothing else. The realisation that she was totally alone consumed her, whatever was she going to do now?'

CHAPTER SEVEN

Years earlier on the day Violet and Vonny died,
Davey had stormed into the club in a foul temper. At
various times the staff had all suffered in one way or
another as a result of his violent mood swings and
knew to stay well out of the firing line if the he
showed any sign of kicking off. Davey made his way
to the office and as he did so noticed Stevie
McNamara leaning on the bar chatting to Sylvia Dent.
Sylvia, a lively young girl from somewhere up north,
was employed to serve drinks to the punters but she
also offered any extra a man could wish for. Davey
knew of her little side-line but it hadn't bothered him
before, now as he looked her up and down just the
sight of her disgusted him. Sylvia never did find out
just how lucky she had been that day, thankfully
Davey had personal business of his own to attend to.
If he hadn't then the woman's face would definitely
have taken on a different appearance by closing time.
"Stevie get your fuckin' arse in here now!"
"Okay Boss, won't be a minute."
"I fuckin' said now! That's unless you want to crawl
out of here on your hands and fuckin' knees."
Stevie instantly knew he was in deep trouble and
racked his brains desperately trying to think of what
he had done to rile his boss up. Knocking on the
office door, he once again looked down at his hands
and noticed that they were shaking. Closing the door
he silently waited but Davey just stood with his back
to him and didn't turn around as he muttered.
"What do you know about Violet O'Malley?"

"Only what I told you before boss, honest!"

"Wrong answer pal!"

Davey spun around effortlessly and before Stevie had time to think about what more he knew and what he'd kept back from his boss, the skin at the bridge of his nose split wide open. Davey had delivered a head butt with such force, it had knocked Stevie to the floor. His head now felt as though it belonged to someone else, the room began to swim and looking around he noticed the blue and red carpet as it began to form weird abstract patterns in front of his eyes. Davey towered over him, his mean expression instilled terror as he pushed the hair back from his face with both palms. It would take a long time before Davey would be able to push Violet and the past to the back of his mind, he hated the thought that a common brass had made a fool of him. No one made a fool of Davey Wiseman, not without paying the price. Seeing Sylvia brought back memories and the mere thought of Violet had caused this outburst. Being out of control wasn't something that ever happened to Davey Wiseman and he knew he had to get a grip before doing his trusted employee some serious damage. Stevie was still on the floor, one hand clutching his nose the other reaching out for something he could use to help him get to his feet. Davey stared at the man but didn't apologise, he never said sorry to anyone, it just wasn't his style. Instead, he offered his hand and helped Stevie to his feet. Removing a large bundle of bank notes he passed them to his victim and motioned for him to leave. Stevie McNamara never returned to the club, all phone calls went unanswered and when Brian,

61

another doorman at the club, was sent round to his house, he found the property empty and a 'To Let' sign hanging in the window.

A decade later the world was Davey Wiseman's oyster. The three clubs he had possessed while Violet was on the scene had long since gone and in their place were four more, each one bigger, brasher and better located than the first. True they were all still based in the Soho area and although it was a location he hated, Davey also knew this was where the big money was spent. Every club had a different theme and the decor would be reflected in accordance with how much revenue it generated. The Royal in Brewer Street, had become very upmarket and was generally frequented by gamblers. It brought in the most income and was plush in every sense of the word. Davey didn't carry out much business at The Royal but it would always be the club he was most proud of. Top to Tail had a small facade but opened out into a vast area once inside, thus earning itself the nickname of the Tardis. Old Compton Street wasn't one of the best locations but the club still attracted a higher profile of clientele and it wasn't unusual to see celebrities drinking at the bar. Its main attraction was the lap dancers, dancers that never adhered to the no touch policy and by doing so, earned a very lucrative living. The street outside catered for all sexual desires with the front seating area of the many gay bars acting as pick up points. Rent boys paraded up and down, willing to provide their services to the hordes of married men who couldn't bring themselves to venture inside. Davey's third club was situated on

Tisbury Court where during daylight hours clothing rails could be found scattered along its narrow length. Loud voiced vendors touted at extortionate prices, in the hope of selling hip clothing to tourists and visitors. The club, aptly named The Judge's Den, was on a smaller scale and far seedier than the others. It was also on Tisbury Court that the many local prostitutes could be found, women who would pound the pavement each night and as The Den employed most of them, it was perfectly situated. At its widest point the court measured no more than eighteen feet and was flanked on either side not only by clubs such as The Den but also peep shows with shop fronts, decorated in bold pinks and purple. Outside each stood a man or women who was employed to try and engage the passing public with sayings like 'Come on in and experience the dream`.

For generations, Soho had been known for the sale of flesh but the oldest trade in the world now sickened Davey to the core but not enough to stop him from accepting the women's hard earned cash. Davey allowed the day to day management of The Judges Den to be carried out by Frieda Cousins and Friday night was set aside to collect the takings. Frieda, herself a former brass, ran The Den with an iron rod. A gaunt woman in her mid-forties, who stood six feet tall in her bare stockings and who only ever dressed in black, which frightened most of the punters not to mention the working brasses. Miss Cousins as she liked to be referred to had been on the game since she came to London some twenty odd years earlier. A bad experience with a pimp named Danny, had seen

Frieda hospitalised for over a month and on being discharged she had begun to work for Davey Wiseman. He had always treated her fairly and as much as he loathed these women and what they did for a living, showed Frieda more respect than she had ever been shown in her life. In Frieda's eyes that made Davey a God and he could trust her to carry out any task that needed doing, no matter how distasteful. The extent of her love for the man had no bounds and the sad excuse for a woman would have died for him had she been asked.

To Davey's pleasure, Frieda seemed able to handle most of the aggravation that came with running The Den, the only exception being Jimmy Loftwood. A regular, he came in at least once a week and always brought his own entertainment. The exclusive use of a small room out back being the only reason he set foot in The Den. His antics sickened even the hardest of brasses as none of his escorts were ever over twelve years old. Occasionally Jimmy would overstep the mark and go too far with a young guest and Davey would be called to sort out the mess, a mess he didn't want Frieda to know anything about. Frieda would see money pass from the big man into the small hands of his guest, other times she noticed he left alone and Frieda didn't dare to imagine what had happened to the child in question. Whoever Jimmy Loftwood was, she knew he must have a terrible hold over Davey.

Last but by no means least, was 'The Pelican', a place where Davey spent the majority of his time and a place most of London's underworld visited on a weekly basis. Situated in Greek Street it was private enough to carry out business that had to be kept secret and Davey was known as a trustworthy and respected host. A rapid growth of the four clubs saw Davey's bank balance soar but with success came many pitfalls and one particular pitfall bore the name of Neil Maddock, Detective Inspector Maddock to be exact and he hated Davey Wiseman with a vengeance. Years earlier when he had first joined the force and was little more than a Bobby on the beat, he had been made aware of a new wide boy working out of Soho but as long as the man's misdemeanours were kept to a small scale, Neil had no real interest. As soon as Davey started to make a name for himself and his level of criminal activity quickly rose to bigger and more violent crimes he suddenly became very interesting to the man. The two men's careers had begun around the same time but where Davey's had soared, it had taken years for Neil to reach the level of Detective. He saw all the trappings of fame that Davey enjoyed while Neil struggled to make his mortgage payments each month. Five years later and on his last promotion, DI Maddock decided it was time to end Davey Wiseman's career once and for all. It was no easy feat and took several promotions and over a decade before Neil would come anywhere close to feeling Davey Wiseman's collar and even then the DI failed dismally. Davey Wiseman seemed to be as slippery as an eel but Neil Maddock would never give up trying and it would take many more years before he found out the real reason for his failure.

Davey lived like a King and had every trapping wealth could provide but the old saying 'money can't buy happiness' was especially true in Davey Wiseman's case. The man was lonely but he couldn't discuss his feelings with anyone, not even his closest friend Billy. The two had been friends for years and often spent the evening drinking together at Billy's own club where women were never on the menu, at Billy Jacksons, it was strictly men only. It was to be on one of their evenings that Davey found out just how deep his friend's feelings towards him went.

The Saturday in question had been a particularly bad day, nothing had gone right and Davey just wanted to wind down and relax. Thinking a few laughs and drinks with his old pal would be a good way of relieving his stress, he made his way to The Bull Dog Club over in Bethnal Green. For many years The Bull as it was known to regulars had been owned by one or more of the Jackson family, at the moment it was in Billy's hands. Davey hadn't been to the place for several weeks and couldn't believe the changes his friend had made to the decor. Stepping through the street door, the inner curtains were parted by two scantily dressed boys. Their toned bodies were clad in tight black leather hot pants leaving little else to the imagination. The dance floor heaved with men, twirling and hip shaking to the high pitched sound of Erasures 'Sometimes'. Billy caught sight of his pal before Davey had a chance to make it across the floor as he was having great difficulty in avoiding the mass of sweating men eagerly trying to tempt him to dance. Billy found his pal's predicament highly amusing and couldn't stop himself from laughing.
"Are you having a Turkish? You know something

Bill? You really piss me off sometimes, why do you have to surround yourself with all these fuckin' Muppets?"

"Don't get your knickers in such a twist Davey boy, it's only a bit of fun."

"Yeah right, at my fuckin' expense you cunt!"

Billy placed an arm around his guests shoulder and led him to the bar.

"Come on let's get a drink and you can tell me all about your day."

A few minutes later the comical episode was forgotten and Davey had managed to calm down. The two friends were deep in conversation when a young boy sashayed over to them and suddenly stopped in front of Davey. Ryan Burton had only just turned sixteen although he'd been a regular at the club for the last year and he liked older men with a passion. They both turned to face the youth but it wasn't Billy who held the boys fascination. Pouting his lips, Ryan looked Davey straight in the eye as he spoke.

"Fancy a shag babe?"

Davey's face instantly turned a bright shade of scarlet but it wasn't out of any kind of embarrassment. Davey was angry, very angry and for a second he even assumed Billy had put the boy up to it.

"No I don't you queer little cunt, now fuck off out of it before I give you a right fuckin' slap!"

The boy didn't move and with his hands perched on his hips he continued to stare.

"Did you hear what I fuckin' said or are you trying hard to mug me off?"

Still he didn't move, instead uttering the words that

were to be his downfall.

"Don't knock it till you've tried it love."

As quick as a flash Davey was pushed aside and Billy now stood only inches from Ryan's face, so close in fact that the boy could feel the club owners breath on his cheek.

"You must be on some kind of fuckin' death wish you little cunt!"

Ryan didn't have time to answer, nor did he see the knife that Billy was holding until it was too late. The steel blade flickered under the light of the overhead mirror ball a second before it sliced through the young man's cheek. Billy Jackson always kept the blade razor sharp and it laid open the flesh with the ease of a butcher's knife. Deafening screams rang out above the music and for a moment people stopped dancing and turned around but when they saw who was involved the dancing suddenly resumed. Billy ran a good place, drinks were cheap and anything sexual was allowed to be carried out so for that reason alone the place was popular but the patrons also knew the dark side that was Billy Jackson and no one dared to be overly interested in what he did. Davey, for all his own violent capabilities, felt uncomfortable that his friend had cut the boy in front of everyone. He quickly took a step back as the boys blood began to flow and at the same time Billy flicked his wrist to summon a doorman.

"Get this cunt out of my sight and clean this fuckin' mess up, someone could slip over!"

Looking down at his feet and the sticky red liquid that had begun to congeal, Davey was dumb founded. His friend never ceased to amaze him as Billy's priorities were always the complete opposite of any other normal human being. No one took any notice of the violent floor show that had just taken place, after all it was nothing new. Everyone continued to dance and after the kid had been forcibly pushed through the fire exit it was business as usual.

"Since when have you carried a blade?"

"For a while now, anyway don't fuckin' sweat over it, the little cunt was winding me up."

"Maybe he was but a slap would have been suffice wouldn't it?"

Bill only shrugged his shoulders. Several drinks later, the two friends were sitting in the quiet of Billy's office but Davey, bothered by his friend's earlier actions, couldn't let the matter drop.

"Why'd you do it Bill? I mean the lad was pissing me off but did he fuckin' deserve that?"

"It's not a case of whether he deserved it. I won't have any of my guests, especially you, offended. Anyway the cunt was taking a proper liberty and trying to mug you off."

"Maybe he was but it wasn't anything I couldn't have handled myself."

"I don't doubt that for a second but you know how I feel and........"

Davey stopped his friend mid sentence.

"Okay Bill let's leave it, before you say something you shouldn't."

"You know how I feel about you Davey and I respect the fact that you're hetro but if anyone is ever going to turn you, then that person will be me and no one else."

The two men laughed. Davey was well aware that

Billy's feelings went far deeper than friendship but both knew it would never be more than that.

Six months earlier Davey had hired a new member of staff due to a feeling of uneasiness. His wealth, now in excess of over nine million, was starting to become a weight around his neck. The streets weren't as safe as they had been in the past and Billy was continually nagging him to get a minder.

"You're a sitting duck Davey my boy, any fuckin' crack head who fancies his chances could roll you over."

"Let the fucker try, I know I may have a few grey hairs now but I can still take care of myself."

"And so you can Davey Boy but if one of those wanker's has a gun pointed in your face, you wouldn't stand a fuckin' chance."

Finally accepting that his friend was talking sense for once, Davey arranged for some new boys to be sent over from Bethnal Green. The Jacksons had a large workforce spread out all over London and Billy was more than happy to supply his friend with a few trusty faces. Davey met up with six of them in The Pelican, chatting and buying each a drink, he wanted to see who he would be happy spending the majority of his time with and one stood out from all of the rest. Gilly Slade was in his early thirties and had gained a reputation in the East End for being a good all-rounder. After finishing an eighteen month stretch for robbery, he was now on the market for some permanent work. Davey dismissed the others and the two sat down at one of the small tables tucked away in a corner.

"So Gilly, tell me a little about yourself?"

"I'm sure you already know all there is to know Mr Wiseman or I wouldn't even be here."

He found the man's straightness a breath of fresh air, Davey himself had always been direct and it was a trait he liked to see in other people.

"Alright, you've got the job."

As Gilly Slade got up to leave, Davey asked one last question.

"Tell me one thing Gilly, is that story about you true or just a fuckin' myth?"

"What story would that be Mr Wiseman?"

Davey smiled.

"The one about your name?"

Gilly looked his new boss straight in the eye.

"Yes its true Mr Wiseman."

Peter Slade had been a bad boy from the time he could walk and by the age of fifteen had already spent three months in a Detention Centre. On his release the need to lay his hands on some ready cash was great and saw him rob the wife of one of the most feared gangsters in North London. It was inevitable he would be caught but his punishment had still been extreme, even by underworld standards. Four men had grabbed Peter on the main high street and bundled him into the back of a transit van, from there he was driven to the banks of the Thames, his body was tied and he was thrown into the water. He had sunk like a lead weight and it was a miracle he survived, those who knew of the incident said he must have been part fish. In reality, one of his captors had felt the punishment way too harsh and had been reluctant to tie the ropes on Gilly's arms too tightly.

After escaping, the villain he crossed had been amused when told of the tale and had decided that no further action would be taken. The nickname of Gilly stuck and shortly after, being called Peter became a distant memory.

Davey soon had his new employee carrying out all manner of tasks, collecting dry cleaning, driving and general dogs body, were all in the man's unwritten work description. Gilly hadn't thought working for the infamous Davey Wiseman would be like this and he soon started to feel like a gofer. Today he was acting as chauffeur and when ordered by his Boss to go and collect someone he decided it was the final straw.

"Gill pop over to The Bull and pick up Billy will you."

Saluting, he walked out of The Pelican and climbed into the car. The five minute drive gave Gilly time to think and he made up his mind he wasn't going to stick around much longer, this wasn't the kind of work he'd signed up for. When he arrived at The Bull, Billy was already outside and he jumped into the car before Gilly had time to properly park.

"How's it going Gilly boy? How do you like working for the wonderful Mr Wiseman?"

"Its fine Mr Jackson thank you but it's not what I thought it would be."

"What do you mean, the tight old bastard not paying you enough?"

"No it just, well I thought I was supposed to be his minder but all I do is run errands and clean the car!"

"Time my boy, give it time. You're a good lad so just

hang in there. Everything comes to those who wait or so I'm told, well that's unless you were born with the name Jackson, then like me, well I never wait for anything I just take it!"

As the car pulled up outside The Pelican he slapped Gilly on the shoulder before slamming the door and disappearing inside. The two old friends were half way through a bottle of Davey's finest malt when Billy brought up the subject of his pals new minder.

"So how are you finding Gilly then?"

"Good, he pretty much does what I tell him, so I can't complain."

"Yeah but are you asking him to do enough?"

"Oh for fucks sake Bill, you're not going to start with the queer sex talk again, are you? You'll fuckin' turn my guts and I ain't had my dinner yet."

Billy's eyes widened in mock horror.

"Moi? Of course not you prat, I mean are you asking him to do what he's really here for?"

Davey studied his friends face and gave the question some thought before answering.

"Can I trust him Bill?"

"Of course you fuckin' can, I wouldn't have sent him over to you otherwise."

CHAPTER EIGHT

2014

The twelve thirty train from Romford into Kings
Cross arrived on time and stepping from the carriage,
Shauna could not only hear the noise of the crowds
but she could feel it. It had been many years since
she'd last been in the capital, she had hated it then
and she still hated it now. Shauna hadn't expected to
feel excited about the return to her home turf and she
wasn't disappointed. Black cabs were lined up
outside the station like sentries and she signalled to
the first driver that she was looking to take a journey.
"Where are you going, sweetheart?"
Shauna shuddered at the man's too familiar greeting.
"Belgravia Square please."
"Your wish is my command princess."
She wasn't anyone's princess and she bit down on her
lip in annoyance. It may have been the glare he
received or just the lack of communication whenever
he tried to strike up a conversation, either way the rest
of the journey was taken in silence. Shauna looked
up at the tall grey buildings which loomed down on
her and it felt almost claustrophobic.
"Whereabouts do you want to get out Miss?"
"The Utopia Hotel."
The cabbie eyed her in the rear view mirror.
"Very classy, if you don't mind me saying."
Shauna didn't reply and was relieved when the taxi at
last pulled up outside the main entrance, where a
smartly dressed porter waited to carry her luggage

inside. Lifting her bag from the seat, she handed over the fare and gave the driver one last contemptuous look before slamming the door. The hotel, set in a quiet corner of Belgravia square was small but none the less imposing. When she'd made up her mind to put the plan into action, Shauna had decided it would begin in style. Mrs O'Dwyer's inheritance had come in handy and she felt sure the woman would want her to enjoy it. Entering the lobby of The Utopia, Shauna stopped for a moment and slowly cast her gaze all around. Standing totally still she was in awe of the splendour, the marble floors and crystal chandeliers were fabulous and she realised that this was a side of London she would never have seen if it wasn't for her inheritance. Quietly she whispered 'Thank you Mary' but as she headed over to the main reception, a girl no older than herself, gave her a snooty look. Without a word her eyes silently asked 'How can the likes of you afford to stay in a place like this?'

"May I help you?"

The girls tone made Shauna feel uncomfortable but she wouldn't allow herself to be belittled. With her head held high she gave the girl a steely glare, which made the recently promoted receptionist turn her gaze away from Shauna and back to her computer screen.

"Yes I have a reservation under the name of O'Malley."

"Oh of course madam. Certainly madam."

Amazed at the change in the woman's attitude made
Shauna felt sad, sad that money was more important
than people but if it served her purpose then she
wasn't about to complain. The girl proceeded to ring
a small bell that summoned a young man employed to
carry her bags and show her to the suite. If Shauna
had been impressed with the lobby she was even
more amazed with her room. It was grand, the
grandest place she had ever seen, the carpets were
deep enough to give the feeling that her feet would
disappear and running her hands over the bedspread
she wondered at the fabric, so soft and rich in colour.
God how the other half lived!
The Bell Boy stood waiting for his tip but made no
comment, he'd seen it all before and this girl though
pretty, was no different from the rest, a high class
hooker if ever he saw one. Shauna handed over a
pound coin and held open the door for the boy to
leave, he wasn't impressed with the measly tip but he
supposed it was better than nothing. Shauna's plan
would take time to come to fruition and Mary's
money wouldn't last forever but for once in her life
Shauna had decided to spoil herself. She slept well
that night and after a sumptuous breakfast provided
by room service, left early for her first appointment of
the day. The salon stood in Bond Street, the kind of
place frequented by celebrities and Shauna knew the
fee would be astronomical but she didn't care. This
transformation had to be good, very good. Walking
through the highly polished brass door with its ornate
etched glass, she was greeted by a beautiful young
woman, who would have been at home on any
fashion catwalk. With Shauna's appointment

checked, she was asked if she would like to take a seat on one of the sumptuous leather couches.

"I will inform your stylist that you have arrived Madam."

Watching the girl walk away, she marvelled at her micro mini skirt and legs that never seemed to end. After waiting a few minutes a man flounced over to the couch, his physique was so thin that even his tight trousers looked two sizes too big for him and Shauna was sure he was wearing makeup.

"My name is Marco and I am your stylist for today." Seating Shauna in front of a gigantic gilded mirror, he didn't try to hide his campness as he lifted her hair this way and that.

"What is it that you want me to do darling?" Shauna had to try very hard to stop herself from giggling, the man's Latino accent was so strong that she was having trouble understanding him but at the same time he was hilarious.

"I want it all cut off and coloured, please."

Marco chuckled at the woman's attempt to copy his accent.

"Marco will make you look like a million dollars darling."

"I didn't think for one minute that you wouldn't, you cheeky boy."

They both laughed and a friendship began, a friendship that would help keep her transformation in perfect condition for the next year. When Shauna stepped out of the salon she was unrecognisable, gone were the long ebony tresses that had been a significant part of her beauty. In their place was a short modern bob the colour of copper. Marco had said the shade of titian he chose was perfect for her but he couldn't have known that she was now a carbon copy of Violet. The look was exactly what Shauna had hoped for and walking back to the hotel she received more than her fair share of admiring glances.

The next few weeks saw her making frequent visits to the Soho area as she knew it was Davey's patch. Always keeping a low profile, she wore a raincoat with the collar turned up and a woollen hat pulled down low around her ears. It wasn't her intention to be noticed but to gain a feel of the place and the people. By now she had left the splendour of The Utopia and had rented a small bedsit in North London. It was nothing to write home about but it was clean and dry and Shauna, so wrapped up in her plans, didn't notice the lack of decoration. For days she walked up and down the tiny streets hoping for a glimpse of her target, it had been easy to find his clubs but after so many years she realised his appearance would have dramatically changed. Mr Simmonds had provided excellent information but no photographs, after discovering what kind of man he was investigating, he had refused to take any pictures. At their last meeting his parting words had been 'I'm good at my job Miss O'Malley, probably the best, but I'm not on a death wish'. Shauna had appreciated his honesty and was grateful that he had been able to provide her with any information at all. On one of her regular trips to Soho she stopped at a small newsagent to buy cigarettes, a habit recently acquired and a habit Jackie Silver would be mortified about if she ever found out. The shop, no more than ten feet wide but which appeared to go on forever in length, was stacked to the ceiling with cigarettes, soft drinks and magazines. Shauna thumbed through a few before settling on a glossy fashion issue. Taking the magazine to the till she met the gaze of an elderly gentleman standing behind the Formica counter.

"Good morning Miss and what a glorious day it is."

For a moment she didn't reply, this short grey haired man was the first person, other than Marco, to have engaged in any real form of conversation in all the time she had been in London. Oh she'd had contact with people when purchasing items or asking for directions but no one had bothered to really pass the time of day until now.

"Yes, yes it is a beautiful day."

Looking closely at Shauna the man continued.

"Please don't think me presumptuous but haven't I seen you in the area before?"

Immediately Shauna's guard went up and she viewed the man suspiciously. Noticing her expression he realised his rudeness.

"I must apologise, I've offended you. I can assure you it wasn't my intention, it's just that I don't get to have a conversation with many people and that can make for a very long day indeed."

Shauna smiled and relaxed, she knew she couldn't afford the luxury of trusting people but this sweet old man just wanted to be friendly. Several minutes passed and they continued to converse about nothing in particular before Shauna said goodbye and left the shop. Her visits to Soho continued and Shauna would often call in at the newsagents and have a chat with her new acquaintance. It was during one of their conversations that she discovered the shopkeeper was looking for an assistant.

"My wife complains all the time that she doesn't see enough of me and with my daughter Susan the way she is, Madge needs all the help she can get."

Shauna felt like she had won the pools.

"It must be hard trying to find someone who is trustworthy?"

"Tell me about it, I can't put a notice in the window or I would be inundated with all sorts of local low life. I don't mean to sound nasty but you know what this area is like."

"Yes I can appreciate you have to be careful and if you don't think I'm being too forward, I may know just the person you are looking for."

"Really, please tell me more Miss."

Shauna proceeded to introduce herself.

"It's me I'm talking about. I'm sorry, you don't even know who I am. My name is Francis Richards and I moved to London a few months ago after the death of my parents."

"I'm sorry to hear that my dear."

"Yes it was all very sad but they were quite elderly and having me late in life, I don't think they expected to be here by the time I was thirty."

The man saw a great sadness in this girl, he had felt it the first time she came into his shop but until now hadn't quite been able to put his finger on the reason.

"Well, if you're willing to learn and don't mind hard work Francis, then the job is yours."

Shauna beamed from ear to ear.

"Thank you, thank you so much and please call me

Fran, all my friends do. Would you like me to give you some names and addresses, so you can get references?"

Shauna knew that in offering this information, she was taking a real gamble but she also knew that it was important to appear honest. As far as she was concerned it was a foregone conclusion that if needed she could ring Jacks, Shauna was sure her friend would give her some kind of backup.

"No, that won't be necessary. I always go on my first instincts and I knew from the moment we first met that you were a nice girl."

Shauna smiled at the man.

"Thank you for the compliment Mr?"

"Oh how silly of me, it's Cecil, Cecil James and my wife's name is Madge. You'll also get to meet Susan our daughter but they're both away at Madge's sisters at the moment."

Shauna walked around the shop and fingered the magazines and stationary items as she talked.

"I'm so pleased I chose this place to buy my cigarettes from Cecil, I think I'm going to like working here."

"There's just one thing I forgot to mention Fran."

She knew it was too good to be true, here came the but.......

"It's only small, a one bedroom flat above the shop but it goes with the position. The rent will be heavily reduced of course. To be totally honest Miss Richards I get a handsome discount on my insurance if I have someone living on site due to the alcohol and tobacco that is stored in the stock room inside the flat. Is that a problem?"

Leaning forward Shauna planted a huge kiss on the cheek of this wonderful human being, a man who had just given her the perfect cover to carry out her revenge. Her first week of work passed by quickly and she'd had little time to search for Davey. By now she knew his clubs well enough but had never managed to spot him entering or leaving. Working eight hours a day there was little time for investigative work but she could wait, she had all the time in the world. At the end of her second week Shauna was yet to take a day off but she didn't complain as she liked the job and her employer too much to risk any kind of a disagreement. Cecil was aware that the young woman needed a break and more than pleased with his new employee, didn't want to risk losing her.

"Fran I want you to take the day off."

"No I'm fine Cecil, honestly."

"I'm not asking you young lady I am telling you, now get you coat and off you go. We all need a little time to ourselves now and again. Good job Madge isn't here, she would have my guts for garters if she found out you hadn't had a day off yet."

"Thanks Cecil, I suppose I could do with some fresh air so maybe I'll take a walk."

Strangely Soho was not Shauna's destination, something had been drawing her back to the Mile End Road and the flat that had once been her home. Boarding the Central line at Oxford Circus, she sat back for twenty minutes and eight stops later she emerged from Mile End Station. It felt like going back in time, very little had changed and Shauna could feel the stirrings of a knot beginning to form in the pit of her stomach. Walking the familiar streets, in her mind she started to relive the last few days before her whole world had fallen apart and was amazed that everything was so clear as if it had happened only yesterday. Shauna could visibly see every room in the flat. The dirty kitchen where Violet sat huddled up the corner in her filthy housecoat, drugged up to the eyeballs. The damp bare hallway where Vonny's skinny little frame could be seen running along the landing with a nappy so full it had hung down in a point between her legs. The rancid living room with its matted carpet and peeling paper was next to appear but Shauna instantly became scared, too scared to continue and stopping her walk, she leant against a low brick wall. She didn't want to mentally go into that room and pleaded with her own mind to stop now but still she pushed the door open and once again reeled at the sight. She could feel her shoulders being shaken quite firmly and suddenly she looked up into the face of a middle aged woman.

"You alright love? You gave me such a fright when you passed out."

Realising she must have fainted, Shauna slowly stood up and rested once more against the wall.

"I'm fine thanks, I just need to sit here for a minute."

The woman who had come to her aid looked concerned but at the same time she needed to be off or she would be late for bingo.

"If you're sure, only I can't be late. You see Edna, my old pal, gets the right hump if I'm not on time."

"Honestly I will be fine."

Unconvinced the woman began to walk away, turning back to view Shauna every few steps until she crossed the road and disappeared around the corner. Her weekly stroll to the Lyceum had been interesting tonight and at least she would have a captive audience at the Bingo. The old girls who gathered there could sometimes be nosy cows but at least she would be the centre of attention today, especially when she relayed the story of coming to the rescue of a young woman who had collapsed. Of course she would have to exaggerate things a little bit but then who didn't and besides, it would all make for a much more interesting tale.

Shauna was now beginning to feel better as she took in big gulps of air and at least her mind was back in the real world and no longer in that rat hole of a flat. She was now sure of one thing, the vision of her baby sister lying on the floor only strengthened her determination that Davey Wiseman would pay dearly. His comeuppance, she hadn't quite worked out yet but Shauna knew it had to be good, so good in fact, that should he live he would never be able to forget it.

CHAPTER NINE

Monday mornings were always busy in the shop and today of all days Shauna had overslept as the alarm for some reason, had decided not to go off. Cecil would be expecting her at nine and although it was only the second time she'd been late for work, it riled her. Shauna knew how lucky she was to have landed this job and how easy going her boss was. Mr James never criticised or spoke out of turn and she would bet her life on it that he wouldn't mention her lateness today. A shower was out of the question there just wasn't time, splashing her face with water and cleaning her teeth was all she could manage until tonight. Quickly pulling on a jumper and jeans she made her way downstairs. As usual the counter was abuzz with people eager to pay for their papers, magazine and cigarettes as they were all in a hurry to get off to work. Cecil smiled as Shauna stepped behind the counter but the two didn't have time to chat until the morning rush had finally slackened off at just after ten.

"Lovely day Fran!"`

"Yes it is Cecil. Cecil about this morning, I'm....."
The grey haired man dressed as always in his home knitted cardigan, placed a hand on her shoulder.

"My dear girl, we are all entitled to a lay in once in a while."

"Oh it wasn't a lay in, my alarm clock just didn't go off."

"Please Fran, it really isn't a problem. You're here now and that's all that matters."

85

Before Shauna could answer the door flew open with a bang and a woman's voice could be heard shouting from outside.

"Susan! Just calm down will you. Your father won't be best pleased if you break the glass in his door."

"Sorry mummy."

A rather plump dark haired teenager girl ran into the shop with a smile on her face that could lighten up even the greyest of skies. Spying Cecil she proceeded to let out a high pitched squeal.

"Daddy!!!"

Cecil opened the counter flap and with both arms, embraced the podgy little girl.

"Hello my darling, did you have a good time at Aunty May's?"

"Alright, but I missed you daddy."

"I know you did sweetheart but you're home now. Come with me and we'll go out to the back and put the kettle on."

Taking her hand, Cecil led the girl through the beaded curtain and into the rear kitchen. Shauna smiled to herself, what a sweetie, it was plain for all to see that Cecil was obviously besotted with his little girl. When she was offered the job, he had touched on the subject of his daughter but hadn't gone any further, now she understood why. Madge James walked into the shop lugging a large case, her face lined and tired from the years of constant caring.

"Can I give you a hand with that Mrs James?"

Madge eyed Shauna suspiciously as she recalled the conversation she had with her husband. Cecil had telephoned her about their new employee but she'd been very unsure about the matter.

"We don't know anything about the girl Cecil, she could rob the shop and clean us out."

"Now Madge, don't be like that. I always go on my first instincts and Fran's a nice woman, you'll see."

"I'll reserve my judgement until I meet her."

Cecil could read Madge like a book and knew she was only miffed at not being in the shop when he offered Fran the job. He also knew she was full of hot air and would come round as soon as the two women got to know each other.

"Mrs James?"

"No it's quite alright I can manage, where's Cecil?"

"He's just gone to make some tea, I expect you're parched?"

Just then Susan came through the curtain and smiled at Shauna.

"Hello sweetheart, I'm Fran and I'm sure were going to be the best of friends."

"My name is Susan."

"Yes I know it is. My! Haven't you got a beautiful smile!"

The small girl blushed and embraced Shauna with a bear hug.

"Susan! Stop that at once, you'll scare Fran."

"It's okay Mrs James, I think she's great, aren't you sweetheart?"

Susan's face beamed from ear to ear as she gripped her new friends hand and hung on for dear life.

Madge looked at Shauna in amazement.

"Very few people want anything to do with my daughter Miss Richards. I had her at a late stage in my life, you do realise she has Down's Syndrome?"

"Yes of course I do Mrs James, though what that has

87

to do with anything I really don't know. It's a shame people don't see behind the disability to the ability and find out what the person is really like before making a judgement."

Madge smiled and nodded to Shauna, perhaps Cecil had been right. Maybe this Fran, whoever she was, was just what they needed. From then on Madge and her daughter visited the shop every day, each time it got harder and harder for her to drag Susan away.

"Susan go and get your coat on, Susan if I have to tell you again!"

"I don't want to. I want to stay with Fran."

"Oh no you're not young lady! You will put on your coat and do as you are told."

Shauna didn't want to interfere but she liked the girl and loved her being around.

"Mrs James, I don't mean to speak out of turn, but Susan really isn't any trouble. I enjoy having her here and I'm sure you could do with a little time on your own?"

Madge James was about to protest, but thought better of it, after all wasn't she the one who spent her whole life caring for her daughter? Didn't she deserve some time to herself now and again?

"Are you really sure Fran? She can be a real handful if she has a mind to."

"Positive, now get going. What do you fancy doing? Why not get your hair done, spoil yourself for a change. Well go on then....."

Madge looked at Susan and then back to Shauna.

"You know something, that's just what I'm going to do."

Giving her daughter a glare that silently said 'You

had better behave' she left the shop. Susan spent the rest of the afternoon with her new friend and Shauna taught her lots of things, things her mother and father never gave her the chance to do. Cecil had been to the accountants and arrived back at the same time as Madge and by then Susan had refilled the shelves and was having her first lesson on the till. Madge immediately noticed her husband had a look of panic on his face when he realised she was alone.

"Don't start worrying Cecil, she's alright. Fran offered to mind her while I got my hair done."

Cecil couldn't stop staring at his wife, she looked so relaxed. He saw the woman he had first fallen in love with, after all these years he'd thought her lost but she'd just been hidden under a mountain of worry and stress. Opening the shop door he placed an arm on his wife's shoulder.

"I'm not worried in the least. I can't think of a better person to care for our girl."

Susan's raucous laughter could be heard as soon as they entered.

"No Susie! Not that button, this one."

Laughter broke out again and Shauna had tears streaming down her face. Madge and Cecil stared in amazement, here stood their daughter, laughing and joking like anyone else.

"Look Susie, your Mum and Dad are back."

Susan lifted her head, her brow furrowed in concentration.

"Fran teaching me the till."

Cecil winked at his employee as he walked towards his daughter.

"Yes I can see that. You do realise Fran that you'll

be out of a job if this continues."

Everyone laughed and as Shauna looked at each of them in turn she thought to herself that this was how families should be, this should have been her and Vonny if only Davey Wiseman hadn't appeared on the scene and robbed them of a life together. Suddenly she wanted to cry, cry for the sister that was lost to her and the feeling of loneliness that now totally consumed her.

Madge's lone outings soon grew from once to twice, sometimes three times a week. Cecil saw and liked the changes in his wife, she had time for them both, relaxed time to be lovers again instead of just Susan's carers. Shauna noticed he had more of a spring in his step and knowing she had contributed to this made her feel good. The James' anniversary was nearing and Shauna decided to offer them the chance of a break.

"Madge? I've been thinking, why don't you and Cecil go away for a few days and I do mean just the two of you?"

"I'd say yes with bells on but there's no chance of that happening."

"Why?"

"Oh Fran! How can we with Susan?"

"I'll take care of her, she likes being with me and I know I could manage."

A grin began to spread across the women's faces, both knew exactly what the other was thinking.

"Cecil wouldn't go for it, I know he wouldn't."

"You leave him to me Madge, go sort something out and be back before I shut the shop tonight."

Shauna didn't have to offer twice, as quick as a flash Madge had her coat on and was closing the door just as Cecil emerged from the back kitchen with Susan.
"Where is she off to in such a hurry?"
"She needed to sort something out and so do we, sit down Cecil."
Twenty minutes later everything was arranged and on her return Madge couldn't believe their Guardian Angel had managed to talk her husband into a holiday. Over the next few days the atmosphere in the shop was electric. Madge couldn't hide her excitement every time she thought of her forthcoming break and Susan was looking forward to the prospect of spending time with Fran. A week in the sun had been booked and the day Madge and Cecil left for Spain saw Susan move into the upstairs flat and it wasn't long before she started to pester Shauna about the way she looked.
"Fran?"
"Yes love, what is it?"
When she didn't reply, Shauna raised her head from the magazine she'd been reading and noticed Susan smoothing down her dress and staring down at the frumpy shoes on her feet.
"I know what you want Miss James, a makeover! Though what your Mum will say, I'm not so sure?"
Nodding her head, Susan excitedly clapped her hands. Luckily the following day happened to be late opening for most of the shops and although Shauna didn't think Cecil would be too pleased if he found out, she decided to shut the shop early. The two set off as soon as the newsagent blinds were pulled and the closed sign displayed. Catching the tube up West,

Shauna led her friend to one of the big department stores on Oxford Street and when she saw all the trendy clothes displayed in crisp neat lines in the window, Susan squealed. Mary's money came in very handy that day but Shauna didn't care, all the money in the world couldn't make up for the look on her little friends face. Carrying the over laden bags back towards the tube station, they passed a small beauty salon and the temptation was too much for Shauna to resist. The stylist and beautician set to work, the long hair which had always been tied back tightly in a ponytail had gone, in its place a short and very trendy bob not dissimilar to Shauna's. You couldn't hide the fact that Susan had Downs but with makeup and a manicure to match, the new image gave her the confidence she'd lacked for so long.

Madge and Cecil's plane arrived at lunchtime and after dropping their cases off at home, they hurried back to the shop. Shauna had just finished serving a customer and Susan had gone to make some tea, when her parents came in. Shauna could see the break had done them both the power of good and Madge's deep tan made her look years younger.
"Hello you two, did you have a good time?"
"It was wonderful, but now I just want to see my little girl."
"Of course you do Madge, she's making some tea."
Cecil and Madge both spoke in unison.
"Making tea?!!!!"
"Yes that's right, you'll be surprised at how much Susan can do when she puts her mind to it."
The beaded curtain moved sideways and out stepped

a pretty, confident young woman, so different from the one they had said goodbye to only a week earlier.

"Daddy!"

"My! Don't you look pretty, look mum, look at our beautiful girl."

Both her parents started to cry, which brought a tear to Shauna's eye but Susan just giggled.

"Don't cry, don't cry, there, there."

Madge looked up at Shauna.

"I don't think we will ever be able to thank you Fran, you've done more in a week than we've ever managed to accomplish."

"I don't need thanks, the look on your faces is enough, besides it wasn't all me. Your daughter can be a very determined young lady when she sets her mind to it."

Life at the shop continued but not quite as before, Cecil gave his daughter a proper job working alongside Shauna every day and all the regular customers soon came to know and love her. Madge started to take her daughter on regular shopping trips but this time she was proud to be with her young companion, instead of trying to hide her away all the time. The family now adored their employee, a young woman who only came for a job but had completely transformed their lives. Shauna on the other hand loved the James' but realised that with her good deed done she must know start to distance herself. It began in a subtle way with starting to take more time off and going out more in the evenings. The family now so happy together, hardly noticed the changes or if they had didn't mention anything.

Too much time had been spent organising other people's lives, it was now time to get on with the task Shauna had come to London for. As much as she would have liked to stay in the warm bosom of the James' lives, she owed it to Vonny to see things through to the end.

CHAPTER TEN

Several months had now passed since the holiday and the James' were over the moon with their new way of life and the freedom they were experiencing. Finally their only child was part of the family business, albeit a small part and both Cecil and Madge had more time for each other, quality time that they hadn't had in all the years, not since Susan had come into the world. Shauna's hours had been renegotiated and she now worked five days a week plus the odd evening babysitting when her employers fancied a little time alone. She didn't mind being with Susan and realised by the grin on his face, that her boss was getting more at home than free time, he was acting like a love struck teenager. Her shorter working hours meant she should have started to progress with her detection work but still every visit to the clubs drew a blank. Starting to feel this whole episode was a mistake, she made up her mind to return home to Jacks and decided that closing time on Friday was as good a time as any to hand in her notice. Shauna knew it wasn't going to be easy to leave the James', in such a short space of time her attachment to them had grown from liking to real love and knowing they were now able to cope still didn't make the decision any easier. Deep in thought at the prospect of leaving, the sound of her boss's voice startled her back to reality.

"Fran? Sorry my dear if I made you jump, it's just that before you go up to the flat I needed to have a word?"

"Sure Cecil, I'll just swap the closed sign over and

I'm all yours."

It had been a long day and Shauna was tired, she hoped whatever Cecil wanted, wouldn't take long. "Is there any chance you could open up on Monday morning? It's just that me, Madge and Susan are going away for the weekend. Actually it's the first proper holiday we've ever taken as a family."

"No problem Cecil you can rely on me."

There went her resignation, she couldn't spoil their weekend so it would have to wait until Monday but dragging out the inevitable only made her feel depressed. Saturday passed slowly, it was unusually quiet customer wise and Shauna missed the hustle and bustle of the weekday people but most of all she missed Susan's incessant chatter. By closing time she had written her resignation and decided to spend the evening packing but after a late supper and a bottle of cheap wine, nothing got done.

As Sunday was her day off it gave Shauna the chance to have one last look, although she didn't hold out much hope. London had been home for over a year and in all that time not one single glimpse, what chance did she have of everything falling into place in twenty four hours? The weather turned out to be glorious and even though the day turned up nothing new, she enjoyed herself just strolling around.

The newsagents opened early on Monday morning. For Shauna it had been a restless night and after tossing and turning into the small hours, she finally decided to get up. Making a quick breakfast, she splashed her face with water, dressed and made her way to the shop. After stocking the shelves ready for the morning rush and with the last of the papers placed in their correct order, Shauna stood up and resumed her place behind the counter. Seven o'clock on the dot saw the door open to the first of the day's customers, a customer she hadn't seen before.

"Can I help you sir?"

The word Sir came out in rather a high pitch as she instantly recognised who was standing before her.

"Just this newspaper please."

In all his glory and as bold as brass stood the reason she had come to London, the one reason she had for living. Frozen, not daring to moving a muscle, she stood totally still.

"Are you alright Miss?"

His words brought Shauna crashing back down to earth, her face reddened as she answered.

"I'm sorry, I seem to have lost the plot there for a moment."

As he gazed at her his face paled, he felt as if a ghost had walked over his grave.

"Excuse me for asking but do I know you Miss, only your look familiar?"

"No! No I don't think so, I haven't been in London very long and I can't remember you coming into the shop before."

"Maybe, it's just that you just remind me of someone."

Paying for his paper he left without another word and Shauna's hand trembled as she placed the money into the till. All this time spent searching with no result and then just as she was about to hand in her notice and give up he was suddenly within spitting distance and she hadn't known what to do. This certainly changed her plans, she couldn't possibly leave now, not when she was so close she could almost taste him. Shauna turned the shop sign to closed and went into the back kitchen to make a drink, she needed peace and quiet to think about what had just happened. With a hot mug of coffee in hand, she mentally went over the events of a few minutes ago and had to concentrate hard not to spill the drink as her hands were shaking so badly. He really hadn't changed, at least not as much as she thought he would have. His hair was now grey in places and his clothes were obviously more expensive but he was still Davey Wiseman, the one person she hated most in the world. Davey's walk to the club was a blur, several people on the street called out as he passed but he was oblivious to them, he couldn't get the young woman out of his mind. He knew Violet was dead, of course he did, she had been for years but this girl was her double, could have been her twin if it wasn't for the age difference. He told himself not to be so stupid and started to read the headlines of his paper as he entered the club.

"Janice! Bring me a coffee love, I'll be in my office."

"Okay Boss, won't be a tick."

Janice Shackleton had been a member of staff at the club for more years than she cared to remember. After a brief marriage that had only lasted two days, she had thrown herself into her work and become one of The Pelican's most trusted employees. Davey sat behind the large mahogany desk in the quiet of his room and tried to concentrate on the day's news. The only sound came from Hilda's old vacuum cleaner as she sucked up the mess caused by customers the previous night.

"Here you go Boss. I made it milky just how you like it."

Placing the cup down Janice noticed her boss's face and was struck by his paleness.

"You alright boss, only you ain't half gone a funny fuckin' colour?"

"Yeah I'm fine, just a little under the weather that's all."

The rest of the day passed in a blur, every time he tried to talk to someone or concentrate, the image of the girl from the newsagents would pop into his head. By four o'clock he'd downed half a bottle of Jack Daniels but he still couldn't shake the image of her face from his mind. Davey made his way home before the club got busy and on reaching his apartment continued drinking long into the small hours. It was a night of anxiety and when sleep finally came it was restless, he turned over and over again, with visions of Violet and the filthy squat she called home. When the alarm clock flicked to five am, Davey finally fell into a deep sleep, only to wake again at five forty.

Filled with anxiety, he got up, preferring to be tired rather than having to endure more bad dreams. After showering, he dressed in a smart navy Savile Row suit and began to make breakfast. Muesli, fresh strawberries, toast, in fact the whole works went into his culinary creation but when the preparation was complete he found he had no appetite at all. The penthouse apartment had been the first expensive item he'd purchased after the money started to roll in and being only a couple of miles from Soho, it was within walking distance of his clubs. The rooms, all colour coordinated in subtle creams and gold, normally had a calming effect, but he felt anything but calm this morning. His heart and soul had been put into the decoration, choosing furnishings which had cost thousands and making the place his own personal sanctuary. It was no sanctuary now, today he felt as if he was suffocating, he needed air, needed time to think. Gilly always collected him in the Mercedes at nine o'clock sharp but when the intercom bleeped Davey was not feeling his usual self.

"Ready Boss?"

"It's okay Gill, I'm walking today. I'll see you at The Pelican later."

Gilly didn't argue, he knew far better than to question his boss. When the man said jump, you asked how high but Davey Wiseman walking? Well that was a first.

"You alright Boss?"

"Yeah fine."

The intercom went dead. Gilly got back in the car and having a free half hour, decided to get himself a full English, Cardiac arrest on a plate was what Davey called it but Gilly didn't care, he'd never been able to stomach the rabbit food his boss called breakfast. As Gilly Slade tucked into a large plateful of greasy food, Davey had begun his walk and for some reason was compelled towards the newsagents. He couldn't get the girl out of his thoughts, maybe his mind was playing tricks on him. So what if she did resemble Violet, that was all it was, just a resemblance but he needed to see her again, needed to convince himself that he was just being stupid. By the time he reached the shop it was almost nine thirty and after having second thoughts, he turned to walk away. It only took a few steps before he turned around again, he had to go in, had to if he was ever to sleep well again. The shop as normal was extremely busy and several people had formed a queue. Davey stood at the back enabling him time to study the woman whilst being hidden from her view. Shauna was at the counter taking money and only looked up to hand back each customer their change, she didn't see Davey, which he was grateful for. It really was remarkable, her hair and bone structure, even her eyes were the same. Before he realised, the queue had moved along and he now stood directly in front of Shauna. Without looking up, she asked what he would like.

"Just this paper please."

She hadn't forgot the voice from yesterday, the voice from all those years ago and could feel her knees begin to buckle. Suddenly she could hear Vonny egging her on, pleading with her not to falter now. Their eyes met and a smile spread across her face.

"Hello again, twice in two days people will start to talk."

He laughed and the tension he'd felt since yesterday began to lift, stepping to one side, he waited while Shauna served the last few customers and when the shop was empty Davey at last spoke.

"I'm amazed at your looks."

"Thanks, well that's if it was a compliment. I assume it was?"

"Yes but I didn't mean it like that, it's just you

remind me so much of someone I used to know. I remember you said that you didn't come from London but do you have family here?"

"No I don't I'm afraid, look can I get you a drink?. I'm due for a break and we can have a chat, it's nice to have a little more conversation than the usual 'Can I help you'."

Before he had time to answer she disappeared behind the curtain. Shauna knew that if Cecil found out she'd left a stranger alone in the shop he would have been angry but this man was no stranger. Making the drinks had given her time to compose herself and think of an explanation. She decided to stick with her original story, just in case Cecil and Davey's paths ever crossed. Emerging a few minutes later with two steaming mugs of instant coffee she handed him one. "Here we are, I'm afraid it's only instant."

Davey smiled

"As long as it's wet and warm."

"So Mr?"

"Wiseman, Davey Wiseman."

"So Mr Wiseman, I look similar to someone you know?"

"Not similar, identical and its someone I used to know, sadly she's dead now."

Shauna could feel the anger starting to surface.

"Oh how sad, were you close?"

"No not really and it was a long time ago, let's not talk about that, tell me about yourself."

Shauna introduced herself as Fran Richards and proceeded to tell him all about the death of her parents and the move to London from Essex. When she'd finished she looked into Davey's face and noticed he was smiling.

"You have had it tough Fran, I'm sorry."

"Don't be, you didn't know them."

"No, but I feel I'm getting to know you."

She felt flustered, collecting the mugs Shauna disappeared into the kitchen. This wasn't supposed to happen, admittedly her experience with men had been limited, well in truth it had been non-existent but she was a hundred percent sure he was coming onto her. With no ground rules set out she didn't want to risk not seeing him again and decided to play along for a while. Davey had been impressed by this beautiful creature and was about to invite her to dinner when the shop door opened. Cecil had taken Susan for her weekly swimming lesson and both were deep in conversation about how well the lesson had gone as they entered. On seeing Davey at the counter, Cecil immediately became silent. Davey recognised the man, over the years he had popped in from time to time and was on nodding terms with the owner.

"Afternoon."

"Hello. Is Fran serving you or can I help."

"No she's already looking after me thanks."

With the coffee cups washed, Shauna was now back behind the counter and could hear the hostility in her employer's voice. She started to panic, not wanting confrontation as she didn't want to risk not seeing Davey again but she couldn't say anything either. Davey tipped an imaginary hat to her and much to Shauna's regret walked out of the shop.

"What the hell was he doing here Fran?"

"Nothing. It was quiet so I made him a coffee, you know how the time drags when it's quiet, we just had a chat, that's all."

"Fran you're such a trusting sort, I bet you don't even know who he is?"

"Yes I do actually. His name is Davey Wiseman and he seems really nice."

Cecil's eyes bore into Shauna, it was a look she had never seen him use before and one she felt uncomfortable with.

"Seems is the word! He's one of the most vicious gangsters in the area. He may come over as all sweetness and light but he's dangerous Fran, please for your own safety stay away from him."

She realised her boss was only thinking of her and it made her feel good inside that he cared but she wouldn't let Cecil or anyone else stand in her way. What made it more difficult, was the fact that she couldn't tell him, couldn't confide in him. Susan hadn't said a word and didn't say much for the rest of the morning, not until Shauna went up to the flat for her lunch.

"Daddy, I don't like that man."

"Me neither darling but there's not a lot we can do to stop Fran liking him, is there?"

Davey walked back to The Pelican with a spring in his step and nodded to anyone who called out. The sun was shining and he felt good, he decided that he liked Fran, liked her a lot and wondered to himself if she was what he'd been looking for all these years. Gilly, seated at one of the small tables, had been waiting for his boss to arrive and was generally pissed off. Thinking out loud that maybe the infamous Davey Wiseman was getting soft in his old age, he jumped up as Davey walked in.

"Fuckin' jumpy Gill!, done something you shouldn't?"

"No Boss, I was dozing and you startled me."

"Fuckin' dozing? You wanker, I don't pay you to sleep, now get your arse round to Jake the Florists and order me a bouquet of red roses. Tell him I want thirty and they'd better be good, not the fuckin' rubbish he usually palms off on his punters. Take them over to the little newsagents on Dean Street and give them to a woman named Fran."

"Who's Fran?"

"Don't be fuckin' nosy, just do it, oh and write this on the card."

Tearing a scrap of paper from one of the bar order pads he wrote.

'WHAT TIME DO YOU HAVE LUNCH?'

"Don't fuckin' scribble it either, use your best hand and Gill, wait for a reply."

Gilly Slade did as he was told but all the way to the florist his mind was in overdrive, the request had riled him, he was no one's pimp and if Davey wanted to get laid he should sort it out himself. The bouquet was gorgeous and Shauna felt flattered but so that Cecil didn't hear, she silently mouthed the words 'one o'clock'. Gilly left the shop and walking back to the club he mulled over his meeting with the woman and what his boss could possibly want with a nice girl like this Fran. She wasn't the slutty type he was normally attracted to, she didn't have her knickers on show or her tits hanging out. Actually he felt a bit sorry for her, she really shouldn't get in with the likes of Davey Wiseman. Unfortunately there wasn't much he could do about it, so he returned to The Pelican and relayed her message to his boss. The news had Davey grinning from ear to ear for the rest of the afternoon.

CHAPTER ELEVEN

Even though the smile remained on his face for the rest of the day, Davey didn't attempt to meet Shauna for lunch. Not wanting to seem eager, he decided that tomorrow would be soon enough.

Billy was due at The Pelican to discuss business and it was something Davey couldn't get out of, he wanted to, wanted to go straight to the shop to see her but he would have to wait. This emotion was new to him and no one had ever made him feel like this. His light hearted mood hadn't gone unnoticed and to The Pelican staff it came as a breath of fresh air, usually Davey's orders were barked out but today his tone was soft and everything he asked for sounded more like a request.

"Gill! Go collect Billy will you?"

"Okay Boss, is he at The Bull?"

"Yeah should be but give him a call and let him know you're on your way just in case."

Thirty minutes later and The Bull came into sight, as normal Billy was in the car before Gilly had parked and was full of his usual banter.

"Hello there my boy and how's it hanging today?" Gilly looked into the rear view mirror. He hated it when Billy said anything that held a sexual innuendo as it was hard to tell if he was joking or coming onto you. Gilly Slade had never been able to stomach queens, he was no queer basher or anything but God help any bloke that ever tried to touch him. With Billy it was different, as Gilly had to show respect even when he felt none but he still couldn't be sure how he would react if his passenger ever tried to take things further.

"Fine Mr Jackson, how's yours hanging?"

Billy laughed and winked in Gilly Slade's direction, knowing he could be seen by the driver in the rear view mirror.

"You're a cheeky fucker young Slade but I like you all the same. So how is the old bastard? I ain't seen him for a few days."

Gilly smirked as their eyes met in the mirror which intrigued Billy to the point of excitement.

"Come on spill your guts, what's he been up to?"

"I don't think I can say, in fact I know I can't or he'll fuckin' kill me."

"Good lad, loyalty is what I like to see and in any case, I'll get it out of the old bastard when I see him."

The car pulled up outside The Pelican and without another word Billy Jackson slammed the car door shut and disappeared inside. Gilly drove to the underground garage, parked and then went to join the boss and his friend in the club. As he entered the bar area was deserted except for Janice who was bottling up.

"Where's the Boss Jan?"

"He's in the office but he doesn't want to be disturbed."

Gilly knew this meant him and it really stuck in his craw. He wasn't included in any business dealings and nothing illegal had crossed his path since he'd started to work for Davey. The money he received was good and he didn't want for anything but there still wasn't anything that could match the excitement or thrill of a good robbery. Gilly decided that when it was time to drive Billy back, he would offer his services to the man, tell him he wasn't happy with Davey and that he wanted to get back into his old line of work. Sitting down he waited to be summoned, all the time mulling over what he was going to say. The situation didn't arise as he was called into the office moments later and was just able to catch the tail end of a conversation as he entered.

"If this comes off Davey we'll both be millionaires. Oh I forgot, we already are."

The two friends began to laugh but instantly stopped talking when Gilly walked in.

"Take a seat Gill. Now Billy and me have a bit of business coming up, you interested?"

"Depends what sort of business!"

Davey rolled his eyes upwards and at the same time puffed out his cheeks.

"Well fuck my old boots! You whinge to Billy here that you don't want to be an errand boy, then when I offer you a bit of action you get all fuckin' picky. Son if your bottles gone just say so."

Gilly looked from his boss to Billy, then back to his boss again.

"Of course my bottle ain't gone, it's just a bit of a surprise that's all."

"Good! I'll let you know what's happening but for now you can go, me and Billy are going to make a night of it so it might be a late one."

Gilly Slade didn't move from the chair much to Davey's annoyance.

"Didn't you hear me, fuck off out of here."

109

Leaving the club, Gilly made his way to the car and felt peeved at the way he'd been spoken to, especially as it was in front of Billy Jackson. Several minutes later his mood had lifted when he thought of the work to come. Thinking over the offer in his mind, he knew it was his chance to be recognised and if all went well, the boss or Billy would probably have plenty more jobs for him. Back at the club the two men had laughed when Gilly Slade closed the office door and Billy had grinned as he looked at his friend.

"You're a right cunt sometimes Davey."

"Don't know what you mean, he either wants a fuckin' job or he doesn't. You've got to tell it how it is Bill, you should know that. You can't have the tail wagging the fuckin' dog."

As if in mock surrender Billy Jackson placed his hands palm upwards.

"I know, I know. Anyway forget about that, what's put a smile on your boat? I ain't seen you so happy in months, come to think of it I ain't ever seen you so happy!"

Davey both smirked and winked at the same time but said nothing to his pal.

"Come on spill your guts, I'm dying to know."

Reluctantly Davey told his friend all about the woman he'd met and about the way he was feeling. He was still talking five minutes later and Billy Jackson was hanging on his every word but his final statement shocked not only Billy but Davey too.

"I think I could fall in love with this one."

"Don't be a tosser, you just need a good screw that's all."

"No I don't Bill, if that was all it was I could nip

outside and give Janice one over the bar. This one is more than sex, I get fuckin' hyper just thinking about her."

Billy studied his friend up close and jokingly placed his palm on Davey's forehead.

"Nope, no temperature."

"Fuck off Bill, I'm trying to be serious here."

"How can I take you serious my dear boy when you haven't even taken her out yet?"

Davey's face suddenly broke out into a wide grin.

"Well that is about to change, I'm meeting her tomorrow actually!"

Conversation between the two dwindled and it was several seconds before either spoke again. Suddenly they both looked in the direction of the door as music began to blare out from the bar area. Janice and the other staff were preparing for the evening rush of punters and the place would soon be full to the brim.

"I'm fuckin' starving Davey, how about getting a bite to eat?"

"Yeah alright but you're paying!"

"Don't I always, you're the tightest cunt I've ever known. Actually, I think you're the tightest cunt in the whole of London."

"And just how many tight cunts have you ever known?"

The two friends burst into laughter before walking into the main room which was beginning to fill up. Billy giggled loudly when he saw Janice slap an elderly but sprightly man around the face.

"Fuck off you old bastard, if you want that kind of service go elsewhere."

The man slouched away and Janice continued to serve

the punters as if nothing had happened.

"She's a fine bar woman Davey my boy but I wouldn't want to meet her down a dark alley, still, if I was that way inclined, a shag wouldn't go amiss." They both grinned as they left through the main door and began their short walk to Chang's Chinese restaurant. The place was typical of the restaurants in Chinatown, with its plain exterior hiding many secrets inside. Billy popped his head around the door to see if they could get a table.

"Hey Chang any space left?"

"For you Mr Jackson, no problem."

To the front of the restaurant, which was decorated in typical Chinese style, sat the tourists and anyone of non-standing in the community but a short distance in was an area set aside for celebrities and anyone who was anyone in the city. Without question, Billy Jackson and Davey Wiseman were shown to the back, Chang Yung had been warned about the two men even before he had opened the place back in nineteen ninety. He had accepted the advice gratefully and in all the years since he'd been trading, had never turned either of the men away and likewise never received any trouble. The men were led to a quiet table in the corner and a banquet of at least twenty dishes followed soon after. Billy never one for manners, dived straight in.

"Steady on Bill, you not eaten for a week?"

"I always eat well when I'm excited and I'm excited! Anyway, you know I love this fuckin' chinky nosh." Davey stared as his friend shovelled in fork full after fork full, his own appetite non-existent.

"Come on, what's the matter? Its fuckin' blinding

grub and all you can do is look at it."

"I know Bill but I'm just not hungry."

"Not that fuckin' girl again, you're starting to get right up my nose. Just fuck her and forget about it."

"I told you, it's not as simple as that."

"It's as simple as you want to make it and what the fucks got into you? She's just another piece of skirt and probably not that special once you get inside her knickers anyway."

"You wouldn't say that if you saw her, then again, you ain't into women are you?"

Billy rolled his eyes upwards signalling that he was now bored with the conversation and the gesture annoyed Davey.

"If you don't want to fuckin' listen, why did your bring me here?"

"Because I like us to spend quality time together you know that."

"And we do but for fucks sake Bill, I have to have a life of my own. For too many years it's been one fuckin' job after another and now I've found something, someone that isn't sullied and isn't connected to the villain community and I like it."

Billy shoved a spare rib into his mouth but at the same time waved his hand in an attempt to dismiss his friend's words, the action was a step too far and instantly riled Davey.

"You cunt! Well you can pig out all you like because I'm off."

Davey stormed out of the restaurant and his companion didn't attempt to stop him. Billy had never seen his friend like this before, whoever this girl was, she was bad news but Davey would just

have to find that out for himself. Billy Jackson
continued to eat, oblivious to the strange looks he was
receiving from the other diners close by.
Outside in the cold night air Davey calmed down and
couldn't for the life of him work out why he'd reacted
that way. Deciding a slow walk back to the club
would clear his head, he set off but half way down the
road he had a change of heart and headed in the
direction of home. The journey would be
considerably longer but the fresh air might help him
to sleep. As he walked along, he started to made
mental notes of where to take Fran tomorrow. The
first date was lunch so it shouldn't be too fancy.
If things went well and she agreed to join him for
dinner, he would book a classy place, maybe
somewhere up West. While Davey enjoyed his
leisurely stroll, Shauna lay in bed worrying over what
would happen tomorrow and for some reason Vonny's
voice just wouldn't shut up.

The fresh air must have done some good as Davey
slept soundly but it wasn't a luxury Shauna had as
she'd relived every detail of that fateful day. She saw
Violet and Vonny in her dreams but unlike before
they were both talking to her, both mouthing words
that she couldn't hear. Their skin began to
disintegrate in front of her eyes, showing the pure
white bone of their skulls and with every word they
uttered, tiny maggots fell from their mouths. Shauna
must have screamed out and awoke to find the bed
soaked in perspiration. Never before had anything
like this happened and it had frightened the life out of
her. She wanted to call Jacks, tell her to come and

114

take her home but knew she couldn't and right at this moment Shauna felt more alone than ever. Finally when dawn broke she realised she'd been awake for most of the night, petrified of falling asleep, terrified that she would see them both again. In the past she had been ecstatic whenever Von came into her dreams but this night, had that been a warning? Maybe she was just anxious about today so settling for the latter she decided to get up. Opening the wardrobe, Shauna chose a smart pair of jeans and a lamb's wool jumper. She wanted to look smart but not give Davey the impression that she had dressed especially for him. Shauna wasn't supposed to know he would take her out today but she did, unable to explain the certainty, alarm bells started to ring in her head but she mentally pushed them away. Her thoughts of Davey Wiseman hadn't changed and having a premonition that today would be a day she wouldn't forget in a hurry, she walked into the kitchenette and made coffee. After taking a leisurely bath she then went down to the shop to find Cecil was already behind the counter when she entered.

"Morning Fran."

"Morning Cecil, ready for the rush?"

"As always my dear, as always!"

Things hadn't been exactly strained between them lately but she knew he wasn't happy since Davey had come into the shop. Cecil always kept his opinions to himself, which made it sometimes hard to work out what he was really thinking. The morning passed quickly and at twelve fifty five Shauna collected her coat and bag, her whole body felt as if it was trembling but she realised it was only nerves.

"Going out for lunch Fran?"

"Yes, I need some shopping so I thought now was as good a time as any."

Cecil eyed her suspiciously but he didn't comment as she left the shop.

<u>CHAPTER TWELVE</u>

That morning Davey had been awake since six, a million butterflies churned in his stomach from sheer excitement, it was going to be a great day, he could feel it in his bones. Having no appetite breakfast was out of the question, the only thing he could concentrate on was the thought of Fran. After a long hot shower, he dressed in one of his most expensive suits and stood gazing across Hyde Park daydreaming. The intercom buzzed at nine o'clock and Davey whistled as he went to answer.

"Ready Boss?"

"Err, no Gill not today, I won't be coming in. Go over to The Royal and Top to Tail, make sure everything's running smoothly. If you've got any problems phone Billy, I won't be available at all today."

Gilly was speechless. In the year he had been working for Davey, he had never known the man to take a day off. A tyrant when it came to his clubs, he always had to have his finger on the pulse.

"You alright Boss?"

Davey smiled to himself. Was he such a bastard that when he was in a good mood everyone thought he must be ill?

"Couldn't be better, now piss off and I'll see you tomorrow."

Gilly Slade didn't understand but it wasn't for him to question why, or was it? He checked on the clubs as he'd been told, then drove over to The Bull. Billy sat holding court in his plush office, a young lad of no

more than sixteen being the centre of his attention.
When the doorman informed Billy who had arrived,
the young lad was told to get lost. Reaching the
office, Gilly passed the young boy coming out and
felt sorry for him, the kid was just a baby and as far as
he was concerned, Billy was nothing more than a
paedophile.

"Morning Gill, what can I do for you?"

Choosing a seat directly facing Billy's desk he
suddenly wondered if this was such a good idea.

"I know I may be out of order Mr Jackson, and please
say if I am, it's just that I'm concerned about Davey.
He ain't half acting strange."

Instantly the smile disappeared from Billy's face.

"I bet it's that fuckin' whore again."

The penny dropped as Gilly recalled the flowers he'd
been sent to buy on Davey's behalf.

"Mr Jackson her name wouldn't be Fran by any
chance would it?"

"How did you find that out?"`

Gilly repeated his orders of the previous day, which
made his hosts eyes light up. Now aware of where to
find the woman in question, Billy was eager to have a
little look for himself but didn't share his plans with
Gilly.

"It's just something he needs to get out of his system,
don't worry he'll be back with us before you know it.
Now haven't you got any fuckin' work to do?"

"Yes of course, sorry to have bothered you Mr
Jackson. Err, you won't tell Davey I was here will
you?"

"Well I wouldn't usually tolerate anyone going
behind Davey's back but I can see it was only

118

concern on your behalf so, Scout's honour it'll be our little secret."

"Thank you Mr Jackson."

Gilly didn't like Billy's tone and couldn't get out of the office fast enough, which made Billy chuckle. Davey's oldest and best friend decided to leave it a couple of days until he paid the bitch a visit, if she thought she could take his Davey away from him, she could fuckin' think again.

Davey Wiseman left home at twelve thirty, giving him plenty of time to walk to the newsagents before Fran started her lunch hour. His feet felt as light as a feather as he stopped off at Jake's to collect three dozen red roses that had been ordered earlier that morning.

"Anymore and you'll be a regular Mr Wiseman, people will start to talk."

"You just keep the quality the same Jake and I'll be in every day."

The florist gave a nervous laugh but underneath he was praying it wouldn't be the case. If Davey Wiseman became a regular, nobody else would come into his shop. It wasn't just the fact he was a gangster, an offer of payment wouldn't have gone amiss. Davey always choose the most expensive blooms and it had cost Jake fifty pounds in the last two days alone. If this carried on he'd be bankrupt by the end of the year.

"Thanks again Mr Wiseman, see you soon."

Shauna came out of the newsagents and turned left towards the High Street shops. Her admirer had been hiding out of sight in a neighbouring doorway and as soon as he saw her he began to follow. Quickening his pace he caught her by the arm several seconds later and startled, Shauna spun round on her heels as she came face to face with the person she hated most in the world.

"Hello Fran, where are you off to?"

"You know very well that it's my lunch break Mr Wiseman and you've just scared the hell out of me!"

"I'm sorry, it wasn't my intention. I thought we could go for something to eat."

"I, I don't think so."

Firmly holding her arm, Davey led her in the opposite direction.

"Fran you have to eat and I'm here to make sure you do, there's a nice little Italian down the road, and you'll enjoy it."

Davey wasn't used to being told no, he always got what he wanted and he wanted this woman. Shauna knew he was trying to bully her and that she had to take control, had to make him see that she wasn't like the women he normally dated. Shaking her arm free from his grip, she turned to face him.

"I don't take kindly to being told what to do, now if you don't mind I have shopping to buy."

Davey was taken aback, whatever had possessed him to think he could force her to do anything, he wanted to kick himself.

"Fran I'm sorry, can we start again?"

Knowing she had him just where she wanted, she smiled and nodded.

"Yes we can but never ever presume to know what I want Mr Wiseman."

"I won't I promise, now how about that lunch? And please call me Davey."

The small restaurant decorated in traditional Sicilian style, was quiet as they entered. Ricardo Maranchini did most of his trade in the evenings and gladly welcomed the lunchtime custom that was until he recognised the male diner. Showing the couple to a small table by the window, he gave them both a menu and disappeared into the kitchen. Ten minutes after being seated Davey was becoming increasingly annoyed at the lack of service. He'd wanted everything to be perfect and now this little grease ball was about to ruin everything. Excusing himself with the ruse of using the toilet, Davey made his way to the back of the restaurant and entered the kitchen. Ricardo was deep in conversation with the chef and didn't notice when one of his waiters walked up to the diner.

"Excuse me Sir but customers are not permitted in the kitchen."

Without a word, Davey grabbed the man by the throat and pushed him up against the wall.

"Listen cunt! I'm here with a lady so get your fuckin' arse out there and treat her and me come to that, with some respect. Capiche?"

Unable to speak, the waiter dropped to the floor and nodded his head vigorously. Davey then smoothed back his hair and re-joined Shauna at the table as if nothing had happened. The rest of the lunch went well, Shauna found herself laughing at his silly jokes and surprisingly, enjoying his company. Glancing at her watch she was horrified to see that it was two

121

thirty.

"Oh my God look at the time, I should have been back at work half an hour ago."

Getting up from the table she hurriedly put on her coat and without thinking bent and kissed Davey on the cheek.

"Thanks for a lovely lunch."

He didn't want the date to end and grabbing her hand asked if he could take her to dinner that night. For a second she didn't reply, which made him nervous but then she nodded and told him to collect her at eight.

Cecil didn't speak when she arrived back at work, he felt too angry with her to have any kind of real conversation and nearly an hour later, when Shauna couldn't stand the atmosphere any longer, she finally asked what was wrong.

"Cecil, if I've done something to offend you then please say."

He looked her in the eye then turned his back and continued to stack the shelves. Shauna thinking he hadn't heard her, was about to repeat herself, when he spoke.

"You haven't offended me Fran, I just feel that you were a little deceitful."

"Deceitful? How on earth have I been deceitful?"

"When you left for lunch I realised you'd forgotten your gloves. I came out of the shop and was about to call after you, when I saw him."

"Oh, I see."

"No you don't see Fran, I tried to warn you but you took no notice. He's a dangerous man and he'll end up hurting you or worse!"

Shauna felt somewhat sad that they were falling out

122

Over something that really was none of his business but a quickly as the feeling had surfaced, it was replaced by anger.

"I didn't try to deceive you, I didn't know he was waiting outside but if I had have known, then it was for me to decide if I went to lunch with him or not." This was becoming a habit, not once but twice in a single day had a man tried to tell her what to do, well she wasn't having it. Cecil began to speak but Shauna instantly stopped him.

"Please I haven't finished yet. I know you care about me and I'm grateful for that but I must make up my own mind regarding who I do or do not see. I love you and your family Cecil, please don't make me feel as though I have no choice but to leave."

"I would never do that Fran. I, we, all think too much of you to ever put you in a position where you would want to leave. I won't mention the subject again but please, just be careful, I really am only thinking of you."

"I know you are and I promise I will."

Cecil walked across the shop floor and hugged her tightly. The rest of the day passed quickly and as soon as her shift ended, Shauna disappeared up to the flat. A leisurely bath complete with a glass of wine was followed by five minutes of frantic clothes searching. Nothing in her wardrobe was suitable and she had to reluctantly settle for a little black dress that Jacks had given her years earlier. With hair freshly washed and her makeup applied to perfection, Shauna was truly stunning, she just hoped Davey would agree.

The doorbell rang at eight and she nervously guzzled down the last of the wine. Stepping out onto the pavement, Shauna smiled at her escort.

"Ready Miss Richards?"

"Sure am Mr Wiseman."

Leading her by the arm, Davey opened the front passenger door of the car. He had given Gilly the night off, tonight was for the two of them and he didn't want to share her with anyone. They drove over to Le Gavroche in Mayfair, Davey got out, walked round the car and opened her door. After passing the car keys to a young man dressed in a smart suit, they entered the restaurant and Shauna couldn't believe her eyes. The walls were covered in olive green silk and the table linen was of the finest quality. Fresh flowers overflowed from crystal vases and Shauna had never seen anything like it, even The Utopia paled into insignificance compared to this but she wouldn't allow herself to show how impressed she was. Once seated the Head Waiter handed them both a menu and Davey's face froze when he realised it was written completely in French but Shauna just leaned forward and clasped his hand in hers.

"Can I order for both of us, it's a long time since I practiced my French?"

Davey felt relief like he'd never known, wash over him.

"If you'd like to that would be nice."

Word perfect Shauna ordered two Soufflé Suissesse, followed by Filet de Boeuf. The waiter congratulated her on her fine pronunciation of his native tongue, in French of course and Davey didn't have a clue what they were talking about, he was just glad that he hadn't been made to look a fool. Fran really was a classy lady, the classiest lady he had ever known. He gazed at his beautiful companion for several seconds before a troubled expression covered his face.

"Is there something wrong Davey?"

"Not wrong exactly, it's just your perfume!"

"You don't like it?"

"No not at all, in fact it's lovely. It's just that I've smelled something very similar but I can't for the life of me remember where."

"It's a very popular brand, maybe one of you staff or someone else you know wears it."

"Maybe."

Inwardly Shauna smiled, Violet's old favourite had sent his mind into overdrive, just as she'd hoped. The food came and empty plates were taken away, conversation flowed until they were the only two people left. Neither wanted the night to end, so Davey suggested the casino. He didn't say he owned the place but when they arrived and people fell over themselves it was obvious, that and the fact Mr Simmonds had already told Shauna all about The Royal. Handing her a pile of gambling chips worth over a thousand pounds, Davey told her to go and play to her heart's content. Approaching the roulette table, she placed a one hundred chip on number one and waited for the wheel to spin. Her return came to three thousand five hundred pounds. Shauna's second bet was on number three, she gently pushed a pile of red chips onto the green baize and sat back in her chair. The croupier spun the highly polished dish and the tiny white ball flew like a bird before finally settling. The croupier called out red number three and at the same time realised that the beautiful woman in front of him had just won thirty thousand pounds. Nervously he moved his eyes to where his boss was seated but Davey Wiseman just grinned and nodded his head, giving the go ahead to pay out. People were starting to gather round, unable to believe the luck of this first time player. Noticing she had an audience, Shauna stood up from the table, gathered up the chips and walking over to Davey, placed them on the bar in front of him.

"It's fine sweetheart, it's yours."

Shauna wanted nothing more than to take the money, it would help her and Jackie enormously in the future but she knew she had to be polite, show him that she wasn't greedy or out for what she could get, so as much as it went against the grain she declined his offer.

"No Davey I couldn't."

"Yes you can Fran. I gave the chips to you so if you won then the money is yours."

Shauna's expression suddenly hardened and it was a look Davey had seen before.

"I'm sorry. If you don't want them that's your choice, I won't be the one to tell you what to do." Remembering the incident earlier that day she laughed and nodded her head. Davey motioned with his hand and a male teller appeared. The man was told to cash in the lady's winnings and bring over the money. The couple left the club shortly before four am and Shauna wasn't looking forward to getting up early in the morning. As they drove along Davey began to chat.

"You did really well at the tables tonight, you must have gambled before?"

"No, honestly. Until tonight I had never set foot inside a casino."

As the car pulled up outside the newsagents Shauna started to get anxious. What if he wanted payment for the evening, payment in kind? She had known the situation would arise but now when it actually came down to the nitty gritty she didn't know what to do. Davey switched off the engine and turned to face her.

"Fran I really have had a nice time."

"Me too Davey. I would invite you in but it's late and I have to be up early."

"That's fine, I mustn't keep you up any longer but I really would like to see you again Fran, that's if you want to of course?"

Shauna thought but only long enough to cause him to worry before she smiled sweetly.

"Yes I would and thank you."

Shauna felt a huge weight lift from her shoulders, she hadn't relished the thought of fighting him off. Luckily it hadn't come to that and he simply kissed her on the cheek and said he would call her tomorrow. She walked up to the flat and once inside Shauna removed the manila envelope and tipped the cash out onto the bed. Thirty thousand pounds sure did look a lot and she had never actually seen that much money in her life before. Someone up there must have really been looking out for her tonight and tilting her head upwards, she blew a kiss. Shauna now felt happy and contented that everything was going to plan, for the moment at least!

CHAPTER THIRTEEN

The following morning, Gilly once again pressed the intercom buzzer at nine sharp but it took two further attempts before Davey finally answered.

"Oh fuck off Gilly! I've only had a couple of hour's kip, come back later."

Gilly smirked to himself, he had an idea that Davey may have got lucky the night before.

"You've got big business today Boss, we don't want to be late."

The intercom nearly blew off the wall as Davey's voice bellowed through it.

"Don't fuckin' tell me what to do you cunt, now piss off back to the club until I phone you."

Realising his boss hadn't got lucky and was once again in a shitty mood, he didn't argue any further. Davey crawled back to bed, he was now paying the price for having a brilliant evening. Shortly before dropping off to sleep, he muttered under his breath 'I'll fuckin' sort that bastard out later.` Gilly made his way to The Pelican and taking a seat in the corner, began his wait for Billy Jackson. While Davey drifted off into a much needed slumber, Shauna had managed to drag herself out of bed. She knew it was going to be a long day and wasn't looking forward to it. Her head was thumping through sheer lack of sleep and the last thing she wanted was a shop full of noisy customers. For the first time in her life she had bags under her eyes and looking in the bathroom mirror, knew she looked as bad as she felt.

"Good morning Fran! Oh my, late night was it?"

"Yes it was Cecil and my head is pounding."
It had been years since he'd suffered a hangover but could still remember the agony of the morning after and it made him feel sorry for his employee.
"Did you mix the grape and the grain or was it sheer volume?"
Shauna's face was ashen, she really did feel terrible but still managed to smile at her boss's comment.
"Believe it or not, I only had two glasses of wine all night. It was after four when I got to bed and that I can assure you, is the only reason I feel this way."
Cecil laughed.
"Listen Fran, once the morning rush is over Susan and I can manage. Go and get some sleep and come back down after lunch."
Susan walked over to Fran and placed her palm on her friend's brow.
"Poor Fran, poor Fran."
Even in her delicate state Shauna had to laugh but she was still grateful for Cecil's offer. Once the hectic period had passed, she didn't need to be told twice and within ten minutes of leaving the shop, was tucked up in bed and had instantly fallen asleep.

Billy got to the club around ten and when told Davey hadn't yet arrived, he flew into a rage.
"What the fuck is he playing at? This is a fuckin' major deal and he can't be bothered to show up!"
Gilly had to be careful with his reply, he hadn't personally suffered the Jackson wrath but he'd been witness to plenty that had.
"I think he had a late night Mr Jackson."
"A fuckin' late night! Are you pulling the piss or

something Gill?"

Gilly started to panic, most of the time Billy Jackson was alright but he was now getting agitated and Gilly didn't know what to do if he kicked off.

"Shall I phone him?"

Walking towards the office, Billy glanced over his shoulder and shouted.

"No! I'll call the selfish cunt myself and he'd better have a fuckin' good explanation!"

Davey's mobile phone rang several times before he groaned and rolled over to answer it.

"Yes!"

"Don't fuckin' yes me, what the fuck are you playing at? We're about to cut the biggest deal we've ever had and you're lying stinking in your fuckin' pit?"

Davey knew his friend always got nervy before a deal, they didn't both need to be there but Billy always wanted the back up of his partner in crime.

"Calm down. Send Gilly to collect me in ten minutes and...."

Before he'd finished speaking Billy had hung up. Once more Gilly drove to the apartment but this time collected his boss as ordered. The short drive back to The Pelican was made in silence, he sensed Davey wasn't in the mood for conversation. The only exchange of words came at the end of the journey when Davey Wiseman ordered him to park the car. Davey walked through The Pelicans main door and when he saw his friend pacing the floor, he smiled to himself as he visualised the imaginary steam coming out of the top of Billy's head.

"What the fuck are you grinning at you cunt! I've been fuckin' standing here with a shed load of fuckin' big ones and you can't even turn up on time. Any cunt could have walked in here and turned us over." Gently placing a hand on Billy's shoulder, Davey spoke in a calming tone which had in the past, always soothed his friends rage.

"Calm down, I'm out of order I know, now let's just get down to business shall we?"

Billy knew there was little point in carrying on. He had learnt in the past you couldn't tell Davey Wiseman what to do but after all these years it still pissed him off. Gilly entered to see the two men sharing a drink and knew he had missed any action that might have taken place.

"Right Gilly, drive Mr Jackson over to Walthamstow for the deal. Are you both carrying a piece?" Billy loudly sighed.

"Is the pope fuckin' Catholic? You really do ask some fuckin' stupid questions Davey."

"Now the meet's in half an hour, that's plenty of time to get there and case the place. Remember if it goes tits up, neither of you are to come back here. Lay low for a couple of days, then contact me."

Both men nodded their acknowledgment but neither uttered another word. Gilly collected an unregistered van from the garage and the two men set off. As soon as the vehicle was in motion, Billy turned to face his accomplice.

"Was he out with that tart last night?"

Knowing he couldn't ignore the question, wouldn't dare ignore it, Gilly felt fear start to rise from the pit of his stomach. If he didn't reply he could end up with a gun in his face, to Billy Jackson, people were disposable and the only exclusion to that fact was

Davey.

"I don't think she's a tart Mr Jackson."

"So the answers yes then and for your information Gilly they are all fuckin' tarts, whores that just get paid in a different way."

Gilly didn't reply as he didn't want to antagonise the man. They drove onto a small trading estate at the rear off Walthamstow High Street and Billy scanned the lockups looking for Rohine Importers & Exporters.

"There it is Gill, now pull up outside and switch off the engine."

Sitting in silence for almost half an hour, they watched people come and go until Billy was satisfied it was safe.

"Wait in the van. If I ain't back in twenty minutes start the engine and get the fuck out of here fast." Removing the holdall from the back doors, Billy walked up to the roller shutter and pressed the bell. He saw the close circuit television camera focus in on him and looking into the lens he grinned. The roller went up and a small man, who to Billy looked like he'd just come from the set of a martial arts movie, stared back at him.

"I have an appointment with Wang Low."

The man didn't speak and waving Billy inside, closed the shutter behind them both. Gilly watched as his accomplice entered the building and he started to get nervous, not knowing what the business was or even who the contact was. Placing his hand inside his jacket pocket he caressed the pistol, it gave him some reassurance but he wasn't happy with the situation. Fifteen minutes later, Billy still hadn't come out and

Gilly was beginning to think that the first bit of business he'd done in a long time was about to turn sour. Taking a pen from the glove compartment he started to doodle on the back of his cigarette packet. Writing Rohine Importers, he casually swapped the letters around and couldn't believe when he read the word heroin. The cocky bastards were advertising their wares and no one had picked up on it. Gilly laughed as he spoke out loud 'The cheeky tossers'.
Inside Billy had been thoroughly frisked, before being led up a steel staircase and along a corridor into Wang Low's office. Secretly he had enjoyed the frisking and jokingly was about to ask the body guard if he would like a full time job but thought better of it. Billy and Wang shook hands, and then quickly got down to business. The guard sliced into one of the bags and Billy Jackson was offered a sample. Placing a finger inside the package, Billy pressed down then removed his hand. The tip of his finger now appeared white and he rubbed it vigorously along the front of his gums.
"Blinding stuff Wang."
Neither of the Chinese men spoke and after handing over the money, Billy walked out of the lockup carrying a large holdall. Placing the bag in the back of the van he joined Gilly up front.
"Drive my boy, everything is as sweet as a nut."
"I thought it was Charlie not H, Mr Jackson."
"It is Gill. These chinks have connections from afar afield as Afghanistan and fuckin' Colombia and the slit eyed little bastards will deal in anything."
They made their way to The Bull but on arrival Gilly wasn't invited inside.

133

"Go back and tell your Boss everything went down without a hitch"

"Is that it Mr Jackson?"

Billy glared at his driver.

"This is the twenty first century boy, not the fuckin' OK Corral. I suppose you wanted to go in there all fuckin' guns blazing?"

"No, it's just that I thought there might be a bit of action."

Shaking his head Billy got out of the van and entered his club. Back at The Pelican the usual early clientele were already buzzing around. Gilly made his way to the office, eager to tell Davey about the success of the deal as he knocked on the door and waited to be invited in.

"Come!"

"Mission accomplished Boss."

Davey nodded but didn't look up from his paper and Gilly couldn't believe that after they had just carried off a major drug deal his boss wasn't the least bit interested. The cut and thrust of underworld business now held little thrill for Davey, he had more money than he could poke a stick at and only participated to keep his friend happy. Billy Jackson was more than capable of carrying out any form of criminal activity on his own but for reasons known only to himself, he wanted and needed his best pal by his side.

"Phone Billy and tell him I'll be over tomorrow night as arranged, then you can take a couple of days off."

Closing the office door, Gilly walked to the bar phone and relayed the message as he'd been told and then after saluting in Janice's direction he left the club.

After receiving the call and stashing the goods, Billy

Jackson was in a mood to celebrate. Downing a large quantity of brandy he had slept like a baby on the office couch and woke with the mother of all headaches just after lunchtime.

The next morning and against his better judgement, he decided to take a look at the whore who was distracting his friend. Driving over from Bethnal Green, Billy walked into the newsagents just as the clock struck four. Cecil had popped out for a while with Susan, leaving Shauna alone to run things. She didn't mind though, now looking and feeling a lot better than she had yesterday, Shauna just felt glad to be alive. Billy browsed the racks for a few minutes admiring the tanned young torsos on display. Selecting a gay magazine from the top shelf he approached the counter to see what held the attraction for Davey. Giving her the once over, he reluctantly had to admit that she was beautiful.
"Hello Sir how can I help?"
He had chosen the soft porn issue on purpose as he wanted to embarrass this girl, wanted to see her face colour up. Billy's plan backfired when Shauna didn't bat an eyelid over his choice, and instead she placed the bold colour issue into a brown paper bag.
"That's four pounds ninety five please."
There and then he decided that he didn't like her, she was a cool customer, a bit too cool for his liking and he would make it his personal project to get rid of her. His vendetta and the fact that he'd been to see for himself what this precious Fran looked like, had to be kept secret. If Davey ever found out he would hit the roof but then there was no reason why he ever should

find out. Accepting that he couldn't say he didn't like her, he had to think of an alternative but whatever happened he'd make sure he got her out of his mate's life and sooner rather than later. Shauna handed her customer his change and he left the shop without so much as a thank you but after months of working and living in a place where so many never even gave you the time of day she didn't think anything of it. Davey wasn't due at The Bull until later so Billy decided to go back and spend the rest of the afternoon holed up in his office. A little light relief would de-stress him and the magazine he'd just purchased would help the task in hand get under way.

After what felt like the longest day in history, Shauna finally locked the front door and turned the sign to closed just as the telephone started to ring. Wearily she walked behind the counter and picked up the receiver.
"Did you enjoy your evening Miss Richards? I must say you looked very sexy last night."
Grinning to herself as she recognised his voice, she decided to wind Davey up a little and in a squeaky voice, made out she was Madge.
"Who is this please?"
Shauna could hear the embarrassment as he began to cough before apologising for his mistake and asking if he could speak to Fran. Shauna giggled and Davey smiled to himself when he realised she was joking.
"Very funny Fran, aren't we the amusing one. So how are you?"
"I'm fine and yes I had a wonderful time, although I suffered for it all day yesterday."

Forgetting his prior engagement he asked if he could see her later.

"I would love to Davey but I'm still so tired, you don't mind do you? Maybe tomorrow or even the day after?"

"Tomorrow would be great, shall I pick you up at say, eight?"

"I'll look forward to it."

As she hung up leaving Davey with the receiver still glued to his ear Shauna knew it was going to be child's play reeling him in.

Replacing the handset Davey remembered Billy and was now glad she had declined his offer. The friends had exchanged a few cross word of late and it would be good to make the peace. As Gilly had been given the day off, Davey ordered a cab to take him over to The Bull. As usual the place was packed to capacity with wall to wall men, young, old, tall and short and remembering his last visit, he chose not to cross the dance floor. Instead he opted to walk the long way around, passing the highly polished mahogany bar which ran the whole length of the club, he finally reached Billy's office and as usual his friend was more than pleased to see him.

"Davey my boy! Result or what?"

Looking onto the desk, Davey saw the magazine his friend had purchased from Shauna and as he ran his hand over the title he smirked.

"What's this? You dirty fucker! I bet you've been in here all afternoon knocking one out ain't you?"

"So! It helps me to relax, maybe you should give it a try now and again."

Davey slowly shook his head and they both laughed

before taking seats on either side of the desk.

"I have been in contact with the Pimlico crew and they can take half the load, I reckon in the next few days we will have moved the lot."

"Good work Davey, how much do you think it will bring in?"

"About 900K, give or take a few grand."

"Not bad, not bad at all but I think we should leave it a couple of months before we go again. It doesn't pay to get too greedy!"

Davey Wiseman looked at the man in amazement, he had never been one to shy away from a deal but with this one still so hot you could fry an egg on it he was stunned that Billy was already talking about the next.

"I think we should hold off for a lot longer than that Billy, anyway how did Gill perform?"

"Did as he was told but I think he would have liked to have seen a little action, the prick!"

"They are all the same Bill, if they don't get to pull out a fuckin' shooter, it wasn't a good job. I think some of the daft fuckers are in it for the aggro more than the payoff."

"That's why Davey my boy, there will always be Bosses like us and wanker's like Gilly Slade. Anyway, enough of this, fancy a drink or are we seeing the little girlie again tonight?"

Davey shook his head in a negative gesture and Billy noticed that he looked tired.

"I'll stay for one, and then I'm off. I need an early night, fuckin' late ones knacker me these days. Tomorrow alright to collect the stuff?"

"Tomorrow's fuckin' brilliant."

Opening a bottle of Scotch the two friends talked

about the old days, how times were changing and both were in agreement that the new faces of crime were not in the best interests of anyone, boys in blue included. Finishing his drink Davey said his goodbyes and after hailing a cab, made his way home, desperate to get some sleep.

CHAPTER FOURTEEN

On the dating front things had moved fast between
Davey and Shauna. Both were eager to see each
other as often as possible but with very different
motives. Even though Billy hadn't been introduced
to her, he was beginning to get upset at the lack of
contact he now had with his friend as their once a
week boys night out no longer happened. Every time
Davey received an invitation to go over to The Bull
he made up some excuse why he couldn't make it.
He preferred to spend his time with Fran or if it
happened to be on one of the rare nights when they
didn't see each other, then much needed sleep took
priority. Davey didn't realise he was hurting his
friend, he didn't give it a second thought and was
totally unaware of the emotional stress and anger his
actions had unleashed. After one particular let down
Billy flew into a rage so severe he trashed the office
while cursing and screaming every name under the
sun, all directed at Fran Richards. Billy imagined that
every tiny thing that had gone wrong in his life was
Fran's fault. If the club had a slack night it was
blamed on her, if his coffee wasn't hot enough it was
blamed on her. Never once did it cross his mind that
Davey preferred to be with his new love instead of
hanging around in a gay bar drinking. The terrible
hatred Billy had for Shauna was the exact opposite to
the feelings Cecil now had for Davey. After
witnessing his gentle and polite manner whenever he
was in Fran's company, his attitude had begun to
soften towards the man. Cecil had a new respect for

Davey but his previous dislike had rubbed off on Susan and the fact that she didn't get to spend as much time with her friend didn't help the situation.

The shop door flew open just before closing and Davey ran in, grinning from ear to ear he had to stop for a moment to regain his breath. Shauna had been out the back washing up the cups and mugs and as she emerged from behind the beaded curtain, was a little surprised to see him.

"Hi Davey, we weren't seeing each other tonight were we?"

"No Fran, it's just that I've been offered two tickets to see Motown The Musical and I know how much you wanted to go."

Shauna pulled a face as she'd never imagined she would get the opportunity. Accepting there was no choice to make, she sadly shook her head, she'd given her word to Susan and a promise was a promise. Nodding in the young girl's direction she quietly whispered in his ear.

"Davey I'd love to go but it's my night with Susan and I can't let her down."

Susan, who was stacking shelves, glared over and scowled at Davey which made him feel uncomfortable.

"That's alright love, I realise it's a bit short notice and you have other commitments. I'll see if I can swap them for a later date."

Placing her arms around his neck, she gently kissed his cheek.

"You are a darling."

Far from being disappointed, it made Davey admire

141

this beautiful woman even more. They arranged to meet the following evening and Davey walked out of the shop leaving his girlfriend feeling as though she'd got the raw end of the deal. Turning to look at Susan, whose face still wore a terrible frown, Shauna tried to lighten the mood.

"Right Miss James, so what's on the agenda for our girlie night in?"

"I don't like that man."

The revelation took Shauna by surprise. Susan was the sweetest girl and never said a bad word about anyone, true Davey was bad but this innocent child couldn't possibly know that or could she?

"Don't you my darling? Well you've nothing to worry about, I have lots of friends but you'll always be the most special."

The ruse of getting tickets at the last moment had been a complete lie. Davey Wiseman could get his hands on just about anything he desired as and when he needed to, he'd just wanted to spend another evening with her but knew without a good excuse she would have been angry if he'd just turned up out of the blue. Throwing the tickets into the nearest bin Davey smiled to himself, now aware that he was falling in love and it was a totally all-consuming love that made him feel like he was walking on air.

The woman was beautiful, caring, gentle and honest, he'd never met anyone like her and wasn't about to lose her for anything, though never in a million years would Davey have admitted to anyone that he was becoming besotted with Frances Richards, besotted to the point of boring everyone to death with his constant talk about her.

Poor Gilly had a daily rundown of where they had been, what she had said, what she had worn, in fact any little detail that his boss could remember, until he felt he couldn't listen to anymore. Along with Billy, he too still hadn't been formally introduced to the new woman in his boss's life and it was beginning to seem as if Davey Wiseman was ashamed of the life he led, maybe even a little scared. Scared that once this woman found out about the prostitutes, the gambling and anything else illegal you cared to mention, she would just up and walk away.

Shauna and Susan spent a wonderful evening together but the whole time Shauna had other things occupying her thoughts. She made her mind up that on their next date she had to try and get deeper inside Davey Wisemans head, she was also aware of exactly how to go about it. The following afternoon, Cecil again told her to leave off a little early so she could get ready for her evening out. Shauna decided to make the most of the offer and a long hot soak was followed by a facial and manicure. By the time she stepped out of the flat wearing one of her new outfits, she looked a million dollars and Davey's eyes were on stalks as he opened the car door.

"Where to princess?"

"How about showing me your clubs? I'd like to see where you spend your days."

Davey began to get nervous as he'd already taken her to The Royal and totally unaware that she knew he owned it, he couldn't now admit it was his. Top to Tail wasn't the kind of place you took a lady and The Judges Den was totally out of the question as he wasn't about to introduce her to the filthy whores that

walked the street outside but who also worked for
him.

"They aren't the sort of places you're used to Fran,
they're seedy and the types of people who use them
are not your typical newsagent customers."

"I don't care. If we're as serious as I think we are, we
shouldn't have any secrets. I want to be in your life
and that means every part of it."

Her statement was a kind gesture and made him feel a
little more at ease but words came easily and Davey
didn't know how she would react to the reality when
she was actually faced with it. Wracking his brains,
he couldn't come up with an alternative so the safest
bet would be The Pelican, he just prayed it wasn't too
busy.

"I'm glad you want to be part of my life Fran and I
will take you wherever you want to go but I just hope
you won't be disappointed."

"I'm never disappointed when I'm with you Davey, I
feel like I've known you my whole life."

They drove in silence, he wasn't looking forward to
this one bit. Fran, his Fran had told him everything
about herself, even reliving the painful loss of her
elderly parents. He had liked it when she'd said they
were serious and true if they were to have a future
together he had to include her in his life. Finally he
came to the resolve that letting her have a glimpse
inside his world was a risk but a risk he was prepared
to take if it meant keeping her. Davey's prayers were
not answered and as usual the club was heaving with
a mixture of Soho's low life. Fran saw the worry
etched on his face and gently squeezed his arm.

"Honestly it's fine. I wasn't expecting the Ritz and

wherever you are I want to be too."
Sheepishly he led her to the bar and Janice came
straight over to serve them.
"Evening Boss, what can I get you?"
Eyeing her employers date, Janice was impressed at
his choice. This woman was definitely a dramatic
change from his usual brassy type, in fact she
couldn't recall ever seeing him with such a classy
bird and this one really was top of the tree.
"What would you like to drink Sweetheart?"
Smiling at the barmaid Shauna asked for a gin and
tonic and Janice immediately warmed to the woman.
As they had approached the bar Janice was expecting
her to be snooty and standoffish but she was the
complete opposite. Shauna made a point of being
friendly with anyone who had contact with Davey, it
would make infiltrating his life much easier if she
was on good terms with all that knew him. Gilly
entered the club a few minutes later and on spying his
boss, headed straight over to him.
"God, what's he doing here tonight?"
"Who are you talking about?"
"See the bloke coming over, he works for me and he
can be a real pain in the arse at times."
Again Shauna gently squeezed his arm.
"Don't be like that Davey, I want to meet the people
you spend your time with."
He shrugged his shoulders and when Gilly reached
the bar Davey began the introductions. Gilly was
mesmerized, he hadn't looked her in the face when
he'd delivered the flowers for his boss but now that
he had, well she was absolutely gorgeous, absolutely
fuckin' gorgeous. Shauna held out her hand.

"Hello Gilly, nice to finally meet you. I must say your Boss didn't describe you as well as he could have, you're far more handsome."

Gilly Slade, standing over six feet tall and built like a tank, felt the first stirrings of a blush. Davey noticed how at ease Fran made his employee feel and considering he had never mentioned Gilly to her it was a nice gesture. Janice lent over the bar, whispered something in Davey's ear and Shauna saw his expression instantly change as he nodded his head.

"I'm sorry Fran but I need to take a phone call. Gill, make sure the lady's kept safe while I'm gone." Davey headed towards the office leaving her alone with his minder, the situation provided her with a perfect opportunity. Shauna had to be careful how she played this, if she came on too strong he'd clam up but at the same time she needed information and this man was the key. Shauna eased into the conversation with questions about the club, how busy it was, did it open every night etc? But getting nowhere she soon changed tactics and tried to veer the questions to more personal matters.

"So Gilly, how long have you worked for Davey?"

"About a year but it seems like a life time."

Shauna sensed his discontent and was on the verge of pursuing the matter further, when Davey returned.

"Sorry about that Fran but it was important, anyway Gill don't let me keep you if you've got something to do."

"Nothing in particular."

Davey's blank expression and piercing eyes told Gilly all he needed to know, so swiftly making his excuses he left his boss and walked from the club. With nowhere in particular to go Gilly decided to call it a night and make his way home but for some strange reason he couldn't get Fran Richards out of his mind and for the life of him he couldn't see what she saw in Davey Wiseman. Gilly hoped that he would see her again soon and Shauna was thinking the exact same thing but for a very different reason. Davey and Shauna stayed at the club for a while but as the punters became more rowdy he felt desperate to get his date out of this hell hole, a hell hole he alone had created and up until tonight had been more than happy with. Leaning over, he had to almost shout to be heard.

"Fran I'm absolutely starving, what say we get something to eat?"

"Fine by me!"

"What do you fancy, French, Mexican?"

"What about the Italian we went to on our first date, I really liked it there."

"Your wish is my command."

Davey hoped that the service had improved since last time and Ricardo felt his stomach lurch as they entered the restaurant but he would make sure this time they wanted for nothing. His waiter had been left traumatised and Ricardo didn't want a repeat performance. Davey and Shauna were shown to a quiet romantic booth situated along the side wall of the restaurant.

"So Miss Richards, what is your opinion?"

"About what?"

"My club, did you think it was terrible?"

Shauna frowned and shook her head.

147

"Why on earth would I think it was terrible? Davey for an assertive man you don't seem to have a lot of confidence in your business!"

"Of course I have confidence, I wouldn't last a second in my world if I didn't Fran, it's just that it's such a different world to the one you're used to."

"They say a change is as good as a rest so perhaps it's time for a little change in my life Mr Wiseman."

Time flew by as they chatted and no topic was forbidden though their conversation was kept mostly to life in general. It got late and Ricardo wanted to close up for the night but he was too frightened to approach their table and by one o'clock had fallen asleep behind the small wooden bar. Finally Davey went to settle the bill but he couldn't see the man anywhere. Placing two fifty pound notes under the candle on their table, they slipped outside and giggled as the door gently closed behind them. Pulling up outside the shop Davey switched off the engine and turned in his seat. Shauna froze, she had known this moment would arise but had hoped it wouldn't be so soon.

"Davey I know what you're about to suggest and I...."

He cut her off before she had finished talking.

"Fran I'd like nothing more than to take you upstairs and make love to you but it's got to be what you want too. If you feel we should wait then its fine by me, I'd wait forever if I had to."

Relief washed over her and leaning across the car she kissed him goodnight then disappeared inside her flat to safety.

Gilly Slade woke early the next morning and as

Shauna opened up the newsagents he was already
standing outside.

"Hello there, its Gilly isn't it?"

He felt tongue tied as he tried to speak, he'd spent the
whole night thinking about her and now he didn't
know what to say.

"Yes, yes how are you? I've just come to get a paper
before I collect the boss, although in all honesty I
don't know how happy he'd be if he found out I was
here!"

"Gilly, do you always talk so fast?"

"No, no only when I'm nervous."

"Well there's no need to be nervous with me, would
you like a coffee before the shop gets busy?"

"That would be great. If you're sure it's not too much
trouble?"

"No trouble at all. Just keep an eye on the till and
give me a shout if a customer comes in."

Shauna disappeared for a few minutes and returned
carrying two mugs but they had only just begun to
chat when the first customers entered the shop.

Shauna didn't want to lose the possibility of a link
into Davey's world but knew it would be like this for
the next hour at least. Turning to Gilly she asked if
he would like to meet for a drink sometime.

"Davey would shoot me if he ever found out and I
mean literally."

"Well I won't tell if you don't!"

He smiled, not able to believe his luck that a beautiful
woman like Fran would give him a second glance.

"In that case I'd love to, once I've dropped Davey off
I'm free until early afternoon."

"What about the wine bar across the road at say one

o'clock?"
"One o'clock it is then."

The morning passed in a blur and Shauna was late leaving for lunch. She didn't arrive at the bar until one fifteen but unbeknown to her Gilly had been there since twelve thirty. After delivering his boss to The Pelican he'd returned home for a good wash and brush up and was now seated at the table, looking very smart in a suit and tie. When Shauna saw him she realised he had mistaken her offer of a drink as a come on, she had to nip this in the bud but at the same time still try to keep him happy.
"Hi Gilly, don't you look smart, got a hot date later?" It was difficult to imagine that this hard man, this gangster's bodyguard, could get embarrassed but he did, for the second time in as many days this woman had made him feel like a school boy.
"I do believe you're blushing Gilly Slade."
"I just like to make a good impression, that's all."
"Well you've certainly done that. Have you got a girlfriend, no of course you haven't. I can tell you're a trustworthy man and if you had a young lady then you wouldn't have agreed to meet me."
With these words Gilly felt his heart sink, he'd read the situation all wrong and now felt like a total idiot.
"Do you know something Gilly, I've been in London for nearly a year and I still hardly know anyone, people here seem so unfriendly. That's why when I was introduced to you, I thought that perhaps we could be friends? I know Davey wouldn't understand but there's no reason why he has to know, he doesn't have exclusive rights over me and sometimes it's nice

150

to spend time with other people."

Gilly soon relaxed and began to enjoy her company, if he couldn't have her on a sexual level then he would happily accept her as a friend. Fran was interesting and more importantly was interested in him, something few people were and he liked it. Shauna hung on his every word and even let out a few little gasps if he mentioned even the slightest thing regarding the underworld. It didn't take long for him to tell her about the recent deal he'd been involved in and about how well off he would soon be. Shauna guessed it was Davey who was really behind the deal and that Gilly only played a small part but she still made out she was impressed.

By the end of their lunch date Shauna was happy, she'd nurtured a true informant and the beauty of it was that he didn't even realise. They agreed to meet the following week and Gilly left the bar feeling valued. Shauna had promised she wouldn't breathe a word to Davey, it would be their little secret and over the next few weeks she would discover from her new acquaintance, more and more about Davey Wiseman and his criminal life. There wasn't anything she could use against him but it was the build up to a bigger picture that she was interested in. It didn't cross her mind that to reach her goal, she had to ride roughshod over people and their emotions, she didn't feel the hurt she had caused Jackie Silver, nor did she bother about the hurt that Gilly Slade would soon begin to feel.

CHAPTER FIFTEEN

Shauna's first year in London had passed quickly but to Jackie it had seemed like an eternity and even though her work at Sunrise continued, her life was empty without her girl. Other members of staff had noticed how her level of care, care that had once been her trademark, was now seriously lacking. She was never late and carried out her duties to the letter but something inside Jackie had died. Previously a favourite among the children she was now just another worker and the situation suited Jackie fine, if she didn't get involved then she couldn't get hurt. Mr Brackson had been quietly informed to the changes in Jackie Silver but it hadn't been necessary, he'd noticed the differences himself over the last year and it made him feel sad. After deciding it was his responsibility to get to the bottom of whatever was troubling her, not just because he was her senior and he had a duty to the other staff and children but because he was her friend. Summoning Jackie to his office he waited apprehensively for her knock at the door.

"You asked to see me Jim?"

"Yes Jackie, take a seat. Now I don't really know how to put this but I'm going to give it my best shot anyway. It's been brought to my attention that there seems to be a few problems."

Jackie frowned, she hadn't noticed the transformation in herself and didn't understand what he meant.

"Sorry, are some of the children being disruptive or is it one in particular?"

Jim Brackson wished with all his heart that he hadn't opened up this can of worms, it was going to be more difficult than he'd first thought and he wouldn't intentionally hurt her for the world. He liked Jackie, no it was more than like, he was fond of her to the point of love whatever that was. If this conversation was going to cause upset, then the upset would hurt him as much as her but his position as area manager had called for him to intervene and intervene he must. Some days Jim would rather have been employed as just a carer and today was definitely one of those. Management could at times feel like the loneliest place in the world and it made him so isolated from Jackie and the other staff.

"It's not any of the kids Jackie, it's you."

"Me? I don't understand, whatever have I done?" Suddenly this was all too much for her and she burst into tears, the tears flowed freely as all the pent up emotion she had felt since Shauna left, came flooding out. Jim didn't say anymore, he let her cry until there were no tears left.

"Feel better now?"

Jackie sniffed loudly and gratefully accepted the box of tissues he eventually offered.

"I'm sorry, I really don't know what came over me. I haven't been myself for several months now, I don't think I've ever felt this low Jim and I burst into tears at the drop of a hat which isn't like me."

"No it certainly isn't."

"I just can't seem to shake it off, in the past when someone said they were depressed, well I was the first to pooh pooh it and say pull yourself together but it's like a big black cloud hanging over me and it just won't go away."

"Jackie, take some time off, a few weeks away from this place will do you the world of good. I can arrange for all the leave you need and it will give you time to get back on track."

"Will head office allow me to?"

"Bugger head office, they won't have a lot of choice in the matter. If it's between holiday leave or another member of staff away indefinitely for stress reasons, I can assure you they won't argue. Get your stuff together and get out of here, when and if you want to come back, your job will be waiting."

"Thanks Jim, you're a good man."

"Stop with the compliments, you'll have me blushing. Just take care of yourself, you're a special member of staff and Sunrise is a nicer place when you're in it."

Leaving the office, she collected her coat and bag and made her way home. Sitting alone in the small flat Jackie's mind whirled as she recalled all the events of her life, every last detail of their lives relived over and again and each time it ended with the feeling of total loss. There was only one thing for it, Jackie Silver had to find Shauna and lifting the receiver she dialled a number.

"Simmonds Detective Agency, how may I help you?"

"Mr Simmonds you probably don't remember me, my name is Jackie Silver and you helped a friend of mine about a year ago."

"I help a lot of people Madam."

"I'm sure you do and now I'm one of those people, I wondered if we could meet up."

The woman sounded desperate and Simmonds beady eyes opened wide as he thought of the overpriced fee he would be able to charge, whilst of course helping a damsel in distress and although he couldn't recall this particular damsel, she did sound distressed. He arranged to call at the flat the following day and Jackie spent the next twenty four hours on tenter hooks.

Dead on eleven the car pulled up and Jackie, who had been watching from the window, opened the door before the little man had a chance to ring the bell. Gerald Simmonds remembered the woman as soon as he saw her, he also remembered it wasn't one of his better cases. If he had to delve any further into the gangster's life, it was going to cost an awful lot more than last time.

"Miss Silver, how very nice to see you again!"

Jackie welcomed the man inside and after fixing them both a drink invited him to take a seat. She didn't feel comfortable with him, didn't like his manner or the way he started to sweat profusely every time he glanced in the direction of her breasts but she didn't have an option if she wanted to succeed in her quest.

"I couldn't picture you yesterday Miss Silver, not until I pulled Miss O'Malley's file. It wasn't one of my best investigations, nasty man, nasty business. Anyway enough of that, I'm sure you don't want to find anyone that distasteful?"

"That's exactly what I do want, I would like all the information you found for Miss O'Malley.

Everything no matter how small, now what will it cost me?"

On his last visit a few stubborn wisps of hair, which he styled in an unflattering comb over had made both

Jackie and Shauna giggle. Twelve months on and the comical strands had finally given up the ghost and Gerald Simmonds scratched his now totally bald head as he thought about her request. Snapping shut his shiny leather brief case, Jackie could see he was clearly annoyed with her.

"I'm sorry but I can't help you, client confidentiality and all that. If you had told me on the phone what you wanted, it would have saved us both a lot of time."

Gerald stood up and began to put on his coat but it was now Jackie's turn to become annoyed. Taking a deep breath she raised her voice and used her best school mistress tone as she spoke.

"Sit down you silly little man. What's the difference between giving me the information you already have and me paying you to find out everything you can about Davey Wiseman all over again?"

The mere mention of his name sent Simmonds into another bout of sweating. He had hated the whole assignment and towards the conclusion of the investigation had imaginary or not, felt in fear for his life. He wasn't about to go through that experience again for anyone but at the same time he didn't relish saying goodbye to his fee. Gerald thought for a second before placing his briefcase back down onto the sofa. Nervously pushing his glasses back along the bridge of his nose, which immediately slipped back down again, he reopened the case.

"Put like that I can see your point, I would only be telling you something that you had instructed me to find out anyway. Also I'd rather not have to spend time in that particular area of London again, shall we say seven fifty?"

Inwardly Jackie groaned this man really was a little weasel. He made her skin crawl but she smiled sweetly and shook hands on the deal.

Two days later she had received all the information she needed to start her search for Shauna. Arriving in London, Jackie booked into a small but respectable guest house in Victoria. Lying on the crisply made bed, she tried to work out where to begin and realised her search could turn out to be far more difficult than she'd first thought. Although Simmonds had provided all she needed to know about Davey, obviously there was nothing in his report about her girl, it would be like looking for the proverbial needle in a haystack but she had to at least try. Luck was on Jackie's side and it would only take three days of treading the pavements of Soho to find what she was looking for. Walking along the same street as yesterday, Jackie stopped when she saw a small newsagents and decided to buy some sweets. She had already passed the place several times but until now hadn't taken any notice of it. Stepping inside she walked up to the counter where a petite woman with her back to Jackie was struggling to place a carton of cigarettes on the top shelf.

"Can I help you with that, it looks a little high?" Shauna recognised the voice and instantly froze but she couldn't run out to the kitchen as she was the only one on duty this afternoon.

"No I'm fine thanks."

Jackie Silver also froze, Shauna wasn't the only one who had a good memory. She studied the young woman, the hair colour had changed and was much shorter, the sombre clothing had been replaced by a younger and more colourful style, it couldn't be could it?

"Shauna? Shauna is it you? Shauna it is you isn't it?"

Turning slowly to face her friend, Shauna O'Malley had tears in her eyes. She was angry with Jackie, really angry at her but also happier than she had felt in a long time. Placing her finger vertically across her lips to silence the woman, she briskly walked to the door and turned the sign to closed. The two women hugged for what seemed like an eternity before Shauna finally broke the bond.

"My name's Fran now Jacks but what the hell are you doing here? On second thoughts don't answer that! Jacks we really can't talk here, my cover could get blown and I'm so close now. Can you come round to my flat tonight after dark? I live above the shop, ring the side door bell and I'll explain everything then."

Nodding but confused Jackie Silver walked out, leaving Shauna shaking from the fear that at any moment Cecil or Madge could have walked in and everything would have been ruined. As soon as night fell, Jackie headed back over to Soho and ringing the bell couldn't wait to see her friend again.

"Come on in and make yourself at home Jacks, I think this may turn out to be a long evening."

Taking a seat on the comfy sofa, Jackie handed Shauna the wine she had purchased on her journey from Victoria.

"Thanks."

Shauna walked over to the small kitchenette, really just an alcove in the living room with a sink and cooker but it served its purpose and passing her friend two glasses, she asked what had brought her to London.

"What's brought me here, are you kidding me? You walk out of my life leaving just a note and you don't expect me to look for you, did our relationship mean that little to you?"

Shauna could see the pain in her friend's eyes and instantly felt guilty.

"It meant the world to me, still does. I love you Jacks, I love you as if you were my own mother but it was inevitable that one day this would all come to a head, it had to and God willing if everything goes to plan, I have every intention of coming home again."

"You take a lot for granted Shauna O'Malley. What makes you think I'd want you back in my life after all that you've done?"

The women sat in silence, each knowing the harsh words Jackie had said were never really meant. Deep down Shauna knew that the heartbreak her friend had experienced over the last year was the only reason she had reacted in such a hostile way.

"Were you really going to come home or are you just saying it to make me feel better?"

"Of course I'm coming home, you're the only family I have. London is a tip and I miss my old life terribly but you have to understand, I must do this!"

"I do try to understand Shauna but it's so hard for me. I'm so scared that it's all going to go wrong. I read Simmonds report on Davey Wiseman and the man is

159

an animal. Do you really think you stand a chance,
going up against someone like that?"

"Please don't worry and in answer to your question,
yes I do think I stand a chance. I'm making such
great progress where Wisemans is concerned. I have
to see it through Jacks so please don't make it any
harder for me!"

Jackie Silver studied her young friends face and
didn't think she had ever seen Shauna so determined
about anything.

"You had better fill me in on all that's happened then
and don't you dare miss anything out."

By the time Shauna had finished, the hands on the
mantle clock showed nearly two am and for the entire
time she spoke Jackie hadn't said a word.

"So here we are. You now know everything."

Jackie slowly shook her head, she really couldn't
believe what she'd just been told and breathing in
deeply, she puffed out her cheeks as she slowly
exhaled.

"So this Davey is in love with you is he? Shauna,
please don't tell me that you've slept with him?"

"Not yet I haven't but I will, I have to if I want to
finish this."

Jackie placed her hand across her mouth, she hated
the very thought of what Shauna was going to do, it
sickened her.

"How can you, you'll be like a prostitute."

"Well if it was good enough for Violet, why not for
me?"

"Don't say such a thing not even in jest, how can you
be intimate with the man that had a hand in killing
your mother and sister? For the life of me I can't

understand how you could do such a thing."

"For the reasons you've just said Jacks. It's the only way I can get close to him, close enough to pay him back for all the heartbreak he's caused me. I don't expect you to understand, you couldn't unless you'd experienced what I have."

Studying the beautiful face before her, the nearest thing she would ever get to a daughter, Jackie, as if for the first time, saw the level of pain and hurt in Shauna's eyes.

"I know love and even though, however hard I try I can't understand, I will always be here for you. How long do you think it's going to take?"

"Well everything's fine at the moment but I'm still looking at a good six months."

"Six months!"

"Jacks, people like Davey Wiseman spend their whole lives hurting people. They would kill their own granny without a second thought, why would someone like that confide in a girlfriend? He needs to trust me and that's going to take time and after all, I have all the time in the world."

The thought of being without her girl even longer didn't bare thinking about but she knew there was no point in arguing as nothing could be said that would change Shauna's mind. All she could do was pack her things and return home the following day but Jackie did accept Shauna's offer of a bed for the remainder of the night as she really didn't fancy walking back to the guest house at this hour of the morning and at least it would give her some precious time with her girl.

Shauna wasn't due into work until two the following afternoon, this allowed the women a leisurely breakfast before setting off in a cab to collect Jackie's luggage from the guest house.

"You really don't have to come to the station with me, it's just going to upset us both."

Inwardly Shauna agreed with her friend but she wouldn't be able to rest until she saw for herself, that the train had pulled out and once again her identity was safe. It really had been great to see Jackie but Shauna's nerves had been on edge the whole time, if Davey had called round while her friend was there, she didn't know how she would ever have explained things. As Jackie boarded the eleven am train Shauna felt relief wash over her but she didn't leave the platform until the carriage had left the station and shrunk to just a dot on the horizon. Suddenly feeling cold, she pulled the collar of her coat tightly around her. For all of her life or for most of it anyway, Jackie Silver had been there to protect her but now Shauna was on her own again. It was true, she had quickly learnt to cope when she'd first arrived in London but now, now having spent time with the only person in the whole world that she loved and with that person now gone, Shauna O'Malley once more felt frightened and alone.

CHAPTER SIXTEEN

Billy's telephone was in constant use. He hadn't been able to get hold of his friend for the last three days and he was either receiving no reply from Davey's mobile or had Janice at The Pelican telling him her boss wouldn't be in that day. After each call Billy was becoming more and more agitated and now had the feeling that he was being pushed aside but he knew the score, knew that the little bitch would only end up dumping his friend when she had gotten everything she could out of him. On what seemed like his fiftieth attempt at calling he didn't bother to ask for Davey, instead he inquired if Gilly was there. Janice called Gilly Slade over to the bar phone and he frowned when told he was wanted by Billy Jackson. "Hello Mr Jackson?"`

"Shut the fuck up Gill and listen, I've just about had a gut full of your Boss, I can't get hold of him and it's really starting to piss me off big style. I want you to pass on a message for me, tell him if he doesn't contact me soon there's going to be trouble."

"I'll do my best Mr Jackson but I hardly see him myself these days."

"What do you mean you hardly fuckin' see him, doesn't he come in to check on the fuckin' place?" Gilly could hear the man's voice rising to a crescendo and felt glad that there was plenty of distance between them.

"Well he hasn't been here for the last few days. I'm the one who has to make sure everything runs smoothly and thank fuck it has been or we'd be right in the shit."

"The tosser, I suppose he's with his fuckin' new whore all the time?"

Gilly wanted to reach down the phone and grab the stupid prick by the throat. His feelings had become strong for Fran over the last few weeks and he hated to hear her called names, especially from some jumped up little faggot. In reality he would never have laid a finger on Billy, Gilly Slade was a lot of things but stupid wasn't one of them. It was all well and good to imagine what he'd like to do but the man on the other end was a killer and Gilly wasn't ready to die just yet.

"All I can do is pass the message on if I see him."

"You didn't answer my question, is he spending all his time with that fuckin' whore?"

Gilly still didn't answer, instead he replaced the receiver back in its cradle. A split second later he removed it and told Janice not to put it back for at least an hour. Billy stood shouting into the mouth piece totally unaware that Gilly had hung up. When he eventually realised he was talking to thin air, his face turned a bright shade of purple and tiny veins stood out on his forehead. Luckily at this early hour The Bull was empty or the punters would have been misled into believing a murder was taking place with all the screaming and shouting coming from the office.

"That fuckin' cunt's hung up on me! He's fuckin' dead meat when I get hold of him."

For reasons unknown and luckily for Gilly, Davey came into the club a few minutes later.

"Boy am I glad to see you Boss!"

"Why, what the fuck's happened?"

He relayed the whole conversation omitting the part when he'd wanted to reach down the line and was somewhat surprised by Davey's reaction.

"That queer cunt's gone too far this time, he's got no fuckin' right talking about her that way and why is this fuckin' phone off the hook?"

Gilly explained that he didn't want to argue with Billy but he didn't want to agree with him either and the only thing he could think of doing was to hang up.

"That's fuckin' great Gill, now he's going to be even more pissed off and once again I'll have to fuckin' sort it out."

Several seconds passed while Davey tried to think of an explanation.

"Right! As far as Billy Jacksons concerned, I've been laid up in bed with a stinking cold Okay?"

"Fine by me Boss, I was just about to skip the country so any excuse is a good one."

On hearing this Davey wanted to laugh. He knew how much people feared his friend and it seemed in the past, he'd been the only one able to calm Billy down but he wasn't sure he could work his magic this time. Lifting the receiver he dialled The Bull's number, it rang only once before being snatched up at the other end.

"Yeah?"

"Hello old mate, how are you?"

"Don't fuckin' old mate me! I've been trying to get hold of you for days. I suppose now you're fuckin' a new bird, you ain't got time for your old pal!"

"Don't be like that Billy, of course I've got time for you. This relationship I'm in is serious, in fact I think

165

it's the real thing, can't you just be happy for me?"
"How the fuck can I be happy about something that's taking you away from me?"
"Nothing is taking me away but you know how it is. I have to spend time with Fran, to be truthful Billy I kinda want to spend all my time with her."
Billy didn't reply but it was a blessing that Davey couldn't see him or he wouldn't have liked the hand gestures being made at the other end by his mate.
"Can you hear me Billy? Now look, I've been off sick for a couple of days and that's why I ain't been in contact, alright?"
"Of cause I can fuckin' hear you and don't give me all that squit about being ill, if she's that fuckin' special why ain't you introduced us?"
Davey had been dreading this question and had to think fast. Billy Jackson, although a good friend wasn't the type of person he wanted Fran mixing with.
"She's really quiet Bill and not used to the club scene, I......."
Once again Davey was cut off mid sentence.
"Well she'll have to get fuckin' used to it won't she, clubs are our life Davey and if she's part of our lives then she's part of the clubs too. When are you seeing her again?"
Davey noticed that his friends tone had softened somewhat and it made him feel uneasy.
"Tomorrow, why?"
"I suggest we all meet up. If it's as serious as you say, well she's bound to want to meet your best mate ain't she? I'll see you both in The Bull around eight thirty."

166

With that he hung up and Davey was left speechless but he knew if he argued or stood his mate up he would never hear the last of it. It was also possible that Billy would create an ugly scene but Davey hoped not, now all he had to do was figure out a way of explaining his extrovert friend to Fran.

It had become the norm for Cecil to let Shauna leave the shop early, giving her extra time to get ready. Over the last few weeks he had slowly warmed to Davey Wiseman and realising that Fran was happy, he figured that to except the situation and not make waves would keep him in everyone's good books, everyone except his daughter Susan. The shop was experiencing the usual afternoon lull and he had just told Shauna to get off home.

"Are you sure it's alright Cecil?"

"Yes of course, you go Fran, oh and Fran, have a good time dear."

Shauna smiled, walked out of the door and turned the corner towards her flat. She'd only taken a few steps when she heard a voice call to her, well it wasn't really a call, more of a whisper and she scanned the street but couldn't see anyone. Gilly stood in the shadows of the connecting shop, he stepped forward only when she was almost on top of him.

"Gilly! What the hell are you doing here?"

"Fran I need to speak to you in private."

The sharp tone, so unusual for him made Shauna step back.

"Sure Gilly, shall we meet for coffee tomorrow?"

"No! It can't wait, I have to talk to you now!"

Her mind immediately went into overdrive, had

Davey found out who she really was,? That was impossible. Whatever it was, it was important enough for Gilly to risk being seen, so she pointed towards her flat and he followed. Once inside the door and with it firmly closed, Shauna turned to face him.

"Whatever is the matter?"

"It's Billy, Billy Jackson. Fran he's trouble and he's out for your blood sweetheart."

Gilly had been standing next to his boss during Davey and Billy's telephone conversation and as soon as the call had finished, he had made the excuse of having to collect the clubs laundry. Shauna didn't have a clue who this Jackson person was but it didn't stop the shudder that ran through her body. Whenever it had happened as a child, Mary O'Dwyer had told her it was someone walking over her grave and Shauna was a little surprised at the distant almost forgotten memory that sprang to mind.

"Gilly I don't know anyone called Jackson!"

"You don't know him but he certainly knows all about you."

"You're not making any sense now Gilly and you're starting to scare me."

"I'm sorry, I'll explain it all but can we have a coffee first?"

After making their way upstairs, Shauna put the kettle on. She was tense and very unnerved to see this man, who stood over six feet tall and was supposed to be a bodyguard, as jumpy as a cat on hot coals. Gilly slowly explained the whole scenario to her, even describing Billy's sexuality and something made Shauna recall the strange customer she'd served the other day. When Gilly described this Jackson character, she knew they were one and the same.

"I think I've already met him Gilly, not formally but I'm sure he came into the shop a few days ago. What I don't understand is what threat he could possibly think I am to him?"

Gilly shook his head, if she knew the real Billy Jackson he was sure she would run a mile.

"It has nothing to do with being a threat Fran. He loves Davey more than anything and not a brotherly love either, it's well known he's besotted with him, has been for years."

"And Davey, you're not telling me he's gay are you?"

Gilly almost choked on his coffee and a mouthful escaped, which he neatly caught again in the mug.

"No of course I'm not! He cares for Billy, always has done but it's never been more than platonic. Billy on the other hand, thinks you are trying to take away the love of his life."

"Well I'll just have to convince him otherwise, won't I?"

"I hate to be the bearer of bad news Fran but I think that's gonna to be tonight!"

They drank the remainder of their coffee and Shauna reassured her new friend, even if she couldn't convince herself that everything would be alright.

Reaching the front door she turned to Gilly with a serious look on her face.

"Davey must never find out you've been here, you do know that!"

Gilly smiled as he hugged her to him.

"Listen if the Boss ever got a hint that I'd been to see

169

you, I'd be a dead man but for God's sake Fran be careful"

"I will and thank you Gilly, it means a lot that you risked your safety to warn me about my own and I promise, my lips are well and truly sealed."

The next two hours passed in a blur of thought and the flat bell rang at eight on the dot. Davey was punctual if nothing else and as Shauna opened the door she apologised for not being quite ready. Showing him into the front room she continued to talk through the open bedroom door as she finished doing her hair. It hadn't taken her long to get to know this man and the way he conducted himself so Shauna was sure there was no way he would let her meet this Jackson man without forewarning her first. "Sorry Davey, we had a bit of a rush on at closing time but I won't be a second."
He walked around the small living room and although it wasn't much to write home about, he was impressed by her neatness.
"Actually I'm glad we're here, there's something I need to have a chat about."
When she entered the room Shauna could sense he was nervous, Davey was constantly twisting his hands and wouldn't look her straight in the eye. Shauna walked back into the bedroom to collect her coat and handbag and called out that she could hear him.
"This flat is so small I can hear you in every room."
Davey began by telling her he had a friend called Billy Jackson. Every so often Shauna would say yes in agreement or okay, just to make him feel comfortable even though what he was telling her

170

wasn't anything she didn't already know. In fact he was somewhat economical with the truth. With Gilly it had been everything warts and all but Davey tried to paint a better image regarding what sort of person his friend was and his final sentence also ended with.

"Did I mention that he's gay?"

Shauna emerged doing up the last button on her coat and looked at Davey with a frown.

"No you didn't but should that make a difference?"

"The fact that he's gay? No of course not but some people are funny about things like that and Billy can be outrageous at times. Well most of the time actually and if you're not prepared for him, it's a bit of a shock."

"I'm a big girl now Mr Wiseman so I'm sure a little campness isn't going to shock me but if you're that worried, perhaps it's best if you don't introduce us yet?"

Shauna saw the alarm come over Davey's face.

"The fact is Fran, Billy wants to meet you. I've been neglecting him recently and we go back a long way. Until I met you, he was the closest person in my life and I wouldn't hurt him for the world."

Shauna O'Malley smiled and draped her arms loosely around his neck.

"I don't expect you to and I'm happy to meet any of your friends especially someone who is as close to you as this Billy bloke. You just seem a bit uptight about it that's all."

"I am and you'll probably understand why when you get to know him. The other thing I'm not comfortable with is the fact that he wants us to go to his club."

"I can't see the problem, I've been to your clubs a few times and his will make a nice change."

"It's a gay club Fran, full of perverts who try it on at the drop of a hat."

She started to laugh, laughed until tears rolled down her face and although he couldn't understand why, the sight of her made him laugh too.

"Davey, if it's a gay club I've got nothing to worry about but you on the other hand should be on your guard. If you drop anything give me the nod and I'll pick it up for you."

Her words caused them both to laugh again and made Shauna's mascara run all down her cheeks. By the time she had reapplied the makeup and they had both composed themselves, it was getting late but instead of leaving for The Bull, they shared a glass of wine and Davey talked in depth about Billy Jackson and how he lived his life. After driving over to Bethnal Green, the pair, much to Billy's annoyance, wouldn't arrive until well after nine thirty.

CHAPTER SEVENTEEN

That evening, The Bull opened and Billy drank over a half a bottle of Jack Daniels before the place had a single customer. By eight o'clock he changed to soft drinks, knowing that if he was drunk when Davey arrived then his friend would walk straight out again. Even though he'd asked to meet this Fran woman he didn't really want to, he had just wanted to see if his best mate would toe the line. Now he was actually going to have to be nice to her and it made his blood boil. Billy knew Davey would forewarn her about the club and that realisation had angered him. Well, he wasn't going to change anything for the whore, in fact he was going to do just the opposite. Calling one of the numerous young boys into the office, he began to describe the atmosphere he wanted in the club that night. By eight thirty The Bull was in full swing, Dusty Springfield blared out from the disco and two semi naked youths twisted and turned as they danced around the podium poles. Men of all ages, who were usually told to tone down their sexual advances, were informed that for one night only anything goes. As nine o'clock came and went, Billy's patience had worn thin and once again he had started on the bourbon. When his friend finally arrived, Billy was well and truly pissed. Pissed from the drink and pissed off at the fact his guests were late after he'd specifically told Davey what time to be there. Billy Jackson expected to be obeyed no matter who the order was given to and in the past it hadn't been a problem, Davey had always gone along with anything

173

his friend wanted but now that he chose to consider someone else, it really riled Billy. Davey parked the car a few doors up from the club on Globe Road and quickly went around to open Shauna's door. Stepping out, she looking the epitome of class and he felt proud to have her on his arm. As one of the doormen opened the main door, Davey whispered into her ear as she passed.

"I'm sorry!"

"What for?"

"For whatever you are going to see or hear tonight." Once again she giggled which at least made Davey feel momentarily at ease. On the drive over, Shauna had decided that whatever this Billy person had up his sleeve, she wouldn't show she was shocked, wouldn't allow herself to react to anything he said or did. As on Davey's previous visit the inner curtains were opened by the same two, almost naked, young men. As they entered the main area the music was deafening, numerous coloured lights flashed in some sort of random hypnotic order and the musky smell of masculine sweat hung in the air. Shauna became mesmerized at the sight of the men before her as she'd never actually seen men dancing together, well at least not in the flesh. Davey had to pull gently on her arm to break the trance she seemed to be in. They made their way along the bar to the private seating area, where Billy could be seen entertaining a group of, in Davey's opinion, underage boys.

"You finally fuckin' made it then!"

"Don't start Bill, let's just have a nice evening shall we."

Pushing his way passed the boys, Billy staggered over

and stopping dead in front of Shauna he stared long and hard into her face.

"So this is the famous Fran is it?"

Holding out her hand, Shauna smiled sweetly.

"I don't think I'm famous but it's nice to finally meet you Mr Jackson, Davey has told me so much about you."

"I bet he fuckin' has, any of it good?"

"All of it I can assure you, now how about a drink to start the evening off?"

Suddenly Billy didn't feel in control. He'd expected to take the lead as soon as they arrived and now this whore was trying to put him in his place, well he wasn't having any of it. Calling to the barman he ordered the drinks.

"Jason! Doubles for me and Davey and whatever the girlie here wants."

Davey felt his hackles start to rise and understood exactly what his friend was trying to do but he wasn't going to put up with it so moving away from Fran he pulled their host to one side.

"For fucks sake Billy, treat her with some respect will you. She isn't a girlie, her name is Fran as you well know and if you're just trying to belittle her, we're going to fuck off out of it right now."

"Calm down Davey my boy, I was just letting her know how the land lies."

"Stop now or I'm fuckin' finished with you Billy, I mean it, push me much further you cunt and our friendship will be over!"

No one ever spoke to Billy like this, least of all his best friend and it suddenly worried him. Realising he had over stepped the mark and knowing that if he

175

wasn't careful, this relationship, the one thing he cared most about in the world, would go down the drain, he turned to Fran and apologised.

"I'm sorry for my rudeness. It's just that I'm not used to female company, can we start again?"

"Of course we can Mr Jackson."

"Please, call me Billy."

Shauna now sure Billy had been her customer a few days earlier, decided not to reveal the fact that he'd already put her through an inspection. Gilly had been right, he obviously saw her as a threat and had wanted to check her out. Billy ushered his guests to a fresh booth that overlooked the dance floor and once again Shauna became mesmerised at the antics of some of the customers. Young bare chested boys gyrated in front of old men, men who could have been mistaken for someone's grandad. Shauna could imagine them at home with their wives and children as to all intent and purpose they resembled family men and it sickened her. Billy watched the woman in fascination, he couldn't make out if she was disgusted or excited. Davey continually tried to make conversation between them both but finally gave up when he had to shout to be heard over the music.

"Is it me or is the music a bit loud tonight?"

Billy laughed and rolling his eyes, looked in Shauna's direction.

"Fran you should be careful with him, he's becoming a right old man."

Davey didn't like the insinuation. Their age difference caused him enough worry without other people adding their opinions.

"No I'm not but I like people to be able to hear what

176

I'm saying."

Shauna didn't reply and it worried Davey even more, maybe she did think he was too old, after all there was an age gap of well over twenty years. He had tried not to make an issue of it before but now he began to wonder if this woman, maybe the love of his life, would soon tire of him. It was typical of Billy to spoil things, why couldn't he keep his fuckin' trap shut. Billy Jackson saw the hurt expression on his friend's face and for a fleeting moment felt guilty. Neither of the men knew that Shauna hadn't heard the remark, she was too engrossed in the floor show to take any notice. Billy suddenly realised that if he wanted to save his friendship, he had to rescue the situation and quickly.

"Shall we go into the office? It's quieter there and we can all have a nice chat."

Mesmerised, Davey had to gently tapped her on the arm to get her attention.

"Sorry darling, did you say something?"

Smiling he knew she hadn't heard a word that either of the men had said and for once Billy hadn't spoilt things. If the age difference was a problem then it would have to be dealt with but not tonight, tonight was for friends, new friends and old. Thankfully the office had long since been sound proofed and they were able to hold a conversation without shouting to be heard. Billy seemed friendly and asked Shauna about her life and whether she was happy in London. It pleased Davey that the two people closest to him, finally seemed to be getting along. As the conversation slowed Billy made his excuses for a moment and left the office. Davey was desperate to find out Shauna's views on the evening so far.

"So?"

"So what?"

"Fran you know very well what I mean, what do you think of Billy?"

"Oh, well he seems very nice, now that we are on a better footing. To begin with I didn't think we'd hit it off but now? Yes Davey, he's okay."

"I'm really glad Fran, it was causing me real aggro thinking that you two wouldn't like each other. He's not the easiest person in the world to get along with and I knew if there was going to be a problem it would've been on his part and not yours."

"Why?"

"If I told you all that he's capable of it would have taken hours and I so wanted tonight to be special and for Billy not to upset you."

"Let me tell you something Mr Wiseman, I can stand up for myself if I need to but it's not always the best policy to go in all guns blazing. Sometimes I find the tactful approach works better."

Davey swept her up in his arms and kissed her passionately.

"I'm in no doubt about that Miss Richards, no doubt at all."

While the romantic couple shared a lingering embrace Billy had been arranging the evening's grand finale. If Davey was under the misconception that his friend had gotten the wrong idea about Fran and that tonight had changed everything, he couldn't have been further from the truth. On leaving the office Billy made his way across the dance floor and headed in

178

the direction of the young lad who had suffered at his hand the last time Davey was socialising at The Bull. Seeing Billy approach the boy tried to make a hasty exit but was held back by two of the doormen.

"Please Mr Jackson I ain't done anything wrong, honest I ain't."

Fear was evident on the boy's face as Billy gently stroked the red scar that now ran the length of his cheek. Handsome would have previously been a word best used to describe the boy but since the wound, he now looked freakish.

"Calm down my lovely, I just want you to do me a favour."

Even with the music playing the sigh of relief was evident to all who surrounded him and he smiled nervously.

"Anything Mr Jackson, just say the word."

Billy placed an arm around the boy and guided him in the direction of the office, all the time murmuring in his ear. Inside Davey was about to go in for another kiss but stopped when Billy entered and coughed loudly.

"Now then you two cool it down a bit, this is a respectable establishment you know, and after all I do have my licence to think about."

Davey rolled his eyes upwards causing Shauna to giggle and as Billy poured more drinks a knock came at the door.

"Enter."

The young lad who had been so willing to do Mr Jackson a favour walked in and headed straight towards Davey.

"Hello again honey, fancy a repeat of the other

179

night?"

Davey couldn't believe his ears and immediately knew that the boy had been put up to it by Billy. He turned on his friend with vengeance.

"Why? Why do you have to fuckin' ruin everything?"

Billy appeared shocked, so shocked that he could have won an Oscar as he placed his hands on his cheeks in mock horror.

"My dear Davey, I can assure you it's nothing to do with me but if he is bothering you we can soon rectify the situation."

Pulling a blade from his pocket he advanced towards the boy and Shauna couldn't believe what she was seeing. She attempted to scream at her host to stop but nothing emerged from her mouth. Again she tried and this time her voice boomed out as if it was bursting from her chest.

"Nooooo!!!!! Leave him alone you bully."

Billy ran his thumb along the blades razor sharp tip, causing a droplet of blood to form which he seductively licked off with his tongue. Returning the knife to his pocket as quickly as he'd got it out, he was sure that if this hadn't done the trick then nothing would. He had wanted her to see the kind of life they led, a violent life and one she wouldn't want to be a part of. The boy on glimpsing the weapon, knew what was about to happen and had ran from the room. Davey should have been shocked at how low his so called friend would sink but then nothing about Billy Jackson could shock him. Gathering up Shauna's coat, he led her swiftly from the office and as they left he could hear Billy calling after them.

180

"It was only a joke Davey. Oh come on Davey don't be such a fuckin' prick!"

No conversation passed between the couple on the drive back to her flat. Davey felt mortified at the stunt his so called friend had just pulled and Shauna was in shock at the events she had been witness to. She couldn't bring herself to speak or look at Davey, she knew the kind of man he was, after all wasn't that the reason she was here but seeing it first hand was a totally different matter. The thought of carrying out her plan now sent shivers down her spine as it dawned on her just how much danger she was in. Shauna had allowed her romance with Davey Wiseman to cloud her judgement and now she had to get things back on track and fast. Davey was seething, he felt embarrassed at Billy's actions and didn't know how to begin to apologise to her, it also worried him that after tonight's antics she would now end their relationship. Stopping outside the shop, the silence continued for a few seconds until finally Shauna spoke.
"Are you alright Davey?"
Shaking his head, he undid his seatbelt and turned to face her.
"I am so, so, sorry Fran. I never in a million years thought he'd do something so fuckin' nasty."
"It's not your fault and in a way I can see why Billy acted like he did."
"Well you're the only one who can sweetheart."
"He's scared Davey, scared of losing you and he will do anything to stop that happening."
"He's overstepped the mark big time, so there's no

181

way I can let this fuckin' go."

"Davey just think about it, don't cut him out of your life. You're angry and I understand that but just sleep on it, nothing seems as bad after a good night's rest." Shauna kissed him on the cheek and got out, bending back into the car she told Davey to go home and she would call him tomorrow. Home was the last place on his mind as rage began to build up inside, a rage so intense that the only place he could possibly go was back to The Bull. The club was starting to wind down when Davey arrived, the music had stopped and the guests were slowly leaving. Billy and was now holed up in the office drowning his sorrows. Far from knocking, Davey almost broke the door down and two bouncers were following in hot pursuit fearful for their employer's safety. Billy looked up as Davey barged in but he wasn't too surprised to see his friend.

"It's okay boys, nothing to worry about."

The doormen looked at each other, shrugged their shoulders and walked out of the room. Davey couldn't believe the nerve of the man and as the doormen left he walked over to the desk.

"You're no fuckin' friend of mine you cunt. The one time in my life I want you to be a true mate and you fuckin' try to set me up."

"She's no good Davey, surely you can see that. I'd never fuckin' hurt you but believe you me, she will!"

"You don't know that, you don't even fuckin' know her. You're just a jealous little faggot who when he can't get what he wants, is prepared to fuck up everyone else's lives."

Lunging over the desk he grabbed Billy by the hair

182

and started to smash his head against the mahogany top. Under normal circumstances Billy would have given as good as he got but the alcohol had taken its toll and with his strength failing, he could do nothing but take the beating. Davey rained down blow after blow until Billy's face became a bloody swollen mess. Exhaustion was the only thing that brought the attack to an end, panting Davey straightened up and pushed the hair back from his face. Walking towards the door he turned to look at Billy and could see bloody air bubbles escaping from the man's nostrils with every breath he took. The only sound he made was a low groan and Davey could once again feel his anger begin to rise. With a vicious tone he couldn't help but have the last say.

"Do you know something Bill? She asked me not to be angry with you, said you were just scared at the thought of losing our friendship. It's fuckin' laughable really, here's you doing any spiteful thing you can to get rid of her and she's worried about you! Well she won't have that fuckin' worry anymore because you and me are finished pal, do you hear me? Fuckin' finished! I never want to see your ugly fuckin' mug again. You don't deserve to breath the same fuckin' air as her, come to that maybe I don't either."

Davey Wiseman left The Bull feeling broken. In just a few hours, a lifelong friendship had ended and he didn't know if this new relationship, the one he'd chosen over Billy Jackson, would even go the distance.

CHAPTER EIGHTEEN

Oddly there had been no word from Davey for over three days and Shauna was beginning to get concerned. Not concerned for his safety but the fact that her plans could now be in jeopardy and the incident at The Bull had made her more determined than ever to take revenge on Davey. Men like him and Billy Jackson thought they could treat people however they liked and not suffer any consequences, well not this time, she would make sure he paid and paid dearly. Karma always came back to bite you in the arse and now it was Davey Wiseman's turn, for Vonny, for Violet and for all the evil acts that Davey and Billy had committed over the years. She had only set out to get Davey but if she could bring down Billy as well then it would be a bonus and besides, the world would be a much safer place if neither of them were able to hurt another soul again. Shauna wouldn't allow herself to contact Davey, it wasn't her place and she had to show him that she didn't run after any man. Suddenly an idea sprang to mind, she would phone Gilly and find out everything that had been going on and Davey would be none the wiser. Waiting until after Cecil had left the shop, she called The Pelican but unfortunately it was Janice who answered the phone.

"Pelican, how can I help?"

In a voice that was a comical combination of Scottish and Irish, she asked to speak to Gilly Slade. Janice could be heard calling out, her loud voice booming as it echoed around the empty club.

"Gill? Phone!"

"Who is it?"

"How the fuck should I know, another of your tarts I expect."

Picking up the receiver, he placed his hand over the mouth piece.

"Fuck off Janice, they can hear you."

The barmaid shrugged her shoulders as if to say she couldn't care less and continued to bottle up.

"Hello, hello is that Gilly?"

"Depends who wants to know."

Shauna resumed her natural voice and told him to just say yes and no to her questions.

"Can we meet?"

"Yeah, whenever you want."

"At the wine bar tomorrow, say two o'clock?"

"Yeah."

Without a goodbye Shauna replaced the receiver into its cradle and continued with her work but she couldn't concentrate on anything for the rest of her shift. The next day she made her way to the wine bar at one forty five. She had decided to be early but Gilly didn't arrive until nearly twenty past two, just as she thought she'd been stood up. As if being chased by the devil himself, the bar door suddenly flew open and a red faced Gilly Slade ran in, puffing and panting.

"Sorry Fran, we had a delivery turn up at the last minute."

"Its fine Gilly, I'm just glad you came. How is Davey?"

"Haven't seen him."

"What do you mean you haven't seen him, for how

long?"

"The last time was the day you met Billy, since then he hasn't left his flat but the phone at Pelican has been ringing off its hook."

"From who?"

"Billy Jackson, Fran whatever went on?"

Shauna relayed the night's events, minus the beating Billy had received which she wasn't yet aware of and Gilly just stared open mouthed until she had finished.

"Fuck me, no wonder Billy ain't been off the blower. This could mean fuckin' trouble big style, take my advice and stay out of it Fran."

"How can I Gilly? My relationship with Davey is more important than some silly argument he's had with a friend."

"This is Billy Jackson were talking about here, he's a dangerous fucker Fran and you don't know what he's capable off."

"Maybe not but I still can't give up on Davey, help me Gilly, tell me what I should do."

Gilly Slade shrugged his shoulders, he didn't know what to tell her but he could clearly see the worry etched on her face.

"As I said before Fran, the only advice I can offer is to get out. If that's not an option, then I can't help. I'm here if you need me, and should it be after hours, this is the number of my digs, better not call me on my mobile."

Shauna accepted the note he had hastily scribbled onto the back of a napkin and with little more to say they sat in silence for a few minutes as they finished their drinks. Making the excuse of having to get back to work and after promising to phone him again the

186

following week, Shauna left. The afternoon dragged and the only thing she could think of was Davey. Cecil had noticed how withdrawn she was and asked if there was anything troubling her. Suddenly all the months of deceit and lies overwhelmed her and she started to cry.

"Fran love, whatever is the matter?"

Shauna knew she couldn't confide in Cecil, couldn't confide in anyone and would now have to invent yet another fictitious story.

"It's Davey, we've had a row and I haven't seen him for three days."

Cecil hugged her to him and stroked her hair just as he did with Susan when she was upset. He was only glad that his daughter was out shopping with Madge today, seeing her new pal cry would really have upset her and when Susan was upset it affected everyone.

"Fran all couples argue, it's part of being in love and making up is the best part. Have you called him?"

"No I hate talking on the phone when there's a problem, things don't always come across as you mean them."

"Surely you know where he lives then?"

"Well yes but I can't just turn up on his doorstep!"

"Why not?"

Shauna thought about what Cecil said and knew it was the only thing left she could do.

"You're right Cecil, I'll go tonight after work."

"Good girl, wear one of your pretty new dresses and he won't be able to resist you, now what about a nice cuppa to cheer us both up?"

Smiling, she dried her eyes and went to put the kettle on.

187

After closing and alone in her flat, Shauna came to
the conclusion that the only way to save the situation
was to sleep with Davey. Once she had resigned
herself to her fate, it didn't seem so bad. Shauna
bathed and expertly applied her makeup. It took half
an hour to decide what to wear and she tried on most
of the clothes in her wardrobe before settling on the
sexy little black number she had brought a few days
earlier. After liberally applying perfume, she called a
taxi and by eight o'clock Shauna O'Malley had paid
the driver and with a shaking hand had pressed the
intercom of Davey's apartment block. He didn't
answer but the main door clicked open anyway so she
entered. It took her a few minutes to reach the
penthouse where she found the door ajar. Hesitantly
she walked in to find Davey in his dressing gown
holding two glasses of champagne.
"How did you know it was me?"
"Easy, the intercom has a video camera. You just
caught me, a few minutes earlier and I would still
have been in the bath."
Shauna threw her bag and gloves to the ground and
marched over to where he stood.
"Lucky me, now what the hell are you playing at?
Billy Jackson causes trouble and it's me who has to
suffer, you've just cut me out Davey!"
"Fran I'm sorry but I needed a few days alone to
think, Billy's been the closest thing to me for years
and giving that up is hard."
"Giving it up, don't be ridiculous. You just had a
silly argument, you can't throw years of friendship
away over one incident."
Davey placed the glasses on the table and turned to

face her.

"Fran you have a lot to learn about me, I never let anyone get away with taking a liberty. A bad trait I know but one way or another I always have to get my own back. There is an invisible line that you don't cross and Billy stepped over it with both feet. I'm not saying I won't do business with him again but that's as far as it goes, anyway enough about him come here and give us a kiss."

Shauna knew her fate was now sealed, there was no going back this time. Slipping off her coat she could see his eyes as they scanned every curve of the tight fitting dress. Davey wasted no time, he'd waited long enough. Unzipping her dress and allowing the sheer fabric to fall to the floor he caressed her breasts. Shauna let out a gentle moaning sound, she had practiced the noise over and again until she was convinced it sounded believable. Unclipping her bra, he slowly moved his hands down her body and after placing a thumb in either side of her panties, they were expertly pulled to the ground. Standing before him naked, Davey then handed her a glass of champagne before leading her through into the bedroom. Sweeping Shauna up into his arms, he gently placed her slim body onto the silk sheets and lay down beside her. Davey gently kissed her breasts as she willingly gave herself to him. Slowly he moved down kissing every inch of flesh until she thought she was going to explode. Her natural instinct was to part her legs and Davey gently nuzzled her mound. Shauna had never had a sexual encounter of any kind but she had to admit that a man going down on her was a feeling beyond belief. Davey

Wiseman had slept with many women in his life, women he had taught and women who had taught him a thing or two and as he expertly began to lick her folds of skin Shauna moaned loudly and this time the sound was one of genuine pleasure. Just as she was about to climax Davey stopped and moved his body upwards. He was slow and considerate but even Shauna couldn't have imagined the pain she would feel. Her whole life had been a roller coaster of emotional pain but excluding her childhood years she hadn't felt physical pain in a long time, until now. With every thrust he made, a burning agony shot through her body but just when she thought she couldn't stand it a moment longer, he stopped. Cupping her face in his hands, she saw the frown of concern on his forehead.

"Fran, why didn't you say?"

"I didn't think you'd want me if I told you, I'm sorry if it wasn't very good."

"Very good? It was bloody fantastic and for me to have been the first and I hope the last, makes it even more special."

Laying together their bodies entwined, it wasn't long before she once again felt his erection. He tenderly kissed her neck, slowly moving down her body until he reached the soft moist place that again sent her into another world. Shauna had never known such pleasure and begged him to stop. Entering her for the second time was less painful and she finally understood what all the books and magazines had tried to explain over the years, only one thing marred her first taste of sex, the fact that she hated the man who was making love to her.

Three hours later Shauna woke and slipping from his arms she quietly dressed. Making her way into the lounge of Davey's apartment she removed her mobile and in a whisper, dialled the cab firm to collect her. As she pulled on her coat, Shauna suddenly became aware of the room she was in and was amazed at its grandeur. He had obviously spared no expense when it came to his home and it crossed her mind that in different circumstances, she would have been in the perfect relationship. He treated her like a princess, why couldn't he have treated Violet the same way? Shauna opened the door as quietly as she could and when the lift reached the ground floor she waited impatiently for her ride. The need to get out of the apartment was rapidly growing and she couldn't take the risk that the cabbie may press the intercom and wake Davey.

Letting herself back into her flat, a feeling of disgust suddenly overwhelmed her. Shauna felt dirty, as if she had sold her body in return for revenge and it didn't feel nice. Running a hot bath, she scrubbed herself until her skin was red raw. The clock on the bedroom dresser now showed midnight and climbing into bed Shauna wrapped the sheets tightly around her and cried herself to sleep. The alarm burst into life at five am and she sat bolt upright with fright.
Splashing her face and after dressing quickly she left for work. Cecil had opened the shop by the time she entered and his smile made her feel even more sneaky and worthless than she had felt last night.
"Morning Fran, what a glorious day!"
"Yes it is and before you ask, I went to see Davey and

191

yes, everything is now fine between us."

"I am glad to hear that. I hate to see you unhappy sweetheart and as much as I had my reservations about him in the beginning, well I can see that he cares a great deal for you."

Shauna didn't answer and a few minutes later the morning rush thankfully began, making it impossible, much to her relief, to carry on with the conversation. From time to time Cecil snatched a fleeting glance at his employee and noticed she had lost her usual glow, something was troubling her and he wished he knew what it was. Being a true gentleman prevented Cecil from asking, if and when Fran wanted to talk she would but she didn't and the rest of the day passed slowly. At four forty five on the dot the telephone rang and Shauna being the nearest picked up the receiver.

"Hello."

"Hello darling, I just wanted to thank you for last night."

She felt her skin crawl, it had been all day! Every time she thought of last night and what she had allowed herself to do. Now he was on the phone Shauna felt even worse, reliving every moment of him touching her, invading her.

"Davey you don't have to thank me, it was, shall I say, a natural progression in our relationship."

"Natural progression! That sounds so cold Fran, are you regretting it?"

Realising her thoughts were starting to come through in the tone of her voice, she quickly rectified the situation, after getting this far and sacrificing so much, she wasn't about to throw it all away now.

"Of course not, it was wonderful."

"I'm glad, now when can I see you again?"

She had to think on her feet and fast as she definitely couldn't face a repeat performance so soon. Explaining that her period had started when she had got home and her stomach cramps were such that she just wanted to crawl into bed got her out of the situation. It wasn't a direct lie, she was due any day and at least it gave her breathing space. The line was silent for several seconds and Shauna thought she could actually feel his embarrassment.

"Oh right, being a man I tend to forget about things like that. To tell the truth, I've never been in a relationship for very long so women's problems haven't cropped up in conversation. Shall I call you tomorrow?"

"That would be great Davey."

She hung up without waiting for a reply and thankfully her shift finished a few minutes later. Finally she could go home and be herself but pacing the living room floor, Shauna became more and more agitated. The need to unburden her guilt was overwhelming and she could only think of one person who would be able to help her. The battery to her mobile had died so waiting until darkness Shauna slipped out to use the phone box on the corner of the street. Her hands trembled as she tapped in the number, maybe she wouldn't receive the warm reception she so desperately needed.

"Jackie Silver is not available at the moment, please leave a message."

"Jacks it's Shauna, if you're there please pick up, oh please pick up!"

Seconds later Shauna heard a clicking sound as the answer machine switched off and breathed a sigh of relief when her friend finally spoke.

"Shauna! How are you love?"

Hearing Jackie's voice now made matters worse and Shauna began to cry but trying to talk as she sobbed her heart out made it impossible for Jackie to understand what she was saying.

"Shauna love calm down, I can't understand a word darling."

In her own soothing way Jackie continued to talk until the crying subsided and as always, she was Shauna's saving grace. She didn't judge but listened intently as Shauna described the events of the past night. When she finally finished telling her story, Jackie let out a sigh.

"I know you said it was what you were going to do but even so, did you think you wouldn't feel anything? And I don't mean physically."

"I didn't think and that was the problem. I'd planned it down to the last detail, even down to what I'd wear but I didn't think of how it would affect me afterwards. I suppose I'll have to learn to live with it but now that it's happened once, it's inevitable that it will happen again. I suppose that's what's scaring me."

"Oh love why don't you come home?"

"I can't Jacks, at least not until its finished."

Jackie knew when she was flogging a dead horse and gave up trying but it didn't stop her wanting to reach out and hug this lonely desperate child. The women talked for a while until Shauna began to feel better and then they said their goodbyes at least for the time

194

being. Walking slowly home Shauna felt numb and once inside the flats hallway, she leant back against the cold paintwork of the front door and broke down.

After the beating he had received from Davey, Billy became reclusive, spending all of his days and most of his nights holed up in the office. Staff at The Bull avoided him as much as was humanly possible and would take turns when summoned by their boss. Even a simple task like fetching a coffee would turn into a nightmare and several employees had emerged covered from head to foot in the scalding hot liquid. If Billy wanted to vent his anger on someone, then he did and sod the consequences. Today it was Ryan Burton's turn and after being summoned to the office, he sheepishly stood outside waiting to be ordered in. The scar on his cheek still hadn't healed and he gently touched the rough edges. When Billy's voice boomed out Ryan nearly jumped out of his skin, turning the handle he stepped inside knowing that to keep the boss waiting was asking for trouble.

CHAPTER NINETEEN

"You wanted to see me Mr Jackson?"
Billy sneered as he spoke and from past experience
Ryan knew it wasn't a good sign.
"You really are an ugly cunt Ryan."
"And whose fault is that?"
Billy was out of his seat in a second and the boy had
no time to escape. Suddenly he was thrown up
against the wall and Billy roughly grabbed the hair on
Ryan's head with his hands. Pushing both thumbs
into his victims eyes made the young lad scream out
in pain but the noise only heightened Billy's feelings
as his act of torture began.
"What have I done, pleeeeease Mr Jackson what have
I done?"
"You're a cunt, you're all cunts that's what you've
done. You all think I don't know that you take the
piss out of me but I do! Well not anymore!"
Suddenly the knife appeared and at the sight of it
Ryan emptied his bladder.
"Please Mr Jackson I'll do anything just don't hurt
me again."
"On your fuckin' knees boy!"
Ryan didn't need to be told twice, he knew what was
required and quite frankly would have serviced the
whole of the club if he'd been asked, anything to stop
another vicious onslaught. His hands were shaking as
he unzipped Billy's trousers and released the man's
penis. As Billy Jackson thrust his erect cock into the
young boys mouth Ryan began to splutter and choke.
The noise being made and the sensation turned Billy

on like never before but he stopped after a few seconds knowing that if he killed the boy then Ryan was likely to bite down hard. It was something he'd heard happened in the moments before death and he wasn't about to take a chance on losing his member for anyone. Taking a step back he zipped up his trousers and when he looked down Ryan Burton's eyes were full of tears.

"Fuck off out of it before I do you some real damage."

Ryan didn't need to be told twice and was on his feet and running out of the office before Billy could change his mind. Now feeling calmer Billy Jackson walked over to the CD player and after choosing one of his favourite discs, sat back in his chair while he decided what plan of action to take.

Whispers of the men's fall out had spread quickly around the club not to mention out on the street and the staff knew that it was a powder keg waiting to explode. It wasn't a case of if but when and everyone was on their guard. Nine days and many phone calls later Billy finally got hold of his friend. Davey had just walked into The Pelican when the telephone rang and being the only one there, as Janice hadn't arrived yet, he reluctantly answered it.

"Hello?"

"About fuckin' time, I've been trying to get you for days."

Davey shook his head, this was all he needed. He had been able to avoid Billy while holed up in the sanctity of his apartment as it had always been an unwritten rule that neither of them invaded the others private space. Davey had recently changed his mobile number, they never visited each other's homes and they both had unlisted residential numbers that they purposely hadn't swapped. Billy was nothing if not persistent but even he didn't break that rule, it would have been rude and intrusive towards his friend and as far as Billy Jackson was concerned, it was something you just didn't do.

"Look Bill, I meant what I said the other night, we're finished as far as friendship goes!"

"Don't be like that Davey boy, we've got to much history between us. I know I overstepped the mark and I apologise but think on, haven't I always been there for you?"

Davey knew deep down that the words he was hearing were true and in all honesty he couldn't be bothered with another row so he reluctantly decided to let the man believe at least for the sake of business, that his apology was accepted and they were still friends.

"Okay Bill, forget about it. We'll let bygones be bygones."

"I knew you would see sense eventually my boy! Now we need to get together, there's a deal in the offing so how about you come over to The Bull tonight?"

"How about you come over to The Pelican instead?"

"Fine my friend, your wish is my desire. Nine alright?"

"Nine will be fine."

Conversation over, Davey replaced the handset. Billy now felt happier and his bad mood lifted instantly, much to the relief of his employees. Still aware his friend hadn't completely forgiven him, he readily accepted that he would have to be on his best behaviour for the next few days. Back at The Pelican, Janice walked in to see Davey standing by the telephone rubbing the back of his neck apprehensively with his index finger. Recognising the sign she had seen many times over the years as the quirky little habit only occurred when he wasn't happy, she asked if he was alright.

"Anything the matter boss?"

The tone of his voice wasn't aggressive but it was definitely one of boss to employee and there was nothing friendly in his manner.

"Yes and no but nothing I can't handle. Bring me a coffee and when Gilly gets here send him straight in."

With that he walked towards his office and Janice saluted in the direction of his back. Davey had no plans to see Shauna that day but now he was uptight and needed to relax. He decided to go and get a newspaper and as he set of for the shop he passed Gilly on his way out.

"You're fuckin' late, wait in the office till I get back!"

With the morning rush over Cecil, Susan and Shauna were enjoying a chat when Davey Wiseman walked through the door.

"Fran! Why you always tell me you're rushed off your feet, prone to a little exaggeration are we?"

Walking towards him, Shauna smiled as she hugged him. Glancing over her shoulder as they embraced, Davey said good morning to Cecil and Susan but Susan only scowled at him. Shauna had explained to Davey, that for some reason the girl hadn't taken to him but it didn't cause him any sleepless nights, in fact he took great pleasure in winding her up at every opportunity, unbeknown to anyone else of course. This morning was no different and out of the sight of her father, he blew her a kiss. Susan slammed the bundle of papers onto the counter and stormed into the back kitchen with Cecil following in hot pursuit, concerned at the unexplained outburst of temper.

"Susan!   Whatever caused that little tantrum?"

"Nasty man."

"Now Susan, don't be so selfish, you have to allow Fran other friends you know."

"Bad man."

"You would find out how nice he is, if you gave him half a chance."

It was useless, no matter what her father said, it was impossible to talk her around and she refused to go back into the shop until Davey had left.

Later that day and at the agreed time Billy arrived at The Pelican and waving to Janice, he then walked straight into the office. Davey, already in position behind his desk, was chatting away to Gilly. The conversation was about nothing in particular as the real business wouldn't begin until Billy Jackson got there.

"Davey my boy!   Nice to see you and how are you keeping Gilly?"

"Fine thanks Mr Jackson and yourself?"

"Never fuckin' better, never fuckin' better, nothing like a good deal to get the fuckin' red stuff flowing hey?"

As always Gilly's palms immediately began to sweat,

it was something that happened whenever he was in this man's company. Unsure as to whether Billy would slap you on the back or pull a knife on you, Gilly had the opinion he was a loaded gun waiting to go off and he definitely didn't want to be in the line of fire. Davey was eager to get the meeting over with and nodded for his former friend to begin.

"Right Bill what's the plan of action?"

Billy Jackson began to walk up and down in front of the desk.

"This one is going to be double the amount and........."

Before he could finish Davey cut him off and his voice wasn't friendly as he spoke.

"You're having a fuckin' laugh! I thought the last lot was big enough, you can't off load that amount of fuckin' Charlie onto the street without any questions being asked."

"Are you getting fuckin' wobbly my friend?"

Davey felt like grabbing the little prick round the throat, not only had he tried to wreck the most precious thing Davey had in his life but he was now willing to put his liberty at risk as well.

"Fuckin' wobbly? You cunt! I've never walked away from a job yet but I ain't got any intention of spending the rest of my life in the nick either. You may well sort the fuckin' deal out but it's me who has to get rid of the bastard stuff and it's my fuckin' neck on the block when the Old Bill come sniffing around."

Billy started to jump up and down, which made Gilly even more nervous. Turning towards his friend, he clapped his hands together in a theatrical manner.

"Calm down Davey boy, I've already thought about

201

it. We just hold some of it back for a while, simple!"
Gilly didn't like what he was hearing, Davey's
reputation was legendary and if he wasn't happy then
anything was likely to happen. He continued looking
from his Boss to Billy and back to his Boss again,
unable to believe what was going on but knowing any
doubts he had could be discussed with Davey in
private after Billy Jackson had left, he remained
silent. Glaring at his accomplice and through gritted
teeth, Davey uttered the words that made Billy realise
he was treading on very thin ice.
"It's anything but fuckin' simple but I have no choice
but to trust you. I'll warn you this much Billy, if the
cunt goes tits up because you're fuckin' greedy, then
you'd better have your fuckin' running shoes on. I
have more to lose than I've ever have and God help
the bastard who puts that in jeopardy."
Billy stopped for a second to study his friends face
and he didn't like what he was seeing. There was a
distance that had never been there before and he
suddenly felt like a stranger. Billy Jackson was
mentally ill but no one except Davey would ever have
the guts to mention that fact. His actions were always
unpredictable and Gilly Slade waited to see what
would happen next. Out of the blue Billy burst into
laughter and walking over placed an arm around
Davey's shoulder.
"Have I ever let you down?"
Davey shrugged the man's arm away as just being in
the same room as him was starting to make his skin
crawl. They had fallen out before but this feeling
forced him to admit that their friendship was truly
over, a month ago that notion would have saddened

202

him but now he felt nothing.

"First time for everything Billy, first time for everything!"

"It will be fine, you worry too much my son. Now I'm sorry to say I have to love and leave you, got a hot date with a nice little blonde and I'm going to shag the arse off him."

Slapping Davey on the back and acknowledging Gilly with a nod, he then skipped from the office. As soon as the door closed Gilly stood up and his eyes narrowed as he looked in Davey's direction.

"Fuckin' shirt lifter! I'm a bit fuckin' worried about this one Boss."

"You and me both Gill."

"Then why the fuck are we going through with it?"

"Gilly you can walk away anytime you want and my advice to you would be to do exactly that. As for me, can you imagine what the state of my reputation would be, once Billy put it about that I had shit myself over a deal."

"Fuck him Boss! Everyone knows Davey Wiseman and your history has every cunt in the East End pissing in their boots at the mention of your name."

"Gilly, half of that is exaggerated but I play along as it allows me to run my businesses with the least amount of hassle or interference. I can't afford to take the chance of it being put at risk and all going down the pan, just because Billy Jackson has a big fuckin' mouth when he's put out."

"I meant what I said Gill, if you want to walk away there's no shame and I won't think any the less of you."

"No chance Boss, if you're in, then so am I."

203

The job wasn't something that would have bothered Davey in the past, but since meeting Fran and falling for her in a big way, he'd become more aware of his freedom. Freedom which he knew could be taken away in an instant and all because of Billy Jackson's greed. In the past Davey Wiseman and Billy Jackson had little or no trouble from the Old Bill, unless they stepped way over the mark. Most of the local CID officers drank in one of Davey's clubs and a few who batted for the other side even spent time at Billy's. On the whole they were not a bad bunch, the only exception being Neil Maddock, a man who couldn't be bought for any amount of cash. From the day Davey opened his first club, which was more years than he cared to remember, Maddock had been on his back. The high ranking policeman on Davey's payroll had been his only saving grace and the one person that had stopped Maddock from charging him at every given opportunity.

For reasons unknown to anyone, Neil had taken a dislike to Davey at their first meeting but he'd found out early on his wings were being clipped by someone in a higher position, still it hadn't stopped the man making himself the promise that one day Wiseman would be brought down and Neil would be the one to do it. Davey had been forewarned that the detective was out to get him but as the years passed and when nothing had happened, Neil Maddock became the butt of many jokes between Billy Jackson and Davey. For some strange reason, and he couldn't explain why, the detective had come into Davey's thoughts and not in a comical way. Gilly was still sitting in the office and after several minutes of

silence, noticed that his boss had a faraway look on his face.

"You alright Davey? You've gone a bit quiet."

Turning to his employee but staring into a void, he slowly moved his head from side to side.

"I had the feeling someone just walked over my grave Gill, a ghost that's been following me for most of my life."

Gilly Slade didn't have a clue what his boss was on about and didn't want to delve any deeper to find out. He smiled in a 'don't let it bother you' kind of way and the matter dropped as quickly as it had been mentioned. Knowing he had just shown his vulnerability in front of Gilly, Davey began to laugh in the hope of rectifying this show of weakness.

"You get off home Gilly, I'll see you in the morning."

"Do you want me to wait and drive you?"

"No I'm fine and besides, I've got a few more old ghosts that need laying to rest."

Davey held up a half finished bottle of malt and Gilly knew his Boss was intending a late one and would probably spend the rest of the night here on the office couch.

"Alright Boss, see you tomorrow."

Davey was nothing if not loyal and Gilly had genuinely grown fond of the man, seeing him pained just didn't sit well but there was little he could do about it. Davey downed the remaining malt and then decided to rest his eyes for a bit but when sleep finally came it was fitful and full of bad dreams.

CHAPTER TWENTY

Due to the lie regarding her period, Shauna gained a ten day reprieve and managed only having to sleep with Davey twice in the following month. It was becoming harder and harder to concoct stories as to why she couldn't do the deed and she knew that sooner or later he would start to get suspicious. It wasn't the fact that she didn't fancy him, quite the opposite in fact but with that realisation came disgust, after all she was only doing this to get revenge wasn't she? Shauna and Gilly still met up weekly but as yet he hadn't given her anything concrete to go on. It was mostly anecdotes of jobs they had carried out in the past but it was the future she needed information about. Shauna laughed in all the right places as her new friend recalled his tales but deep down she was becoming bored with the stories. Gilly didn't seem very good at anything, not as a story teller and least of all as an informant but she had to appear amused to keep him on side.

"So how is your Boss treating you?"

"Okay I guess, he doesn't let on a lot but I think he's got something up his sleeve."

"Like what?"

Gilly was obsessed with Fran and now trusted her with most things but he knew this time he had already said too much. He realised that he couldn't tell her about the meeting but he still had to answer her question and thinking fast he replied.

"I'm not sure but Billy's been calling a lot lately and the Boss has been taking all of his calls."

This was music to Shauna's ears but she needed more details, knowing she couldn't come right out and ask Gilly, she had to think of a way to snoop on Davey. It came to her in a flash, if she slept with him again and stayed over, maybe she could get him out of the apartment long enough to find out what she needed. Shauna couldn't leave the wine bar quick enough and Gilly seemed a little upset at her abruptness.

"I'm sorry Gilly but I have to go now."

"Why what's the rush?"

"There's something I forgot to do, same time next week?"

"Same time next week."

After slipping on her jacket, Shauna bent over and gently kissed his cheek. He watched as she left and wished with all his heart that he could sweep her up into his arms and tell her how he felt. With work being the last thing on his mind Gilly Slade consumed another drink after Shauna had left and the warm alcohol helped with the heartache he was beginning to feel. All he had to look forward to that afternoon was being stuck in the club and having to listen to Janice's mind numbing chatter so he told the barman to refill his glass. Downhearted and unsteady on his feet, he finally made his way back to The Pelican over an hour later. Shauna ran back to the newsagents to relieve Cecil for his lunch and get him out of the shop as quickly as possible. Dialling the club, she hoped Davey would pick up but it was Janice who answered. This time Shauna didn't put on a voice and she was recognised immediately.

"How nice to hear from you Fran, I'll see if he's in." Janice used the small internal switchboard, making the phone ring in Davey's office.

"Yeah?"

"It's Fran on the phone, do you want to speak to her or are you out?"

"Don't be fuckin' stupid, of course I want to speak to her."

Janice was instantly annoyed by his manner. Of all The Pelican staff, she had always been the one he treated with respect but now here he was talking to her like she was a piece of dirt on his shoe. Huffing under her breath she pressed the button and connected her boss to Shauna.

"Just putting you through Fran and be careful he's a bit tetchy today."

Shauna laughed, knowing he would never be tetchy as Janice called it, at least not with her.

"Hello there and who is in a bad mood then, Janice's words not mine."

"Me? She can be a right cheeky cow at times, anyway what can I do for my princess?"

She cringed at his term of endearment.

"I've been thinking, you know a lot about me, down to every curve on my body but you don't know if I can cook."

"I'm not seeing you for your culinary talents Fran, your talents definitely lie elsewhere."

"Well that's nice I must say! Seriously, how about I come round tonight and fix us dinner, perhaps stay the night?"

Davey's face was a picture of bliss, it was the best idea he'd heard all day.

"I'd really like that, what do you want me to get?"

"Absolutely nothing! I'll bring it all with me but it's

209

going to be about six by the time I get there, so can you be home to let me in?"

Glancing at his watch he saw that it was already two thirty, he had a business meeting that was due to start in half an hour and it would certainly carry on until early evening.

"Fran I'm going to be late tonight, what if I get Gilly to drop my flat fob off to you at the shop?"

The suggestion was like music to her ears, now she could nose around to her heart's content and unwittingly, he had laid everything on a plate for her.

"That will be great, see you later then."

Davey replaced the receiver and called out to Gilly but it was Janice, still narked with her boss over his earlier treatment, who came into the office.

"He's not back from dinner yet."

"Well when he does deem to show his ugly mug, tell him to get his arse in here pronto!"

Gilly casually walked in as the two were talking and immediately joined in the conversation.

"Did I hear my name mentioned?"

When his words came out slightly slurred Davey could immediately tell why Gilly had been late back.

"And just where the fuck have you been? As if I need to ask."

"To lunch."

"Fuckin' lunch! Why can't you grab a sarnie like the rest of us?"

Gilly's face reddened at the remark. He had always called his midday meal dinner time but after meeting Fran and hearing her call it lunch, he'd decided he liked the word better. It sounded good, kind of refined just like her but of course he couldn't tell the boss that.

"Take this over to Fran if you're not too pissed, then come straight back or would you like to stop off for a spot of supper?"

Janice laughed out loud, which embarrassed Gilly even more. He snatched the apartment fob from his boss's hand and stormed out. Twenty minutes later and now a little more sober, Gilly entered the newsagents in search of Fran. She was nowhere in sight so he stood around waiting and eventually Cecil appeared from behind the curtain. The two men had met on several occasions when Gilly had been delivering flowers for Davey so there was an instant recognition between them.

"Hello there young man, is it Fran you want? I'm afraid she's taken the rest of the day off but I'm sure that she's up in her flat as I've heard her stomping about."

Smiling Gilly nodded his thanks and left the shop. When the bell rang Shauna was in the middle of washing up and she quickly dried her hands before going to answer the door.

"Hi again, Davey asked me to bring you this." He handed Shauna the fob.

"Thanks Gilly, I'm cooking for him tonight but to tell you the truth I don't think he knows what he's letting himself in for."

He smiled at her words but wished that it was him she was cooking for, his boss would never appreciate her the way he could. Once again he felt the overwhelming urge to sweep her up in his arms and kiss her but deep down he knew it would never happen, couldn't happen unless he wanted to end up

211

dead somewhere.

As soon as her visitor had left, Shauna flipped through the magazine to find her list and holding a pen, she gently nibbled its end while thinking of what to add. A recipe and ingredients came first but now for the most important things. Wracking her brains she tried to make notes of what she should be looking for but it turned out to be harder than she thought. After ten minutes she gave up, deciding that the search would now have to be carried out purely on instinct. Leaving the flat at just after four, Shauna headed for the supermarket. Luckily all the items she had neatly written in little columns were in stock and some thirty minutes later she emerged carrying two bags heavily laden with meat, fruit and vegetables and after hailing a cab, she rode the ten minute journey in silence.

The apartment block looked gloomy and uninviting as the taxi pulled up outside, Shauna had to admit that this feeling was probably more to do with the reason she was here rather than the building itself. She didn't attempt to get out, instead she craned her neck to look up at the penthouse. The complex housed around twenty units and every one of them carried a million pound plus price tag. Reflecting Shauna thought how far Davey Wiseman had come up in the world since the flat in Mile End Road and her face hardened as she weighed the situation up, maybe he hadn't come that far at all, just a bigger flat, a bigger ego and an even bigger bully!

"Excuse me Miss, but are you getting out or what?" Shauna snatched up her bags and opened the door,

throwing a twenty pound note at the driver she
snarled.

"What's your problem, I've paid for your time
haven't I?"

Walking to the entrance she looked back and could
see the cabbie still cursing as he pulled away. Now
well aware of which direction to go in, she pressed
the brass button and the mirrored lift took her directly
to the penthouse. Nervously, Shauna placed the fob
onto the electronic device and when the door opened
she stepped inside and connected the security chain.
Placing her shopping bags onto the hall floor she
proceeded to walk from room to room calling out
Davey's name just to be sure. He had told her he
would be late home but she wasn't about to take any
chances. Satisfied that the coast was clear Shauna
began her search and decided that the best place to
start would be the rooms she had never had an excuse
to go into before. The small study took her far longer
than expected as she cautiously and methodically
went through every drawer and shelf. Careful to
replace everything just as she'd found it, her search
which had taken an age, turned up nothing and she
prayed the other rooms would reveal more. In the
spare bedrooms she found wall to wall storage and
once again she methodically opened every nook and
cranny but apart from clothes and several pairs of
shoes they held nothing of interest. Shauna hesitated
when she reached the bathroom, surely he wouldn't
have anything hidden in there but then again, nothing
concerning Davey Wiseman would surprise her so
she entered just to be on the safe side. The room was
clinical in its decoration and after checking the only

213

cabinet in the room and finding nothing, she walked out. Shauna began to relax as the lounge and master bedroom were now the only places left to look and she had good reason to be in either one of them. Davey's sitting room was vast and walking towards the massive window that spanned the whole length of the reception room, Shauna looked out and could see right across Hyde Park. The antique furniture, placed around the walls was of the highest quality and she could tell each piece had been specifically chosen for this very room. It was all so different from the bare boards and stinking mattresses she and Vonny had been forced to live with. Once again she recalled her childhood and the pain they had all suffered at Davey's hands. She quickly erased those images from her mind and carried on with the task in hand but still her search turned up nothing of value. Finally after closing the bedroom door behind her, Shauna leant against its rich mahogany wood and let out a deep sigh, how could a man like Davey keep no business papers of any kind in his home? There were no signs of a secret drawer or none that she had been able to locate, no safe behind a picture like in the movies. The answers she strived for were probably locked away at one of his clubs and she knew that was a nonstarter as beady eyes, too many to count, watched your every move at The Pelican and she imagined it was the same at his other places. Now accepting that the exercise had been a complete waste of time, she removed the safety chain from the front door and then entered the bedroom to have a shower and get ready before Davey returned. Standing naked in the massive cubicle she held her face in her hands as the piping hot water rained down onto her body. Back when the first seeds of revenge had formed in her mind, Shauna had known that hurting him was to be her raison d'être, her whole life's work. Nailing the bastard, hopefully as painfully as possible brought a wry smile to her face. There was only one stumbling block, where did she go from here? Right from the beginning she had known that it could never be a physical revenge, firstly she wasn't strong enough and secondly there was no way she would allow herself ever be taken down to his level. Men like Davey Wiseman only knew violence, well she would teach him that emotional pain was far worse than he could ever have imagined. After tracking him down and making him fall in love with her she really didn't know which way to turn or what to do next. It would have been easy to forget it, allow herself to feel something for him but that would mean Vonny, her dear sweet little Vonny had died for nothing. In the silence of the apartment Shauna O'Malley suddenly cried out.

"Dear God in heaven help me, please help me!"

By the time she heard Davey enter and close the front door, Shauna had dressed and stood waiting in the kitchen, ready to serve him dinner. He walked in carrying a huge bouquet of red roses and placing them on the island unit, he hugged her to him.

"It's been a very long day but it was worth it to come home to you."

"Why thank you kind Sir, now if you would like to take a seat I shall serve dinner."

The meal was a complete success with Davey eating everything she had placed in front of him. They drank the two bottles of wine she had bought and as he opened a third from his own rack, Shauna knew she didn't have to worry about sex tonight. Fetching the bottle, she saw him wobble on his feet and a few of his words came out slightly slurred. Eventually they made it to the bedroom, where Davey collapsed on the bed and was soon snoring softly. Gently removing his clothes and covering him with the duvet she slipped in beside him and instantly fell asleep herself. Early the following morning Shauna slowly opened her eyes. Gently getting out of bed she quietly washed and dressed as she didn't want to disturb him and by the time Davey eventually woke and made his way into the kitchen, Shauna was standing at the high tech stove cooking bacon and eggs.

"That smells so good baby."

"It is the least you deserve after the night you gave me."

He frowned at her words and she knew he hadn't got a clue what she was talking about.

"Don't tell me you can't remember? You were like a real stallion last night."

Typical of the man that he was, Davey knew he'd been drunk but thought he must have given a fabulous performance and Shauna was sure she could visibly see his chest swell.

"Of course I can remember, it was brilliant, now what's on the menu I'm starving."

Taking seats and eating their breakfast, Shauna visualised a similar scene from her childhood. The only difference being the fact that there now sat two at the table where previously there had been four. She couldn't believe she was sitting eating breakfast with the man who had destroyed her family, not much of a family she had to admit but at the end of the day it was the only one she'd had. Now years later she had cooked him breakfast, actually cooked food for him, just as her mother had before her.

"Anything wrong Fran, you've gone quiet all of a sudden?"

Startled back to reality, she gazed into his eyes.

"No of course not, I'm just a bit tired, you wore me out."

As he placed the last forkful into his mouth Davey smiled, he really couldn't remember anything about last night, nor could he remember ever being this happy. Oblivious to the fact that she had left the table, he looked up to see her walk in clutching her coat and bag.

"And where do you think you're going?"

Shauna shook her head and at the same time giggled.

"To work silly, some of us have to make a living. Call me later."

Stepping from the building, she looked up at the sky, it was grey and overcast but she still decided to walk to the shop. Something in the early morning air made her feel a little better about herself and she was desperate for anything that made her feel better. Shauna O'Malley knew that after this morning they had gone a step further in their relationship, she also knew that one way or another, the end was not too far off and the thought sent a shiver tingling down her spine. Inhaling deeply, she pushed the thought to the back of her mind, whatever happened she had to see it through to the end.

CHAPTER TWENTY-ONE

Davey was dressed and ready and waiting by the time Gilly came to collect him. He was in a fantastic mood and Gilly's imagination ran wild at the thought of what had happened the previous night. Every time he thought about his boss mauling and pawing Fran it sickened him to his stomach.

"Where to this morning?"

"The Pelican but stop off at the newsagents first."

As he sat back on the soft leather seat of the Mercedes, Davey wore a smile like a cat that had got the cream. God, Gilly wished he would leave her alone, he was nearly twice her age, old enough to be her father in fact. Davey Wiseman didn't notice his driver's sullen face and even if he had it wouldn't have made any difference, the way he felt today nothing could upset him. The car drew smoothly to a halt outside the shop, Davey climbed out and almost danced inside. Shauna, as usual stood behind the counter, a line of around ten people formed a queue in front of her, all waiting to be served before going about their daily business. He didn't mind waiting, would have been happy to stand and look at her all day but in reality it was only a couple of minutes before he reached the front.

"Good morning again sweetheart."

Shauna raised her head and seeing the look on his face, realised she had finally caught him, hook line and sinker. This hard man, this gangster and killer was like putty in her hands, nothing more than a kitten. Shauna could actually visualise it and it gave

219

her a feeling of strength to know, that within her own hands, she held the power to love or figuratively speaking, squeeze every last emotional breath from his body and she hoped it would be the latter.

"Hello darling, what can I get you?"

"Just this paper, oh and maybe dinner tonight?"

"Dinner but I was going to have an evening in."

His face took on the expression of a disappointed school boy, making her cave in to his request.

"Okay but not too late, all these late nights are wearing me out."

"Pick you up at eight?"

"See you then."

On her walk this morning, Shauna had run through the events of the previous night and had come to the conclusion that it wouldn't be long before Davey wanted to move their relationship forward. If he asked her to move in she could never allow it to happen but then again, she was hoping it would all be over long before that situation arose. Davey left the shop in the same mood in which he had entered and would spend the rest of the day wearing the soppy expression of someone in love. Greek Street was quiet today and Gilly pulled up right outside the club. About to get out he was shocked when his boss informed him that he was going straight out again.

"Where are we off to Boss?"

"We are not going anywhere! I'm the one going out and you can sit and fuckin' wait, understood?"

Gilly didn't like the idea, he didn't like being left out of business, if it was business Davey was doing.

"How are you getting there?"

"Where?"

"Wherever it is you're going to."

Just a look from Davey was enough to tell Gilly that he had overstepped the mark.

"None of your fuckin' concern now make yourself useful and help Janice bottle up."

His boss's words instantly embarrassed Gilly, Davey had a knack of building him up and involving him in deals one minute, then pulling the rug from beneath his feet and reducing him to a pot man the next.

Davey walked alone which was highly unusual and a few minutes later he reached his destination on Wardour Street. The shop facade, painted entirely in black to make everything on display stand out, claimed to be one of the oldest buildings on the street. The window looked good but the item Davey wanted had to be more than good, he would accept nothing less than perfect. As he walked through the door a buzzer went off, alerting the proprietor that a customer had entered. A small bespectacled man climbed a spiral staircase up from the basement but stopped in his tracks when he saw it was Davey.

"Mr Wiseman, how nice to see you, it's been too long."

"Hello Abe, how are you?"

As soon as the words were out of his mouth, and he saw the man lift both palms upwards and shrug his shoulders Davey knew it was the wrong question to ask. Abe Steinman had been a jeweller in the area for as long as Davey could remember and every time their paths crossed the man did nothing but moan about his wife and ungrateful daughters. Abe was a Jew and Davey hated the way the man talked and everything that reminded him of his own father but he didn't hate Abe enough to stop using the place.

"That wife of mine is nothing but a greedy over bearing shrew, well she's really done it this time I can tell you. I've done with them all Mr Wiseman, they are bleeding me dry and I.........."

"I'm sorry to interrupt you Abe but I need a ring and I'm in a bit of a hurry. It has to be eighteen carat gold, solitaire stone, and the best you have."

"Mr Wiseman, it won't be cheap, as you know good solitaire stones come at a premium."

"I don't care what it costs but it has to be good and I know you wouldn't dream of ripping me off, now would you?"

It was a well-known fact that Abe Steinman would sell his own mother for a price but the man standing before him was one person he wouldn't dare cross, not if he valued his life. This customer would get the best deal he could offer because as much as he detested his family, he wanted to live long enough to tell them how he felt.

"Come follow me, I think I have just what you're looking for."

The narrow staircase led down to a small room that held just one table. Abe Steinman disappeared behind a curtain for several seconds and re-emerged carrying a brown briefcase. Removing its contents, he handed a tiny package to his customer, which Davey opened and tipped out onto the table to reveal four magnificent rings. Abe Steinman walked around the table and began to inform Davey, as to each ones size and value.

"They are all around four carats in weight and range

between twenty to fifty thousand."

The price didn't faze Davey in the least but he was bright enough not to reveal that fact.

"Hot?"

"No not at all Mr Wiseman, you are definitely one person I wouldn't sell dodgy tom to, although if that's what you're looking for I have...."

"No! It has to be the best for my princess and it must be legit. So why the difference in price?"

"I was waiting for that question, let me explain. Contrary to most people's beliefs, the size of a diamond isn't the most important thing. You can have a huge stone that's full of flaws and inclusions and a smaller one that is as near to perfection as you are likely to get. The smaller one wins every time, now each of these rings all look about the same size I admit but in my humble opinion one stands out from all of the others."

Offering Davey his eye glass, Abe asked if the man would like to try and pick out the star. Davey knew absolutely nothing about jewellery but still accepted the challenge. The first three appeared almost identical and the only thing he noticed were small black speckles that could only be seen with the eyeglass. On examining the fourth ring, Davey immediately knew it was the one and handed the ring along with the eye glass back to the jeweller.

"Spot on Mr Wiseman, you are not Jewish I think but you certainly have an eye for a good stone."

Davey didn't know if he was more pleased at choosing the right ring or being mistaken for not being a Jew.

"I'll take it but you might have to resize it for me at a

223

later date."

"Not a problem!"

Abe Steinman's face beamed, he hadn't shifted anything so valuable in weeks but his smile quickly faded as Davey removed his credit card.

"No, no Mr Wiseman, you know I deal strictly in cash!"

"Sorry Abe but this has got to be above board with no question of a comeback and I want proof that I paid for it."

The jeweller knew better than to argue with the likes of Davey and with a heavy sigh accepted his defeat graciously.

"Fine, fine! I'll place it in one of my finest leather boxes'."

"Thanks Abe and one more thing, I don't want a word of this getting out. Understood?"

"On the life of my family you have my word."

Knowing there to be little love lost between Abe and his family Davey gave the man a steely glare before picking up his package and leaving the shop. He hadn't gone five paces before Abe Steinman was on the telephone, not because of who he had served but to let other gem merchants know what a massive stone he'd just sold. He didn't realise that the news would spread like wild fire and before the day was out Billy Jackson would be informed.

The Bull only opened to the public at night but trusty regulars were allowed in to spend their days drinking and chatting. Deals were carried out and information exchanged regarding which firms were doing what and to whom. Tiny French was the exception, he didn't belong to any firm, probably because no one would have him and he crept about eavesdropping on conversations, before moving on to inform anyone that might be interested as to what he'd just heard. Billy allowed him to frequent The Bull, through no sense of loyalty or liking but simply because he got to know first-hand anything that was going down and it was Tiny who revealed Davey Wiseman's intension within hours of the ring being purchased. Billy was dozing on the leather couch in his office when someone knocked at the door.

"Enter and whoever you are, you'd better have a fuckin' good reason for waking me up!"

"Sorry to bother you Mr Jackson, it's just that I heard something today that you might be interested in, maybe not but I thought I'd better come and........"

"For fuck sake Tiny, spit the bastard out."

"Yes sorry Mr Jackson. Well it seems your friend Mr Wiseman has just purchased a fifty grand diamond ring from Abe Steinman, all above board I might add."

"What the fuck's that got to do with me? Piss off out of here you little scroat before I do you an injury."

Tiny was full of apologies and bowed several times as he made his exit. Walking towards his desk, Billy started to get angry, very angry. To think that bitch had his best friend spending hard earned cash and on a fuckin' ring of all things. He wanted to speak to Davey and fast but knowing that the reception was poor in the club, he was forced to use the desk phone which he hated. Dialling The Pelican, Janice was on the last step up from the cellar when the telephone rang. Stomping over to the bar, she snatched up the receiver and shouted down the line in a none too friendly manner.

"Pelican!"

"It's Billy, is he in?"

"I think so Mr Jackson, I'll just put you through."

When his barmaid informed him that Billy was on the line, Davey didn't imagine in his wildest dreams it would have anything to do with his morning's business.

"Hi Bill, how's it going?"

"How's it going? You cunt, when was you going tell me, after the fuckin' honeymoon?"

Davey immediately understood and at the same time he in turn became angry.

"Listen Billy, if you're on about the ring, I think you should stop right there. What I choose to do is my fuckin' affair and I don't appreciate you interfering."

"Fuckin' interfering! You are making the biggest mistake of your life and you think I'm interfering. Everyone but you can see what's happening Davey, when the fuck are you going to wake up to the fact that she's using you?"

Davey slammed down the handset, he wasn't interested in Billy's opinion or anything he or anyone else had to say. He felt like going over to The Bull and once again beating the shit out of Billy but instead he instructed Janice that if anyone called, he was out for the rest of the day.

Back at The Bull, Billy couldn't let the matter drop but he knew there was no point in trying to reason with Davey any further so it would now be down to him to put a stop to this once and for all. Billy was

226

furious and grabbing the keys to his car he set off for
Soho. It was just after three and Shauna was busying
herself restocking the shelves when the front door
flew open. When she saw Billy flick the Yale to
locked and turn the sign to closed she started to get a
little nervous.

"Billy? Are you alright?"

"Stop the fuckin' niceties. I don't fuckin' like you
and I don't give a flying fuck what you think of me
alright."

"Billy what's the matter, is it Davey, is he alright?"

"He will be once you've fucked off out of his life you
conniving little whore."

Shauna was confused, they hadn't got off to a very
good start but why he was angry now, she hadn't got
the foggiest idea but she needed to calm him down
and fast or her plans could be in jeopardy and then all
of this would have been for nothing.

"Billy I really don't know what you're talking about
or what you want but if I've done something to offend
you then I'm sorry."

"You're sorry? You bitch! You know he's bought a
ring and a fuckin' big one at that!"

"No Billy I didn't know, though I suppose you've
ruined the surprise now."

"Shut the fuck up and listen. I want you out of his
life and out of London fuckin' pronto, understand?"

Shauna couldn't believe what she was hearing.

"You listen to me Billy Jackson, you may scare the
little boys that you hang about with but you don't
frighten me! So if you don't mind I would like you to
leave now."

As he slowly walked towards her, Shauna began to

tremble. The hard shove hurt, as Billy pushed her up against the shelves and pinning her arms back, his words made a hissing sound as he snarled into her ear.

"Oh you would, would you? Well I'm warning you bitch, get out of his life and quick or else."

Even though she was now totally consumed with fear Shauna still wouldn't keep quiet.

"Or else what?"

"Or one dark night when you think you're fuckin' safe I'll come for you and by the time I've finished no man on this fuckin' earth would want to touch you!"

With that Billy turned and quickly walked out of the shop leaving Shauna's heart racing as she ran to the door and locked it as fast as she could. Perspiration ran down her back and her whole body trembled as she slid to the floor. Gilly had been right, Billy Jackson was a nutter, a one hundred percent nutter and there was absolutely nothing she could do to stop him. At least she was grateful for one thing, now aware of his hatred she would at least be on her guard. Shauna knew she couldn't tell Davey what had just happened, not if she didn't want World War Three to break out and that realisation just added to her feeling of helplessness. Everything would now have to be pushed forward, she needed results and she needed them fast.

CHAPTER TWENTY-TWO

It had taken ages for Shauna to get ready as she couldn't stop thinking about that visit from Billy and by the time Davey rang the doorbell she was a nervous wreck. Davey didn't get invited in like he usually did, instead she hastily closed the door behind her and looked around for any sign that she was being watched. As he stepped forward to kiss her on the cheek Shauna quickly opened the car door and climbed in before he had chance. Davey frowned as he walked around to the driver's side and once he was seated turned towards her with a look of concern on his face as he asked if everything was alright.

Shauna's tone was sharp as she snapped her reply. "Yes!"

"Fran whatever is the matter, you're acting really jumpy?"

"It's, it's nothing, I'm just a bit uptight that's all."

"Why, what's brought this on?"

She knew she had to offer some kind of explanation, Davey wasn't the type to let things lie.

"I had a bit of a weird customer this afternoon. Cecil had gone out and I was on my own, and, well he just scared me a little, that's all."

"A little! I'd say a fuckin' lot by the look on your face. Who was it?"

"I don't know Davey. I've never seen him before, now can we just forget about it, please?"

"If that's what you want princess but God help him if I find out who he is. If he comes into the shop again promise you'll phone me straight away?"

Shauna didn't reply, she was just glad that yet another lie had been believed.

"Fran?"

"Okay I promise, now can we go and eat, I'm starving?"

Entering the restaurant, Davey noticed there were only two other people there and it pleased him. He had planned for the evening to be special, romantic even and a restaurant full of noisy diners would definitely have ruined things. On seeing his customers, Ricardo almost tripped over in his haste to greet them.

"Mr Wiseman, Miss Richards how nice to see you both again."

After holding out a chair for Shauna to sit down, Ricardo handed them menus and took their drinks order. By the time the starters arrived Davey could see Shauna had begun to relax and he was about to talk of their future, when the door opened and two men walked in. Davey made a sighing sound followed by 'For fucks sake` which made Shauna frown.

"Friends of yours?"

"You could say that, in a manner of speaking."

The men walked by the table and the one in front nodded his head to Davey as they passed but the acknowledgment wasn't reciprocated.

"That wasn't very nice Davey, he was only being polite."

"You wouldn't say that if you knew him sweetheart."

"So why don't you tell me about him then?"

"He's just someone from my past, there really isn't

anything to tell."

"Why don't you ever share things with me Davey?"

"Share things? Of course I do, I want to share the rest of my life with you."

"That's not what I meant and you know it."

Davey laughed, which made Shauna angry, he reached out to touch her hand but she pulled away. All she had gone through today and he couldn't even take her seriously, at this rate she would be ninety before she found anything out.

"Don't be like that sweetheart. Look his name is Maddock, Neil Maddock and he's local CID. Happy now?"

"No not really, how do you know him?"

"Years ago, when I opened my first club, he took a dislike to me, ever since then he's tried to find a way to send me down."

"Davey, people don't just dislike you without a reason, nor do the police fit people up just because they take a dislike to them."

"My darling Fran, you are so naive. The world I live in is far from normal, in fact it's about as corrupt as you can get. Luckily I have a guardian angel, so Maddock's never been able to pin anything on me but I doubt he'll ever give up trying."

"He can't hurt you if you don't do anything wrong."

He smiled at her sweetly, she really was so innocent. "Now can we forget about the boys in blue and concentrate on our evening?"

Shauna wanted to delve deeper and was about to ask more when Ricardo brought their main courses. Deciding to postpone her questioning until later, she started to tuck into her food and by the time the desert

231

menu came, she felt totally stuffed and Davey couldn't help but laugh.

"You've eaten too much, haven't you?"

"I know but it's just so delicious, I'm glad I'm not married to an Italian or I would be as big as a house." Davey once again reached for her hand but this time she didn't pull away.

"I'm glad you're not!"

"What?"

"Married to an Italian or anyone else come to that or you wouldn't be here with me now."

Shauna's face began to colour up, knowing he was about to bring the ring out, she didn't want to spoil things by turning him down. Making her excuses, she left the table to go to the ladies, keeping her head down as she went. Neil Maddock's table was almost in front of the toilet door and Shauna had to walk around it to gain entry. She could feel his eyes on her and lifting her head, she looked directly into his face.

"Miss, you really should be more choosey about the company you keep!"

"I beg your pardon and what business exactly is it of yours?"

"None but I would hate to see a nice girl like yourself, get mixed up with a low life like Davey Wiseman."

"Thanks for your concern but if you took the time to get to know him, you would soon realise that underneath he's a really nice man."

"They are all nice love, that's until you cross them." Neil Maddock laughed out loud, which infuriated Shauna. Marching into the toilet, she slammed the door behind her. The bathroom was cool and sitting on the small chair in the corner, she tried to gather her thoughts. Not only was she about to be proposed to by the man that had beaten her as a child but also the man that had killed her family. Was she mad, she had actually defended him to one of Her Majesty's finest and the only explanation she could come up with was the fact that she was losing her mind? Shauna didn't look in Neil 's direction as she returned to the table, instead she focused straight ahead to where Davey was sitting. Ricardo's restaurant was only small and Davey had seen the conversation but hadn't been able to hear what was said. None the less, he was as mad as hell and as Shauna went to sit down, he couldn't wait to question her.

"What did he say to you?"

"Nothing worth repeating."

Davey's voice took on a menacing tone as he spoke and he suddenly gripped her arm causing Shauna to wince.

"Fran I need to know what he said, every single word."

Seeing the frightened expression on her face, he released her arm when he realised he had been far too heavy handed.

"I'm sorry love, I didn't mean to hurt you but it's important that you tell me."

Shauna knew this was a perfect moment to act, a perfect time to make him confide in her and she forced her eyes to fill with tears.

"You're sorry! You're no different to that animal Billy Jackson."

Shauna swiftly stood up and grabbing her coat ran from the restaurant. Quickly pulling notes from his wallet, Davey threw them onto the table and ran after her. The street outside was empty and he had to strain his eyes to make out the small figure disappearing into the distance. Nearing the river Shauna saw a bench situated under one of the many trees that lined the bank, if everything panned out he would follow her, if not then she didn't have a clue what would happen next. Luckily he did and even though Davey didn't have a clue where she'd gone he continued to search the streets until he found her.

"Oh Fran, I'm so very sorry. I had no right to be rough with you."

Shauna didn't speak, she couldn't look at him and instead her eyes focused on the dark waters stretching out in front of her. Taking a seat on the bench, Davey placed his arm around her shoulder and pulled her to him.

"I want to tell you all the things you long to know but I warn you, it's no fairy tale. When I've finished, it's up to you if you decide to end things between us but believe me, as much as it would break my heart if you did, I would understand."

Shauna still didn't say a word knowing she was on the verge of hearing all she'd been waiting for, words she knew would seal Davey Wiseman's fate and ultimately get her justice for her mother and sister. He didn't know the turmoil that had her mind spinning out of control and when she didn't speak, he took it that she wanted him to continue. Davey Wiseman talked like never before and even he was a little taken back at his own frankness.

"It all started a long time ago when I opened my first club and met Billy. Until then I'd been a bit of a wide boy, you know, just trying to make a few quid here

234

and there but it didn't take me long to be known as a face, someone to be avoided at all costs"

Davey told her all about his clubs, his businesses, the legal deals and the not so legal deals. He told her about the beatings and far worse that they had inflicted, even down to Neil Maddock and James Loftwood. The only thing he left out was Violet and she knew he would never speak of that. His life revelation lasted for what seemed like hours and in all that time the woman by his side, remained silent. Finally, as the first of the birds began to sing, he turned to face her.

"And that Miss Richards is Davey Wiseman, not a pretty picture eh? Not the person you thought I was am I?"

Here sat one of the hardest men in London with his heart pounding so fast he thought it would burst, waiting in anticipation for a reply, like a small child. No situation in all of his life had ever made him feel this nervous but then this was no ordinary situation. He knew that whatever her decision was, one way or another it would change their lives forever.

"I may be naive but I'm not stupid Davey. It doesn't matter what you've done in the past or even what you do in the future, I just wanted you to be honest with me and now that you have we can finally go forward. We've all done bad things in our lives and I guess most of us will go on to do even more but if you can share them with someone, trust someone totally, then you'll never be alone. Davey I needed to know I could trust you, I want to spend the rest of my life with you but I knew that could never happen until you opened up to me."

Reaching into his jacket pocket, he brought out the tiny leather box and snapping the clasp open, turned it towards her. The early morning sun reflected every facet and Shauna thought it was the most beautiful thing she had ever seen.

"Fran, will you marry me?"

Caught up in the emotion, she heard herself say yes, she also heard Vonny's voice scream inside her head but for once Shauna chose to ignore her sister. Davey held her so tightly that she felt like she couldn't breathe and gently pushing him away, she inhaled the morning air as she looked into his face. Arm in arm, they strolled along the river bank and Davey knew he was the luckiest man in the world. The moment she had agreed to marry him Davey had made a decision and he would allow nothing to get in their way, not Billy Jackson, not business, not anything. One of the trendy riverside cafes had just opened up for the day and Shauna motioned to Davey with her eyes.

"Exactly what I was thinking Fran, for some reason I could eat a horse."

Shauna's appetite was zero, she couldn't take her eyes off of the ring and nor could she stop thinking about the commitment she had just agreed to.

"So darling, do you want to set a date?"

His words startled her back to reality and raising her head, she met his gaze.

"Slow down Davey, I haven't got used to the idea of being engaged yet and I want to savour every moment. I want to let people know that in the not too distant future, I am going to be Mrs Wiseman but there is one thing worrying me, how do you think Billy will react?"

236

Davey sighed deeply, he hadn't given his oldest friend a thought until now.

"He won't like it but to be honest I don't give a fuck. The only person in the world that really matters to me now is you and if Billy can't accept that, well that's his tough luck."

Shauna glanced at her watch and knew she was going to be late for work, somehow she didn't think that Cecil would mind. Fleetingly she felt guilty at the deception, she knew her employer would be genuinely pleased for her and it hurt to think she could lie so easily to a friend. After Davey had consumed, much to his own amazement, a full English breakfast, they continued to walk. Heading in the direction of the newsagents they passed the florist which had supplied all of the bouquets over the couple's courtship and Davey dashed inside and grabbed a large bunch of red roses.

"Settle up with you later Jake?"

Jake knew he would never see any money and was becoming resigned to the fact he was Davey Wisemans personal supplier of expensive blooms but when all was said and done there was little he could do about it. Running ahead of her, Davey started to walk backwards as he held out the flowers.

"Davey they are beautiful but if you're not careful you are going to fall over someone."

"Never! Today I'm invincible, today I feel like I could walk on water."

As soon as the small shop came into view, Shauna felt relieved. She had now been acting for over twelve hours and couldn't no matter how hard she tried, stifle the yawn that fought to escape. Kissing her goodbye, Davey said he would call later. Shauna slowly entered the shop and told Cecil of the nights events, his congratulations were genuine as he kissed her on the cheek.

"My dear that's the best new I've heard in ages. Have you been up all night?"

"Yes and to tell you the truth, I'm nearly asleep on my feet."

"Then take the day off, go to bed and I will see you in the morning."

"Are you sure Cecil?"

"Positive, it's not every day we have news like this and believe you me you're going to need all of your strength. Davey Wiseman doesn't do anything in small measures, this wedding will be huge. I can't wait to tell Madge, she will have her outfit by the end of the week you mark my words. Now off you go and get some sleep."

Shauna did as she was told and on returning to her flat, climbed into bed and pulled the covers over her head, this might have been what she'd longed for but it was all now turning into a nightmare.

CHAPTER TWENTY-THREE

Shauna eventually managed to drift off to sleep but it only lasted for a short while, before she heard Vonny's voice within her head.

"Shauna, Shauna! Wake up, please wake up!"

Shauna didn't want to wake up, she didn't want to talk to Vonny or think about what she had done. She rubbed her eyes but there was no point in trying to ignore her sister, Vonny was angry and she wasn't about to shut up for anyone.

"Shauna, whatever have you done. The way you're carrying on, well, you know you're going to end up here with me and mum, don't you?"

"Vonny I'm so tired, can't we have this conversation later?"

"NO WE CAN'T! He's a bad man Shauna, you know he is."

"I know Von but I'm almost there, can't you see that?"

"The only thing I can see is that you are going to get hurt. Why don't you go back to that nice lady, she'll take care of you."

Shauna could feel the anger begin to build up inside her.

"I don't need anyone to take care of me. Vonny I have to do this, for myself as much as for you. Now please let me get some sleep, I'm really not up to talking right now."

Vonny didn't reply and Shauna snuggled under the duvet once more but no matter how hard she tried, sleep wouldn't come and she tossed and turned over and again. Frustrated and desperately tired she finally decided to get up and after making a coffee she stared out of the window. It was a beautiful day and not wanting to waste it, she quickly dressed and then left the flat.

Hailing a cab, Shauna hadn't a clue where she was going but when the driver asked her where to, the words 'Bow Cemetery' came out of her mouth. Although Shauna hadn't been there since the day of the funerals, she remembered the cemetery and immediately walked towards the grave. Stopping directly in front of the plot, she saw the small wooden cross, all that marked the last resting place of what had been her only family. Violet and Vonny's names were burnt into the faded rotten wood. There were no marble or granite headstones to mark the plot as the funerals had been paid for by the state, so the luxury of a proper headstone had been out of the question but it didn't bother Shauna, she didn't need a fancy lump of stone to know where her nearest were buried. Without the love and care of a family to regularly tend it, the small piece of land had become overgrown. The grass and weeds made it seem even sadder and more desolate than she remembered. Shauna knelt on the damp turf and began to pull at the unwanted foliage with her bare hands. Slowly at first, then suddenly with speed, she ripped faster and faster at the greenery. The tears started to flow and her body let out huge racking sobs but still she couldn't stop pulling at the ground. Shauna didn't feel the pain or see the droplets of blood forming on her finger tips. Only one image filled her mind, the image of Vonny's body, crawling with maggots. She wanted to dig up the earth and pull her free, hold her in her arms so it could be like it used to be. Suddenly her vision changed to the day of the funeral, she could clearly see Mary O'Dwyer and her own tiny hands as they gripped tightly onto Mary's coat. Shauna felt the utter loss and despair all over again but this time it seemed so much worse, this pain felt almost physical. The heartbreak that had consumed her as a child had been truly horrendous but it was nowhere as intense as it was now.

"Excuse me Miss but are you alright?"

The male voice brought her tears to a sudden halt and Shauna raised her head to see an elderly gentleman in a trilby hat, carrying a large bunch of chrysanthemums. He slowly ambled over to where she was kneeling and looking down gave her a warm and friendly smile.

"It's hard isn't it? I lost my wife four years ago and it still isn't any easier. People say time heals but I don't think so, you learn to get on with your life but the pain never really goes away."

His words cut Shauna like a knife and as another round of sobs emerged the man tenderly touched her shoulder.

"There, there, best to let it all out."

They knelt together on the ground until Shauna's crying had subsided.

"Looks like no one has been here in a very long time?"

"No, no they haven't. It's the grave of my mother and sister, they died when I was a little girl."

"That's sad my love, would you like some help to

241

tidy it up a bit?"

Shauna tried to smile and attempting to dry her eyes with the palms of her hands, she left brown mud stains across her face.

"Do you mind?"

"Not in the least. By the way, my name is Fred, Fred Armitage."

"Shauna O'Malley."

"Nice to be acquainted Shauna. Look here, these will come in handy, I always bring them along to cut the stems."

Fred removed a pair of kitchen scissors from his coat pocket and began to snip away at the remaining foliage. When he had finished he got to his feet and removing two yellow flowers from the bunch, laid them onto the grave.

"That looks a treat doesn't it? Now let's get you up off your knees, if the damp gets into your bones you'll know about it. I always bring a plastic carrier bag to kneel on, with my arthritis I can't take any chances."

Bending over her he pulled a large handkerchief from his pocket and as he wiped her eyes Shauna softly took his hand in hers and thanked him.

"No need for thanks, glad of the company actually. Anyway, it was really nice to meet you Shauna O'Malley, it can be a very lonely place here."

"Likewise Mr Armitage, maybe we'll meet again one day."

"I do hope so, now you take care of yourself."

Shauna left the cemetery with a lighter heart. It was good to know there were still kind people in the world, good people, people who wanted nothing in return for their kindness. Somehow it made it all the more important to seek justice for Vonny, her sister might have been a kind and caring woman but she had been cruelly robbed of the chance. What right did the Davey Wisemans of this world have to do that, why should they be free to make people suffer and never suffer themselves? They had no right, none whatsoever, and Shauna was now determined to see that he paid the full price for his actions. She hailed a passing cab but the driver was reluctant to take her when he saw the state of her hands. She hadn't realised they were in such a mess and seeing the earth and blood she slipped them into her pockets, whilst trying to explain that she had left her trowel at home and would he please be kind enough to take her home, knowing that if she'd told the truth and said that she had just tried to dig up her dead mother and sister, the cabbie would have left her high and dry without a second thought.

When she was at last back in the sanctuary of her flat, she paced the floor. Shauna didn't know how to deal with the situation she had gotten into, didn't know where to go from here and there was no one anywhere she could ask for help.

Her weekly meeting with Gilly was scheduled for later that day and for a few seconds she contemplated cancelling but decided not to. There was only a slim chance but maybe he would have some information for her and she couldn't risk not hearing something that might just help. Shauna showered and put on fresh clothes before setting off. The wine bar was empty as she stepped inside and today was one of those days when she wished it had been brimming with people. The barman greeted her with a cheery smile and without asking, poured her usual glass of dry white wine.

"Is your friend not joining you today?"

Shauna really didn't feel like making polite conversation but forced herself to be civil.

"On his way I expect, I'll take my drink over there to the booth. Can you send him over when he gets here?"

"Sure."

She pushed herself into the corner of the seat, happy in the knowledge that she was invisible to anyone passing by. Gilly was late, very late, two o'clock came and went and Shauna was about to leave when he finally arrived.

"Another late delivery?"

Gilly was a little taken back by her tone, Fran was never nasty and he knew she must be troubled.

"What's the matter? You've obviously got something weighing on your mind."

A single tear escaped as she slowly told him all about the night before, about the proposal, her answer and the argument about honesty and truthfulness. She ended up confiding all about her relationship, her doubts on marriage and the prospect of her life with Davey. Her revelations were genuine, even if she was a little economical with the truth but there was no way she could ever tell him who she really was or why she was actually in London.

"Whoa there girl!!! That's heavy stuff Fran, are you sure you know what you're doing?"

"Of course I don't, I haven't got a bloody clue, why

do you think I'm in this state?"

"Well, all I can say, is I've never seen you so miserable and the Boss so happy."

"Maybe you haven't but his happiness is at whose expense?"

Gilly hated to see her acting this way. He wanted to tell her how crushed he was when she'd told him about the wedding, wanted to tell her he was totally and utterly besotted with her and that he lived for their weekly dates but he said nothing, absolutely nothing and instead he just listened.

"Gilly what do you know about Neil Maddock?"

"That sack of shit! Who told you about him?"

"Davey. As I said, we had a long conversation about trust and he told me all about his past, good and bad."

"Really? Well I don't know much, only that the Boss is shit scared of him. He's alright while he has his protector but we all know that won't last forever."

"Yeah, that's true. He said last night he had someone watching out for him, who is it?"

"None other than Superintendent James Loftwood. Mind you, you won't hear Davey call him that, he only refers to him as Jimmy."

Shauna already knew the name but not that he was a Superintendent, everything started to fall into place. She had needed to know who this Loftwood character was but even she hadn't thought he would be so high up the ladder. Gilly was now scared that he might have opened his big mouth a bit too much and Shauna saw his worried expression.

"It's fine Gilly, Davey already told me his name and that he was in the force. What I don't understand is why someone so high ranking would want to protect a man like Davey?"

Gilly now didn't mind revealing a bit more, not once he knew she already had half the story.

"Loftwood likes young girls, very young girls, in fact the younger the better. When Davey first started out, his clubs were even seedier than they are now and Loftwood was a good customer. Davey was no fool and made sure that each of the man's visits were recorded. Even today Loftwood still uses The Den from time to time. I don't think he's a hundred percent sure about the recordings but he's got his suspicions and while there's a chance they exist it's in his best interest to watch out for Davey for as long as he can."

"What about Maddock, surely he can't be stopped forever?"

"In our world Fran almost anything or anyone can be bought but Maddock is the exception, he's as straight as they come but there are plenty of others who are only too happy to help out and take a back hander. Several times Davey has been hauled in and Maddock does everything by the book but as soon as he brings charges against him, the evidence or statements mysteriously disappear. Neil Maddock doesn't know exactly whose behind it, only that it's someone very high up. I suppose he's too afraid for his career to push the matter."

"So what you're saying is it's only a matter of time."

"I suppose if you put it like that, that's exactly what I'm saying."

After this last revelation the conversation dwindled, both Gilly and Shauna sat deep in their own thoughts. The discussion had made Gilly Slade realise that if it was only a matter of time for Davey, then it was only a matter of time for him as well. He didn't care about Billy Jackson but he did care about Davey, the man had been good to him and the last thing he wanted was for Davey to be locked up for years, come to think of it, he didn't want to be locked up either. If life had taught him one lesson, it was that incarceration at Her Majesty's pleasure was not on his list of things to repeat. He scratched his head as he stared into space and Shauna could once again see the look of worry.

"When it's all laid out in black and white and I realise we're heading for a fall, well it makes me think of the deal we have lined up. Davey said I could pull out if I wanted but of course I said no, now I'm not so sure!"

Shauna's ears instantly pricked up, finally she'd hit the jackpot. She needed to know more and pressed her new found friend for answers but the only thing Gilly would elaborate on, was the fact that they were having a meeting later that night. The two said their goodbyes and arranged to see each other again the following week. Gilly headed back in the direction of The Pelican but Shauna didn't go home, she needed time to think and made her way to the riverbank where only a few hours earlier Davey had proposed. Sitting on the same bench, she ran over all that Gilly had told her about the police and the forthcoming deal. This Loftwood character sounded like a real pervert and it made Shauna wonder just how many paedophiles were actually in The Met. The only person that sounded like he may be halfway decent, was the man who wanted to see the fall of Davey

Wiseman almost as much as she did. This was a man that she could go to as Shauna O'Malley and not Fran Richards, a man who would listen to her and realise she was a victim. Shauna knew that she needed more information, much more in fact, before she could risk asking anyone for help but things did seem as though they were slowly falling into place. Two hours later and after sitting on the bench with nothing to do but think Shauna was numb to the bone but she knew that come hell or high water, somehow she had to get into that meeting tonight.

CHAPTER TWENTY-FOUR

As she neared the flat her mind was still buzzing but she also knew these feelings wouldn't last forever, there was finally a light at the end of the tunnel and his name was Neil Maddock. Shauna resigned herself to the fact, that before long she would be paying Detective Maddock a visit and hoped with all her heart it would be sooner rather than later.

Davey had been trying to call Shauna all day without success and as she opened the door to her flat and walked into the front room her mobile began to ring. Having a good idea who it was and not wanting to speak to him, she pushed the phone under a cushion to blot out the sound. Running a bath Shauna lay in the hot soapy water and planned her final actions down to the last detail. After drying her air and then carefully dressing in a stylish black suit and white blouse, she left home and began her walk to The Pelican. A taxi would have been quicker but her nerves were in tatters so she thought the walk would give her chance to calm down. After trying all afternoon to come up with a good enough excuse to barge into the meeting, her mind was still a blank. Reaching The Pelican, she was just about to open the main door when she suddenly stopped, she didn't need an excuse, she was now The Big Shot, the fiancé of Davey Wiseman and if that wasn't a good enough reason to be here she didn't know what was. As Shauna opened the door she relaxed a little but then as if from nowhere and not for the first time since her arrival in London, Shauna wished she was back with Jacks, back where she felt safe, back where she belonged. Gilly sat in the office watching his Boss pace the floor. Davey's unease wasn't about the forthcoming meet or even being in Billy's company again, it was purely and simply down to the fact that he hadn't been able to contact Fran. Now that she'd agreed to marry him, he felt even more protective towards her. Gilly knew the reason for his bosses pacing but couldn't let on that Fran was fine, couldn't say that he'd actually been in her company this very afternoon and that they had shared a glass of wine together. He wanted, in a strange way, to reassure his boss but all he could do was sit and watch the man's anguish. Davey once more picked up the receiver and tapped in her number but again the telephone rang and rang. He replaced the handset just as Billy Jackson walked in and for a moment Fran was lost from his thoughts as he greeted his accomplice with trepidation.

"Billy."

"Alright Gilly? Davey my boy, how's it hanging?"
Neither of the men answered, to have done so would have encouraged Billy to start with his usual sexual innuendos and for differing reasons, neither Gilly nor Davey were in the mood.

"Please yourselves. Right then, let's get down to business."

Davey continued the meeting, explaining that he'd put feelers out all over London and stretching as far afield as Northern Scotland down to Western Wales. They would be able to shift the gear but it wouldn't be easy.

"Well that's good news Davey as I've spoken to Wang and he's confident that the shipment will be here on Saturday night, we go on Sunday if that's okay with the both of you?"

Davey really didn't want this, he didn't want the job, nor to be in this man's company but there was no way out.

"Good a day as any I suppose."

As if seeing Billy for the first time, he decided there and then that this was definitely going to be his last deal. He had often thought of selling up, selling the clubs, associated businesses, even his luxury apartment but that thought had become far more serious since meeting Fran. Daydreaming was now an enjoyable pastime and over the last few months various images had formed in his mind, one in particular had turned out to be a firm favourite. It was somewhere rural with land, maybe a large country house and children running on the lawn. He could see himself and Fran, cuddled up every evening on one of those over stuffed sofas in front of a roaring open fire, could even picture lazy days spent walking the countryside or attending school plays. It was all within reach, he already had enough money for them both to live like Royalty so why risk that dream for the likes of Billy Jackson? Davey knew he had no option but to see this deal through, he was also aware that he couldn't discuss his future plans with anyone, not even Gilly. Hobson's choice in the matter meant he had to just sit it out until after the weekend, then everything would be over and he'd be free to live his life exactly as he wished. The thought made him smile, which was observed by the other two men in the room, particularly Billy, who voiced his annoyance.

"Like to share the fuckin' joke, or are you off on fuckin' planet Mars again?"

The aggressive tone brought Davey back to reality.

"Just drifted off there for a second, now where were we?"

Billy looked over at Gilly seated on the chesterfield sofa and gave the man a steely stare.

"What's he fuckin' on?"

Gilly just shrugged his shoulders, he hated being put in the middle, which was something Billy did all the time. No matter what the argument, he would always side with his boss, so he didn't understand why Billy even tried to involve him. Before he had a chance to answer, Davey's raised voice could be heard.

"I'm not on any fuckin' thing, I have a lot on my mind at the moment, alright!"

"I suppose it's that fuckin' bitch again?"

Both Davey and Gilly glared at him, each wanting to grab him by the throat for what he'd said but naturally it was Davey who acted.

"Listen cunt, you start with all that again and this meeting's fuckin' over. The deal, whatever you thought it was, will be off, got it?"

"Whoa calm down, calm down Davey Boy, can't you even take a joke now?"

Everyone present knew the comment was no joke but all let the matter drop for the sake of business. Davey gave both men a warning look that said 'If either of you even utter her name you're dead', then once again he continued with the matter in hand.

"For fucks sake, can we just get on with it? I want to

be out of here ASAP."

Janice was in the middle of wiping tables when Shauna walked through the door and swiftly looking up she automatically spoke.

"Sorry Madam we're not open yet, Oh hello Fran, nice to see you again love."

"And you too Janice, is he in?"

Janice knew that under no circumstances were the men to be disturbed but she was also scared that if she didn't tell Davey his lady was here, she would really be made to suffer later.

"He is Fran but he's in the middle of a meeting at the moment, can I get you a drink? I'm sure he won't be much longer."

"No need Janice, I'll pop my head round the door and let him know I'm here."

Shauna confidently walked towards the office and Janice sighed as she rolled her eyes. Billy wasn't going to like this, come to think of it the boss might not like it either. She wanted to run ahead and stop the woman and in normal circumstances she wouldn't have hesitated. Many times in the past Janice had become a human barricade to stop over eager women who were trying to bother Davey and on several occasions it had even come to blows. This situation was different and Janice didn't want to interfere, instead she went into the store room and taking a seat on one of the upturned beer crates, she lit a cigarette. At least she would be out of the line of fire if any of the men went into one. Shauna didn't knock but slowly opened the door and peeped around. After winking at Gilly she looked over in Davey's direction.

253

"Just thought I'd call in and say hello but if it's not convenient."

"Of course it is, come on in."

"For fucks sake Davey this is all we need, we are in the middle of some pretty important stuff here you know and then she strolls in!"

Davey glared at Billy but he didn't need to say anything more, the look was enough.

"Fran I've been trying to call you all day, I was starting to get worried."

Now fully inside the office, she leant towards his face and kissed him on the cheek.

"Sorry, I had a bit of shopping to do and you know how it is when you start chatting."

Billy had had just about as much as he could stomach and stomped across the room, stopping abruptly in front of Davey and Shauna. He couldn't believe that after his warning she still had the balls to show her face.

"Are we here to do fuckin' business or for a lovers date? If it's the latter, I'm fuckin' out of here."

"Billy it's okay, me and Fran have no secrets, carry on."

"Not on your fuckin' Nelly! Either she fuckin' goes or I do."

Davey held up his hands as if to say "No contest", and cursing through pursed lips Billy stormed towards the door.

"Call me later to arrange details and don't forget!"

With that he marched out of the office and slammed the door behind him so hard that it nearly came off of its hinges. Gilly began to laugh and it wasn't long before Shauna and Davey joined in but when the laughing finally subsided, Gilly's face became ashen. "Davey he's not going to be pleased with us." Shauna chirped in "Me neither", they all laughed again but deep down she was worried. It was only a few hours since Billy had threatened her and the recollection made her shudder. Davey on the other hand was glad that his partner was riled, it was nice to see him get a bit of his own medicine for once. "You get off now Gill, me and Fran have stuff to talk about."

Gilly left the office with a heavy heart, he wanted to stay, just hang about to spend time with her. Whenever he was in Shauna's company, it was getting harder and harder to leave her. It had come to the point where it was now extremely difficult to hold his feelings inside. Gilly walked out and Shauna discreetly winked as she said goodbye which made his heart do a somersault. She then turned to Davey with a look of concern on her perfectly made up face.

"I'm sorry if I came in at an awkward time."

"Never, I meant what I said, we have no secrets now."

Shauna knew this was her chance and without hesitation jumped in feet first.

"So what was all that about then?"

Davey beckoned her to join him on the rather lavish sofa.

"A few months back Billy and me bought a shipment of drugs, close on a quarter of a million quid's worth. Anyway we got rid and doubled our money, problem is he now wants a repeat performance, only this time he's upped the ante."

"By how much?"

"Almost a million."

"A million pounds!"

"Oh believe me Fran, it's not the money that's causing me sleepless nights. You can't offload that amount of Charlie onto the streets, well not all at once, without asking for trouble."

"Why don't you just say no?"

"It isn't that easy, if I did Billy would spread it round that I'd gone soft and I need the reputation I've earned to survive in this business. Fran......., I promise you one thing, when this one's over that's it, Billy Jackson can take a running jump. I'm just praying we can pull it off one last time."

Shauna slung he r arms around him.

"Don't worry sweetheart, I'm sure everything will be fine. So, how long until it happens?"

"The deals on Sunday but that's only Billy's part, I won't get the gear until the following day but by Tuesday it should all be over."

She hugged him tighter and breathing intently, whispered in his ear 'I'm sure it will be`.

Davey amorously kissed her neck and fondling her breasts, then began to unbutton the front of her blouse, she didn't try to stop him. Inside Shauna fought with her conscience, not knowing if allowing him to make love to her was a last kick in the teeth towards him, or did she feel love for him? Then again maybe it was just regret that things had turned out this way. The loving began slowly and sensuously but after moving from the sofa, he guided her to the desk. With once swift action he swept the objects from the desk onto the floor as his passion changed to pure animal lust. Shauna didn't know if sex should be like this but if it shouldn't, then it damn well ought to be. The only reason she stopped herself from screaming with pleasure was the fact that Janice was unfortunately only a few feet away in the bar. The gentle foreplay of before had disappeared, this time it was hard rough sex that took over both of their bodies. Davey roughly forced himself inside of her and Shauna loved every second as he thrust harder and harder. After it was over and both were totally exhausted, they laid down on the sofa. Davey didn't want the moment to end and wrapped his arms tightly around her when she tried to get up.

"Wow Fran, that was absolutely brilliant, I wasn't alive until I met you, all I ever did was exist."

"Don't be silly, of course you were alive."

"I don't want to sound like a pussy but literally, I've never had anything meaningful in my life, not until you came along. Sometimes I can't get to sleep at night and it really scares me."

"Why?"

"Because I'm so frightened something is going to take you away from me and I couldn't bear that."

Davey didn't notice Shauna's eyes as they took on in a hardened steely glare but her tone remained soft when she sweetly replied.

"Nothing could take me away from you, I think that one way or another we're stuck with each other for life."

The moment was spoilt by a knock at the door and they quickly dressed before Davey called out "Enter". Janice came in and quietly closed the door behind her.

"Sorry to trouble you Boss but we are starting to fill up and I think you've got an unwanted guest."

"Who?"

"That copper who's always trying to give you grief."

"Fuck! That's all I need, where is he?"

"Over by the side bar, do you want me to ask him to leave?"

"No Jan, I'll sort it, just carry on and act as if nothing's happened."

As always, doing as she was told, Janice left the office and was back behind the bar before Davey and Shauna came out. Holding her hand, Davey led her straight to where the man stood.

"Evening Neil and to what do we owe this unexpected visit?"

Neil Maddock discreetly eyed Shauna up and down, she really was a stunner and he couldn't think for the life of him, why someone like her would entertain a low life like Davey Wiseman.

"Just keeping my eye on the ball Davey, don't want you forgetting who I am."

"Detective Maddock that would be an impossibility. Shall we go Fran?"

Leading her by the arm, Davey and Shauna left the policeman standing and Neil Maddock was seething. As they walked away Shauna glanced over her shoulder to where he stood. The area around him seemed empty, which was unusual as the rest of The Pelican was packed to capacity. No one wanted to be seen to be too close to the Old Bill and Shauna thought the man must have the loneliest job in the world. Ten minutes later and they once again found themselves at Ricardo's. Over the past few weeks it had become their own special place and after being seated at a discreet corner table, Shauna tried to make light conversation but everything she said was greeted with just a Yes or a No. The evening had started off wonderfully but with the appearance of Neil Maddock, it had been spoilt and it worried her.

"Don't let him get to you Davey."

"I can't help it, it's like an omen of something bad to come."

She clasped his hand in hers and focusing directly on his eyes, tried to make him relax.

"That's silly. You think that his appearing tonight means something is going to go wrong? Tell me Davey, how many years has he been after you?"

"Twelve or thirteen I suppose, why?"

"And how many times has he caught you?"

"Touch wood, never."

"Then what are you worrying about? Now please, can we just have a nice meal and enjoy ourselves?"

"I'm sorry love."

For her sake he tried to act normally but however he looked at it, the night was sadly ruined, he knew it and so did Shauna. Davey couldn't concentrate on anything but the imminent deal and the ironic sudden appearance of Detective Inspector Neil Maddock. He tried to make small talk but each time his mind wandered back to the Boys in Blue, finally they both decided to call it a night. Unsurprisingly neither had an appetite so after finishing their bottle of wine, they left. Davey dropped Shauna off at her home and then returned to his apartment. Climbing into bed, he hoped that if he would get a good night's sleep, things would seem better in the morning but it wasn't to be, his recurring nightmare once again returned with a vengeance. Images of cell doors slamming shut invaded his mind over and over again, until he felt he was slowly going mad.

CHAPTER TWENTY-FIVE

The following morning Shauna was behind the counter a good half an hour before the shop was due to open. Her sleep had been broken as many times in the night as Davey's but where his were due to nightmares, Shauna's had been a battle of conflicting choices. Unable to make a decision, she thought that doing some work may take her mind off of the situation. After making a coffee, she proceeded to replenish the stock and by the time Cecil arrived, every shelf had been filled to the brim.

"My, you've been busy. I really wasn't looking forward to that today but what do I find? My star employee has already done the job for me, thank you Fran."

"You're welcome Cecil, I've always found if you've got something on your mind, a little work therapy can help."

"And did it?"

Shauna mulled over the question for a moment, she hadn't realised that all the while she'd been working away, her mind had been running on auto pilot and the decision had been made without her even noticing.

"Yes Cecil, yes it did."

"Good, now how about another refill before we get busy?"

He collected her mug, before disappearing behind the beaded curtain. Fifteen minutes later and the shop was abuzz with people who popped in daily to collect their early morning essentials of fags, milk, newspapers and lottery before heading off to work. Today was no exception but Wednesdays were always the bleakest, everyone seemed miserable at the prospect of three more days of toil before the weekend. Today Shauna joined in with the sombre mood, she didn't feel happy, only empty and the thought of what she was about to do, scared the life out of her.

Again, she spent her lunch break by the river as she had come to find it a sanctuary amongst all the madness that is central London. Today was cloudless and calm but she still wrapped her coat tightly around her body, trying to stop the shivers that ran through her. It didn't work, as the more she tried to warm herself, the colder she felt. Her mind was doing cartwheels as she finally started to take in the enormity of what she was about to do. Within the next couple of days, her life would change completely, no more Davey or Gilly, no more Cecil or Susan, no more job, no more flat, in fact no more Fran. Clenching her fists in anger, Shauna felt the sting of tears and wanted to hit out at the world, a world that always seemed to have dealt her a bad hand, a world that always snatched away any little morsel of happiness she found. What Shauna wanted to do and what she had to do, were two totally different things. None of this emotional stuff should ever have occurred and Shauna was angry with herself for letting it happen. She wanted to forget about all the hurt, all the pain and stay with Davey. It would make life so much easier to build a future with him and never reveal the past but she knew that wasn't an option. Her whole life or her adult life at least had been lived with only one aim, vengeance for Vonny. If she backed down now, then what had her life been about, if she changed her mind, could she ever live with herself? Shauna knew the answer, whatever the future held, she had to carry on.

She returned to work with her coat wrapped tightly around her while the rest of London basked in the late summer sun. The afternoon passed slowly, there was little shelf filling to do and customers were thin on the ground. With nothing to occupy her but her own thoughts, by close of business her nerves were in shreds. Cecil cashed up the days takings and after bidding her good evening got into his car and headed off to the bosom of his family. Pulling on her coat, she set the alarm and then slammed to door shut behind her. Shauna didn't return to her flat, instead she hurried in the direction of Soho as fast as she could. She kept her eyes down not wishing to observe anything that might distract her or spoil her concentration at what she had long accepted was her fate. Shauna felt that she was the loneliest soul on the earth, she wasn't, cameras followed her every movement. She silently prayed that someone, anyone was looking out for her but most of all she prayed that her guardian angel Vonny was guiding her. After stopping only once to ask for directions she was pointed towards Charing Cross and the Agar Street Police Station. The large building looked grey and foreboding as she slowly approached and Shauna stopped for a moment to gather her thoughts before walking up the front steps. Suddenly her nerves got the better of her and she swiftly turned around and walked back down again. However hard she tried, she couldn't walk away, something pushed her on and she knew that it was now or never, knew that if she went home without seeing it through, then it really would all be over. Shauna heard Vonny's voice in her head, making her snap back to reality. "Go on Shauna, now's your chance, it's what we've been waiting for. After all these years you can't let me down now can you?"

"I know darling, I know, I just had an attack of the jitters, that's all."

A uniformed bobby approached as he ended his shift and gave her a strange look. Suddenly she realised that he had seen her talking to herself. Shauna sheepishly smiled but at the same time she could feel her cheeks redden with embarrassment. Once again she climbed the steps, only this time she pushed on the entry bell all the while aware that she was being watched on the CCTV. Big Brother seemed to be everywhere these days and she sadly wished she had a big brother looking out for her. Finally she heard a click as the heavy door was released and she quickly stepped inside. The desk sergeant was a tall thickset man but his manner was pleasant, which at least made her relax a little.

"Can I help you Miss?"

"Possibly, I'd like to see Detective Maddock if he's available."

"If you'd like to take a seat, I'll buzz his office and see if he's in. What name should I give?"

"Shauna, Miss Shauna O'Malley."

She walked over to the bench as the sergeant called

his superior and began to speak, he turned his back to her but as much as he tried to speak in hushed tones, his voice was as big as his size and Shauna could clearly hear every word.

"Fuckin' hell Neil, I don't know who she is but she's tasty and the least you can do is come down and check her out. Sorry, I meant see her. Lord knows we have enough brasses and thieves in here, when someone decent comes in the least we can do is show them some respect."

Finishing the call he turned around and informed Shauna that Detective Maddock would be with her shortly but it was a good ten minutes before he actually appeared. The glass security doors at the end of the hall clicked open and a weary looking Neil Maddock emerged but on seeing Shauna his face seemed to instantly come alive.

"I'm amazed Miss Richards, never in a million years did I expect to see you here."

"Don't be amazed, it's not a social visit."

Neil Maddock took a seat beside her and Shauna could see the man was tired, not in the usual sense but maybe just tired of life itself.

"I didn't imagine for one minute that it would be you but you've obviously come for a reason. It's been a long day, so if you've got something to say, can you get on with it?"

His abruptness shocked Shauna but not enough for her to leave, after all she knew it was now or never.

"Firstly Detective my name isn't Fran Richards my name is Shauna and if you have some time to spare and a quiet place, I think I have a story to tell that you'll want to hear."

Neil was on his feet in seconds and ushered her into a small interview room situated just off the main reception. After offering her the obligatory refreshments which she declined, he switched on the recording device, sat back in his chair and folded his arms. It was a gesture that implied to Shauna he didn't really want to be here and hoped it wouldn't take too long.

"Detective, I have something to tell you that you've been waiting years to hear but it has to be strictly off the record. If anyone saw me coming in here tonight, then I happened to be reporting a stolen purse. My life will be at risk with what I'm about to reveal, so there is no way on God's earth I will allow you to record it."

"Let me be the judge of that Miss O'Malley, if that is indeed your real name?"

Shauna felt like she was being patronized, treated like a child and she wasn't going to stand for it. Her tone, learnt from Jacks, had all the authority of a school mistress as she raised her voice to speak.

"Thanks but no thanks! This is either done on my terms or not at all. Take it or leave it!"

Neil knew he had no choice and nodding his acceptance turned off the recorder but Shauna could see he wasn't happy. Staring up into the corner of the room she instantly saw the camera and panic was evident on her face.

"There's nothing to worry about, they don't record sound and are only there as evidence in case anyone kicks off."

Nodding her head but not entirely convinced, Shauna took in a deep breath and then began her story and nothing was left out. She told him about Violet, Davey and Vonny, about the violence, neglect and the drugs. As harsh as it seemed, when it came to the death of her mother and sister, Neil Maddock was becoming bored. When Shauna moved on to Jacks and the care home, he interrupted.

"I'm sorry for the losses you've had and life really has dealt you a shitty hand Shauna but I can't see where this is going. There is no way I can charge Wiseman with murder, I'd be a laughing stock if I took this to the C.P.S."

Shauna was taken aback and started to get angry, angry at this ignorant man and angry with herself for stupidly thinking someone could help her.

"Well I'm sorry I've wasted your valuable time, I'm sure you have much more important things to attend to but the least you could have done was to let me finish what I came here to say."

Neil Maddock suddenly felt sorry for her and apologised for his rudeness. When he gently asked her to continue it was more out of pity than the thought that he would finally get a result on Wiseman. Shauna resumed her story, explaining that she needed to tell him of her past so that he understood she was genuine and why she also wanted to hurt Davey Wiseman in the worst possible way. Neil nodded but didn't say anything until she reached the part about the drug deals past and present and suddenly the detective was on the edge of his seat. Once again he had to interrupt her, only this time it was through sheer excitement.

"It has taken years Miss O'Malley, years and years to finally have any real chance of nabbing that bastard."

Shauna looked him directly in the face, searching for an answer somewhere but couldn't for the life of her understand how someone with no personal score to settle, could waste their life hunting down another human being.

"You're not the only one to have waited years but a word of warning Mr Maddock."

"Please call me Neil."

"Okay Neil! Davey Wiseman has a friend in a very high place, why do you think you've never been able to catch him? Have you never wondered why evidence disappears and witnesses go into hiding?"

"Of course I have but everything was always so well hidden that I could never get to the bottom of it."

Shauna gave a childish grin, suddenly she felt the powerful one, the one with all the answers.

"Then allow me to tell you why, because James Loftwood is in his pocket."

"Loftwood!"

"A liking for young girls, the younger the better and who were all supplied by Davey I might add. That sick bastards also recorded all the twisted things that were done to those poor children. The evidence is stashed away somewhere safe and keeps Loftwood well and truly under Davey's thumb."

Neil Maddock didn't answer, he couldn't and instead he just stared at Shauna open mouthed. Finally it had all fallen into place. All these years and he'd never been able to find out who it was, then out of the blue some young woman walks into the station and tells him all he ever needed to know.

"I had to tell you Neil, as any action you may take, will as you know be scuppered at every opportunity by Loftwood."

"My God I'm struggling to take all this in. I mean I can't believe what I'm actually hearing. After all these fuckin' years, Woops! Apologies Miss for my swearing."

"Well it's all true I can assure you."

"Thank you Shauna and I really mean that. I could have been chasing Wiseman for the rest of my life and I would never have got anywhere."

"What will you do now?"

"I'm not sure, can I call you later?"

"No! It's far too risky but I can pop in again tomorrow if that's any help?"

"Means cutting it a bit fine if the deals on Sunday but I suppose it's got to be that way."

Shauna stood up from the table fully aware of what had just occurred. Walking towards the door, she was about to leave when he spoke again.

"Take care Shauna, I can't imagine what it must have taken for you to come here. I also know how much danger you have put yourself in."

She smiled gently in his direction and noticed how lined his face was, noticed again how tired he looked.

"Thanks for the concern Detective but you couldn't possibly imagine what it took for me to come here, not in a million years."

It was way past nine o'clock by the time she arrived home and finding Davey waiting outside her flat in his car, didn't help. He saw her approach in the rear view mirror and immediately jumped out.

"Where the fuck have you been? I've been worried sick."

"Calm down, I'm here now. Actually I've been sitting in the police station for the last hour."
Shauna could see the colour visibly drain from Davey's face as a hundred different scenarios raced through his mind.
"Police Station! Why?"
She grabbed his arm and led him towards the front door.
"I went shopping after work and some bastard stole my purse."
"I bet Neil Maddock loved that?"
"Who?"
"You know, I introduced you to him at The Pelican."
"Oh him, no I only saw the desk Sergeant and what a nice man he was. Said he'd do all he could but there wasn't a lot of hope. I'm to call in again tomorrow morning just in case someone has handed it in."
Davey was happy with her story and again everything in his world looked rosy, everything apart from the nagging doubt that the ensuing deal could all go so very wrong. All day long it had kept creeping back into his thoughts and it was starting to get him down. Shauna could sense his worry and tried to lighten the situation.
"I'll fix us both a stiff drink and then I think we should take a long hot soak together with plenty of bubbles."
"Now you're talking."

That night they made love like never before and unlike the first time, when it had been a little uncomfortable and with restraint or like the night in his office when it had been just raw sex, this time his touches were electric and she felt like she was on fire. Shauna gave her all, mostly because it would be the last time she would ever feel his touch or his kisses upon her body. On his part, he had wanted to leave her with a lasting memory, should anything go wrong. As their passion drew to a close, they lay silently entwined in each other's arms. In their total absorption of each other, the bedroom curtains had been left open and now the perfect light of a new full moon shone through. The only sound came from the constant stream of traffic passing by but as the night wore on even that would diminish. Eventually they drifted off to sleep and for the first time in weeks they both found peace. Davey didn't have his recurring nightmare and Shauna, now that the final phase of her plan had been put into motion, was not in a state of turmoil.

Well before six the following morning, Davey had dressed and returned to his apartment. It was going to be a tense few days and he needed to keep alert and be on the ball. Shauna still in a deep slumber didn't hear him leave and when she opened her eyes, she panicked for a second when she realised he'd gone. She calmed down when she saw the note laying on his pillow and propping herself up on one elbow she opened the envelope and gently removed the sheet of paper. As Shauna read his words a single tear trickled down her cheek.

'My daring Fran, last night you were amazing and I know that after this weekend the rest of our lives will be spent like this. I love you with every part of my being. Your Davey XXXX.'

Burying her face into the soft pillow, Shauna sobbed her heart out. She knew that by her own hand, she was about to destroy the only chance of happiness she'd ever had and accepting that she would never see him again was going to be harder than she could possibly have imagined. When the tears had subsided, she tried to understand how she had come to feel this way. Hate, a terrible loathing hate was all she'd ever felt for this man so how in God's name had she allowed that to change? Was it really possible to love someone and hate them all at the same time? Suddenly her thoughts were interrupted by Vonny's tiny voice screaming out, becoming louder and louder with every word 'Traitor, traitor, traitor!!!' Calling out to no one, Shauna begged for forgiveness.

CHAPTER TWENTY-SIX

While Shauna and Davey had been in the throes of passion, Neil Maddock sat alone in his office. The next few hours would be crucial if he was to collar Davey Wiseman once and for all. After Shauna had revealed who Davey's guardian angel was, Neil knew he would be forced to seek help from outside of his own station. Calling in old favours made him feel inadequate but desperate times called for desperate measures and help would come in the form of a certain Graham Myers.

Superintendent Myers was known to socialize with James Loftwood but there was little love lost between the men. It was helpful that Neil and Graham had completed their basic training together and become firm buddies back when they both wore the blue uniform. Even though Neil's career had taken years to progress, Graham had risen quickly to the position of Super but the two had still remained friends. It wasn't a deep friendship and they would often go months without seeing each other but whenever their paths crossed, it was just like the old days. By the time Shauna returned to her flat, Neil had already been phoning around for almost an hour, trying to locate Graham. As a last resort he had reluctantly called the man at home but was unsure of the reception he would receive. Graham Myers walked into the kitchen to replenish his wine glass, sitting out on the patio he hadn't heard the landline ring and glanced around to see where his wife was hiding.

Normally his mobile would have been glued to his side but after a particularly stressful week he had decided on some down time in the hope of getting a little relaxation. Hearing her laughter, he made his way into the hallway and saw she was indulging in her second favourite pastime of chatting. Suzy Myers had a knack of being able to listen at the same time as speaking but on seeing her husband standing in the doorway, she smiled and pointed to the receiver with her finger.

"Anyway Neil it was really nice to hear from you but Graham has just walked through, so I'll pass you over."

Handing the phone to her husband, she returned to the kitchen and the more mundane task of making dinner. Neil Maddock needn't have worried, as soon as Graham heard his voice and realised it was serious, his old loyalty shone through. Not wanting to discuss the problem over the phone, they arranged to meet at The Prince of Wales pub in Barnet. Neil set off straight away and reached the pub well before his friend so he ordered a whisky to calm his nerves. This information was huge and the fallout would be immense. Leaning back into the snug sofa he closed his eyes for a moment and didn't hear Graham Myers stroll over.

"Nice to see you Neil, it's been a while."

Neil Maddock stood up from his seat.

"Yes Sir it has."

"Come on Neil, drop the formalities, we're not on duty now so sit down for God's sake."

"Old habits die hard I'm afraid. Right let me get you a drink before we start because by the time I've finished telling you what I've got you'll need several more."

The bar was crowded with Friday night drinkers and it took a few minutes of jostling through the hoards before Neil was served and could return to the table. Placing the drinks onto the highly polished surface, the two men just looked at each other and it was Superintendent Myers who spoke first.
"Off the wagon I see?"
"First in a decade and after the day I've had, I think I deserve it!"
Graham smiled but didn't push the matter any further. "So Neil, what's so important that you drag me away from the family on my weekend off? Friend or no friend it had better be good, because I'm missing one of Suzy's famous roasts for this."
Normally Neil would have laughed but his face remained stony which made Graham realise there must be big trouble in store. It took Neil Maddock half an hour to relay the story told to him by Shauna. He left out the part about Loftwood until the end, knowing it would shock Graham to the core and seal Davey Wiseman's fate. Graham Myers exhaled deeply and at the same time ran a hand through his receding hair.
"Jesus Christ Neil, when you drop a fuckin' bombshell, it's certainly a big bastard."
"Yeah tell me about it but I didn't know who else to turn to. The deals going down tomorrow and without your help, Loftwood will make it disappear again. Graham I've waited years to get this bastard, Billy Jackson is a bonus but if we can bring down

Loftwood as well!"

"Hold your horses Neil. I can help with this Wiseman bloke and any accomplices he has but the Superintendent is another kettle of fish altogether."

"So what are you saying Graham, we just let him scupper the collar once again?"

"No that's not what I'm saying. I will supply all the men and back up you need. When the time is right, pull them all in and then call me straight away. I will speak to Loftwood before he acts and have a friendly chat, I don't think you'll have anything to worry about. In fact I can assure you, you won't."

"But there's no way he'll listen, remember Wiseman has a lot on him, stuff that's far more damaging than anything we could ever produce."

"He won't have an option and besides, he will have more chance of getting his hands on any evidence once the villains are locked up. The Super can get as many warrants as he likes to search Wiseman's premises and maybe I'll suggest that perhaps he calls it a day. Whether he likes it or not he will be forced to resign and there will be no black marks against the force, hey presto everyone's happy."

Neil Maddock slowly shook his head, it always amazed him how the big boys stuck together.

Graham Myers instantly recognised the look on his friends face.

"I know what you're thinking and it isn't a case of the Boys at the top sticking together. If Joe public get wind of this, the force's good name would become a laughing stock and I can't afford for that to happen Neil. Our reputation with the masses is at an all-time low as it is without any more shit hitting the fan."

"I realise that Graham and believe me, I am grateful for your help, it's just....."

"Just what?"

"When we joined up, I know we both took the oath seriously and I'm well aware that all forces have bent coppers but a top brass in a villain's pocket not to mention the fact that he's a paedophile and he gets away with it?"

"Don't be stupid man, there will always be rotten apples but without the likes of good men such as yourself, well I dread to think. I guess it's a bit like life Neil, it's all about balance, black and white, yin and yang, good and bad."

The two men sat in silence for a few moments as they contemplated what would happen next and it was Graham Myers who broke that silence to resume the conversation.

"Any idea how you're going to handle it?"

"I've been thinking about that and its causing me more than a little concern. If I nick Billy Jackson, then Davey will get wind and do a runner but if I let Jackson go so I can nab Wiseman, then I've lost Billy."

Graham Myers rolled his eyes.

"Neil sometimes you amaze me, it's as simple as this! I'll set up surveillance and record this fuckin' Billy character collecting and delivering the stuff, and then we will hold off until you've collared Wiseman."

"Graham surely you're not naive enough to think we can actually film him with the stuff in his hands are you?"

"Of course not but if we've got him on film and we threaten him with a fifteen stretch, believe you me he'll spill his guts faster than he can shit."

"Maybe but you don't know them, they've been friends for years and there's the honour among thieves bit. It would be much simpler if they were Jack the lad wide boys but both men are well hardened serial villains, serious evil bastards."

"Neil I've never met a villain yet, who when faced with a long stretch wouldn't trade their own mother for a lighter sentence."

Neil Maddock raised his eyebrows, pursed his lips and at the same time shrugged his shoulders.

"Well we've just got to take a chance, that or let them and Loftwood get away with it once again."

Graham finished the last of his drink and stood up but before leaving he fumbled in his pocket for a pen and looked around for anything he could write on. The only thing to hand was a beer mat and after scribbling something down he then passed it to Neil.

"My personal mobile number, we can't take any chances. When it's time to go, we don't want to risk anyone getting wind of what's about to go down."

"But I already have your number?"

"Not this one, this is kept for anything top secret and believe you me, it's needed more and more these days."

Without another word Graham left the pub, hopeful that his dinner would still be salvageable. Neil didn't go home, he returned to the station to make sure everything was in order before the big day. Knowing that he couldn't have any involvement in the surveillance annoyed him but he wouldn't risk the operation, he'd waited too long to put Davey Wiseman behind bars, much too long.

Shauna left the flat early and began her walk back to the police station. She wanted to get the meeting over with as soon as possible and as she walked along she wondered how many other people would be turning traitor today. Entering the station she was greeted by a different sergeant. He was a small man with sharp features and he didn't make any effort to be friendly towards her. He made her wait for several seconds before eventually raising his head from the computer in front of him.

"Yes?"

"Good morning to you too! I have an appointment with Detective Maddock."

"Name?"

Unlike the warm and friendly greeting she had received last night, this officer was hard face and Shauna didn't trust him one bit.

"I would rather not give it thank you, please just tell him the lady from last night is here. He's expecting me."

The Sergeant turned his back to Shauna and dialled his superior. The previous night's alcohol had forced Neil to fall asleep at his desk and he only woke after his desk phone had rang a few times. His neck was stiff, his tongue felt like sandpaper and to top things off, his head was pounding with pain. Reaching into his coat pocket he pulled out a crumpled pack of cigarettes then changed his mind when he realised he was still in work. Replacing it he then retrieved a packet of mints that had been festering in his pocket for weeks, quickly slipping two into his mouth he picked up the receiver.

"Yes?"

"Desk sergeant here Detective, there's a lady in reception, won't give her name but says you're expecting her."

"Tell her I'll be down in a couple of minutes."

With that the phone went dead, much to the annoyance of the sergeant. Turning to face Shauna, he pointed towards the wooden seat that lined one side of the wall.

"Take a seat over there, he's on his way."

"Thank you!"

The bench was hard and Shauna hoped Neil wouldn't keep her waiting long, she needed to get out of this place or she'd go crazy just thinking about what the hell she was doing here. True to his word Neil Maddock quickly appeared, though his appearance when he entered left a lot to be desired.

"Sorry Shauna, those stairs are a killer first thing in the morning especially if your knees are shot to pieces, middle age hey? Tea, coffee?"

He ushered her into the same room as last night and once again proceeded to check everything was definitely set up to be recorded.

"Neil, you know better than that!"

"Hey, you can't blame a boy for trying and it's only in case I miss anything."

"Not a chance, now turn it off!"

They both smiled at one another and sat down in the same seats and positions as before.

"Now then Shauna, let's run over what you told me last night, you don't mind if I make a few notes, only the old grey matter isn't quite as sharp as it once was."

Shauna smiled and nodded her head.

"I doubt that very much but I don't mind, although I'm not signing anything."

"I wouldn't dream of asking you, let's start with Billy Jackson's part in all this shall we?"

Deciding this could be a lengthy chat, Shauna slipped off her coat and made herself more comfortable.

"I know very little about the actual deal, a small industrial estate in Walthamstow, something about a Chinese firm and that it's cocaine. Sorry I can't give you more but there was never a good enough reason to press Davey for details."

"That's fine, I'm sure we can locate the place, now what about Davey?"

Shauna gulped, shopping Davey made her feel like she was the most treacherous person ever to walk this God forsaken earth.

"Billy collects sometime on Sunday, and then takes the stuff back to The Bull. They'll wait to make sure everything has gone smoothly, and then Davey collects it on Monday. It won't be around long though, I know he's already got people lined up to shift it."

"Don't you worry about that Shauna, I'll personally make sure the bastards are caught this time."

Suddenly her nerve started to go and she knew she had to get out of there.

"I think that's about all I know, now if you don't mind I need to get off. I told Davey I was popping in this morning regarding my purse and you never know who's watching."

Neil Maddock got to his feet as Shauna pulled on her coat.

"What will you do when this is all over?"

The question stunned her, revenge had consumed her to such a degree that she hadn't given the future much thought and now it was only a few days away, she realised she needed to make plans and fast.

"I don't know, I really don't know."

The Detective walked towards the exit with her and as the desk Sergeant released the main door Neil touched her arm.

"I don't suppose I will see you again, take care of yourself Shauna, it's a bad world out there."

"No one could hurt me anymore than I already have been but thanks for the concern and make sure you do the same."

As soon as she had left the building Neil didn't give the young woman a second thought even though she had just given him the biggest break of his career. The only thing on his mind was getting in contact with the Superintendent and doing it as quickly as possible. Graham Myers, seated at the head of the large conference table, was finding it increasingly difficult to stifle a yawn when his mobile rang. The monthly statistic meeting was coming to a close and he'd been expecting this call all morning so after making his excuses he left the room.

"Myers."

Neil again relayed everything Shauna had told him but there was very little new information.

"Don't worry Neil, I'll know the location before the day is out and as for the other, I've sorted you out a team of my finest. They are all trustworthy loyal men and will be waiting at a location close to The Bull on Monday. I realise you've waited years for this Neil, that's why I want you to lead the investigation, they

282

won't move an inch until you say so."

"That's great Graham and thanks for all your help."
Graham Myers returned to the boardroom with a wide
grin on his face. After meeting his old friend in the
pub, he knew this was going to be big, much bigger
than two scheming little cunts like Wiseman and
Jackson. They were buying direct from an importer
and seizing a haul this size could be his ticket all the
way to the top. He liked his old friend, he was even
grateful for the information but if Neil Maddock
thought for one minute that Graham would trust him
to see it through, he was mistaken. The
Superintendent wasn't about to take any chances, his
best man Ryan Toft had been placed on the team and
at the first sign of trouble or if Neil couldn't handle
things, Ryan had been instructed to step in and take
over.

While Myers and Maddock both leaned back in their
chairs with smug grins on their faces at the thought of
the operation, Shauna sat alone on the bench by the
river. She had to make plans of where to go and what
to do and the only person she could think of was
Jacks. Removing her phone from her handbag
Shauna nervously dialled. Still on leave from
Sunrise, the phone rang only twice before Jackie
Silver answered.

"Hello Sweetheart, how are you? I must say I wasn't
expecting this!"

"Hi Jacks, long time no hear."

"Shauna? Oh Shauna love I've missed you so much."
Shauna felt a lump in her throat at the reminder of all
the hurt she had caused her friend, a friend she had in
fact always thought of as a surrogate mother. After

everything she had done to Jackie, the lady still greeted her with all the love in the world.

"I know, I've missed you too Jacks but listen, it's all going to be over in a couple of days and I need a little help."

"Anything darling, anything at all, you know you only have to ask."

Shauna told her trusted friend what she wanted her to do and after a hurried goodbye, ended the call. She walked back to her flat as quickly as possible and all the time her eyes darted from side to side as she looked for anything suspicious. Maybe it was her imagination but Shauna knew that sooner or later she would be hunted down like a frightened animal. Not having arranged to see Davey because he'd said he would be too tense and uptight about the impending business he had, business that in reality he didn't want to be involved in, she spent the following two days holed up in her flat pacing the floor and praying for her phone to ring and put her out of her misery.

CHAPTER TWENTY-SEVEN

As with their previous deals, Billy was once again expected at The Pelican to collect Gilly. Davey had deliveries and as usual his staff were all busy preparing the club. He didn't want them to see how uptight he was so he locked the door to the office as he nervously paced the floor. Finally he came to a halt and pulling his mobile from his pocket tapped in the number.

"You've reached The Bull darling, how can I help you?"

Davey felt his skin crawl, why couldn't Billy have a female to answer the telephone instead of those effeminate little faggots he surrounded himself with.

"Put Billy on."

"Who should I say is calling?"

"Mind your own fuckin' business and do as you're told you little cunt."

Before pressing the button through to Billy's office, Davey heard the boy whisper "Sorry for breathing love". The line clicked and Billy picked up the phone in his office.

"Yeah?"

"Bill it's me, a slight change of plan I'm afraid. I want Gilly off the job, so can you find a replacement, like pronto?"

"Bit fuckin' short notice isn't it but I suppose I will have to, whys he off?"

"It's a personal choice, a little of his and a lot of mine."

"Okay by me but he doesn't want to think he's getting

a fuckin' cut!"

"Don't worry he won't. There isn't any need for you to come over now, so as long as everything goes smoothly I'll see you tomorrow."

Billy didn't reply and replacing the handset he cursed under his breath. A few minutes after the conversation ended Gilly arrived and Davey was in no way looking forward to letting the man down but he knew it was for his own good.

"Come in Gill, I'm glad you're early I need a quiet word."

"What's up Boss?"

"Nothing for you to worry about but I'm pulling you out."

Inwardly Gilly felt nothing but relief but unable to show it he feigned shock.

"You what? For fucks sake, why?"

"There's no real reason I can give you, just a gut feeling. You're a good bloke Gilly and I don't want to see you going down."

"No one's going down. What the fuck gives you that idea?"

"It's just something that's been nagging away at me for the last week or so, maybe it's nothing but if it is, I don't want to take you with me. I need you to hang around for the next couple of days, if everything goes to plan I want you to get the fuck out of London. I'll give you a wedge to see you through but for fucks sake Gilly, I'm telling you, get out of this bastard game, it's no way to live."

Davey expected an argument but he didn't get one. Gilly mulled over what his boss had just said and remembering his conversation with Fran, he knew that for once in his life he was being given, what he thought was good advice. He also knew that for the first time in his life he was listening and would do exactly as he'd been advised.

"Yeah you're right Davey. I can't be doing this in ten years' time, nor do I fuckin' want to and that's if I could manage to stay on the outside. Do you think Billy's going to kick off when he finds out?"

"It's already been sorted Gilly, now take a couple of days off and if everything goes to plan, I'll see you Monday."

Gilly headed straight for the door. He didn't feel any disappointment and actually felt that he was being given a second chance and there was only had one person to thank for that.

"I appreciate this Davey, more than you'll ever know."

Hardness once again came over Davey even though inside he was feeling very emotional but it was something he would never allow the man standing before him to see.

"Fuck off Gilly, before I change my mind."

Gilly Slade left without another word but to anyone who bothered to take a sideways look, the smirk on his face said it all. With nothing to do for the next two days, he planned to lay low and spend his time thinking about Fran. He couldn't possibly tell her how he felt, he wouldn't do that to Davey and above all else he couldn't risk the embarrassment of rejection. Gilly decided that when the deal had happened and everything was back to normal, he'd get off somewhere, make a new life and try to forget her.

At the agreed time Billy set off from The Bull to carry out the business in hand and took along the young lad who had earlier answered the phone to Davey. Simon was tall, thin and blonde and at just eighteen years of age, he was exactly how Billy liked them. Billy was also well aware that if anything went wrong Simon would run a mile, so he was no good as back up. On the other hand, the Beretta Billy had discreetly concealed inside his jacket pocket would be more use than ten Simons put together if things turned nasty. The Walthamstow site was deadly quiet but then he didn't really expect any different at two in the morning. Billy vaguely noticed the courting couple canoodling in a door way but dismissed them as probably a brass and her punter. Having already called ahead, he pressed the intercom beside the roller shutter. As before, the same oriental man answered but this time he welcomed Billy inside and the two men climbed the steel staircase and entered the small office.

"Good to see you again Wang, how's it hanging?" Wang Low didn't even think about responding to Billy's pathetic attempt at pleasantries, he couldn't stand the man, he despised him in fact and was only here because it was business.

"You got money?"

"All here as agreed, want to count it?"

"No need Billy, money not there, you die, simple!" He swiftly motioned with his head and two heavily built men started to carry out the merchandise. Billy wasn't allowed to leave until the money had been inspected but he too had no intention of leaving until his van had been loaded and the goods he'd purchased had been checked. Removing a small liquid filled test tube he proceeded to slice randomly at one of the packets and tapped a small amount of the contents into the tube. The colour changed immediately and Billy Jackson grinned from ear to ear. With the deal now completed the men bowed their heads to one another and Billy left the unit and got into his van.

Ryan Toft, hidden behind a darkened window in the building opposite, filmed their every move. There was no way the local CCTV that was supposed to record the area could be relied upon and supposed was a term used lightly as more often than not the cameras weren't working or the image quality was so poor, that its use as evidence would never have held up in a court of law. The courting couple had relayed Billy's arrival and the fact that he had a passenger in tow, Ryan had in turn relayed the information back to Graham Myers via an unregistered mobile phone. They were only able to identify Billy as entering with a holdall and seeing the van being loaded up by two men of Asian origin. The importers premises had been checked out for any history and the dossier Chief Inspector Myers received on Wang Low and Rohine Import and Export made for very interesting reading. The gang traded in any drug imaginable from crack to heroin, cocaine to cannabis, right down to the modern low level stuff that the kids were now into, in fact they traded in anything illegal that had a street value. Interpol already held a file on the men and Myers, if he had been carrying out his duties correctly, should have notified them about the undercover operation. He didn't, there was absolutely no way he would allow them to come in at the last minute and take all the glory. Of course after the event he would take great pleasure in calling and explaining he had some of their most wanted villains in his cells, he would also tell them that he had the men bang to rights with little chance of getting off. As soon as Billy drove away, the team were told to 'Go Go Go!' Officers seemed to emerge from everywhere and the shuttered door was forced open in seconds. SOCO along with a sniffer dog team was sent straight in to scour the place and amazingly after Ryan had sprinkled out the contents of a small plastic bag, seconds before the team entered, they quickly came up with their evidence. The find of coke had been a smokescreen to give Chief Inspector Myers reason to hold Wang and the others for an extended time. As it turned out it was unnecessary as the place was full of drugs but that hadn't been known in the planning stages. The arrested men were taken on a lengthy drive to a small station in Suffolk as the risk of anyone finding out about the collars had to be kept to a minimum. Myers had an old friend who was now the head of a small rural police station and who somewhat fortuitously, owed Graham a favour from way back. The Chinese were locked in cells with no questions asked and collection had been arranged for twenty four hours' time, when they would be returned to London and charged. Billy, oblivious to the events that had taken place only minutes earlier, was now in a very happy mood. Driving back to The Bull, he told Simon he was going to whisk him away for a holiday really soon.

"You can pick any country in the world so long as it's

somewhere hot. I want to see that beautiful fuckin' body of yours tanned all over."

Simon was stunned, Billy was known as a good lover but not for his generosity.

"How come Mr Jackson? Done some business?"

The question changed Billy's mood in a second and as quick as a flash he back handed the boy around the face, Simon reeled from the blow which brought tears to his eyes.

"Don't be fuckin' nosey, cunt!"

Neither of the men spoke for the rest of the journey and as soon as The Bull came into sight, Billy stopped the van and told Simon to get out. The young boy didn't need to be told twice, he slammed the door shut and running as fast as his legs would carry him, didn't stop until Davey and The Bull were no longer visible. Pulling up alongside the curb, Billy wasn't able to leave the van and its contents unattended and pressed on the horn several times. Two young muscle bound men emerged from the building and under his watchful eye, started to unload the precious cargo and take it inside. Piled up in his office, Billy surveyed his white treasure and thought this was how Midas must have felt. Calling Davey, he could feel the adrenalin rushing through his veins.

"Hello."

"It's me, all present and correct."

Those were the only words spoken but had nonetheless been recorded as evidence by Myers. The phone bug had been in place within three hours of him meeting Neil Maddock, although Neil had never been privy to the information. The only two people on the planet who knew of the tap were

Graham and his trusted man Ryan and God willing that was the way it would stay until the trial. Even after Billy's call Davey didn't feel any easier, he wouldn't be happy until the collection was over. He was glad that he hadn't arranged to see Fran tonight as he knew he'd have been lousy company and one bad date in a week was enough. It was three thirty in the morning and deciding to take a walk, Davey set off along the Charing Cross Road. He passed Top to Tail, who were ushering out the last of the nights punters but he didn't bother calling in. Instead he took a left into Duncannon and carried on for a couple of minutes before finally turning into Villiers Street. As The Embankment and home came into sight, he called in at the all night off licence, where he purchased a bottle of his favourite whisky in the hope that it would knock him out for at least a few hours. He desperately needed to sleep, anything but think about what had just occurred but even after consuming half the bottle, Davey was still sparked and awake at ten that morning. Holding his thumping head in his hands, he felt as if an pneumatic drill had been hammering away inside and reaching for some aspirin, swallowed several in an attempt to ease the pain. Three hours later, and just before he was due to leave for his meeting with Billy the headache had finally started to lift. Davey knew that even though it had seemed a good idea at the time, to use whisky to relieve his anxiety was foolish. Billy had spent the remainder of his night at The Bull, asleep on the office sofa surrounded by his precious cargo.

By noon the following day he had started to become

anxious for his friend to join him, he always hated this part of a job because the waiting around was so fuckin' tedious. Davey didn't arrive until nearly one thirty and on entering the office his eyes opened wide when he saw the stash sitting in the middle of the room.

"Fuck me Billy, there's enough here to get all of the East End off of their fuckin' nuts."

"Not quite my boy but maybe next time!"

Outside, discreetly and as quiet as mice, it seemed like the whole of The Met were surrounding the club. An arsenal of automatic weapons, good enough to grace any terrorist threat, were being unloaded while dogs were quickly released from vans. Suddenly the office door burst open and both Billy Jackson and Davey Wiseman were faced with wall to wall armed police. Chief Inspector Myers then stepped forward, followed closely by Detective Neil Maddock.

"I'm sorry to say gentlemen that there won't be a next time. Well, not for very many years to come at least."

Neil slowly walked around the stash in the centre of the room and nodded his head in satisfaction, his face beaming as he read out their rights.

"Cuff them both and take them in."

Billy, in a moment of panic, suddenly tried to remove the Beretta from inside his jacket but his hand didn't even reach his front. Instantly a dozen safety catches were released and he was faced with automatic rifles pointing directly at him. Billy lifted his hands to surrender and seconds later his gun had been wrenched from its holster. Typically of Billy, even restraining hand cuffs didn't stop him launching into a torrent of abuse and he began to scream and curse as he spat at the two men who now held him.

"You sad cunts! Get off on this do you? You fuckin' slag's, I bet collaring us makes your little dicks go hard, that's if you could manage a hard on between you."

Suddenly Billy lifted his leg and with every bit of strength he could muster, stomped down on the calf of one of the policemen. The assault was so vicious and forceful that the shin bone was heard by all as it snapped. The policeman crashed to the ground screaming and Billy immediately tried to make a run for it but he didn't have a hope in hell as within seconds he had been knocked to the floor. Four Officers proceeded to put the boot in and Billy Jackson rolled abound in agony all the while screaming abuse. Neil Maddock gave it a few seconds before he brought the assault to an end.

"That's enough boys, we don't want the cunt complaining about his human rights and all that shit!"

Billy was hauled to his feet and the barrel of an automatic rifle pushed into the side of his neck. An ambulance was summoned and the injured officer was tended to by the paramedics but strangely the arrest just carried on as if nothing had happened. Davey remained silent throughout, what had just occurred was normal practice in his world and with Billy being the way he was, well nothing ever shocked Davey. Neil Maddock walked over to where he stood.

"You really are a couple of low life cunts Wiseman and it's been a long time coming but I've finally fuckin' got you."

Davey just smirked, there was no way he would give

this toe rag the satisfaction of knowing that inside he was bricking it. The two men were taken away separately in unmarked police cars. Much to his disgust, Davey was accompanied by Maddock, who for the entire journey tried to get into his head and wind him up but the prisoner didn't utter a single word until they reached the station. After being helped out of the car, the idea of not knowing who had grassed him up was too much even for Davey. He spun furiously around so that he was face to face with the policeman and spittle flew from his mouth as he spoke.

"It was Gilly fuckin' Slade, wasn't it?"

Neil Maddock began to laugh, a deep gut wrenching laugh that made Davey's blood boil.

"Davey you couldn't be further from the truth if you tried, shall we say a certain young lady was more than a little helpful, very, very helpful in fact."

The colour instantly drained from Davey face, he became so white that D I Maddock was adamant he was about to pass out. Quickly glancing around he called for assistance from the first rookie constable he could see.

"Oi! You! Give us a hand. Take him straight down and under no circumstances is he to speak to anyone, do I make myself clear?"

The officer did exactly as he was told and within minutes Davey found himself staring at a hard concrete bed as he heard the cell door slam behind him. The interviews began immediately but both men being hardened to the life they led, refused to cooperate. Their high flying briefs were not called, instead they were offered the services of two duty solicitors but Davey along with Billy Jackson Davey just smirked, there was no way he would give wouldn't even look in the direction of their representatives. Both men remained tight lipped and after several hours of hard pressure, they were given up on.

The evidence gathered was damning enough and quite adequate to see them both receive sentences long enough to please Neil Maddock and promote Graham Myers all the way to the top. Both knew that if they were released before it was time to draw their pensions, they would be lucky. Davey Wiseman was charged with attempting to supply a Class A drug on a national scale and remanded to Wormwood Scrubs. Billy Jackson's charge was the same and just for good measure, GBH and attempting to use an unlicensed firearm against one of Her Majesty's Officers was added. Eager for the men to be kept separate, Billy was shipped off to Belmarsh and there was a ban imposed preventing any contact between the two men. By eleven thirty that night Davey had been processed and escorted to his cell at The Scrubs. His mandatory entitlement to a phone card, which should have been withheld on Myers's orders, had somehow been handed out on his arrival. A quiet word with the night guard, whose mother had worked in Soho for many years, a fact which the man didn't want becoming common knowledge, brought privileges. Fifteen minutes later Davey had access to a phone and was calling the only person he could think of. Gilly Slade had been tucked up in bed for over an hour and it took several rings before the noise woke him. Groggily he picked up his mobile and glanced at the screen.

"Hello?"

"Gilly don't speak just listen. It's all gone tits up and I'm in The Scrubs. I don't know where they've taken Billy and I don't fuckin' care but I need to see you as soon as possible."

"Okay Boss, I'll be there first thing, for God's sake try and chill, I'll do everything I can."

Davey didn't reply, hanging up and with his shoulders slumped he slowly walked back to his cell. He had never been a man to show his emotions but when the lights went out he couldn't help himself. A single tear ran down his cheek, Fran, his Fran, the only woman he had ever truly loved, had stabbed him in the back and he couldn't for the life of him understand why. How could someone you loved with all your heart, someone you were going to marry and spend the rest of your life with, do that to you? He had wanted to have children with her, grow old with her but moments later his eyes narrowed and all he wanted to do was to kill her.

That night Gilly was having trouble getting to sleep as thoughts of the call ran through his mind and he knew that there but for God's grace, it could have been him banged up. A shiver ran down his spine and not knowing what had happened didn't help matters. He was uneasy with the fact that maybe the boss thought he'd had something to do with it. Turning off the light he tried in vain to sleep, one way or another he'd find out tomorrow.

James Loftwood lay soundly next to his wife who

was gently snoring. When the bedside telephone burst into life Laura Loftwood rolled over onto her side signalling that she had no intentions of answering. Her husband sighed in annoyance as he propped himself up on one elbow and reached over to grab the receiver. It took him several seconds to put a face to the voice on the other end but when Graham Myers mentioned Davey's name any colour he may have had drained from his face. James Loftwood now sat bolt upright, he listened intently and the only contribution he made to the conversation was a succession of whispered yes and no's. Hanging up he wiped his forehead with his palm and could instantly feel that it was soaked in sweat.

CHAPTER TWENTY-EIGHT

Driving through the large wooden gates that formed
the entrance into Wormwood Scrubs, a chill ran down
Gilly Slade's spine as he remembered his own time
spent behind bars and the old saying 'If you can't do
the time, don't do the crime' came to mind but then
again, you never thought you'd get caught. Staring
up at the grime looking building he knew no amount
of money in the world could ever get him to swap
places with Davey Wiseman. Entering the Porta
cabin, which was situated on the car park and was a
poor excuse for a waiting area, Gilly registered his
visit with a plump grey haired woman who smelled of
moth balls and very cheap perfume. Purchasing a cup
of tea from the small cafe area run by The Friends of
Prison Visitors, he took a seat and began his wait to
see Davey. The system which was renowned for
almost grinding to a halt was remarkably quick today
and the cup was only half empty when his name was
called out.

"Peter Slade for inmate 74079."

Gilly stayed seated, after all these years he wasn't
used to being referred to as Peter and didn't realise it
was him they were calling until the receptionist
repeated his name in an overly loud voice.

"Peter Slade for inmate 74079, please make your way
to the reception!"

In his haste to stand up the cup tipped its contents
over his trouser leg and as he swore all the other
visitors turned around to look. Gilly's face reddened
and he felt a complete twat. With his head bowed, he

walked back over to the lady who had booked him in on his arrival.

"Yes?"

"You called my name, Gilly, I mean Peter Slade."

The woman eyed him suspiciously as she handed over a slip of white paper.

"Take this to the main gate, ring the bell and wait for a guard to answer."

He took the slip and without a thank you, walked swiftly out of the Porta cabin. After pressing the bell Gilly leaned against the wall and was about to light a cigarette when a small door inserted into the large gates, opened up. He handed over the piece of paper as he'd been told and was led into a somewhat windy tunnel area. The guards inside offered no conversation, which suited him fine as he had never felt comfortable with anyone in uniform, least of all screws. Two officers and a sniffer dog stood in a small room just off the main entrance. Gilly was led inside and roughly searched by one of the men, the final insult being the dog nosing his crutch.

"For fucks sake mate, I'm only here for a visit."

"And so is every other fuckin' lowlife that walks through here and many try and bring in a lot more than a few coppers for a cuppa, so if you don't like it, you can piss off!"

Gilly glared at the man but didn't answer back, he needed to see Davey too much to risk an argument before he'd even got inside. The drug search was soon over and he continued along to the visiting room which was dismal. The worn out furniture, faded carpet and faceless people, not to mention the disgusting smell of stale sweat was depressing.

Walking over to the small canteen, he purchased two teas and remembering his own experience, bought a selection of chocolate bars as well. The area started to fill up with other visitors and as Gilly glanced around he realised he could probably tell most of their life stories. It was the same in every nick in the country on visiting day, mothers travelling for hours to see their wayward sons, wives with snotty nosed kids who would repeat this day over and over again for most of their married life. There were brasses visiting their pimps with the remainder of a black eye from some unsatisfied punter and Gilly's mind was instantly made up, he wasn't ever coming near another place like this again and after today he was getting out of London as fast as he could. The teas were cold by the time Davey and the other inmates were herded in but nodding to his visitor Davey sat down at the Formica table and drank the cold sweet liquid.

"How's it going Boss?"

Davey didn't answer, his eyes filled with water, making Gilly look away in embarrassment. The Boss was always so fuckin' hard, chilled, in control and composed and Gilly didn't think he could handle seeing the big man cry. Immediately Davey wiped his face with the back of his hand and sniffed loudly, causing Gilly to once again look him in the face.

"What the fuck went wrong Boss?"

"You won't believe what I'm going to tell you but it's the truth all the same."

"What?"

"Fran, that's what, the bitch! She stitched me up like a fuckin' kipper."

Gilly couldn't believe what he was hearing. Swallowing hard and knowing he had to show solidarity towards his boss, he shook his head in astonishment.

"I'm finding that hard to take in, I mean she'd never do something like that. Are you completely sure?"

"Well I'm telling you it was her. I heard it straight from the fuckin' mouth of that cunt Maddock."

Not knowing what to say next Gilly silently recalled all the secret meetings he'd had with Fran, all the things he'd told her about Davey and all the things she already knew, much more than he would ever have been willing to reveal. There was only one conclusion, unknowingly, his boss had hammered the nails into his own coffin. How could Fran, the woman he loved with all his heart do this? Gilly felt such a fool every time he thought about it. He wanted to change the subject, needed to take his mind off of her, so instead he asked after Billy Jackson.

"Had any news on Billy?"

"That queer fuckin' cunt can rot in hell as far as I'm concerned, he's part of the reason I'm in here. If he'd just left things alone after the last time but oh no! The greedy little bastard wanted a repeat performance."

"Davey you need to be careful, he could still sell you down the river."

"I'm well aware of that Gill but we ain't got a hope in hell of getting off with this one and besides, the only thing I can think of at the moment is finding that bitch and making her pay. I don't know how yet but believe me I will."

In the time Gilly had worked for Davey Wiseman,

he'd seen his boss in many violent rages but today it was different, he could actually feel the hatred coming from the man's body in waves.

"How, how will you find her?"

"It's not going to be that fuckin' hard! I've got people out looking for the whore as we speak and as soon as she surfaces she's fuckin' history!"

Gilly suddenly felt afraid, afraid for Fran and afraid for himself. He couldn't imagine her not being in his life and knew he had to get to her first but Davey's next sentence shocked him, really, really shocked him.

"I need your help Gill."

"Anything Boss, anything at all you know that. Do you want some stuff brought in?"

Davey stared at the man, sometimes Gilly Slade could be a thick bastard.

"No you prick, just listen. I want you to go to the clubs and close them down but leave The Pelican until last. Tell Janice to take all the keys around to Smart & Jenkins my solicitors. Tony Smart will take over from there."

"Okay, it's as good as done Boss."

"Whoa! Not so fast, I haven't finished yet."

Gilly had an inevitable hunch that he knew what was coming next and prayed that he was wrong.

"In the left hand drawer of my desk is the entry fob to the apartment, you'll find a safe in the dressing room. The combination is 1212 and inside there's a hundred odd grand. It's yours but first you have to find that bitch and kill her. Do you hear me?"

Gilly wanted to vomit as his stomach started to churn over and over again.

"Slow down there a minute Boss, you want me to top Fran?"

"What's wrong with you, gone soft on me, lost your guts?"

Gilly stared open eyed at the floor and slowly shook his head. He desperately needed the money to make a new start but to kill Fran? Now that was a whole different ball game. The idea of doing a runner with the money crossed his mind but the thought was gone as fast as it had entered his head. No one ever crossed Davey Wiseman and got away with it, it was a known fact and something Gilly wouldn't ever seriously contemplate doing.

"No I haven't but Fran, are you serious Boss? I mean don't you even want to find out why?"

"Not interested she's just a two faced whore like all the rest of them and I should have listened to Billy when he tried to warn me. My mistake and now I'm paying the price, so are you gonna help me or not?"

Gilly wished he was somewhere else, anywhere but here. His mentor and boss sat staring at him, waiting for a reply and he knew he had no choice but to answer and promptly.

"Of course I will. You've always been good to me Davey and if it wasn't for you then God only knows where I would've ended up."

"Good, now go and fetch some fresh tea while I work out how I want you to handle this."

Doing as he was told, Gilly was grateful for a few minutes away from the man. He couldn't stop thinking about what he'd been asked to do. It was true, Davey Wiseman had been good to him, really good but Fran was the love of his life, how could he even imagine hurting her? Returning to the table, Davey instantly saw the worried expression on his face.

"Gilly I know what's going through that head of yours but the bitch can't be trusted. If she could stab me in the back after I asked her to marry me then she would betray anyone, can't you see that?"

"Yeah okay, I know. I'll do whatever it takes, what have you got in mind?"

Davey sighed with relief, for a moment he'd thought his trusted Gill was about to let him down. He didn't care what happened to himself, as far as he was concerned he was done for and in all honesty he felt as if his heart had been ripped out but he did care about making her pay. In the few minutes it had taken for his visitor to replenish their drinks, he had mulled over what Gilly had said about finding out why. Davey decided he had to know, if he was ever to have any peace again, he had to know.

"Find her. I'm sure she will have left the Smoke by now but she's somewhere out there and I know if anyone can find her you can. I want her brought here, tell her if she agrees to see me then nothing will happen to her."

It was now Gilly's turn to sigh with relief, perhaps Davey had relented after all but the relaxed smile that had slowly begun to spread over his face immediately disappeared with Davey's next sentence.

"After I've seen her, you can dispose of her in any way you want, just let me know that it's done. When it's over, get the fuck out of London and don't ever come back."

"Davey if you want her dead, why the fuck do I have

to bring her here?"

"I thought about what you said and for once you're right, I have to see her one last time. There are things that need to be said and there are people in here who owe me big time so I should be able to wangle a private room for the visit."

Davey eyed his visitor with a steely glare.

"Are you happy about this Gill, I mean does it sit well?"

"Sure Boss, no problem, like I said whatever you want."

Gilly cursed himself, why couldn't he keep his big mouth shut? Leaving the prison, his heart felt far heavier than when he'd arrived. Racking his brains he tried to think of a way out of this impossible situation but no ideas were forthcoming. Driving around for what felt like hours didn't help, so he made his way over to The Royal. The place wouldn't be open until the evening, so of the four clubs, this would be the easiest to close. The only other person on the premises apart from Gilly was the manager Bob Crawley.

"Hello Gill, long time no see. How can I help you?"

"I'm sorry Bob but this place is closed until further notice."

"What? Closed but why?"

Gilly knew he had to take a hard line or shutting the clubs down would take days instead of hours.

"Mind your fuckin' own, now I want the keys and last night's takings. Someone will be in touch as soon as we are ready to reopen."

Bob knew better than to argue, he handed over the cash and keys then walked out of the place that had

been like a second home to him for the best part of
ten years. As Gilly locked the main doors he placed a
'Closed until further notice sign' onto the glass.
Making his way to the bank, Gilly threw the takings
into the shoot and continued towards Top To Tail.
The club was about to open for the lunch time trade
and it took what seemed like an eternity to get rid of
all the girls. He then inform the manager as to what
was happening. Thankfully the previous night's
money had already been placed in the night safe, so
locking the doors Gilly again put up a closed notice.
Moving onto the next, Gilly parked outside and sat in
the car for a few minutes trying to prepare himself.
Out of all of the clubs, The Judges Den had been the
one he had least relished shutting down. The brasses
were active at any time of the day and he knew he
was in for a shit load of abuse by stopping them
earning. The place was dark and seedy and the smell
of stale alcohol and cheap perfume turned his
stomach.
"Well if it isn't young Gilly Slade, the boss sent you
around has he?"
"In a manner of speaking Frieda, can we have a quiet
word in the office love?"
Frieda, ex brass and manager of the Den for several
years wasn't happy. Davey always phoned her if
there was a problem and she wanted to deal with the
organ grinder not his monkey. Gilly knew this was
one woman who wouldn't go quietly and he would
have to share with her a little of what was going on if
he wanted to get anywhere. Not until they were
inside the room, a room Frieda was proud to call her
office but in fact was nothing more than a converted

broom cupboard, did Gilly feel it was safe to speak.
"I can't tell you everything but The Boss is in big
trouble. I've been going round closing all the clubs
on his instruction, it's only temporary but it's got to
be done. Davey said he could trust you to help me
get the girls out and lock the place up?"
The words Gilly spoke were like music to her ears, to
think Davey Wiseman, the one and only Davey
Wiseman, actually trusted her.
"I'd fuckin' die for that man, anything he wants me to
do, I'll do."
Having Frieda on his side made the job a whole lot
easier and although several of the girls started to kick
up a fuss when asked to leave, they soon quietened
down when given a steely glare from the towering
woman before them. With the job done and only the
two of them left in the place, Gilly led Frieda towards
the main door.
"Thanks for that, you've made things a whole lot
easier and I will make sure I tell The Boss how
helpful you were."
Placing the notice on the door, Gilly grinned, brasses
really were pathetic, give them a little compliment
and they would fall over themselves to help you.
Frieda had walked away as happy as if she'd been
given the crown jewels, the thick cow!
After visiting Davey at Wormwood and closing the
three clubs, it was well past five o'clock by the time
Gilly walked into The Pelican. As usual things were
in full swing and he was grateful the place was well
staffed. It gave him one less thing to worry about.
Janice, busy behind the bar, didn't notice him arrive
and it wasn't until he stood in front of her that she

saw the worried expression written across his face.
"Alright Gill?"
"Jan I need to speak to you pronto!"
Usually it took all of his time to get her to do
anything he asked but she knew just by looking at
him that something big had gone down. Holding up a
key she smiled and without uttering a single word
they made their way into Davey's private office,
where Gilly told her what had happened over the past
twenty four hours. Janice was privy to an awful lot of
what went on in her boss's life and little surprised
her. Having worked for the man for well over ten
years, she heard about most of the deals but that was
as far as it went and nothing of what she heard was
ever repeated, anywhere. Believing her to be beyond
trustworthy, Gilly hoped she'd carry out his
instructions to the letter and he wasn't disappointed.
Opening the desk drawer he removed the fob and an
envelope containing ten grand.
"This is for you."
Handing over the three bunches of keys, he informed
her word for word just as he'd been told by Davey.
"The Boss wants you to take all the keys to the clubs
over to Smart & Jenkins, and tell Tony Smart that
Davey will be in touch as soon as he can."
"What about this place?"
"It stays closed until you hear different, ain't ten
grand enough for you?"
"It isn't about the money Gill, this place is my life!"
"You and a lot of others, you ain't the only one losing
out here you know but Davey is in deep shit. We
both know he can usually worm his way out of
anything, so fingers crossed things will probably be

back to normal pretty soon."

Gilly hoped he sounded more convincing than he felt but deep down both he and Janice knew that it would be a long, long time before any of the venues saw another punter. Gilly nervously drove to the apartment, parked the car in the underground garage and then let himself inside the building. He had never been invited to Davey Wiseman's private sanctuary before and was amazed how spacious it was. He had always dreamed of owning a place like this but knew it would only ever be a dream. That was until today's revelations and the offer of some serious cash. There was now a distinct possibility that things just might be about to change on the housing front. He slowly walked from room to room until he found the master bedroom, the door to the left was obviously the dressing room but Gilly didn't go in. All of a sudden he felt tired, sleepy tired and emotionally drained and reasoned that if Fran had survived until now, he guessed she would be alright until tomorrow. The fact that he didn't really have a clue where to start looking for her was the real reason he was in no hurry, that and the understanding that to find her meant he would have to deal with the situation. The thought wasn't something he could even contemplate doing right now and Gilly Slade needed time to think. Climbing onto the massive king-size bed, he was only going to rest his eyes for a few minutes but sleep came quickly and Gilly didn't wake up until after eight the following morning.

CHAPTER TWENTY-NINE

As soon as the arrests were over, Neil Maddock, true to his word had called Shauna. She could hear the euphoria in his voice as he repeated over and again 'I got him Shauna, I finally bloody got him'. It was obvious that he had taken this as a personal vendetta and wanted anyone and everyone to know that at last he was finally the victor. Thinking she would feel relief at the news, it came as something of a shock when all she felt was total emptiness inside and her reluctance to celebrate was a disappointment to the Detective.

"Aren't you pleased that bastard is finally behind bars?"

Inhaling deeply, she didn't answer straight away.

"Shauna?"

"Yeah I can hear you, it's just that I'm finding it hard to be happy about someone, anyone, who is going to lose their liberty for a very long time because of me."

The line was silent for a second and then his tone sounded flat and dismissive.

"Well Shauna, I have a lot of paper work left to do so if you'll excuse me I'll hang up now."

"That's fine Neil and I hope you can finally relax, instead of spending the best part your life hunting Davey Wiseman like I have."

"Just a job to me Shauna, just a job, you take care of yourself now, do you hear?"

"I will, goodbye."

Shauna was a lot of things but naive wasn't one of them, as soon as she had spoken to Maddock the

311

reality hit her that if she wanted to stay alive, then she had to get out of London as soon as possible. She nervously double bolted the door and closed the curtains in case anyone was watching the place. Making her way to the bathroom she picked up a bottle of black hair dye that had been sitting on the shelf in readiness for this day. Just over an hour later Shauna O'Malley had once again emerged and Fran Richards was just a distant memory. At last resembling her true self, she collected a wine bottle and glass from the small kitchenette, walked into the front room and began to write a letter.

Dear Cecil, Madge and not forgetting my beautiful Susan

This is one of the hardest things I have ever had to do and I beg with all of my heart that one day you will be able to forgive me. Time is short so I won't waste it by going into detail but needless to say I will not be returning to work again. When you read the papers I expect you will have a little understanding of what has gone on but believe me, things are never what they seem. I have loved you all like a family and its killing me to have to write this. By the time you receive this letter I will have left London and be out of your lives forever. Maybe one day our paths will again cross and I will be able to explain my side of the story but until that day please, please forgive me.
Fran xxx

Sealing the envelope was difficult, her mouth was dry with fear so hurriedly opening the wine, she took a large swig. The liquid was welcomed for more reasons than the need to secure a letter. The wine tasted good and Shauna refilled her glass several times before she walked into the bedroom. As she lay down on the bed she had shared with Davey a feeling of totally emptiness engulfed her. The tears started to fall and unaware, she fell asleep still crying. Waking with a start, she glanced at the bedside clock and on seeing it was now past seven, began to panic. Leaping out of bed, Shauna quickly changed into jeans and a tee shirt and threw a few things into a holdall. With a scarf tied tightly around her head, she pulled the collar of her lightweight coat up around her neck. Taking one final look at the flat, she closed the front door, slipped outside and began to mingle with the evening crowd. A short walk led her to Soho Square, it was a warm evening and couples were just hanging around drinking and socializing. In ordinary circumstances this sight was no different from any other August evening but these weren't ordinary circumstances and this was far from an ordinary scene. The couples were mostly men, beautiful chiselled young men who lay in the last of the day's sunlight, trying desperately to top up their already bronzed bodies. Shauna had seen the displays so many times over the previous months that it didn't have any impact on her whatsoever, they were just clone gays, each one trying to be a copy of the next. Instead she kept her head down and walked straight through the park to St Bartholomew's.

Luckily, none of the men sent to find her had known of the place or if they did then they hadn't thought to look there. It had been decided by Davey that she would already have left the city so the net had been cast further afield. Shauna pressed the security button on the door and a few second later a rosy cheeked woman beckoned her inside. She was amazed that apart from asking her name no other details were required. After being led to a small room at the back of the house, the woman, who hadn't bothered to introduce herself, quickly informed Shauna of the house rules, and then walked back downstairs leaving her standing alone in the doorway. Peering inside, Shauna saw that the room was bleak and even on a warm night, it felt cold and damp. Curling into a foetal position on the bed, she decided not to venture out again until it was light and plenty of people were around. Fortunately sleep came and the next thing she knew was being woken by the morning sunshine filtering through the window. After cleaning her teeth and having a hurried wash in the tiny basin positioned in the corner of the room, Shauna again donned her head scarf and slipped out onto the street. The nearest shop supplied her with an assortment of sandwiches and cans of drink, enough to see her through until the day after tomorrow when she could at last get out of this grotty hovel. On the second day at St Bartholomew's the room began to feel claustrophobic and Shauna wondered if this was how Davey was feeling. She tried not to dwell on the thought for long but occupying her mind elsewhere became almost impossible. She ended up counting the thousands of tiny flowers on the tired out dated wall paper.

Tuesday night finally arrived and Shauna placed the small holdall by the door in readiness for an early departure. For the last time she laid down on the bed, hoping to grab just a few precious hours of sleep but for some reason she slept soundly and didn't wake until ten on Wednesday morning. Quickly dressing, Shauna was about to open the door when someone knocked, they knocked very hard and peering through the small gap allowed by the safety chain, she come face to face with Gilly Slade.

Departure from St Bartholomew's

"And so Gilly, this is Shauna O'Malley! I told you it was a long story but you now know everything about me, I've laid my whole life open to you like a book, not that it's going to make any difference."

She lifted her head to meet his eyes but the hardened glare she'd seen earlier was now replaced with a look of sadness.

"Oh Fran, I never knew. I'm so, so, sorry sweetheart."

"Use my real name, and I don't want your pity Gilly, I've lived with people's pity for most of my life and I'm done with it. Now just do what you came to do and put me out of my misery once and for all."

Shauna closed her eyes and braced herself for the inevitable bullet but was stunned when all she felt were Gilly's strong arms around her.

"Shauna I could never harm a hair on your precious head, with or without a heart wrenching story like you've just shared with me."

He held her as the tears started to fall and was still holding her when her body began to jerk with wracking sobs. He knew it was impossible but he never wanted to let go of her again and when she finally calmed herself he spoke softly.

"So where are you going to go?"

Shauna couldn't answer at first, she was amazed that

315

he was sparing her life and was almost speechless but somehow she at last managed a whisper.

"I have a friend, my only friend in the world actually and I know she will help me."

"Shauna you have two friends and this one will help you all he can but there's something we must do first."

Gilly explained about Davey wanting her to visit and he could visibly see her start to shake.

"It's not what you think, he can't hurt you in there. I'm supposed to tell you that if you go along then no harm will come to you."

"But?"

"But after he's seen you I'm supposed to kill you once we get away from the place."

"Kill me......!!!!"

"Sweetheart, people like Davey and Billy Jackson are animals and just like a wounded animal they are unpredictable when hurt and you certainly hurt the boss in the most spectacular way."

"And what about how he hurt me?"

Shauna began to cry again and Gilly wanted to hold her but he knew time was running out and they needed to get this over with as soon as possible.

"I know what you're saying sweetheart but men like them have no respect for life, no real feelings and they will cut anyone down without a second thought, surely you realised that?"

"And what about you Gilly? How do I know if I can trust you, how do I know that you're not just like those other two animals?"

He shook his head from side to side and his expression was one of hurt.

"How can you even ask that? I could have killed you as soon as you opened the door."

"I'm sorry Gilly, it's just that the idea of seeing him scares me to death."

"I know it does but after what he did to you, don't you think its poetic justice that he finally gets to know the reason why you shopped him?"

Shauna answered but she wasn't convincing anyone, least of all herself.

"I suppose so, though whether I will get any comfort from that remains to be seen."

Shauna wasn't sure, wasn't sure of anything anymore but if visiting Davey Wiseman would somehow save her life then she had no alternative but to reluctantly go along with it.

Having sworn never to set foot in the place again, Gilly once more found himself in the waiting room of Wormwood Scrubs, only this time he wasn't alone. Shauna was petrified of the place, not only was it imposing but it stank and it was in no way what she had imagined. By the time they were ushered into the visiting area, her complexion had grown very pale. Gilly felt somewhat relieved, he'd thought they would be led into a private room but was glad that for whatever reason he was wrong. He fetched teas and chocolate bars like before, and then joined Shauna at the small table. A few minutes later Davey walked towards them and for a second he did a double take. Fran's hair was now as dark as the night and she looked totally different, different but at the same time strangely familiar. He eased into the chair but didn't speak, instead he stared directly into her eyes.

His piercing glare scared her and forced Shauna to look away. Sitting in this filthy place only feet away from the man she had agreed to marry, the man who had taken her virginity, the man she would send to prison for a very long time, made her feel like a traitor. Suddenly Vonny's face appeared and from somewhere she gathered enough strength to speak. "Hello Davey."

"Fran, I didn't think you'd come."

"Davey, my names isn't Fran, its Shauna, Shauna O'Malley, do you remember me? As for me being here, I didn't have a lot of choice in the matter did I?" The colour immediately drained from Davey Wiseman as the realisation sunk in of who she really was. Suddenly the years fell away and he could picture that dirty squalid little flat, see Violet and the kids and remembered just what he had done to them. As quickly as the image had appeared it somehow disappeared and he raised his eyebrows.

"It's taken a long time for you to get your revenge!"

"I wouldn't have cared if it had taken the rest of my life. Davey when you murdered my Mum, you inadvertently killed my baby sister too."

"I didn't murder anyone."

"Oh you weren't there Davey but you're to blame, as surely as if you'd plunged that needle into her arm yourself. Since that day I've only existed, all I could think of for the last twenty years was making you pay and I've done that now. Just as you took Vonny's life I've taken yours, or what's left of it."

Davey's eyes began to mist over and for once he didn't hold back, didn't care who saw.

"I loved you, wanted to spend the rest of my life with

318

you. God I would have given you anything you wanted in the whole world."

Hearing his words didn't soften Shauna, they only made her angry, so angry that she almost spat out her next sentence as she gazed into his drawn and saddened face.

"Davey, you took away the only thing I ever loved and no amount of money could ever bring her back. Now I've done as you asked and come here but I don't think there is anything more left to talk about do you?"

The eyes that had once made her fall for him were now ice cold and fixed.

"Did you think this would be it, you did didn't you? I knew you were naive but to actually think I would let you walk away from me."

Davey let out a loud haunting cackle of a laugh and Shauna suddenly felt frightened.

"But you said, I mean Gilly said, that if I came to see you then you wouldn't hurt me!"

"Oh look Gill, the little girl's scared now! You played with the big boys Miss O'Malley and now you have to pay the price I'm afraid. All those years ago when you were a snotty nosed kid who pissed the bed, do you remember when I knocked you're head off in the bathroom?"

Shauna sat in stunned silence. He remembered, remembered every rotten cruel thing he had put them through but still he wasn't the least bit sorry for any of it.

"Shocked I can recall all that? Well I can and even back then people had to pay, just like your dirty bitch of a mother did and after all these years I still make

319

them. Only this time the price is much higher. When I do eventually get out of this shit hole and believe me I will, if I've been seen to be soft on you I wouldn't have a reputation to go back to. Oh yes, I definitely have to make an example of you sweetheart."

He brushed the back of her hand with his and she flinched and recoiled. Not wanting to hear anymore, Shauna stood up and stepped away from the table. She couldn't stand to breathe the same air as him and turning she ran from the visiting room. The need to get as far away from Davey Wiseman as she could became overwhelming. Once outside Shauna stopped to take stock of what had just happened and then a strange calmness came over her. With only the glint of a smile she continued to walk with her head held high as she made her way to the main gates. Back in the visiting room the two men sat silent and stony faced but underneath Gilly felt so proud. He admired her, admired her front and the guts it must have taken for her to come here.

"So now Boss you know."

"You know something Gill? Not in a million years would I ever have guessed who she was."

"Does it change anything?"

"Like fuck it does! Let me know as soon as it's done."

Now glad that the visit was at last over, Gilly stood up and pushed his chair neatly under the table.

"I'd best be off, don't want to lose track of her."

Davey nodded and without a goodbye, got up and walked back to the steel door that separated the visitors from the rest of the inmates.

320

Outside in the fresh air Gilly looked around and for a moment the idea crossed his mind that she'd gone but a second later he saw her. Walking towards the car he smiled but didn't say anything. Shauna tried to smile back but it was hard, she was still uncertain as to her fate and whether Gilly would keep his word. Liverpool Street station seemed cold and noisy as they stood together on the platform. Shauna's train wasn't due for a while but Gilly had thought it best to come straight here, the old cliché of safety in numbers being at the front of his mind. He had indeed been right to think that way as the door to Shauna's old flat had been smashed down within ten minutes of their leaving the prison. The two men, who stood over six feet tall and appeared nearly as wide, really weren't the type to be softened by a sob story. Luckily Gilly's first port of call that morning had been to Fran's flat and on finding the St Bartholomew's card, had slipped it into his pocket. Gilly quickly checked for any more clues to her possible whereabouts just in case any unwelcome guests decided to make a visit. The stations loud hailer burst into life, stating it was the last call for the one fifteen to Bournemouth. As Shauna stepped aboard, Gilly handed over her bag and stood in front of the open door.

"Will I ever see you again?"

"Gilly it wouldn't be safe, but I'll never forget you or ever be able to repay you."

Leaning out of the door, she stooped to kiss him, not a peck on the check but a full blooded kiss on the lips. Gilly's heart was breaking but he manly stepped back and breathed in deeply.

"No payment necessary."

As the carriage slowly pulled out of the station, Shauna waved from the window until Gilly disappeared from sight. Leaning back in her seat she sighed, she was going home, it was finally over.

CHAPTER THIRTY

The train compartment was clean and relatively empty and although the journey would only last for two hours, it was two hours too long as far as Shauna was concerned. Once out of London the train sped past trees and green fields and everything seemed so fresh and new. Somehow it felt that with every mile she travelled, her old life was diminishing and a new one was beginning to emerge, only this time things weren't tainted. The need to feel clean, to smell clean air became so overpowering that Shauna pulled open the small window situated above her head and breathed in deeply. Like a dream this was another world, far, far away from the dirty streets and smog that she had lived with for too long now. Walking from the station, she inhaled a large breath of sea air and almost immediately the tears began to fall. The smells and noise brought back all the happy memories of Jacks and their times here, memories she'd had to suppress while she'd carried out her vengeance for Vonny.

To her utter joy, Bournemouth hadn't changed a bit and Shauna was eager to see her old friend. The last few years had been a nightmare but finally it was over and all she wanted was to be left alone in peace. The train had arrived on time and after a few minutes wait at the taxi rank, she was at last on her way home. Everything seemed so perfect compared to Soho and all the other seedy areas she had come to know and hate. The winding road that led to home resembled something from a chocolate box, the flowers were in full bloom and the sky cloudless. Today was special to Shauna, it was the first day of her new life and she wanted to embrace it. The cab driver, on her instruction, stopped a short distance from the cottage and after paying her fare, she slowly started to walk. The last few yards made her feel as if she were going back in time, back to when the only thing that mattered in life was worrying if the sun would shine. Much to her relief the tiny house hadn't altered. The walls were whitewashed and the windows and door still had the same green peeling paint. Standing in front of the rickety garden gate, Shauna was glad the owners hadn't changed anything. A woman wearing a large floppy hat was kneeling in the front garden, swearing and cursing as she pulled at the mound of weeds that had accumulated throughout the summer. The sight of her and the language she used made Shauna giggle.

"Tut, tut and from a lady as well!"

The woman glanced up, and using the back of her hand to blot out the bright sun light, she squinted at her visitor.

"Shauna, Oh my god Shauna is it you? I'm so pleased to see you darling!"

"Yep! Here I am, home at last and it feels great."

As Jackie Silver attempted to stand up, Shauna noticed what a struggle it was for her, noticed the many lines that were etched upon her face. Two years ago Jackie's skin had been smooth, almost ageless and it cut like a knife to see how much the woman had aged in a relatively short space of time. What an earth had happened?

"Jacks we were so lucky to get the cottage at short notice."

"Not really love, I agreed a sale on my flat three weeks ago. There was plenty of equity in it so by the time you phoned I had already rented this place on a long term lease. When you suggested meeting here, I didn't have the heart to tell you I was already coming with or without you. I didn't know if you would ever come back and my health isn't so good nowadays. I thought the sea air might help."

"And does it?"

"A little I suppose but not half as much as seeing your beautiful face again. Come let's get you inside and we can have a nice cup of tea."

Jackie had to lean heavily on Shauna's arm as they made their way into the cottage. With the tea brewed, Jackie couldn't take her eyes off of the beautiful young girl sitting opposite. Her hair had now returned to its raven black, which made her think back to their first meeting at Sunrise. That day now seemed just a distant memory and she thought how Shauna resembled someone much older than her thirty years but after what the young woman had been through was it any wonder? The afternoon was spent reminiscing about all the happy times they had shared in the past and both women were unable to truly believe they were back together again. Jackie explained to Shauna about how she was recently forced, emotionally at least, into giving up her job. She also described the total loss she'd felt when her darling girl had left.

"To be honest love, I think I suffered a mini breakdown."

"I'm so sorry Jacks, why didn't you tell me when you came to London?"

"It was after that and on the odd occasions you called me, well I thought you had enough on your plate without having to worry about me."

Shauna hung her head in shame, she felt dreadful, after everything the woman had done for her and she wasn't around when Jackie needed her.

"It's all my fault."

Jackie grabbed Shauna's arm, her tone was firm but gentle as she spoke.

"Now you listen to me Shauna O'Malley, nothing is your fault. You didn't ask to be born or to suffer the life you were given and you definitely didn't ask for me to love you, that was my choice. As far as my health goes, that would probably have deteriorated no matter how I had lived."

Jackie picked up the tea pot to pour another cup but it was empty.

"I'll put the kettle on and make us a fresh brew, while I'm doing that you can tell me about everything that happened after I left you in London."

Shauna wasn't sure she wanted to relive all that pain so soon but she owed her friend big time and if Jackie wanted to know, then she had to explain. By the time they had finished their second pot of tea, Shauna had relayed and relived every moment of the last two years. She told of her love for Davey, the proposal, the deal and Neil Maddock. Her last recall was Gilly seeing her off at the station this morning and how she now felt totally drained.

"And that Jacks is the end!"

"Shauna I'm sorry for all you've gone through but

you are home now and that's all that matters."

"You don't know what it means to me to hear those words, to hear you say I'm home."

"Oh you are so wrong love. I've waited years to have you to myself, even when we were at Sunrise you were never totally with me. It was as if you were always somewhere else, somewhere that I couldn't reach you but now at last you are free."

That night and many more over the next three months saw Shauna sleep like a baby. She soon settled into life at the seaside and the past events of her life in London began to fade. When Jackie heard Shauna being sick in the bathroom four mornings in a row she prayed that she was wrong but sure enough a test at the end of the week proved Jackie's worst fear was correct.

"So now what are you going to do?"

"Do? What can I do?"

"Oh Shauna love! Why on earth weren't you more careful?"

Shauna began to cry but they were not tears of sadness and for the life of her Jackie couldn't work out why the young woman was so happy.

"I know what you're thinking Jacks but don't you see this was meant to be. It doesn't matter that Davey is the father, all that matters is that I have someone of my own, someone no one can take away. It almost feels like Vonny is coming back to me if that makes any sense?"

It didn't but Jackie knew better than to comment, all she could do was support her girl and see where it all ended, hopefully it would be a happy outcome for a change. The women spent their days in the garden or catching up on old times and the sea air really was a boost to them both.

With Shauna gone, Gilly had returned to Davey's apartment and taken the money and in all honesty he could have lived like a King for several years if he'd wanted but knowing he had taken it under false pretences played heavily on his mind. Most of the cash had gone untouched as Gilly felt he had betrayed his old boss. The money had been payment for taking Shauna's life and it was something he hadn't been able to do, so as far as he was concerned it was stolen and added to the fact that sooner or later he would be forced to suffer Davey's revenge as well, made it even more tainted. With Billy and Davey now incarcerated and Shauna safely out of harm's way, Gilly caught a plane to the Costa del Sol. For six months he tried desperately to mix in with the locals and holiday makers but was never quite able to reach his goal. Shauna was constantly on his mind and he couldn't stop worrying about her. After leaving the country, Gilly had contacted Janice and left his mobile number. Days soon turned into weeks and he often let the battery go flat but something would always pop up to remind him of the past. Thinking it would take at least a year for the case to come to court, he was stunned when he received a call. Lounging by the pool of his apartment block, he jumped when the phone rang and without checking who was calling he hesitantly answered, scared of whom he would hear on the other end.
"Gilly?"

"Who wants to know?"

"It's Janice you tosser, who the fuck did you think it was?"

"Sorry love, I get a bit edgy these days. Any news?"

The trial starts next week, are you coming back for it?"

"Next week! Fuck me that's quick, I thought it would be months away."

He heard her sigh as she waited for a reply.

"Well?"

"Yeah, yeah of course I am. You just took me by surprise that's all."

"Not as much as a surprise as it was for Davey I bet, anyway I had best go as this call must be costing a fuckin' fortune."

With that she hung up, leaving Gilly with the phone still glued to his ear. He didn't feel happy to speak to his old Mukka, in fact he wished she hadn't bothered. Returning swiftly to his apartment, Gilly began to pack a case as thoughts of seeing Davey again raced through his mind.

Back in England, Davey Wiseman paced up and down in his cell at The Scrubs. After a visit from Tony Smart, he was still reeling from news that the case had been brought forward and the prospect of being sentenced and losing the privileges of being on remand added to his misery. Prison Officers had been instructed to stay out of his way until after the first hearing, all obliged knowing that their charge could be as vicious and unpredictable as the notorious Billy Jackson.

Since the arrests, Davey, if left alone, had proved to be almost a model prisoner but this wasn't the case just a few miles down the road. The news had seen most of the wing staff at Belmarsh Prison dancing on the landings. The thought of Billy being sentenced and hopefully moved, was music to their ears. Unlike his friend, he hadn't been upset at the news as Billy Jackson's mental state had deteriorated over the past few months and he now lived in a fantasy world for most of the time. Hearing he was to be reunited with Davey he was ecstatic and on the morning of the trial both men were given an early wakeup call and released from their cells at six am. Dressed in new suits brought in by their solicitors, they were driven into the city. Luckily they weren't able to see the outside world as they approached the Old Bailey and once inside they were led straight down to the holding cells. The small rooms faced each other with only metal bars as a means of restraint. Davey Wiseman sat at the small wooden table staring into space as he waited for his brief and for a few moments he was lost in thought at what the future would maybe hold. When he finally raised his head, the vision across the hallway made him want to throw up. From somewhere Billy Jackson has obtained a tube of bright red lipstick and as he smiled his pursed lips resembled the mouths of the numerous brasses Davey had encountered over the course of his seedy life. The old familiar greeting made him slowly shake his head.

"Hi Davey boy, how's it hanging?"

Davey didn't answer, he couldn't as the sight made his stomach churn. Billy leaned seductively up against the bars and slowly licked his upper lip as he blew kisses in the direction of his old friend but no matter what he did he still couldn't get a response. When the Court Warden eventually saw and heard his antics, the cell door was quickly opened and Billy Jackson found himself moved hastily down the hallway and out of his accomplice's sight. Davey felt grateful at not having to look at the appalling spectacle but until the trial ended, he would be continually forced to listen to the ranting of a lunatic. The two then had a thirty minute meeting with their barristers and were informed that they didn't have a cat in hells chance of getting off with the charge. Davey's brief whispered a message that Loftwood had said he was sorry he wasn't able to help this time. For years this top filth, his ace card, had kept him out of prison but when Davey needed help the most, he had been hung out to dry. Wiseman and Jackson were tried together and both men sat side by side in the dock. Billy kept patting his friend on the shoulder and desperately tried to strike up a conversation but all his attempts at friendliness were ignored. Davey scanned the court room and stopped when he reached the public gallery. The first face he noticed was Frieda, still every inch a whore but Davey knew she wasn't here to gloat. Janice came into view next, good old reliable Jan and for a second Davey could hear her raunchy laughter that had cheered him up so many times over the years. Along with his employees sat a few old faces that Davey knew had come to gloat, and would undoubtedly cheer when he was sent down but it didn't bother him in the least. Lastly and just before the Judge entered, Davey spied Gilly

Slade. Slipping in late and sitting on the back row, Gilly had hoped not to be noticed but he was out of luck. As Davey's eyes met his, Gilly could feel himself begin to shake and the slight smile covering his old boss's lips did little to help.

Privately and before the case started, Judge Michael Smeeth had been informed that both men were serious players and an example had to be made. Even before he had placed the wig onto his head, he had known in his gut what the verdict would be and had mentally already sentenced them. The first day held nothing but setbacks after the usher informed the court he had reason to believe that certain members of the jury had been bribed. The selected twelve men and women were duly asked to leave and a new jury sworn in, one that Davey hadn't been able to get at. Davey, now aware that the slightest hope of a reduction in sentence had just flown out the proverbial window, sat back and closed his eyes. He tried his hardest to relax but feelings of sheer rage ran through his veins. Sitting beside him, Billy still kept trying to talk even though he'd been threatened with contempt several times. Finally when he could stand it no longer, Davey suddenly turned and glared directly into Billy Jacksons face.

"If you don't shut the fuck up and shut up now, I'll be up for murder let alone drug dealing, alright?"

His friends voice was music to Billy's ears, he'd waited months to hear it

"I knew you couldn't ignore me forever. I've missed you so much Davey, I wrote to you every day but they must have held back my letters."

Davey shook his head.

"No I got every fuckin' purvey one!"

"You did?"

"Yeah and they went straight into the fuckin' bin unread. I hope they fuckin' throw away the key as far as you're concerned, I can't bear to fuckin' look at you, you cunt!"

For once Billy Jackson was speechless, tears streamed down his cheeks much to the amusement of the guards and most of the faces in the gallery. Over the course of the following ten days, several key witnesses had been brought before the court. Neil Maddock had revelled in his own personal appearance, knowing that the tabloids and associated media would be all over the shop once sentencing had been passed. His smart new suit and shirt had cost a small fortune but he had figured it was worth the cost for his five minutes of fame.

As agreed, Shauna's name had been kept out of the procedures. Detective Maddock stated that he'd received an anonymous tip off from a disgruntled ex-employee, who had been only too happy to spill the beans on the deal. For some reason, only explainable by Davey, his barrister didn't argue with the explanation, Shauna's name wasn't even mentioned. After giving his evidence, Maddock began to think he'd gotten off lightly but as he stepped from the witness box shouts of 'filth' came from the gallery above. Order was called for but it took several minutes for the proceedings to resume.

Throughout the trial Judge Smeeth had trouble concentrating. Whenever he looked at the defendants and saw Billy's bright red lipstick it took all of his

333

resolve not to laugh. He wasn't sure if the man was indeed insane as he'd been told, or if he was just trying to appear that way in order to receive a lighter sentence. Either way it made no difference, Billy Jackson had been deemed fit to stand trial and that was exactly what would happen so Michael Smeeth didn't care if the man came to court in a sparkling evening gown and stilettos, the case would still be heard. For Davey the rest of the trial passed by in a blur and he had to be nudged by a warden when told to stand for sentencing. As the foreman read out guilty on all of the counts for both men, Davey's shoulders visibly sagged. The Judge wasted no time with the two, as far as he was concerned they were both scum and not worth making him late for his planned game of golf.

"David Abe Wiseman and William Gerard Jackson, you stand before this court on the charge of attempting to supply class A drugs on a national scale. A jury of good standing has found you guilty as charged and I have no alternative but to sentence you both to fifteen years imprisonment. Furthermore I wish for it to be added to the court papers that I suggest you are both made to serve out your entire sentences without the opportunity of parole."

Immediately the court turned into a circus as the sound of uproar echoed around the room. Friends and associates screamed that this country was unjust and enemies, many of whom had suffered at the hands of one or both men, were wildly cheering. Billy let out a high pitched, almost Hyena sounding laugh that continued down into the holding cells and didn't subside until he was finally placed into the prison escort van. Davey was led from the dock with his head hung low, his world had collapsed and he looked at no one. Informed that transport wouldn't be available for over an hour, he was escorted into the lower cells to find an uninvited guest.

"Hello Davey. I'm terribly sorry to hear the verdict." Davey Wiseman's eyes opened wide, barging past the man he stormed over to the table and placing both hands palm down he inhaled deeply as he slowly spoke.

"Jimmy you're a cunt and now you've got the nerve to stand there offering your fuckin' condolences?"

"I had no choice, they had me by the short and curlie's. I've even lost my pension you know."

"Fuckin' pension! You bastard! If I have my way, you'll be dead long before you reach that age now fuck off out of here before I break your bastard scull!"

James Loftwood immediately left, he didn't wish his old acquaintance well or even look back. Having felt duty bound to pay the visit, he was now glad it was thankfully over. James knew his life was a mess at the moment but he hoped one way or the other he could bounce back, unlike Davey Wiseman. Gilly stayed behind in the court until everyone else had left or at least that was what he thought but when he eventually walked from the room Tony Smart approached him.

"Peter Slade?"

Gilly spun around on his heels expecting to see a gun pointed in his face and his brow furrowed as he tried to place the man standing in front of him.

"Tony, Tony Smart? I am Mr Wiseman's solicitor."

"I know who you are but what the fuck do you want with me?"

"I'm sorry Mr Slade but I have been asked to pass on a message and as you very well know, you do not say no to Davey."

"So what's the message then?"

"I haven't got any idea what it means and I am ...."

"For fucks sake just spit the bastard out will you?"

"Here goes then and these are Mr Wiseman's words not mine, "I've upped the ante on Shauna to two hundred thou, once she's been taken care of you are next."

Gilly didn't wait to hear more and ran from the court room in a blind panic. Back at the hotel, he threw his clothes into the suitcase and was about the check out when suddenly a thought hit him and he stopped dead in his tracks. Rapidly pacing the floor he tried to think of what to do, there was no way he could run when she was totally oblivious as to what the future held for her. Whatever happened he had to find Shauna quickly and warn her that the danger had just increased beyond belief. The only problem was, he didn't have the foggiest idea of where she could be.

CHAPTER THIRTY-ONE

As part of her exercise plan, it was a morning ritual for Shauna to walk to the local newsagents and collect the daily paper for Jackie. Mid morning when the older woman sat down with a cuppa to have a read Shauna would start to trawl the internet on Jackie's Laptop scouring the pages looking for news, any kind of news on Davey and the case. On the 6th of January the two women had as usual finished their chores and taken up their comfy seats in the lounge to begin the search. After such a long time with no news, Jackie had started to naively believe it had already been dealt with and they could just get on with life and Shauna didn't have the heart to burst her friends bubble. Shauna clicked on the news page of the Telegraph and as she read she chatted away about nothing in particular but soon stopped mid sentence.

'FIFTEEN YEARS FOR NOTORIOUS LONDON DRUG DUO'

Shauna instantly felt the hairs on the back of her neck stand to attention. Neil Maddock had told her they would both get long sentences but fifteen years! She suddenly felt more scared than ever before. At the abrupt halt in conversation, Jackie glanced up from her newspaper with her glasses perched on the end of her nose.

"What's the matter love?"

Shauna slowly shook her head, she couldn't speak and holding her belly as she stroked the child inside she leant over and passed the Laptop to her friend. Concentrating deeply, Jackie bit down on her bottom lip as she read.

"My! Fifteen years, well at least it's done now."
Shauna's head began to spin as her stomach turned
over.

"I'm sorry Jacks but I need to be on my own. I think
I'll go to my room and have a lie down if you don't
mind."

Curled up on her bed she began to sob. Over the past
few weeks and with still no news she had tried to kid
herself that it hadn't really happened but it had and
now it was back and her life was once more falling
apart.

"Shauna?"

No sound emerged from her room, she loved Jackie
with all her heart but at this moment she wanted and
needed to be left alone. Slowly the door opened and
Jackie's head appeared from behind.

"Please Jackie I just can't....."

"I know you want to be on your own love but there's
something else here I think you should see."

She handed over the newspaper and pointed to the
personal add section.

"I carried on reading when you came up here and I
wouldn't have taken any notice if it wasn't for the
unusual name, the same one your friend has."

Shauna hurriedly looked up and down the columns
and immediately stopped when she saw his
advertisement.

DESPERATELY TRYING TO FIND Shauna O
CALL GILLY ON   0768........9

Shauna didn't speak but nervously tapped her closed
lips with her index finger as she read the advert
several more times.

"What are you going to do love?"

Shauna looked up into her friend's face and again noticed all the lines of worry, worry that she and she alone had caused and then Shauna saw something new, panic, sheer and utter panic.

"I have to contact him Jacks, I really do because I just know he would never try to contact me unless it was absolutely necessary."

Lifting herself from the bed, Shauna took her coat from the wardrobe and started to leave the room, turning back she smiled at her one true friend.

"Don't look so worried, I'm coming back. It's just that I need to be alone so I'm going to go into the garden."

Standing up, she now had a real waddle as she walked. Her back was constantly aching but at the same time it was comforting knowing that the discomfort was all down to the tiny life that she had made, a beautiful little person that she couldn't wait to meet.

Gilly Slade was asleep in his room and cuddling a half bottle of scotch when his silver state of the art, all singing all dancing mobile began to blare out Bob Marley's 'No woman no cry'. Call it old school but Gilly loved reggae and it always brought a smile to his face when his phone rang.

"Yeah?"

"Gilly it's me."

He should have checked the number but as he jumped from the bed, a searing pain shot through his skull and he was suddenly aware he was going to have the mother of all hangovers in the morning. Groaning, he pushed hard on his closed eyelids, trying to relieve the pressure as he spoke.

"Thank God! Shauna listen, you have to get away, disappear in fact. You are now in more bloody danger than you could possibly imagine."

"Gilly calm down, it's all over now or haven't you seen the news?"

"For fucks sake, of course I've seen it! I was at the trial and when the verdict was read out Davey's expression said it all. He had people looking for you when he got arrested but now there's a price on you head and it's a big one. There are certain people who weren't interested before but for two hundred big ones will make it their business to find you."

"Two hundred thousand?"

"Oh yes sweetheart. You upset a lot of people and none more so than Davey. He never lets go and he will track you down if it takes forever. Now listen to me Shauna, I'm leaving the country tomorrow and I can have a fake passport and ticket waiting for you at Heathrow if you want me to. My flight is from the south terminal at two o'clock. Please Shauna, if you value your life you will be there."

Gilly hung up, it was now up to her to make the decision and he just prayed it would be the right one. Shauna slowly walked back into the cottage in a daze, she felt as if she was being pulled in two. On one hand was the knowledge that to leave would break Jackie's heart and she had already done that too many times in the past but on the other she knew that to stay, would seal her fate and possibly place her friend's life in danger too, not to mention there was also her baby to think of. Walking up to the path, she stopped at the back door for a moment to compose herself. Stepping inside Shauna saw Jackie sitting by the fire and knew there was no way she could tell her friend the truth, it would only end up with Jackie begging her to stay and she wouldn't give in until Shauna had agreed. Making light of the situation had to be the best way to handle things, at least for the moment.

"I'm back!"

"Thank god, I've been so worried, how did it go?"

"Fine, completely fine. Do you know sometimes I could kill that Gilly Slade, he was missing me pure and simple, that's all it was."

Jackie's face was illuminated by the glow of the fire and Shauna thought she maybe saw the slightest hint of a smile but she wasn't entirely convinced that her friend believed her.

"Thank the Lord for that, I was so worried. Shall I make us both a nice cup of cocoa?"

"That would be lovely Jacks, really lovely. Then I think I'll have an early night I'm absolutely exhausted."

Half an hour later Shauna slowly climbed the stairs but instead of getting into bed she quietly packed her bag and slipped it inside the wardrobe. Her sleep was peppered with bad dreams and it was just after three before she finally dropped off. The following morning she woke to the sound of birds singing and smiled to herself, the bad news of last night didn't register straight away. Hearing Jackie pottering about downstairs brought it back to the fore that once again she was being forced to leave. After showering and getting dressed, she made her way down stairs to the small dining room which had already been laid for breakfast and just as she sat down, Jackie emerged from the kitchen.

"There's fresh tea and toast all ready. I should be back by early afternoon."

"Early afternoon? Where on earth are you going?"

"It's a hospital appointment for my arthritis. I would cancel but it took months to get, you don't mind do you?"

"Not at all, I'm going to have a lazy day and when you come home I want to hear all about it and you never know, you might meet a hunky young doctor!"

"I doubt that at my age and even if I did, the mind's willing but I'm afraid the body's too knackered."

The two women giggled like schoolgirls and after Shauna helped her friend to put her coat on, she hugged her closely.

"What's that for?"

"No reason, I just love you very much that's all."

The cab arrived to collect Jackie but even before it had driven off Shauna was making a call to another taxi firm. She had a thirty minute wait and after finding a pad and pen, began to write a letter. Of all the goodbye notes she'd written in her life, this one really broke her heart but Shauna didn't know what else to do. Just to disappear without explanation would leave her friend, her best friend, worrying and in a state of panic for the rest of her life and after all they'd been through, it was something she wasn't prepared to do.

My Darling Jacks

By the time you read this note, I will be long gone. I wanted more than anything for us to be together especially with the baby due soon but yet again fate has dealt me a bad hand and it just wasn't meant to be. I'm sorry that I lied to you last night but I needed to hold off hurting you for as long as possible and anyway, I know you would have only begged me to stay. Gilly told me I'm in grave danger and I have to get away. I can't put you or my child at risk, you both mean too much to me. The man I hate and love, yes Jacks love, can you comprehend that I could still love him after all he did to me? He has people looking for me and they won't stop until they find me. I know there's no point in crying over spilt milk but I wish with all my heart that I could turn the clock back. I foolishly thought that once everything was over I would be able to get on with my life but I realise now that I'm tied to Davey Wiseman one way or another for the rest of my life. I won't be able to see you or contact you ever again Jacks but I hope you remember me with love and enjoy the happy memories of all the good times we spent together. Try not to worry, you know I will be alright and somewhere out there, I don't know exactly where yet, I shall always be thinking of you.

Love you forever

Your Shauna xxxx

Leaving the hire car exactly where he'd been instructed, Gilly locked the doors and placed the keys into the secure box on the wall. The thought crossed his mind that he would probably never drive a car in his home country again and inwardly he smiled. The thought didn't bother him in the least, there were far too many other things to think about. Gilly had arrived at the airport with plenty of time to spare and after unloading his luggage and checking in, decided to take a walk around the small selection of shops. Every airport seemed to be the same with tiny places selling books, coffee and suntan lotions but on seeing a florist he stopped. It brought back memories of all the times he had called in at Jake's to purchase flowers for her. Selecting a large bunch of red roses, Gilly thought to himself that this time it was different, this time they were from him and not from Davey. The beautiful blooms were a dark shade of crimson and he hoped she would recognise the love with which they had been bought. Finding a seat in the airport bar, he placed the flowers on the table, ordered a drink and eagerly waited for her to arrive. Over the next hour many people passed by, people from all walks of life, all countries, colours and creeds. Families desperately trying to control over excited children, honeymooners who oblivious to anyone else only had eyes for each other. Gilly watched them all and he noticed something that he hadn't seen in a long time, most of the people were smiling. His life for the last few years hadn't called for a happy face but now he could look to the future and he felt his mouth begin to crease up at the corners. As one thirty came and went and the tannoy announced the last call to Florida, he knew she wasn't coming. Throwing the bouquet into the nearest bin and with his smile now gone, Gilly Slade slowly walked through to departures and boarded his plane. He had to find a new life but it wouldn't be the fairy tale he had hoped for, how could it be without her?

CHAPTER THIRTY-TWO

The knock at the front door was loud enough to wake the dead. Shauna picked up her case and after slowly looking around for one last time, she walked from the cottage. The cabbie had already taken up his position behind the wheel so after placing her bag onto the cars back seat she climbing inside, clicked the seat belt into position and sighed deeply. The taxi pulled away sharply and at speed but it didn't faze Shauna, she had too much on her mind. As they passed the open fields her sadness felt like a huge black cloud that slowly began to wrap itself around her. She couldn't believe that after everything she'd gone through and all the effort she'd put in, that fate would be so cruel. There wasn't a happy ever after, he'd beaten her once again and now she was being forced to walk away from the only person in the world who had ever really loved her.

Several minutes later something occurred to her, the driver hadn't spoken to her or asked where she wanted to go to. Straining to look into the mirror, Shauna's eyes met his. He was vaguely familiar and she racked her brains trying to remember where she knew him from, in a nanosecond it came to her.

"Shit! I know who you are, stop this car and let me out or I'll........."

Barry McCann had heard it all before. He had worked for Davey on and off for years but he wasn't choosey in the slightest, as long as he received payment he would work for anyone.

"Or you'll what sweetheart?"

The so called cabbie began to laugh in a mocking way and Shauna was now far more scared than she'd ever been in her life. The car suddenly began to speed up and even though she had a seatbelt on Shauna was still thrown sideways across the back seat. With tears streaming down her face she screamed out that she was pregnant but her revelation fell on deaf ears. The journey seemed to take an eternity but she realised it as just her fear taking over making it feel like forever. As quickly as it had begun, the drive came to a screeching halt. Trying to open the door in an attempt to escape she was out of luck when the handle wouldn't budge. Barry McCann slowly climbed out of the driver's seat and walked around the vehicle. When he opened the rear door Shauna gasped at the size of the Man. Barry stood over six feet tall and must have weighed in at twenty plus stone so she didn't stand a chance. Dragging her out he proceeded to frog march her towards a dimly lit farmhouse. There was no sign of life only a deathly silence and she knew that wherever this place was, it was totally remote. Eventually after a struggle Barry managed to unlock the front door and he forcefully shoved her inside. The first thing Shauna experienced was the musty sickening smell of damp. The place hadn't been inhabited for years and she slowly shook her head in realisation that this was where her life would end, a dirty derelict building that no one had visited in years.

"I know you don't give a fuck about me but what about my baby?"

"Makes no difference to me sunshine, it's not my kid. I've been given a job to do so as far as I'm concerned its end of story and in any case, I never concern myself with people's feelings."

Barry marched Shauna along the hall and then roughly grabbed a handful of her hair. Pulling her head back made her instantly stop in front of the entrance to a basement. The wood creaked loudly as the door opened and after he'd flicked on the light switch he pushed her forward. Shauna stumbled down the rickety staircase and reaching the bottom she came face to face with a makeshift campsite. A bed, table and a single chair had been placed in the centre of the room. There was no window and just a bare bulb shone down to illuminate the space.

"So what now?"

"Now, you just sit and wait. It might be months or it could turn out to be years you'll just have to be patient. Mr Wiseman wants you kept captive until he's released."

"But I will be giving birth in the next few weeks!"

Barry shrugged his shoulders as if to say 'So what'. Walking confidently back towards the stairs he turned and grinned revealing a mouthful of rotting yellow teeth.

"Now you can scream all you want little lady but we are miles from anywhere so no one will hear you. I shall call in twice a week to make sure you have food and water and if things go wrong and your time should turn into years, preparations have been made for my replacement. Mr Wiseman has given strict instructions and he's also been very generous so there is no way you will be able to talk me or any successor into letting you go. Bye for now!"

With that Barry McCann spun around and strode back

up the stairs and Shauna heard the key turn in the lock and then three or four bolts as they were drawn across the door.

Meanwhile back in Bournemouth, Jackie opened the front door and called out to Shauna as she walked in. The appointment had taken far longer than she'd thought it would but on the plus side there had been several hunky doctors and she couldn't wait to describe them to her younger friend. The normal sound of the radio blaring out was absent, in fact the house was as silent as a graveyard. The lack of a response from Shauna would normally have seen her call out again but not this time. Her stomach started to churn as she walked from room to room. Reaching the living room, she saw the crisp white envelope propped up on the mantelpiece and instinctively knew that history was once again repeating itself. Jackie didn't open the letter, she didn't need to. Instead she sat down and sobbed until she thought her very heart would break. The life together that they had both dreamed of wasn't to be and she realised she was a fool to ever think it would happen. For a fleeting moment Jackie wished she had never set eyes on Shauna O'Malley all those years ago but then when she thought of her beautiful girl and all that Shauna had gone through she felt guilty.

The remainder of Jackie Silvers life would be spent at the cottage and every day she waited and prayed for her girl to return. She waited until the day she died but her prayers were never to be answered. Her body was found a year later by bailiffs who had come for non-payment of rent. The coroner stated at the inquest that she must have been dead for over a month. There was no family to inform and the girl in the photograph, which was clutched in Jackie's hand, was never identified.

Unlike his friend, Billy Jackson had not been able to handle the amount of time given to him. Most thought he would cope easily, even enjoy the sentence to a degree because of his full on homosexuality but they were wrong. At every given opportunity he picked fights with inmates and screws alike and finally when the system couldn't handle him any longer, he was ghosted in the middle of the night to Broadmoor and detained as criminally insane. His days were now spent with raving lunatics, whose antics shocked even Billy. The only solace he found was in the form of writing to his friend and every evening Billy would put pen to paper to described his day and ask how things were for Davey. He always signed off with his undying declaration of love and each morning he would eagerly await a reply but none ever came. As the days turned into weeks and then months and he heard nothing, Billy became more and more violent. His assessments were all so damaging, that they eventually sealed his fate forever. Billy Jackson would spend the rest of his life in an institute built to keep society safe from the criminally insane.

After the trial, Davey Wiseman had been shipped to Whitemoor top security prison for the duration of his sentence. Davey had quickly adjusted to the routine

349

of prison life and his infamous name had arrived at the prison long before he had. Being known as a serious player meant special privileges were there to be bought and Davey made sure he used those privileges to the full, one of which came in the form of accessing a private room to receive and make telephone calls. Choosing to spend most of his days tucked away from the riff raff, he dreamed of revenge and could actually visualise down to the last detail, every last agonizing second of the pain he would inflict. To Davey Wiseman it wasn't a case of if but when. A light tap came on the cell door and a young, rather frightened looking officer shuffled inside.

"There's a telephone call for you Mr Wiseman."

Davey didn't reply, he just stood up and walked past the guard who sheepishly stepped to one side. The recreational area echoed with the noise of other inmates playing table tennis or watching television and as he passed many called out to Davey but he didn't reply. Continuing along the corridor until he reached the store room, he closed the door then retrieved a mobile from under a pile of cleaning cloths.

"Yeah?"

"Hello Mr Wiseman, Tony Smart here!"

Davey wasn't expecting anything from his solicitors, he had long since resigned himself to the fifteen stretch that lay ahead of him.

"Hi Tone, I didn't think we had any business left to discuss?"

"We didn't Mr Wiseman, well not until today but I have news and it's good."

Davey let out a sigh, the man's voice was already

starting to grate on him and his impatience was quickly picked up on.

"Please bear with me and I will explain it all as quickly as I can. Do you know anyone by the name of James Loftwood?"

"That fuckin' nonce?"

"Pardon?"

"Now you listen to me! He's nothing more than a fuckin' kiddie fiddler, why the fuck would you even contemplate that I could ever be associated with the likes of him?"

"I don't presume to think anything of the sort Mr Wiseman. The only reason I am contacting you is to relay the news that my office received a package this morning from someone of that name. A recording and sworn affidavit were enclosed, both admitting his involvement."

"Involvement! Regarding what exactly?"

"His guilt, regarding his involvement with the Metropolitan Police and the conspiracy he was party to that set you up."

"But he had nothing to do.............."

Davey stopped mid sentence. He knew Lockwood had nothing to do with the collar, so why was he trying to help now? Davey remained silent, he wasn't about to voice his thoughts to Tony Smart or anyone else.

"Mr Wiseman are you still there?"

"Yeah, yeah I'm here."

Tony Smart continued to talk and it took all of Davey's efforts to concentrate on what he was being told.

"James Loftwood committed suicide yesterday.

Connected a hose to his car in the family garage no less, anyway that's beside the point. There was a short note in the package and I was instructed to read it to you. I don't profess to understand it but then I suppose I don't need to, so here goes.

'Davey I know it's a bit late in the day but I couldn't leave this mortal coil without at least trying to help you. The information I have supplied should be enough to get you an appeal hearing. My family will have to live with the shame of me taking my own life but that won't be as hard as some of the things that could have come to light. I know you understand what I'm talking about and I beg you for the sake of my family, if anything else exists please destroy it. Yours Jimmy'.

"Does any of that make sense to you Mr Wiseman?" Knowingly Davey grinned from ear to ear as he spoke "Not really but tell me where do we go from here?" "Well it goes without saying that we will definitely get an appeal and I would hazard a guess that it's just a matter of time before you are a free man again. As soon as I have any more news I will be in touch. Goodbye for now Mr Wiseman."

As the line went dead Davey allowed himself to smirk and then he began to laugh, in fact he laughed until his sides ached. He could wait a little longer to be a free man, in fact he could do with a good alibi when the shit hit the fan and what better alibi than being detained at her Majesties. After making a few more calls Davey returned to his cell a very happy man.

The internet was on fire and the Sunday tabloids had

a field day with the anonymous photographs of James Loftwood and his young escorts. A few hours later a rushed statement was issued by the Metropolitan Police Department to the media. Chief Inspector Graham Myers said that whoever could do this to the late man's family must really have had a grudge against him. Davey Wiseman had a grudge alright, in fact he had several and this was just the beginning.

The End

To be continued!

Printed in Great Britain
by Amazon

80121136R00210